IN THE END, NOTHING

IN THE END, NOTHING

A Short Story Collection

MICHAEL PATRICK HICKS

Also by Michael Patrick Hicks

In the End, Nothing (A Short Story Collection)

Friday Night Massacre

Broken Shells: A Subterranean Horror Novella

Mass Hysteria

The Salem Hawley Series

The Resurrectionists (Book 1)

Borne of the Deep (Book 2)

DRMR Series

Convergence (A DRMR Novel, Book 1)

Emergence (A DRMR Novel, Book 2)

Preservation (A DRMR Short Story)

Non-Fiction

The Horror Book Review Digest

The Horror Book Review Digest Volume II

In the End, Nothing (A Short Story Collection)

Copyright © 2023 by Michael Patrick Hicks

High Fever Books

First Edition: January 2023

Hardcover artwork by Michael Patrick Hicks

Paperback and eBook Cover artwork by Matt Wildasin

Printed in the United States of America

ISBN-13: 979-8-366643-93-1 (hardcover)

ISBN-13: 978-1-947570-18-4 (paperback)

ISBN-13: 978-1-947570-19-1 (ebook)

Contents

This one is for you, reader.

Foreword

One of the questions I've been asked most frequently from those who have read my short stories, particularly *Revolver*, which at the time of this writing has only been available digitally as either an audiobook release, a Kindle ebook, or as part of the *Chronicle Worlds: No Way Home* anthology ebook, is how they can buy a physical copy for their collection. Well, the good news is, *Revolver* is finally available in print format with the release of this volume of short stories, along with a few other stories that have been for sale only as ebooks and were too short to justify a physical print release.

Even though I've produced a fair number of short stories, I don't consider myself a short story writer at all. My prose trends toward the longer end, and even as a reader I lean strongly toward longer pieces, like novellas and full-on novels. Still, I've managed to produce a fair number of shorter works over the course of my writing career, including a handful of flash fiction pieces. I had a mind to begin collecting these works into a single collection eventually, but once I started going through what's been published I was surprised to find I had enough material for good-sized book.

Apparently being published in about a dozen anthologies over the course a few years adds up fast! Who knew? Admittedly, I lost track quite a while back and it wasn't until I saw Jeff Strand discuss his process somewhere online about how he manages and organizes his short story writing in Excel that I realized what a great idea that was and promptly stole it. Thanks, Jeff! I immediately went to work building a spreadsheet to track what I had written and submitted, the word counts for each story, what had been published and when and where, and when I was contractually allowed to reprint them. By the time I was done with that spreadsheet, I realized there was a potential book there after all. Lucky you, dear readers!

What follows, then, are stories previously published by horror presses like Crystal Lake Publishing, Off Limits Press, Death's Head Press, Silver Shamrock Publishing, and others. You may already be familiar with my John Langan-inspired "A Song of the Earth," the devilish "Brujeria," or my foray into erotic horror with "Ministrations," if you've previously read some of the more popular anthologies from these publishers. Maybe you've been reading my independently published short works over the last few years, like my Lovecraft by way of *Chopped* ode in "Consumption" or my zombie story "Let Go."

"Consumption" has seen print before, having been included with my novel, *Mass Hysteria*, as a bonus story, but I've opted to include it here for the sake of completeness (and, selfishly, because I really do love this story; it's one of my favorites!). My tie-in novella, *From the Ashes*, for Nicholas Sansbury Smith's *Missions from the Extinction Cycle (Volume 2)* has not been included, though, since it lives as a part of Nick's Extinction Cycle series and is presently available in print, ebook, and audiobook (narrated by Balki Bartokomous himself, Bronson Pinchot). Funnily enough, though, my story, "Sundown," from the shared world of *Centralia*, is included here despite that story also being readily available elsewhere. (See why a spreadsheet containing contractual rights is a good idea? Thanks again, Jeff!) Other stories will for sure be brand new to you, such as the previously unpublished epistolary story, "Above the Earth, Below the Ground," and a mysterious piece of flash fiction called "White and Black." Whether you're a new reader or not, I do believe you'll find something to enjoy in here.

I believe, too, that this volume is a pretty fair representation of my interests and growth as a speculative fiction author who has worked his way from the Amazon Breakthrough Novel Award finalist in science fiction with my cyberpunk debut, *Convergence*, to the demonic antifascist splatterpunk of *Friday Night Massacre*. Writing fiction hasn't been only about telling a fun yarn for me, oh no. No no no. At times, it's been far from it. Writing has, oftentimes, been a form of therapy for me, and also a bullhorn for me to air my grievances, to work out my issues with the world and the people around me. More than once, I've put my fingers on the keyboard as a way to try and cope with all the shit that's happening out there. It's been an (admittedly safe) arena for me to get loud and angry and, more often than not, spectacularly and bloodily violent.

Some stories herein are meant to entertain you. Some are here to maybe gross you out, or make you think or reflect for just a few moments. And some are here to piss you off. Such is the function of art, I think, in all its various guises. I hope you'll find something in this collection to enjoy and remember, dear reader, and maybe even something you'll want to share with others.

Michael Patrick Hicks
Michigan
November 2022

A Song of the Earth

I

THE LAST OF THEIR LAST-EVER FINAL EXAMS WERE BEHIND them, and their university days, much like their downriver homes, were officially in the rear-view mirror. At least for a little while.

Malicke was eager to put his school days behind him and forget about life. While he wasn't exactly looking forward to the trip itself, there were worse fates than beer, music, and friends, even if it was out in the middle of nowhere. It was all Tessa's idea, and she practically vibrated with excitement in the seat beside him. She rolled her shoulders and danced with her arms as some perky pop-rock came too loudly over the car radio, a fifth of uncapped Jack lodged between her tighs.

Daniel and Cherise passed a fresh celebratory joint back and forth in the front seat. After taking her hit, she twisted around in the passenger seat and offered it to Malicke. He nodded and smiled, reaching for it, and took a healthy drag before handing it over to Tessa. He sank back against the cool leather and relaxed, let the weed mix with whiskey to wash away post-graduation anxieties. His friends were partying. He was just trying to escape his worries.

Cherise had already applied and been accepted to the electrical engineering grad program at U of M and would be starting there in the fall, on top of working full-time as a graduate student research assistant for the department's top faculty member in EMC.

Daniel's co-op with Ford had led to a permanent full-time position following his graduation. Although they had wanted him to start immediately, they'd agreed to push the start date out a few weeks so he could enjoy a small break between his last frat party blow-out and the beginning of responsible adulthood, where his all-night benders would have to wait until Friday or Saturday night if he was to be fresh and presentable for the weekday grind.

Tessa's part-time student job had turned into a full-time position after one of her office mates announced their timely retirement at the end of the term, leaving a cushy vacancy for Tessa to slide into. She'd started working in the English Lit department her freshman year and had assumed many of the responsibilities the full-time staffers were supposed to be doing. She was known and well-liked by both the faculty and staff, which made it only natural for the fresh vacancy to go to her. The department chair and admin put up a dog-and-pony show for HR and brought in a handful of outside candidates, none of whom were seriously considered, simply so they could check off a box before giving the job to Tessa.

Malicke was happy for his friends, even if he felt like the odd man out. He'd made the Dean's List each semester for his last two years and graduated with honors from the school's journalism program. None of that changed the simple fact that newspapers, at least those local to southeast Michigan, weren't hiring. He knew going in that he'd be climbing an uphill battle, but he'd still hoped to land a job at the Free Press or Detroit News. Malicke's father had worked for the Freep, manning one of the paper's many printing presses, and he liked the idea of maintaining a generational foothold within that newspaper. He'd done an unpaid internship with WWJ Newsradio 950, but it had been supremely unsatisfying. He hadn't even gotten to write copy for the on-air broadcasts or do any first-hand reporting, at least not like he'd done for a local Dearborn rag that was more than happy to give him a number of first-page, above-the-fold bylines. The market had dried up, and the corporations that owned the news were scaling back more and more every year, gutting their investigative journalism divisions and relying more heavily on social media and bloggers, people whom were euphemistically touted as "citizen journalists."

The lack of gainful employment had put a cloud over Malicke's mood that he just couldn't shake. Being cooped up in Daniel's Ford Explorer for the damn near twelve hours hadn't helped any, either. GPS had said the drive would be nine and a half hours, but evening rush hour traffic, a car accident and, further down I-75, a rollover, had prolonged their travels. It was amazing, he thought, that you could drive for so long and still be in the same state. More than six hundred miles separated Daniel's home in Allen Park, near Detroit, to Copper Harbor, situated at the tip of the topmost horn of the Upper Peninsula.

It was a long way to drive, but Daniel and Cherise guaranteed it was worth it. They'd hiked and camped the Keweenaw Trail, all 51.7 miles of it, three times before.

Cherise had been reminiscing one night over beers and Tessa said she'd love to give it a go one day.

"How about once the semester is over? We wrap up our exams and go!" Cherise said, smacking her hands together and launching her left hand into the air like a rocket taking off.

Tessa squeezed Malicke's thigh under the table upon hearing that, her big blue eyes wide and pleading. He hated that look because he could never say no to it, and even though the last thing on Earth he wanted to do was hike fifty-some miles through bug-infested woods at the ass end of nowhere, he'd agreed.

He liked Daniel and Cherise well enough, but they'd always been Tessa's friends. Even though they had welcomed him into their tight fold ages ago, he never quite stopped feeling like an interloper. He graciously put up with her friends for the simple reason that he loved Tessa and wanted to make her happy, but he would have been more content to celebrate their mutual graduations with just her at their apartment. Maybe take a long weekend, make love, play some video games, smoke some weed, and figure out some more realistic job options so he didn't feel like such a goddamn bum having his girl working to support both of them. As much as working as a part-time blue shirt at the local electronics store sucked, he swore to Christ he wasn't going to be working there the rest of his adult life, barely making ends meet. And making those ends meet was going to be even more difficult without pay, since he was taking unpaid time off to go hiking instead of working. Tessa had told him not to worry, but he couldn't help it. Worry was in his blood.

He was dozing when Tessa squeezed his forearm, her breath hot on his neck as she whispered to him. "We're here." She pecked him on the cheek, but instead of waking up, he just wanted to hold her close and inhale the scent of her perfume. Grudgingly, he opened his eyes.

Daniel was slowly driving them through town, keeping to the posted 25 mph limit. After so many hours speeding on the highway, it felt like they were crawling along the road now. It gave him time, though, to look around and check out the whitebread scenery. Apparently, even this far north, this small pocket of civilization had discovered the postal service. As they drove by the antiquated looking post office, Malicke noticed the old, weathered posters in the windows. One had apparently been there for quite a while and the sun had turned the black blocky letters of the word MISSING to a pale shade of gray. The photo of the man and woman beneath it was faded and ghostly. He couldn't make any of the rest of what the poster said. He guessed whoever they were they'd never been found, but he didn't pay it much attention. He had his own shit to deal with, his own problems. If anything, disappearing entirely sounded like an OK idea.

A moment later, the GPS announced they had arrived at their destination. Looking through the windows, Calumet didn't seem all that impressive. In fact, it struck Malicke as being little more than a sparser, scaled-down version of the suburbia they had left behind that morning.

"Well, actually, it's just a little bit farther," Daniel said. He glanced back at Malicke and offered him a sympathetic smile in apology. "If traffic hadn't fucked us up so much, we'd have parked at the visitor center and started hoofing our way into the interior from there. But we're really burning daylight, so we figured we'd get a room at the lodge. Good news is, we can get a start bright and early tomorrow, and it saves us a few miles on the loop."

"The loop?" Malicke asked.

"Yeah, Calumet to Copper Harbor and the lighthouse, and then back."

"So, it's fifty miles round-trip?"

"Oh," Daniel said, registering Malicke's confusion through the rearview mirror. "No, no, it's fifty miles there, fifty back. Thereabouts, anyway, maybe just a smidge more."

"We're hiking a hundred miles?" Malicke asked, wondering why the hell he hadn't thought about clarifying all this earlier. Cherise always just said it was a fifty-mile hike, and he hadn't even given it a second thought, let alone considered doubling the figure she'd given them.

"Don't worry," Cherise said. "We'll take it easy on you two."

Daniel and Cherise exchanged a knowing smirk as they pulled into the lodge, and Malicke's stomach fell into an open pit.

"It's going to be fun," Tessa said, smiling wide as she hopped out of the car.

This just gets worse and worse, Malicke thought, rubbing his eyes. They wanted him to walk a hundred miles?! And they hadn't even told him that? *Fucking rich yuppie assholes.*

II

Malicke started at the hammering sound coming from nearby. He shot up, unsure of where he was, as he took in the small confines of the room.

"Breakfast in five!" Daniel shouted through the door.

"Hey there sleepyhead," Tessa said. She was already dressed in shorts and a white tee, her hair pulled back in a ponytail and ready to go from the looks of it.

"You let me sleep?"

"After last night," she said, a small smile curling across her lips, "I thought you deserved the rest." She leaned over him for a kiss, then smacked his butt through the comforter. "Now we gotta get moving!"

Groggy, Malicke pushed himself up and swung his legs over the side of the bed. The mattress had been lumpy and squeaky, but despite how uncomfortable it had been, he could have easily slept for a few more hours. He stretched, then picked up his underwear, shorts, and shirt from the floor and fished them back on.

Part of roughing it, he knew, was forgoing the niceties of a daily change of clean underwear. They were going to backpack their way through the Keweenaw Trail, and instead of packing an entire wardrobe for the hike, they'd stuck to the essentials, like energy bars, trail mix, plenty of water and water filters, canned foods, waterproof matches, headlamps and flashlights, a first aid kit, sunscreen, bug spray, extra pairs of hiking socks, blister kits, rain gear, sleeping bags, a tent for each couple, cooking equipment and fuel cans. While Malicke did have enough extra clothing to see him through the trip, he figured he was just as well-off wearing yesterday's clothes since odds were, all he was going to be doing was sweating anyway. He had no reason to dress to impress.

He opened the door and saw Daniel standing under the open hatch of his Escape. A moment later, Cherise came out of their room, tying her hair off with a scrunchie.

"Our last home-cooked meal for a while," Daniel said, turning to his friends with his bags of offerings.

A small laugh escaped Malicke at the sight of the brown bags, and he opened one to inhale the scent of egg McMuffins and hash browns.

"Got us coffees, too."

"Oh, bless you," Malicke said, earning a laugh from the other man.

"How'd you guys sleep?" Cherise asked.

"Ooof," Tessa said. "That was rough. My back is killing me."

After a few minutes, Malicke tuned out the pointless small talk and mechanically ate the greasy food, offering only the occasional grunt of agreement or non-committance when prompted. He stared off to a point across from the parking lot, but nobody else seemed to notice or care. Across from the lodge was a hip-high white picket fence and a sign that said SCHOOLCRAFT CEMETERY RESTORATION PROJECT. He could just barely see the outlines of headstones that the surrounding woods had grown around, but a sense of unease crept over him nonetheless. They'd spent the night across from a graveyard, which for as far as a hiking trip he'd not even been looking forward to went, felt like an inauspicious start. Even for one who wasn't inclined toward superstition, Malicke at least knew a bad omen when he saw one.

"Yum!" Daniel said, crumpling the paper sack in one large fist. He squared a beat-up ball cap on his head and tossed the bag into the back of his SUV. "Toss your garbage inside and let's get a-hiking!"

Even with the caffeine starting to perk him up, Malicke absolutely could not muster a similar enthusiasm. In fact, if Daniel got any more eager this early in the morning, Malicke might have to kill him, take the keys, and drive back home.

III

Daniel and Cherise had planned the hike to Copper Harbor to take five or six days, but they'd built in an extra cushion to their travel times. They'd given Malicke and Tessa a checklist of things to pack, and a specific number to bring for each item, so that each person was carrying roughly seven or eight days' worth of supplies. If the hike took longer, and Malicke assumed *they* assumed it would because of his inexperience, nobody would have to risk going hungry or running out of clean socks or fuel to cook with. Once they reached Copper Harbor, they could either restock for the five-day hike back to Calumet or rent a car, or call an Uber to drive back to Daniel's SUV.

As the first ten-mile day wound down, Malicke was already firmly in favor of calling an Uber. Oddly enough, though, this thought ran head-on into an odd point of internal conflict for him. He was exhausted and sore, but also strangely proud of himself. Almost even emboldened. He felt like he'd conquered nature, and idly wondered if this was what all those insane marathoners referred to as a runner's high. He was also seriously ready to sit the fuck down and rest.

On paper, ten miles didn't sound like a lot, but it had been more than enough to place them in the middle of nowhere, out of the reach of any signs of civilization. It was just them and the trees and the bugs, hidden deep in the woods on uneven terrain. And the bats, he thought, as the noise of wings smacking against the cool night air drifted overhead. He looked up and saw what had to be hundreds of them flying through the moonlight.

A spattering noise, and the realization of what that sound actually was, eliminated any of the goodwill nature had summoned from him. It was hard to feel emboldened when it was raining guano.

"Oh my god," Cherise shouted, shaking her arms and

squirming. Her squirming looked almost like a dance that involved jogging in place, and Malicke had to stifle his laughter. "Oh god!"

Cherise hurriedly grabbed and uncapped a bottle of water, then upended it over her head. Her legs didn't stop gyrating the whole time and she looked so ridiculous that Malicke finally lost it. He couldn't hold the laughter back anymore, and that only made Cherise angrier.

"This isn't funny," she shouted. "I just got shit on! And you -- you got it all in your hair! What the fuck!"

Malicke ran his fingers through his hair, feeling the goopy wetness there, and flung the batshit into the weeds, away from the fire. "I'm gonna need some water, too, I guess."

As disgusting at it all was, he had to laugh. Like his mom had often told him, sometimes you just have to laugh or go crazy. Laughing was better.

Tessa and Daniel came out of their respective tents, worried looks on their faces.

"What's all the shouting about?" Daniel asked.

"The bats found us," Malicke said.

Cherise pointed her drenched head to Daniel. "Did I get it all?"

"Fuckers had diarrhea or something," Malicke said.

"Here." Tessa uncapped a bottle of water for Malicke and switched on her headlamp. "Look down," she said, then began helping him rinse away the mess. She poured, and he worked the goopy mess out of his hair with his fingers.

"I can't believe I let you talk me into this," he muttered. "First night in the woods and we get shit on. That's gotta be an omen, right?"

"Oh stop it. You were laughing your ass off about it a minute ago."

"That was before I could feel all this crap on my scalp."

Tessa snorted. "Don't be such a baby."

"It's good luck," Daniel said.

"It's too bad you didn't get shit on instead, then," Cherise said.

And at that, Tessa finally lost it, too. A moment later, even Cherise was laughing.

Later, hands washed with sanitizer and dressed in clean shirts, they heated their dinners of canned stew over the fire Daniel had built and made the gooiest smores Malicke had ever tasted. Daniel rooted around in his pack for a minute and pulled out some red Solo cups and a bulky towel.

"Got us a surprise," he said, unfolding the towel to reveal a bottle of champagne.

Daniel popped the cork and poured as he handed out the cups. Once everyone had a Solo in hand, he held his up in a toast. "To our first successful day!" he said. "To the end of our university days, and to the start of our new lives. We did good, gang. Cheers!"

"Cheers!" the rest shouted, hoisting their cups up and softly clinking the plastic rims.

They savored the champagne and let it settle in their full bellies. The group made small talk around Malicke as the fire began to gutter, but he barely noticed. He'd had a song stuck in his head for the last hour or two, and he let the soothing melody play out while he stared up at the stars. Crickets and toads filled the air with their own songs, and it wasn't long before Malicke joined in, softly humming, absentmindedly, along with them.

IV

HALFWAY THROUGH THE SECOND DAY, DANIEL AND CHERISE led them farther off the trail and deeper into the forested interior of the peninsula, following the deer paths.

"You guys are gonna love this," Daniel said after Malicke meekly asked about the change in direction. A short while later, they stepped into a wide sandy trail.

"This used to be a river," Cherise said, "way back when. I don't know when it dried up, but its trail is still on the maps. No name, though, which is kinda weird, right?"

Malicke swatted at a mosquito and grumbled, "Maybe nobody wants to be here."

The others laughed. They were all used to Malicke's temperament and his sometimes-complainy humor, particularly when he was tired and hungry.

"Is this what you wanted to show us?" Tessa asked.

"No, that's up ahead still. Cherise and me, we found it last year, looking over some old maps from way back when. We didn't really have time to explore it, but I figure since we have an extra night... We're almost there! Just wait. I don't want to spoil it."

Malicke and Tessa exchanged a glance. She shrugged her shoulders and gave Malicke's hand a gentle squeeze. "Lighten up, hon. Try not to be so hangry—it's an adventure!"

He let her get ahead of him a bit, content to watch the sway of her hips and the long, lean shapes of her tanned thighs reaching out from her frayed denim shorts.

The walk was peaceful, at least, and the group had lapsed into a comfortable silence. Malicke followed behind them, an odd but comforting sense of being pulled lingering over him. He wasn't sure what Daniel and Cherise had in store for them, but something about it felt right. For the first time since leaving school, he actually felt like he was on the right track, and that he was heading toward something. Apparently, Daniel's enthusiasm for his big reveal was infectious, after all. Even Cherise seemed excited, singing softly to herself as they went, her stride confident and assured, and she already knew what the big deal was.

Nearly two hours later, they reached Daniel's big surprise.

"Oh wow," Tessa said. "Honey, get your camera!"

Wordlessly, Malicke worked the backpack off his shoulders and he dug out his Canon EOS. He'd been looking forward to getting some photographs of the lighthouse at journey's end, or some good landscapes from the taller cliffs of the peninsula along the way, looking out over Lake Superior. He hadn't imagined this, though, and a smile grew over his face.

Malicke was a big fan of what was, in the photography community, known as ruin porn. He'd taken a number of stark black-and-white photos documenting the urban decay of Detroit and Flint, and had gone on group excursions to the Packard Plant, a crumbling former auto factory. He hadn't had a chance, though, to shoot an honest to god ghost town in the middle of the forest.

"It was an old mining town," Daniel said, "back in the late-1800s, early-1900s. Been abandoned for about just as long, too."

"This is incredible, man," Malicke said, studying the geography of it all through the digital camera's viewfinder. He took a series of shots of what was likely a turn of the century bar whose roof was now caving in, weeds winding up the side and between the wooden boards of the walls and door frame. Then he moved a few steps over, looking for a different angle. It was deep into the afternoon, but golden hour was still some time away, so the light was even and the shadows deep. It wasn't dramatic, but it was pretty damn cool to see anyway.

"I'm glad you like it, Mal. Especially since this is where we're camping tonight."

Daniel laughed at the expressions that crossed Malicke and Tessa's faces. Malicke's dubious look was quick to turn to enthusiasm at the realization that he would have many more hours to explore and document the abandoned town.

"It's perfectly safe," Cherise said to Tessa, putting an arm around her. "Just stay out of the buildings. They're pretty rotted and you could step through a board, turn an ankle, or get cut up pretty good."

Tessa's face cleared, a dull blush coloring her cheeks. "It's cool, really. My mind was just…," she shook her head, laughing. "Too many slasher flicks."

"We'll stay away from the ruins, though. Having a building collapse on top of us would certainly ruin the mood," Daniel said.

"Oh, stop," Tessa said, and Cherise smacked at his chest, smirking.

"So," Malicke said, "where's the mine?"

V

MALICKE STOOD AT THE LARGE, WOOD-FRAMED, rectangular opening cut into the face of a densely-treed hill. Daniel had led them little more than a mile along a fairly straight dirt path to where the cut had been made. The late afternoon sun died at the mouth of the mine, casting the craggy, rocky interior in shadow. Malicke could see the photograph in his mind's eye, and he stepped back a bit to capture it on the camera's memory card.

"What did they mine?" Tessa asked

"Copper," Daniel said, sounding surprisingly chipper. He might have been an engineer, but he had a natural teaching streak in him that made Malicke think he'd missed his calling. "It's the whole reason Copper Harbor is named what it is. Where we're at now, it's part of the Keweenawan Rift, which made copper mining one of the most important industries in Michigan back in the 19th Century. This shit's pure copper, too, which is rare. Most other copper towns made their riches off copper sulfides or oxides, but the Rift is all straight-up, hundred percent legit."

Malicke flicked the switch on his headlamp and tentatively stepped through the passage. The day's heat suddenly turned significantly cooler.

"Hey, Mal," Tessa started to say, but he pushed on.

"It's OK," Daniel said. "Nothing but solid earth in there."

Daniel and Cherise followed, Tessa at their heels.

The opening led to a much wider and taller cavern that made Malicke feel small. He'd had to duck his head a bit to get through the framed opening, but once inside he could stand straight up without fear of banging his head against the rock ceiling.

He turned in a circle, aiming his light up and then around to either side, and, finally, straight ahead. He'd never been in a cave before, and the enormity of it astounded him.

"Just watch your step," Cherise said. "There's a drop-off ahead."

"It's amazing when you think about it," Daniel said, "the ancient primordial forces of nature that made all this. The glaciers that carved their way across this land and shaped this peninsula, and the precambrian lava flows that burned through these veins of rock. I mean, it's just amazing, you know?"

Malicke nodded, only half paying attention. Daniel was really laying it on thick, he thought, and had started to tune out the man's impromptu lecturing. He'd taken an elective course in Michigan geography, and while he reluctantly supposed it had been interesting on a purely academic level, he'd largely been bored by it.

Daniel, however, had been keenly intrigued and had, evidently, soaked up all that information like a sponge. He had confessed to Malicke one night that history and geography were his true loves, but neither passion could offer him a starting salary of $80K a year. He hadn't cared much about engineering beyond the paycheck it promised, but for that much money and a beaucoup retirement package, he was willing to tough it for the next forty years. In the meantime, he'd said, he had a Kindle full of history books and travelogues to keep his mind occupied.

After more than a dozen paces, Malicke came to the drop-off Cherise had mentioned. He stood at the lip and looked down, his light finding land about seven or eight feet down. If there had been stairs or a ramp at some point in the past, any trace of it was gone now.

He looked into the darkness past where the light from his headlamp failed to reach. It was deep and impregnable, and there was something both chilling and oddly soothing in that void.

"Let's head back," Daniel said, "get camp set up and do up some dinner."

Malicke turned back toward the group, his feet heavy as he trudged back to the opening.

VI

"Jesus, would you stop with all the goddamn humming?" Tessa said. Her words were a hiss so as not to disrupt Daniel and Cherise in their neighboring tent. She flopped over in her sleeping bag on the air mattress and wormed an arm free so she could smack at the material over her leg and vent her frustration.

"What?" Malicke said, his back to her. Slowly, he turned to face her, rubbing the sleep out of the corner of his eyes.

"You've been humming all fucking day, but now it's time to sleep, Mal. I'm tired, baby. Please, just stop making so much racket."

"I was humming?"

"You've been humming," she said, propping herself up on one elbow to meet his eyes in the darkness. "You, and Cherise, too, on and off. You've hardly stopped humming for the last day and a half. What the hell is that, anyway?"

"What's what?"

She sighed, then took a deep breath. It's like I'm talking to a fucking idiot, she thought, but didn't dare say. "What you've been humming. What is it, a song or something? It doesn't sound familiar at all."

"I don't know," Malicke admitted. "Ask Cherise. Just something I heard, I guess. Honestly, I didn't even know I was doing it."

"Well, stop it. Please. We need to get some rest."

Malicke said nothing, but she could feel his presence radiating outward next to her. She rolled onto her side, pressed her face against his back, kissed him through the t-shirt he wore, and put an arm around his waist. She was too tired to stay angry, and she just wanted to sleep. The muscles in her legs were sore, and she'd just about kill for a foot massage.

Tessa was almost asleep again when his voice pulled her back from the edge of unconsciousness.

"You don't hear it?"

"Hear what?"

"The song."

"What song?" she murmured. Tessa kept her eyes closed, willing him to be quiet and to go to sleep, trying to pull those frayed edges of sleep back to her.

"You don't hear it."

"Go to sleep, Mal."

He shifted beside her, the rustling of his sleeping bag and his clothes surprisingly loud in the small tent. "You don't hear it."

"No, I don't fucking hear it, OK? Just go to—"

Pain exploded along the side of her face and she screamed. Her hand came up to the side of her skull, blood pooling over her fingers. She kicked at the sleeping bag, trying to free herself, scrabbling at the material covering her body.

Malicke was just a shape in the darkness, kneeling over her and holding onto something—was it their lantern?—that he rose overhead and brought crashing down upon her skull.

The sharp edge of the lantern's base split open a second gash in her head and dented the bone beneath. She put a hand up between them to ward off a third blow and felt the joints in her fingers grind together as bone and tendon jammed. The fourth hit landed directly at the center of her face, pulping her nose and lips, and the fifth hit her squarely in the forehead hard enough to rattle her brain.

Malicke straddled her hips and raised the lantern again, blinding her in one eye with his next attack. Soon, the darkness enveloped her and Tessa saw nothing at all. She could only feel. But even that sensation was fleeting.

VII

THE SMELL OF THAT NIGHT'S CAMPFIRE WAS BURNED INTO Malicke's skin and clothes, every bit as much as the dying screams were lodged in his ears. His breath came in ragged gasps, pluming before him in clouds of pure white vapor, and his arms ached from the exertion of murder.

The fire hadn't yet died out completely and the embers cast enough of a glow that he could easily see the dark blood staining his skin, and the flecks of bone and gristle on his soaked shirt.

Behind him, the noise of a zipper screamed into the night and he turned toward it. Cherise stepped out, her face masked in red with hair plastered around her skull. In the hand at her side was a folding knife. Looking beyond her, Malicke could see the unmoving lump of Daniel's body and the splashes of red that darkened the interior of their tent.

"He didn't hear the music?" he asked.

"He doesn't know the song."

Malicke nodded, then began shucking off his sodden clothes. Cherise did the same, and they cast their ruined garments into the dying fire, stoking the flames with fresh fuel.

Naked, Cherise turned her back to him and walked down the central avenue of the ghost town, and into the woods beyond. Malicke followed, unbothered by his own nakedness.

They followed the path for a mile, to the cave entrance cut into the hill, and into the mine beyond. They followed the song and the rhythm of the earth and did as it commanded of them.

Malicke walked to the edge of the drop-off and slowly lowered himself down, until he was dangling off the lip of the rocky ledge, about three feet off the ground from the lower level of the cut. Without even a second thought, he let himself drop, bending his knees to absorb the impact. Then, Cherise did the same, landing beside him.

Together, they walked through the darkness, and although the interior of the cave was pitch black, they needed no light to see by. The song in their heads told them where to walk, what paths to follow, and it guided them precisely. Cherise and Malicke followed the old mining path deeper into the earth, humming an ancient and tuneless melody as they went. Eventually, they came to a massive chasm, the bottom of which they could not see, so deep and covered in shadow was it. A long, and old, bridge made of wood and rope was suspended over the hole in the earth. Fearlessly, they stepped onto the old boards and made their way across, their footsteps raising small clouds of dust. Cold water dripped from the stalactites above, and the groaning of the ropes and the creaking of the wooden slats echoed in the cavern around them, but the protesting of the bridge was quiet beneath the rising volume of the song that drew them further into the underworld.

On the other side of the chasm, the ground sloped gently downward, almost imperceptibly so. The air grew colder still, but neither of them noticed. They didn't care about the stinking piles of long, thin, black pellets they waded through, clumps of which were smashed beneath their feet and, in fresher instances, oozed between their toes. The dust of older lumps of guano drifted into the air, and they breathed it in deeply.

Eventually, the path the miners had cut into the cavern leveled out, but beyond that were large, roughly hewn steps carved into the rocks leading deeper. Malicke went down first, then took Cherise's hand to help the shorter woman down. At the bottom of the ill-made stairs were piles of dusty, moldy clothes that stretched out against the earthen wall. They looked to be mostly adult-sized men's shirts and pants, but there were children's clothes mixed in there, too, and some wooden toys, as well as women's dresses and undergarments.

Still holding Cherise's hand, Malicke followed the trail of ratty, moth-eaten clothes. The rustling of movement echoed through the cave, but pinpointing a source was impossible.

Daniel had said this cave system was part of the Keweenaw Rift, an ancient scar left behind by volcanic forces and the earth's shifting plates. He would have liked to have seen this, Malicke thought; Daniel would have been impressed by the enormity of it all. But Daniel, and Tessa, too, hadn't heard the music of the Rift, a billion-year-old harmony that sang without sense or reason to him and Cherise. It sang to them. It chose them.

In that song, Malicke felt hope. In that song, Malicke found purpose. He sang with it, and of it, and he followed its loose, shifting beat as it guided them further and deeper into the Rift. Cherise's hand was dry and cool in his as they stepped over the bones littering the lake's precipice and waded into the cold, clear water.

She pressed her body to his, and he held her close. Slowly, she let go and stepped away, and then she nodded.

He had no recollection of when or where he had picked up the large rock, but he raised it overhead and brought it crashing down onto the top of her skull. A fresh hairline parted in her scalp and, a brief moment later, blood began to pour down the side of her head.

Cherise hummed louder around the scream her body wanted to produce. She tried to stand, but her legs gave out and she sank into the lake.

Malicke was there for her, though. He held her head down beneath the water, let the sharp nails of her reaching hands cut faint lines into his belly and thighs as she flailed and the water turned pink around them. Her hair floated limply, drifting in the shallow current their movements had made in the water, but the rest of her was still.

He sang the song of the earth as he waded in deeper, rocks stabbing and cutting into the soles of his feet. The floor of the pool dropped away, and he sank into the fetid liquid. Cherise's corpse drifted atop the susurrating underground lake, dead fingers grazing the top of Malicke's hair as his head sank beneath the surface. He hummed to himself, and the earth sang back. He opened his eyes but saw only blackness and the inky hint of movement, felt more easily than seen, as bony fingers reached toward him and caressed his ankles and thighs.

The music grew stronger, its deep vibrato joined by a chorus. He spread his arms and legs until he, too, was floating, and the sea's calmness settled over his mind. The water carried him closer to Cherise, their fingertips nearly touching. He admired the peace she had discovered and he longed to join her. He had delivered her, as the hungry earth had demanded, and it had sang to him all of its plans.

After a time, he waded to the shore, his muscles sore and heavy. His music joined the shrieks of the bats above and the chorus of the dead below. He poked among the bones and found an old, dry femur. He broke it over his knee like an old stick, white dust pluming around him and gluing to his wet flesh. The broken end was sharp, knife-like, and he poked at it with the tip of his finger to test the sharpness. A dot of blood blossomed on the pad of his fingertip, and the earth told him it was satisfied, that this was a fine instrument.

He looked up at the shifting, writhing darkness. He couldn't make out the fleeting shapes of the creatures above, but he could hear them calling to him, their screeching and chittering echoing through the concave hole in the world. He'd heard their noises the last several nights when the bats took the sky to hunt. That was their song, and it was impossible to ignore.

He hummed as he climbed the rough-hewn steps, an ancient song of promise and wonder filling his head. As he retraced his path through the Rift, the song of the earth revealed to him his future. His voice joined with the earth, and he sang with it the song of the emissary.

Malicke gripped the jagged length of bone tighter, longing to drive this old blade of calcium into fresh, supple flesh. He was eager to return to the surface and share his song.

Brujeria

The Spanish-style home carved into the hills of the Pacific Palisades was more of a compound than a mere mansion. Carroll Arendt had bought the 3.5-acre estate in the late '80s for less than seven million, a steal compared to today's property prices.

"You ever been here before?" Marcus Blake said.

He shot a quick look at his date, trying not to get lost in the exquisite lines of her profile. The private access road to Arendt's home was a twisty affair, and he didn't want to ruin his night with Madeline by running his Escalade off the road and into the trees.

Madeline smiled, a joint burning in one hand while the other cupped her knee. "I've not had the pleasure."

"You're gonna love Carroll. I promise."

She passed him the joint, and he took a hit. As much as he loved Carroll's, and let's face it, Madeline's company, his anxiety had been growing progressively stronger over the course of the day. He was less impressed with some of Arendt's friends, and worries of conflict had clouded his day. Not that he'd had fights with any of Carroll's hanger-ons before, but he knew they thought less of him. His movie career hadn't been nearly as successful as Arendt's work as a film director, and he didn't own a home with nearly as many zeroes attached to its price tag. Carroll had been a loyal friend, and even a fierce advocate when studio meddling had sought to replace Marcus's casting, even in glorified cameos. A number of Carroll's friends, though, saw his relationship with Marcus as little more than a charity case. Hell, Carroll had even told him as much one night, during a blurry drug and booze-fueled confession. Carroll was a morose, guilt-ridden drunk, but he never lost sight of his friends.

Despite his nervousness, Blake couldn't help but notice that Madeline had gotten quieter the closer they came to the compound. She was tapping one foot against the floorboard, her fingers drumming an aimless tune against her thigh. The weed had been a good idea, he thought, already feeling looser.

"How'd you guys meet?" she asked.

He looked at her, momentarily confused. "Seriously?"

"Well, I mean, I know you guys did those horror flicks in the woods and he made some serious bank on it. You guys were friends before that, though, right?"

He couldn't help but laugh. "Yeah. Yeah, we were. We grew up in Michigan together, lived in the same sub in a town you never heard of outside Detroit. Carroll, he was always fucking around with his camera, making home movies with his Super 8. I didn't know him from Adam and rode my bike through one of his shots. All of a sudden, I hear some kid yelling, 'Cut, cut, cut!' And he comes running at me! He gave me a few choice words no seven-year-old should know, but I thought, holy shit, this kid's making a *movie*! I talked him down, and next thing I know he's pulling me toward his buddies and his brothers, fucking casting me in his little backyard production. That was my first acting gig, you know."

Madeline's eyes were bright enough to light up a room. "That's amazing."

"Been best friends with him ever since."

The *Dark Cabin* flicks had been good to them, that was for sure, but Carroll had definitely gotten the better end of the deal and made himself into a Hollywood A-lister. Marcus Blake had gone the opposite route. The few big productions he'd been cast in had been commercial failures, but he'd earned his cult status in a string of low budget direct-to-video horror flicks, even as he always felt like he was trapped in the shadow of *Dark Cabin*. Getting arrested numerous times over the course of his first decade in Hollywood for possession of various narcotics, drunk driving, and soliciting prostitutes had made Blake a high-risk investment for studios. Insurance companies wouldn't fund him and studios balked at his casting, kicking him off more than his fair share of productions. Carroll got to make some superhero flicks and a couple of period pieces that had won him a spate of awards. Blake sold signed photographs for sixty bucks a pop at horror conventions and auditioned for supporting character roles in cable dramas. But Carroll had never let success go to his head, and he never forgot about his friend Marcus. Blake knew Carroll was tossing him a bone when he cast him in bit parts in his cape-and-tights flicks, or as a nameless soldier cut down by a hail of Nazi bullets on Normandy Beach, but damn if he didn't sink his teeth into them. It was, after all, a paycheck, and God knew he couldn't turn down one of those.

"Here we are," he said, and Madeline let out a low whistle.

Pulling through the gated entrance was an impressive sight. Dozens of palm trees dotted the massive lawn fronting the tile-roofed stucco mansion. The walled estate was like an oasis in the middle of the woods, the large, wide windows inviting you in.

"This is amazing," Madeline said.

"Ha! Wait until you see the inside."

As he opened his door, his cell phone rang. He unplugged it from the center console, saw his ex-wife's name on the display, and silenced the ringer.

"Ah, hell," he muttered. He mentally kicked himself, realizing it was supposed to be his weekend with the kids, which meant Shelly was calling him all up in arms, wondering where the hell he was. He made a mental note to have Madeline roll another joint for him once they were inside and settled. His phone dinged as the voicemail notification flashed on the display. He swiped it away, in absolutely no mood to have his night ruined with thoughts of children and his bitchy ex's anger management issues.

"You need to take that?" Madeline said, coming up alongside him and looping her arm through his.

"Nope," he said, leaning toward her for a kiss. Her lip gloss tasted like strawberry, and he couldn't help but wonder what other parts of her flesh might taste of fruit. "C'mon, let's go in."

He led her to the carved front doors and pulled one open for her, waving her inside and giving her ass a squeeze as she passed by. She took his hand, their fingers sliding together with a routine familiarity, and he followed.

"Marcus!" Carroll's voice was deep and booming as he stepped into the vestibule with arms spread wide. He leaned toward Madeline, then stopped, as if awaiting permission. She nodded, and his smile grew wider. He gave her a quick hug and peck on the cheek. "You must be Madeline Howard. It is a pleasure to meet you," he said. A moment later, he was wrapping his friend in a bear hug and they were smacking each other on the back.

"Madeline," Carroll said, pulling both her and Marcus toward him on either side as he walked them into the house, "you were absolutely marvelous in *Burgundy's Foal.* Best part of that whole movie, if you ask me. Are you interested in reading a script I have?"

Madeline's hand went to her chest, a blush rising to her face. "I…" she sputtered. "I mean, yes. I would be honored. Oh my god, yes." She laughed, and it proved infectious, Carroll joining in with her. Even Marcus couldn't help but laugh.

"Excellent! Now, to the kitchen! I've just opened up a couple bottles of wine. Or there's some harder stuff if you prefer, and beer, too. Let's go get some drinks and catch up while I work on dinner."

"You cook?" Madeline said.

"Do I cook?" Carroll said, turning to Marcus. "Do I cook? Listen to her."

"He cooks," Marcus said.

Early in his Hollywood career, Carroll had directed a feature about a drug addicted chef at a Michelin-starred restaurant and had brought in a highly regarded chef to serve as a consultant on the picture. Carroll had a fondness for cooking even before that particular movie, but working so closely with Chef Heinrich Schauer had turned that spark of pleasure into a powerful flame and he'd begun taking culinary classes, wanting to build his knowledge further. He'd become close friends with Schauer, the two often cooking together in an apprentice and master dynamic. It had been several years since Marcus had seen Schauer at one of Carroll's shindigs, though. Apparently, the chef had traded the United States for Switzerland, but he'd left behind a strong student in the film director.

"I hope you like tacos," Carroll said.

"I. *Love*. Tacos," Madeline said, pushing closer to Carroll. She looked across him to Marcus and made an O of surprise with her lips. "This is like heaven!"

Her heels clicked loudly against the marble floor as they headed into the kitchen. The closer they drew, the more overwhelming and succulent the smells became. Marcus's stomach rumbled in response, his mouth watering.

"Oh, man," he said. Carroll gave him a friendly slap on the arm.

Carroll had a soft spot for Mexican cuisine, and he made the best carnitas Marcus had ever eaten. Okay, well, second best. The best still came from Chef Gabino Iglesias, a restaurateur who took his food on the road in what was, hands-down, Hollywood's most successful food truck. Schauer had trained Carroll in a lot of classical French dishes and techniques, but it was Gabino who taught him all about the heart and soul of delicious Mexican street food. If Carroll was making his carnitas that meant tonight's movie was a special event.

"You are going to absolutely love this, Maddie," Marcus said.

She turned her face up toward him, eyes wide. She was positively star struck. Not that he could blame her. And that was saying something for a waitress who had served some of the biggest names in the world. When she first began talking to him, Marcus had brushed her off as just another adoring fan. He smiled and behaved politely, listened to her stories about coming to LA to find an acting career, the usual story every-fucking-body in this town had, including his own damn self. But then he saw her waiting to audition and they got to talking. He saw, then, the real her, and realized she was really something special. He might have enjoyed a few modest hits back in the '80s, but he wasn't too full of himself to ignore the fact that he was a working actor. If some well-paying residuals hadn't kept him afloat through various writer's strikes over the years and let him pay off his small bachelor's pad, he'd probably be waiting tables too.

He squeezed her hand, intending to reassure her. Carroll was just Carroll to him, but to Madeline he was a larger-than-life millionaire who had made some of the world's biggest films, movies that weren't just popular with audiences but critically acclaimed and Oscar-worthy. He was one of Hollywood's hottest directors and she would kill to be in one of his films.

Beyond the doorwall, he caught sight of Andrea Michaels and Paul McGinnis splashing in the grotto, her in a bikini that looked like dental floss. Carroll's wife, Joan, was sunning herself on an Adirondack chair and thumbing through a well-worn paperback.

"This house is bigger than my entire neighborhood," Maddie whispered to him, trying to stifle a giggle.

He pulled her close, holding her arms. "It's okay, baby. Just relax. Try to remember they're just people, like you and me, and Carroll especially. He's really not the glitz and glamour kind of guy."

"What about her?"

He followed her gaze to the pool and saw Andrea rising out of the pool, her bronze and toned flesh wet and shiny beneath the dying rays of daylight.

"Well, she's a bit of a bitch, but if you can block her out, you'll really go places here."

She laughed and buried her face in the crook of his neck. Her lips pressed lightly to the curve of his jaw, and he gave her arms another squeeze. "It's just dinner and a movie. Date night. Not a care in the world. We got weed, wine, and tacos. What else is there?"

She smiled and his heart fluttered as he nearly fell into the deep seas of her bright blue eyes.

"Well, look what the cat dragged in," Andrea said, stepping into the kitchen.

"Hi, Andi," Marcus said with fake good cheer.

She snorted and took one look at Madeline. "Be a dear and fetch me a towel, hm?"

"Andi, this is Madeline. Don't be a cunt."

Andrea glared at him, gave him the finger, then tracked water through the kitchen as she went off in search of a towel.

"Wow," Madeline said.

"Sorry," Carroll said. "She'll become less abrasive the better you know her."

"No, she won't," Marcus said.

"No, she won't," Carroll said. "She's just…"

"Andrea."

"Yeah. But she's taking the lead in my tent pole movie next summer, so, here we are."

"Speaking of movies," Madeline said, "can I ask what's on tap for tonight?"

"You can!" Carroll said. "And we'll talk all about that soon! Dinner is ready, so grab some plates and beers and let's eat." He went to the door to holler out to his wife and McGinnis to come inside and stuff their faces.

Dinner was a casual affair as the group drew up barstools around the center island. A large plate of shredded pork sat before them, along with slices of lime, cilantro, cheese, soft tortillas, and bottles of Modelo. Madeline let out a moan of deep enjoyment as she took her first bite, the juices from the taco running down her chin and arms. She took a second bite and her eyes rolled back in ecstatic bliss.

"So," Carroll said, "Madeline asked about tonight's movie and I figure this is as good a time as any for a brief history lesson. In keeping with the Mexican theme, we'll be watching *Brujería* from 1922."

"I don't know that one," McGinnis said.

"That's because it doesn't exist," Marcus said, taking a long draw on his beer. "It's a lost film."

"Oh, it exists. And it's very much been found. *And*," Carroll emphasized, "we are going to be the very first people to lay eyes on the original print in nearly a hundred years. This is cinematic history!"

"What's it about?" Madeline said.

"*Brujería* was produced by one of the poverty row studios, but it had such a troubled production the film itself was thought to be cursed. It was a horror movie about witches," Marcus said.

"It was a horror movie *starring* witches," Carroll said. "The director, Aldofo Perez, was striving for authenticity."

"He was also a Thelemite."

"Mmm," Carroll said, nodding around a mouthful of food. "Well done, Marcus. You remember! Yes, Perez was a disciple of Aleister Crowley's religion, and was even rumored to have ran the Californian branch of the Ordo Templi Orientis for some time."

"I'm sorry," Madeline said. "This is a bit over my head."

"Crowley was a Satanist," Marcus said. "Perez was,

too, and according to the rumors, *Brujería* was his attempt to film the Devil."

"The film was meant to be a documentary of sorts, at least for those in the know. But Perez wasn't hired to make a documentary, and even though he strove for as much authenticity as possible, he had to hide it behind Hollywood artifice."

"Did it work?" This from Andrea, who sat on the edge of her barstool. Marcus had never seen her so engaged.

"During production, a number of cast and crew were purported to fall ill, and supposedly some even died, including the three witches at the center of the film. It was a grueling production and there were constant setbacks. Eventually, its budget spiraled out of control and the studio cancelled the film. Perez tried to salvage what he could and had hoped to edit what he had shot into something cohesive. The result of that was *Brujería*, a short film that runs seventeen minutes and forty-three seconds."

"And, according to legend," Marcus said, "Perez was the only man alive to see that final cut."

"What happened to Perez?" Madeline said.

"He disemboweled himself."

"Okay, now I have *got* to see this film," McGinnis said.

Carroll clapped and pointed at the man like an excited child. "Yes! That's the spirit! No pun intended, I swear."

"He died in a fire," Marcus said.

"No, his remains were found after the fire was extinguished," Carroll said, correcting him with the patience of a school instructor, "but that wasn't his cause of death."

Rather than feel chided, Blake smiled at the gentle rebuke. They'd argued plenty over the years about the legitimacy of Perez's death and the rumors surrounding his demise. Carroll had been obsessed with *Brujería* and its mysteries since he'd first learned about it in one of his film study courses when he and Marcus were attending Michigan State University. Being a horror fan, and horror film maker, he'd had a natural affinity for the potential real-life horrors surrounding various Hollywood productions, as well as the occult lore of Hollywood itself. Carroll had already been well-versed in topics like the *Poltergeist* curse that, rumor had it, was the cause of death for two young girls that had played central roles in the film trilogy, one of the most cursed franchises in Hollywood's already sordid and nasty history. There were also a number of incidents surrounding *The Omen*, including actor Gregory Peck and producer Mace Neufeld traveling on separate planes that were *both* struck by lightning. Creepier still was the death of a set designer, who died in a head-on collision near a road sign reading "Ommen, 66.6 km." He could tell you everything you'd ever want to know, and likely more, about the curses surrounding the making of *The Exorcist*, *Rosemary's Baby*, *The Passion of the Christ*, and dozens of others.

It was *Brujería*, though, that most interested the burgeoning director, and rather than fade with time, his obsession only ever grew.

"Wait," Andrea said, "so, what happened to the movie? How did you get a hold of it?"

"The night Perez was editing his film, the studio caught fire. It spread from the offices and nearly took out the whole lot, and the studio was ruined. Once the fire was put out, they found what was left of Perez. The autopsy report doesn't speculate on how he suffered the injuries he did, but it does rule him a suicide rather than an accidental victim. His stomach was ripped open, and not gently, either. Needless to say, the fire wiped out everything, and *Brujería* was thought to be lost with it, along with a number of the studio's other productions, but few were as noteworthy as Perez's. We only know of *Brujería* because of interviews Perez gave at the time. He was trying to sell the movie as the first Hollywood production starring witches, and there was a bit of buzz surrounding it. And then, of course, the total disaster that followed its production. Nobody ever saw any of the film, but that didn't stop the rumors that, somehow, the film survived."

"Okay. So, *again*, how did you get it?" Andrea said. She was getting antsy for an answer, bouncing one foot on the floor as she squirmed in her chair.

It was a fair question. Marcus knew Carroll had had spent an enormous amount of time and money trying to locate the lost film, hiring private detectives to track down whatever information they could and college students, who he paid to research and compile as many clues as they could find. Although it had been at least a decade since Carroll had directed his own horror feature, he had produced an incredible number of them in the intervening years, hiring occultists, psychics, witches, and Satanists to consult on those films and, likely pry them for any knowledge they might possess about *Brujería* or could possibly discover on his behalf.

As far as Marcus knew, Carroll's endeavors had been nothing but a waste of money. Nobody had been able to track down the three Mexican actresses the film had been centered around, and *Brujería* had taken on such a mythical status that some doubted the movie had ever been shot at all. Most suspected Perez had just been shooting his mouth off in interviews, trying to secure funding for a script he was shopping around, or attempting to inflate the status of his actresses and make them into larger than life figures. It was all promotion by a young unknown director who thought he was a hot shot, and nothing but a glitzy façade to make the flick more than it was, or could have been, to make potential audiences thirsty.

Carroll shrugged. "I've been looking for it for years. Decades. In that time, I've amassed a number of contacts and resources. You remember Schauer?"

Marcus nodded. "Your chef pal."

"He had an incredible network that I was able to leverage. You know how many productions he's catered? Thousands, easily. He's probably forgotten more Hollywood history and trivia than any of us at this table will ever know in our entire lives. I've always been fascinated with the occult, and so was Heinrich. We talked about *Brujería* all the time. I thought I knew a lot of crap about that movie, but Schauer? He was like an encyclopedia! Eventually, I was able to track down the movie to a private collector with a fondness for the strange and occult and, as they say, the rest is history."

"Impressive," Andrea said.

"No," Carroll said, "what's impressive is the check I had to cut him."

Everybody laughed at that, but it felt forced to Marcus, uneasy. Carroll had lost his goddamn mind, his odd obsession overruling any good sense he'd once possessed.

"So how did this film survive the fire? And how did this collector of yours get ahold of it?" Marcus asked.

"I don't know how it survived, frankly, but your two questions could very well be related. I asked him those very same questions myself."

"And what did he say?"

"He sold his soul for it."

There was more laughter at that, except for Carroll. His face remained impassive, serious.

"He admitted he hadn't watched the film out of concern for its power, based on its history, but he had studied the film cells enough to believe its legitimacy. He let me do the same before purchasing it, and I agree. This is it. This is *Brujería.*"

Carroll took stock of the friends assembled before him. Everyone looked happy and full, if not completely skeptical and maybe even a little somber. Their plates pushed away, and napkins folded on the table, it was clear the meal had drawn to a close. He wiped his mouth with a cloth napkin and dropped it on his plate.

"Now, who wants to go see a movie?" He pushed himself away from the table and stood, picking up his half-full beer bottle. "Grab your drinks! Let's go!"

As everyone filed out of the kitchen to follow Carroll into his home theater, Marcus and Madeline lingered toward the end of the procession. She looped her arm through his and said, "Spooky stuff."

Marcus shrugged. "It's just a lot of Hollywood BS. Nothing in this town's real, baby."

He didn't add that the town was practically built off the occult, from Scientologists to Jack Parsons's sex magick rituals, the Manson murders, and new age religions that used powerful psychedelics to reach spiritual enlightenment. In Hollywood, the only god worth believing in was cinema, but people always needed a devil, people like Aldofo Perez and, to a certain extent, Carroll Arendt.

"Well, your friend certainly does know how to set a mood. We haven't even started watching this thing and I'm already getting chills."

"Carroll misses horror, you know? He keeps wanting to get back to it, but the studios are iffy. They want blockbusters. But Carroll, well, he'll always find a way to make horror real, if not for an audience, then at least for himself. That's what all this is about."

Madeline said nothing but leaned her head on his shoulder as they descended the staircase leading to the basement and the plushily furnished auditorium with three levels of sunken floors. She let out a low whistle as they moved along the top row to snuggle on the cream-colored sofa. Andrea and Paul were on the couch below, and in the lowermost row was Carroll's wife, Joan.

"Where's Carroll?"

"Cueing up the projector, probably."

As if on cue, a cone of light blossomed above them, aimed at the enormous floor-to-ceiling projection screen that the entire room was in service to. Carroll emerged from a hidden door beside them and flashed the couple a big shit-eating grin, jogging down the stairs to sit beside his wife. Once he was settled, he hit a button on the couch's armrest and the lights dimmed. Slowly, the white screen went black and the soft hum of the projector was all that could be heard as the silent film began to play.

All eyes were on the hundred-year-old black-and-white imagery before them—a close-up of three beautiful Mexican women, with long, flowing, velvet-black hair that shined in the day's bright sun. They were kneeling in a dirt field, arranged around a large triangle drawn on the soil in salt. Within the triangle were other shapes made from the salt, circles and squares that overlapped, and fat candles that burned brightly and gave off a thick smoke. Their eyes were shut, and although their mouths moved, there was no sound on the old film.

And yet, Marcus swore he could hear a noise of some kind, not the film projector or the hum of the compound's air conditioning, but something *other*.

Shadows moved across the screen as the women took one another's hands and raised their arms. The skin along the backs of their hands split open from unseen forces and black blood slid down their forearms. Their heads bent back, their necks stretched as throats heaved and shoved beneath delicate flesh, and then they stood with a simple grace. Bloody hands went to glossy lips, and they danced around the triangle, drawing closer and closer to one another, and shadows flickered around them.

Madeline shifted on the couch, her hand hot and sweaty in his. Marcus couldn't blame her. There was definitely something creepy about the scene playing out before them, and even though he'd been in scores of horror films over the course of his career, and a lifelong fan of the genre, he was still unsettled. Perez's cinematography was deeply affecting, and the way the practical effects and editing blended together was absolute perfection. Even without sound, there was such a rich mood that it was impossible not to be enraptured.

The cave walls closed around the women—the witches. It took Marcus a moment to realize the scene had changed. *Weren't they in a field?*

The women drew closer as shadows coalesced around them, their bodies pressing tightly against one another as they sucked blood from one another's wounds, their mouths following the lines of blood that stretched down their wrists and arms, until they were disrobing one another.

Marcus felt like a voyeur, a flush of heat rising in his cheeks. Suddenly he was a twelve-year-old again whose mother had just found a stash of *Playboy*s under his bed, guilt and shame competing inside him and churning his guts.

He swore he could hear the women chanting, their voices sensually murmuring in his head. The words were completely foreign and sounded like no language he had ever heard before. Sweat exploded in his armpits and he flapped the front of his shirt to try to cool his chest. The theater felt like it'd gotten a hundred degrees hotter, but he couldn't take his eyes off the screen as the women began to kiss, their tongues finding one another's, bloodied hands grabbing and squeezing bare breasts, fingers finding hardened nipples.

"Jesus," he muttered. "What kind of movie is this, Carroll?"

The eyes of the witches glowed brightly, a startlingly pure white that was wholly otherworldly. He could hear the sounds of their lovemaking in his head as if he were there with them, and even as their mouths were otherwise preoccupied, he could somehow hear their chanting as it grew louder and louder.

He turned to Madeline, saw her legs splayed and skirt hiked up over her thighs, one hand between them while the other massaged her breast through the fabric of her top. He opened his mouth to say something, to either chide her or offer her another hand, he couldn't decide which, when a scream erupted in his head. One of the women on screen was at the throat of another, blood erupting from the woman's neck as teeth tore loose a grisly hunk of meat.

Shadows moved around them, dancing on the walls, and Marcus couldn't tell if that was happening on screen or off. Darkness swirled in the air, clouding his vision, the screen hidden for the briefest of moments, but he could still hear it. He could hear everything.

His hand moved on its own, going to his crotch as he leered at Madeline. He had to force himself to stop, the chanting in his head louder, more insistent and…*hypnotizing*. The word came to him from nowhere and then the disjointed pieces clicked together with a mental *snap!*

The film, he thought. *Oh my god, it's real!*

He darted off the sofa and pushed his way past Madeline. Along the way, he looked down the aisle below, discerning movement in the shadows. The air was impossibly thick, and he could barely make out Andrea and Paul on the next row down. She was crouched between his legs, her head bobbing up and down, and the haze cleared enough that he saw Andrea looking past her partner to stare at him. Her eyes were wrong, the color impossibly vivid and bright and—they were glowing, an ethereal light that briefly cut through the fog.

Oh, Carroll…what the fuck did you do?

Madeline snatched his arm, and he shook loose from her grip. Her hands were inhumanly twisted, her fingers ending in animalistic claws that dug deep trenches in his skin. She smiled coyly at him, too-full red lips parting over what should have been perfect pearly whites. Worms wriggled inside the black pit of her mouth, spilling over her lips and the décolletage of her top. She fell back onto the couch, her laugh muffled by the writhing pink and brown tubes of meat.

Marcus choked, the air thick and acrid. His mind and body took its time breaking through the *Brujería*-induced fog, but by the time either part of him had caught up with reality, it was too late. His lungs ached as he hauled in a mouthful of bitter, greasy smoke that was filling the home theater and making the air scummy. He realized now what the shadows he had seen dancing around the walls and projector screen had been, and as he looked up at the projection booth, he could see the dark gray clouds occluding the cyclopean beam of light.

Tendrils of smoke curled out from between the booth's door and the door jamb. He unthinkingly reached for the door handle, grateful to find the metal cold against his hot flesh, and yanked it open. Although there was no fire, the room was blanketed in a thick, swirling cloud of smoke. He covered his mouth with his arm as he stepped inside, his eyes watering as he scanned the tiny, closet-sized room for the source. His first thought was to turn off the projector, believing the old reel-to-reel machine—the same damn projector Carroll had had since they were kids—was somehow malfunctioning and burning the film, but then he saw it.

Tucked in the corner of the room was a pulsing blob of —well, he didn't know what. It was large and tumorous looking, the flesh of it blackened and cracked, revealing a bright, wet-looking pink interior, an ugly network of varicose veins marbling the surface. Whatever it was looked to be breathing, and he heard an odd and wretched gasping noise coming from it. And then it began to unfold itself.

"You're missing the show, baby," Madeline said, her hand on his shoulder and turning him toward her.

A slick, fat earthworm dangled from her mouth, brown chunks dotting her lips and chin like scabs. He lowered his shoulder and tucked his chin to his chest, shoving into her like he was a high school linebacker again. She sidestepped him, laughing, and swatted his ass as he passed. Let her laugh, he thought. All he cared about was getting away from her.

He nearly tripped on a rock on his way out of the small booth, his hands rising in reflex to grab the wall. The wall was all wrong, though, rough instead of smooth, a dark stone instead of the cream-colored paint Carroll favored. He choked on the stench of sulfur, the smoke making him lightheaded and sick, filling his lungs even as the chorale chanting filled his head.

"No, no, no," he said, feeling lost and dizzy. This wasn't right. None of this was right. The theater was gone, the projection screen gone, the couches, everything, all of it gone. Carroll and Paul were there, though, as were Joan and Andrea.

The women strode toward him, their hands and mouths bloody. The men stayed on the ground, inert lumps, and Marcus saw too much of how messy their ends had been in the flickering light of flames. Joan and Andrea's eyes glowed hot, as if the spirits animating them were burning through their bodies. A forked tongue darted out of Andrea's mouth to lick at the gore staining her lips.

He turned, searching for some escape, and came face to face with Madeline. She smiled, the corners of her bright, white eyes crinkling, and a moment later the pain struck him, his mind once again playing catch up with his body. Her nails dug into the soft meat of his belly, sinking through skin and fat, and then muscle. He grabbed at her wrist, tried to push her away, but it was useless. Her hand sank deeper inside him, and he screamed in agony at the intrusion of her probing claws and the popping of the organs that got in her way.

Joan and Andrea came up behind him, murmuring and laughing as one played with his hair and the other bit into his neck. He sank to his knees, and something inside him exploded as he slid free of Madeline's arm.

In the smoke before him, something massive stirred. He saw cloven hoofed feet, but little else. He didn't have the strength to raise his head and take in the full enormity of the beast just on the other side of Madeline. But he didn't need to see it to know what it was, just as he didn't need to read the autopsy report to know how Adolfo Perez or Carroll and Paul had died. The answer was right there in grainy black-and-white, projected against the black rock of the cave wall.

And then the movie reached its end. The projector

hummed on, and the loose film slapped against the still spinning reel. A cacophony of insane laughter surrounded him as his life force drained away, and he felt so very, very tired.

Marcus's eyes began to close like heavy curtains and, finally, the world faded to black.

Consumption

1

Heinrich Schauer drew the blade across the smooth, silky flesh, his face set with concentration. His eyes were narrowed in focus as the knife's tip found thick bone, slicing down at an angle and then across, separating the soft tissue. His fingers pressed into the fatty outer layer, holding the meat still, as his blade sliced with surety and carved free a long strip of meat.

Marveling at the ugly creature lying prone before him, Schauer promised that not a bit of it would go to waste. He had a generous menu planned, the courses incomparable to anything he had ever created.

Setting the meat aside, he turned his attention to the network of tentacles along the beast's flanks. They, too, were smooth, unlike those of, say, an octopus. While it lacked suckers, the heavy musculature was striated into narrow but pronounced gills. Moving away from the base, the flesh tapered to a jagged point, the thick tentacles ending in a jagged, vicious array of stingers.

Again, the knife bit in, piercing the hide and releasing a milky fluid as he separated the stingers from each long appendage. When he was finished, twelve evenly cut stingers stood atop the counter, their gray skin glistening beneath the white lights. While he doubted their digestibility, the stingers would make for a rather dramatic element in the main course's plating.

He took stock of the rest of the monstrosity, formulating plans for each of the evening's dishes, giving new weight to his previously fluid ideas.

The creature was fatty, but well-muscled. Its meat would be nicely marbled, and the back fat would be excellent for pan-frying. Tentacles lent themselves to numerous methods of preparation, and he immediately found himself mentally flicking through dozens of recipes: battered and fried, stewed with saffron and smoked paprika, or perhaps a preparation more classically Asian, with coconut milk and ginger, or stir-fried with scallions and ginger. He smiled as he struck upon the ideal recipe, one that he had always found to be charming with squid. The recipe would work rather nicely, and even provide a bit of levity as the meal got underway.

Yes, that was it, then. Hors d'oeuvres of deviled… devil? He smiled tightly at the small bit of humor as he wiped his hands clean on a dishtowel.

He prepared the broiler and oven, his ingredients neatly arranged, ready to begin.

2

EACH OF THE SIX HAD RECEIVED A PLAIN WHITE ENVELOPE in the mail, bearing only their name and address, with no return address shown. Each envelope had been sent locally and bore their town's own postmark, with a pre-paid postage rate printed upon it in local currency. Inside, a three-by-four cream cardstock, the typeface simple and unadorned, providing the barest, most pertinent information.

Chef Heinrich Schauer Invites
You To a Twelve-Course Tasting Meal
On the Appointed Date and Time:
Sunday, January 8 @ 8PM
46.559° N, 8.561° E

The guests arrived separately at a Swiss manor situated in a vibrant green field near Lago di San Carlo in the Leventina Valley. To reach the lakeside estate, each of them had navigated through the winding roads of the Gotthard Pass and the Devil's Bridge, named so due to the hazardous River Reuss, which quickly flooded with the spring rains and snow melt from the surrounding Lepontine Alps and led to many drownings between April and May.

Legend said that a Swiss herdsman had found the Reuss so difficult to pass that he wished the devil would build a bridge. The devil agreed, but only in exchange for the soul of the first to cross. The herdsman agreed and sent across one of his goats. This trickery angered the devil, and he drew forth a rock to smash the bridge. Before he could collapse the structure, an old woman drew a cross on the massive stone, preventing the devil from lifting it.

Now, gathered around a great oak dining table, the six sat in silence beneath dimmed, golden light cast from an ornate – bordering on repulsively gaudy – chandelier. In keeping with the evening's dinner theme, each guest had been issued a unique demon's masquerade mask.

One woman wore a red ochre mask with square eyeholes and horn-like hooks on either side that reached down across her cheekbones and, at the top, roped off into a half-dozen points. Another, worn by a male, was the more traditional horned devil disguise.

The third, another woman, wore a leather devil jester mask, while the fourth was adorned by a golden mask with red glittery accents and fat, black, downward-curving tusks.

The fifth's was an odd, earthy bit of macabre: a wooden mask, covered in a shiny black lacquer. The left eye was a smooth triangular cut, whereas the right was more irregular, uneven, lending weight to the shifting imbalance inherent in the mask itself. Above where his left eyebrow would be, the wood was raised into pointy shards. As those rough-hewn bits migrated to the right, the wood roughened further, taking on the appearance of black bark. The bark gave way to raven feathers and thin, stiff roots, and – if one examined it closely, where the bark curved up across his forehead – there, hidden in the coarse folds, was the keen black shine of a raven's eye. On the lower half of the mask, above his lips, were white ornaments that upon closer inspection appeared to be sliced teeth.

The sixth mask was pure white, with giant horns that coiled up, over, and around that man's head, as if he had been fitted with a ram's skull.

A fire warmed the dining room, the occasional loud pop of an exploding knot echoing across the cathedral ceiling. That, and snifters of brandy and glasses of warm, mulled red wine, helped to warm their bones. Silently, they sipped, watching the snow fall beyond the window. Soot-colored sky had given way to inky darkness, the moon hidden by a thick screen of clouds. The wind howled, sending a curlicue of white powder past, the temperature quickly dropping into single digits.

Occasionally, a few of the guests made eye contact and nodded politely, their lips creasing into thin imitations of a smile, but none attempted to raise a conversation or make small talk. Strangers to each other, their faces largely hidden and with only their mouths exposed, several enjoyed the anonymity and escape from the usual. What little could be seen in their eyes made one thing plain – all were outcasts.

A waitress, dressed in a black button-down shirt, a black vest, and black slacks, her face hidden behind a sheer black widow's veil, a raven tricorn mourning hat perched atop her head, circulated around the table, refilling their glasses.

Standing at the head of the table, she said, "If I may have your attention. Thank you. Your first course will be deviled tentacle. The meat was rubbed with a mixture made of Dijon mustard and Worcestershire sauce, coated in bread crumbs and olive oil, and then broiled to perfection.

"Chef Schauer welcomes you with the utmost warmest regards, and hopes that you will enjoy the evening. Your dishes will be ready soon."

Finished, she nodded politely and then presented a crisp turn as she took her exit. The diners nodded expectantly, mouths already watering.

One, the man in the ram's horn, raised an eyebrow, leaning into the group conspiratorially. "Squid?"

The woman seated across from him, wearing the red ochre mask whose arrangement of horns and hooks made it resemble melting wax, tilted her head, her lips turning downward in thought. "Could be octopus."

"Mmm," he said appreciatively. He recalled a dish of *jjukkumi gui* garnished with cucumber that he'd eaten in Singapore. The baby octopus had been marinated in soy sauce, red chili pepper paste, rice wine, sugar, garlic, ginger, and sesame oil. "Guess we'll soon see."

She returned his smile, the muscles in her face more relaxed this time. Not the prudish affectation of a thin-lipped smile he had received earlier. This one was warmer, and as she sipped her brandy, her face growing warmer, her eyes steadily made more contact with his. When he blushed, she laughed at him, a pleasant sound.

Moments later, small, square white dishes were laid before each diner. The tentacles had been sliced into inch-thick circles of meat, the breading a perfect honey brown, as promised by their waitress. Chopped chives garnished the plate, giving the meal a warm, earthy color.

After she finished chewing, the second woman spoke. "This is…" she began, but paused to seek out the right word.

"Strange," the woman in the melting wax mask said.

"Strange, definitely, but delicious."

"It's not octopus," Ram's Horn said.

"Not squid, either," one of the other men said.

Ram's Horn stabbed at another piece of meat, chewing it slowly. The breading and tentacle separated in his mouth, and he let the pulped flesh rest against his tongue, studying the flavors.

He could pick up the sour-sweet Dijon and the tang of Worcestershire, but beneath that was an odd heated-earth flavor. A certain sour note, an almost dusty taste, but not quite the flavor of mold. Not any type of blue cheese, he was sure. Still, he couldn't quite place it, even as an acidic, peppery taste lingered at the back of his throat.

"I'm stumped," he said.

His dining companions agreed, yet despite the peculiar profile of the starting dish, they found it compulsively intriguing and pressed on.

Chef Schauer was known for his eccentricities in the kitchen. He enjoyed surprising his guests with odd combinations, typically keeping the main ingredient a secret from them until after the final dish had been served.

Schauer had a stable of guests that he enjoyed feeding and sampling recipes on. He was rather proud that no two diners had ever shared a meal, constantly rotating his invitations and ensuring their anonymity. While he could not prevent a bit of table talk, guests were discouraged from speaking too openly of themselves or their affairs. The sole focus, they all knew, was the meal.

As with many of his previous tasting meals, Schauer centered the affair with certain macabre fetishes. Food, he believed, was a celebration of death. Eating was a morbid affair, albeit an ultimately enjoyable one. Meals gave sustenance to the eater, but at the expense of another organism's life. Every dish was a complicit act of murder, regardless of whether or not one's personal view of morality and politics allowed them to view it as such.

Schauer, however, was cognizant of the inherently vicious and violent nature of the cycle of life. He demanded a respectful mourning of that passing, a funereal elegance to the act of consumption.

"That was very good, thank you," the man in the wooden mask said. The waitress gave a small nod as she collected his plate. His eyes followed her as she walked their plates back to the kitchen.

Although none of them knew each other, they had each been invited to previous meals by Schauer in the past. Each time, the location and their company had been different, and while none of them had ever been to this particular property before, a relaxed repose settled across the table. Small talk had begun, food and drinks had been had, and their guards were dropping, slightly.

No one asked after anyone's business, nor did any of them trade information or volunteer details of their lives. Instead, they took turns guessing at what the meat in their first dish had been.

"I don't think it was tentacle at all," the woman in the leather mask said. "I'm Irene, by the way." She did not offer her last name, as that would have been a violation of house rules.

"Noel," Ram's Horn said. "I don't know what that was. I know what it wasn't."

"I'm ruling out any sort of cephalopod. Coraline." She scratched at her cheek, her slender fingers reaching beneath the lines of melting wax.

"A mushroom of some sort? The dish reminded me a bit of chanterelles. And, yeah, I'm Laura." She gave a small wave, then readjusted her mask by grasping the downward-curving tusks.

"Joseph," said the man wearing the standard devil horn's masquerade mask. He clicked his tongue against his upper palate. "And I'm ruling out mushrooms."

"Hi, all. Name's Peter. I don't know what the fuck that was, but I enjoyed it."

"Impeccable," Irene said, turning her head to meet Peter's eyes. He gave her a perfunctory smile, which she quickly dismissed.

"What do you think, Coraline?" Noel asked. "What was it?"

She shrugged her shoulders, shaking her head side to side. "The meat was smooth, no suckers on it, so, definitely not octopus. And I agree, it definitely wasn't mushrooms, although the texture seemed somewhat similar. The flavor was earthy, and the meat was chewy." She puffed her cheeks out, at a loss. "I just don't know."

"We have eleven more dishes to figure it out," Joseph said, a wicked grin plastering his face.

In short order, six bowls of consommé were served. The broth was a luxuriant brown, and a single toasted sesame cracker floated in the center, a sprinkle of grated cheese encircling it.

"Gruyere," Peter said.

"But the broth. I'm getting that same earthy taste. Musky, almost."

"Ashes," Noel said.

The five other diners held the broth in their mouth, their eyes considering.

"Not vegetable ash," Joseph said, taking another spoonful.

"Now that you mention it, it does have an almost sulfurous taste. I can't pinpoint it."

"This is going to drive me nuts," Peter said, his soup nearly gone.

3

A SHARP CRACKLING NOISE FILLED THE KITCHEN AS RAW skin hit hot grease and snapped away from the heat. Schauer had taken a strip of back fat off the beast and melted it into a dirty-blonde puddle in a large cast-iron pan. The odor was strong and dangerous, and he inhaled deeply, absorbing the scent of fish, salt, and fat.

In the pot, potatoes boiled, nearly done.

After turning the fish, he began spooning the liquid fat across the pink surface of the salmon. He hummed quietly, completely focused on the task at hand.

Behind him, the creature stirred, a shallow moan burning from its throat. Arms bound to both its sides and the table, torso split wide from chest to waist, it writhed in pain.

In his early studies of the beast, Schauer had found that stress positively impacted the taste of the meat. As such, he deemed it vital to keep the creature alive for as long as possible. In most instances, stress prior to slaughter increased the amount of glycogen and acidity in the meat, making it less tender, less flavorful. Schauer was surprised to find the opposite reaction in the grisly being strapped and splayed across the island counter. Surprised, and overjoyed.

He dumped the water and set the potatoes aside. Although he tended to serve boiled potatoes with boiled fish – not pan fried – he was feeling whimsical. A potato scoop would fashion the meat into small, perfectly round balls. Served with this would be cucumbers dressed with oil and vinegar, a slight callback to Noel's Singapore supper, which he knew the man would appreciate.

Turning to the beast, he ran his hand across the creature's skull, his palm coming away slick. The monster was feverishly hot, no doubt a side effect of Schauer's grueling excavations. He was sure that the beast would be howling if Schauer had not had the foresight to sever its vocal cords. No shared language existed between them, of course, save for the excruciating roars of pain and misery that were common to all.

4

"OH MY GOD, THEY'RE SO CUTE," LAURA SAID. HER blonde head bounced happily as she rolled one of the balled potatoes with her fork. "Sorry, I'm easily amused."

"OK, that's definitely salmon."

"I'm getting ashes, again."

"Yeah, but it's more savory than that. Pork fat, maybe?"

"It does sort of have a bacony component," Joseph said.

"I'm down for anything plus bacon," Peter said.

"That's not surprising," Irene said.

Peter glanced down at his sizeable belly, suddenly self-conscious, his sausage-sized fingers wrapped around the stem of his fork. "What the hell's that supposed to mean?"

Irene blanched, suddenly aware of what she'd said, too late. She stammered, suddenly feeling the alcohol daze. "No, I just mean, you sound like you're from Texas. Isn't everything all about bacon there?"

"We're not supposed to talk about where we're from," Noel said.

"I'm sorry," Irene said, meeting Peter's heated gaze. "Really, I didn't mean anything by it."

Peter was fit to burst, his face burning hot red. He couldn't contain it.

He exploded with laughter, a hearty, gusting noise, his eyes watering.

Irene suddenly appeared more disgusted than bashful. "You jerk."

"I'm sorry, really. I couldn't help it. You looked so fucking earnest. I just…oh, man. Wow. I had you, huh?"

Irene rolled her eyes, her disgust blunted behind the mask. Then she let out a small smirk, a small chuckle. "You did," she said, stabbing at the fish.

She tried not to laugh, but couldn't help it. Peter was still roaring, infecting the others, until Irene, too, was sucked into the sudden honest joy, laughing until her eyes watered.

5

THE SPOON PROBED THE CREATURE'S EYE SOCKET, ITS TIP forcing its way into the hollow cavity. The gelatinous membrane folded beneath the metal curvature of the utensil, yielding but not breaking. The creature, its head tied down to the edge of the countertop, writhed in panic and pain, mouth contorting. The spoon eased around the top curve of its eye and across the sides and down the bottom with a slippery squelch, as if Schauer were carving a grapefruit.

He pressed the spoon further down, the metal cupping the underside of the creature's eye as he pushed down on the fulcrum. The eyeball popped loose with a wet burp and a splash of tears running in a rapid current down the side of the creature's skull, flowing in all directions.

A rope of optic nerve came with it, and Schauer had to wonder at how fucked up the beast's visual receptors were at having one of its six eyeballs dislocated and freed from its stationary orbit.

He held the spoon at waist level, a good few inches of optic nerve pulled taut, and took a pair of scissors to the cord. The nerve bundle was tough and he had to press hard several times, rocking the scissors back and forth, sawing through the nerve until it finally snapped.

He spooned the eyeball into an ice cube tray, very carefully. He didn't want to drop the eye or upset its delicate stability. While not as fragile as egg yolk, he treated it as if it were.

Knowing what to expect, he was able to free the five remaining eyes with ease.

6

As the grandfather clock in the foyer struck nine, the waitress promptly presented the plated entrees.

"Before you: a four ounce filet and a cucurbita medley roasted in orange butter."

"Cucurbita?" Laura asked.

"Gourds," Noel answered. He pointed his fork at each cube: "Pumpkin, squash, zucchini."

"Ah, OK. Thanks."

"Ashes, again," Irene said.

"I don't think it's ashes," Joseph replied. "I'm starting to think this meat has a natural sooty flavor."

"Unless Schauer accidentally burnt everything or is just fucking with us."

"I don't think so, Irene. Joe may be on to something."

"Joseph."

"Apologies," Peter said. "Anyway, I concur. It's not ashes."

Noel lifted the filet with his fork and examined the underside. The meat was cut to squared perfection, the size and shape of a deck of cards. Visually, it was unlike anything he'd seen before. Not a white meat, like pork or chicken, but a sickly gray. It had been grilled, and the exterior bore perfect crosshatching, but as he cut into it the tender meat oozed a faint, milky juice, revealing an ugly, bruised center.

True to Schauer's habits, the meat was grilled to medium rare, but, oddly, it lacked any sort of pink coloring. More to the point, Joseph couldn't think of any animal that exhibited such characteristics. He just hoped it was cooked through enough to kill any parasites or bacteria. The last thing he wanted was a case of trichinellosis or brucellosis. Not that he thought Schauer was capable of making such an amateurish mistake. No, more likely it was bit of trickery by way of molecular gastronomy.

"You think he added food coloring?" he asked, noting how intently Noel was studying his food.

"He does enjoy a culinary sleight-of-hand now and then, but this is above and beyond."

"I feel compelled to eat, but a part of me can't get over the strangeness. The taste, and now the appearance, it's all somehow…*off*. I can't think of a better way to explain it," Joseph said, pushing aside thoughts of E. coli and tapeworm and salmonella.

"Me neither," Coraline said, cutting off small piece of filet and running it through the orange butter. The acid cut through the nutty bitterness of the meat nicely.

She chewed slowly, unable to take her eyes off Noel. His hands were strong, but untarnished by hard labor. Short nails, clean. A faint network of scars topped the knuckles of his left hand, and she wondered, briefly, how his flesh would taste against her lips. She felt a sudden desire to suckle the inside of his elbow, to nibble his shoulder and the side of his long neck before taking a plump ear lobe into her mouth, his hands roaming across her body, strong fingers gripping her thighs.

"Are you OK?" he asked her.

"Oh, yes, I'm good."

"You're staring."

"Lost in thought, I suppose."

"Good food can do that," he said.

"It awakens the senses," Joseph added.

She turned to him, mustering up a plastic smile, wanting nothing more than to stab her fork into Joseph's face, over and over. She could imagine the tines piercing his cheeks, ripping the silverware free in a spray of gore, and then hammering it back into his head, his plasma hot and sticky as it splashed across her, his screams drowning the world as he writhed to escape. He couldn't flee, though. She had her free hand wrapped in his hair, her knees squeezing into his hips, and she was stabbing him again, and again, and again.

She forced herself to turn away, afraid that he would register the homicidal intent in her eyes. Noel was as much of a no-go. She stared at her plate, forcing herself to consume even though eating was now the last thing on her mind.

7

FOR THE FIFTH DISH, SCHAUER PLANNED TO SERVE SMALL, delectable *hachis Parmentier*, arranged in a beautiful, flowery presentation, as if he were serving each guest a corsage.

Standing over the beast, he was absorbed by the creature's inelegant beauty, bordering on pure ugliness. With the spidery arrangement of eyes removed and set into the blast chiller, the head was bifurcated with gory holes.

The cranium was an odd construct, dissimilar from anything he had seen previously and yet strangely recognizable. The skull was warped into multiple layers and planes of bones, an almost hexagonal configuration that was disorienting to study. The dense plates of bone curved and folded back over upon themselves, creating a multistory maze of patchwork lattice.

Its mouth was a brutal affair, hidden behind multiple tusks, some of which reached up across the front of its face while others curved below the reaches of its soft chin. The sharp bones reminded Schauer of a spelunking expedition he had once been on, and he marveled now at the familiarity of stalactites and stalagmites that breached this being's head.

Beneath the gore-stained protrusions was a smeary hole and a thick plank of forked muscle. A tongue. Getting to it required him to saw through the tusks, and throughout the procedure the beast grunted and undulated beneath the heavy leather straps, its muscles straining.

Removing the cage of bone, he got his first good look at the unadorned mouth. His first thought was of a parasite – a disc-shaped funnel filled with pointed teeth, similar to a lamprey, built for sucking. Yet it possessed a jaw and thick musculature and very long, frighteningly prominent incisors built for tearing and rending.

The bone cage was set to the side, near the severed stingers he had removed prior to butchering the tentacles, a plating design crystalizing in his mind's eye.

He drew a paring knife across the creature's cheeks, its milky blood streaming as the meat was peeled away and set aside atop a sheet of brown butcher's paper.

With the heavier chef's knife, he focused on the creature's abdomen, carving free a thick brisket. After loosening the straps enough to turn the beast over, then retightening and securing it in place, he turned his attention toward the meaty shoulders and butchered a shapely chuck. From the lower back, he removed a sirloin cut.

He took the brisket, chuck, and sirloin and placed them in the blast chiller. Turning his attention back to the creature, he carved away at its ribs and around the curve of its back. He set the rib eye roast aside on another sheet of butcher's paper, and began trimming meat away from the bone, cutting it into a tomahawk steak. This he seasoned with rosemary, thyme, and mint.

Finished, he sat atop a bar stool and poured a glass of

white wine. His forehead was slightly glazed with sweat, his once-white chef's coat messed with fresh spatter. He needed a small rest. He sipped and waited, counting down the minutes in his head until the appointed time arrived to remove the meat from the blast chiller. Meat ground better when partially frozen, as the grinding process generated heat. Heat melts fat, and he could not abide losing any of the succulent flavor and juices, or risk making the meat mealy.

One by one, he fed the cuts through a grinder. Working his fingers through the ground mixture to combine them, he was careful not to overwork the meat, for that would make it tough.

He took a good amount of the bluish-gray matter and sautéed it until the color was even and cooked through. While that was cooking, he mashed the baked potato and set the skins aside. When the meat was done, he stirred in the potato mash and poured sauce lyonnaise over it, a compound of the white wine he had opened, and vinegar and onions. He mixed it well, then spooned the mixture into the potato skins he had shaped into cups.

The cheeks were warmed through in a pan with butter and a red wine reduction, thyme, and rosemary. He finished the small cuts with a dash of black peppercorn and Mediterranean Sea salt.

He arranged the cheeks and *hachis Parmentier* on a long wooden board, separating the individual portions with the tusks, cleaned and arranged in a standing crosshatch formation, as if it were a perverse sort of rib cage. Of course, the display stood in mimicry of the creature's mouth, an ode to the cheeks, which he knew would be succulent and tender, perhaps even the best cut from this…*thing*. Schauer was a cheek man. Fish cheeks or beef cheeks were one of his specialties, and always lent themselves toward terrific dishes overflowing with flavor.

This would be no exception.

8

"Tusks!" Lauren said, surprised and delighted. Childish wonder filled her eyes as the serving board was laid between her and the other guests. She dug in her purse, removing an iPhone.

"Anyone mind?" she asked, waving the phone toward the meal. Before anyone replied, she was already swiping the screen to camera mode. The display told her she had no service, but she thought nothing of it. Schauer was famous for interrupting cellular service during his tastings, wanting his guests to focus solely on the food and texture and tastes, and not on social media or phone calls or the silly apps that occupied much of their daily lives.

"Ah, you're one of those," Joseph said, good-naturedly. When no one else objected, he too began taking photos with his phone.

"One of what?" Lauren asked, clueless.

"A voyeur," Peter said.

"When it comes to food, we're all voyeurs," Noel said.

In her mind's eye, with each click of the shutter, Lauren was already picking out in-app filters, Diptic arrangements, and calculating the number of immediate 'Likes' the image would win her. A cold blue filter, maybe, hashtag foodporn.

"Elephant?" Irene asked, a slice of cheek aloft on the tines of her fork, her gaze naturally turning toward Noel.

"No," he said immediately. "Elephant meat is a very dark red, and it's very lean. Not nearly as fatty as the dishes we've been served. It's also quite a bit more gamey, sort of like elk."

"He could be using pork fat. It's certainly tasty enough," Peter suggested.

"I think it's seal," Coraline said.

Joseph shook his head. "Seal meat's pretty dark, too. And sort of fishy tasting. It's definitely got the fat component, though."

"What else has tusks?" Lauren asked.

"Hippos," Peter said.

"Hippo meat's purple," Irene said. All eyes turned to her. "What?"

"Hippos are endangered," Laura said. "And besides, hippos don't have tusks."

"They do," Peter said. "Their incisors are ivory. Big, too, but not as big as these."

A small lull settled over them, as they thought about what the meat was. Eventually, their eyes migrated toward Noel.

"I've never had hippo," he said with a shrug.

9

NORMALLY SCHAUER BLANCHED AT FOOD PHOTOGRAPHY during a meal, and found it obscene. Watching his guests on the monitor, the video feed piped in from a closed-circuit camera in the chandelier over the dining table, he found himself surprisingly pleased. The photos would never make their way into the world, but the obvious admiration of his efforts buoyed his spirits. The snapshots, perhaps, were their way of memorializing the food, and in effect, the creature itself.

He abhorred social media and the instant

documentation of one's life without any pause for reflection. After one gentlemen – Frederick Hansworth – took to Twitter to broadcast his location and alternately praised and condemned Schauer's dishes based on some backwards system of rating that only Hansworth truly understood, Schauer had been forced to install cellular signal dampeners. He hated the false publicity those damned tweets and fucking status updates brought his dinners as they made weak-kneed efforts at capturing his glow within their own pathetic radius, as if they were somehow equal to him. Or, worse still, that he was somehow subservient to them.

Hansworth! Fucking Hansworth.

The name stabbed at his brain, an invective vulgarity. The first and last time he had ever allowed the man into his private domain; afterwards, he had banned the oaf from his restaurants worldwide.

Of course, he had kept tabs on Hansworth. At this very moment, if he so chose, he could learn the location of Hansworth in a heartbeat. Enough time had passed, the dust settled, that anyone who proposed a correlation between Hansworth's disappearance and Schauer's rage would be seen as a mad conspirator, or tabloid gossiper.

Temptation lingered, though, and Schauer's mind turned toward formulating a tasting meal around long pig, his long-simmering hatred for vile Hansworth returning.

He forced the thoughts away. Now was not the time to have tonight's vision clouded by such pettiness. Besides, Hansworth would not be long for this world, with or without Schauer's direct intervention. He took some solace in that, at least, and it sent a small ripple of pleasure through his core.

10

"GOD, I'M GETTING STUFFED," IRENE SAID, PATTING HER prominent belly.

"Only seven more courses to go," Peter said, a wide, wicked grin spreading across his face. He seemed to take great joy in Irene's dramatic eye-rolling.

"No time to cop out on us," Noel said.

He had spent several days consuming an enormous amount of water to stretch his stomach and limited his food intake to a few low-calorie dishes. His wife thought he'd gone vegetarian based on the number of salads and celery stalks he'd eaten.

His lie was only slightly less than the truth: telling her he would be dining with multiple potential business partners in Asia and that they enjoyed their large, multi-course meals. Copping out early would be a sign of weakness. She'd grudgingly accepted the excuse. On the drive here, he'd removed his wedding band and tucked it into the pocket of his sport coat, disconnecting himself from that life in accordance to Schauer's demands of complete anonymity. Ditching the ring felt good, and he allowed himself to slip into the role of some other, better version of himself.

Unfortunately, all that water had expanded more than just his stomach. "If you'll excuse me," he said, pushing his chair away.

The waitress approached as he was halfway out of the dining room, asking him if he needed any assistance and then providing him with detailed directions to the bathroom. The interior of the manor was expansive, and appeared far larger once inside than it had from outside.

Clearly Schauer had not inhabited the manor for long, and seemed to have little intention of staying. As he wound his way through the long stretches of corridor, he peeked inside the rooms he passed and noted that the pieces of furniture in the dining room, sitting room, and foyer were the only ones not covered in white drop sheets.

The noisy clacking of high heels stamping against the wooden floor drew his attention. Turning, he watched Coraline approach. Her figure was even more gracious than he had surmised. She appeared pleasant enough while sitting across from him and largely hidden by the massive slab of oak as they dined. But standing, her long, toned legs stretching the hem of her svelte black dress as she strode toward him…she was magnificent. While he'd certainly noticed her finely-muscled arms and long, elegant neck, and a rather eye-catching bust line, he hadn't realized until now how incredible her figure really was.

"The waitress said the bathrooms were this way," she said, slipping up beside him with an endearing amount of familiarity.

It took him a moment to remember how to form words, the shape of them clumsy in his mouth. He managed to creak out a, "Right. Yeah," before mentally kicking himself.

She smiled, her brilliant teeth shining in the dim accent lighting. Somehow – neither of them was quite sure how – their hands found one another as they slowly walked to the corridor's end.

By the time they reached the bathroom door, a heat had generated between them, and Noel's concerns for his bladder were replaced with a sudden impulse and an utter lack of control.

He pulled her to him, finding her lips with his own, his hands urgently exploring and taking note of the garments beneath her dress. Fingers roamed over a thin line of fabric across her hips, tracing along the warm skin beneath, neatly plucking at the thread and mentally cataloging it as a thong.

Coraline could hardly believe what was happening, but she lost herself to the sudden rapture. Her earlier fantasies crumbled under this new reality as she reached between his legs and cupped him through his slacks, measuring his hardness. A throaty purr escaped her as he gasped in her ear, and she twisted her mouth away from his, finding his neck. She could feel his plasma coursing through the thick cord of subtle blue beneath his flesh as she sucked and licked, wending her way down to the crook of his shoulder, lapping at the hollow of his collarbone as his buttons pulled away.

She was intensely aware of the hand pressing between her legs, reaching fingers brushing at the smooth hint of cotton that covered her mound, tugging the cloth to the side. She moaned, "Yes," encouraging him deeper, her hips rocking against his palm as she rode his strong fingers.

"I've been thinking of this all through dinner," she whispered, tasting the salt of his skin against her lips.

She nuzzled back up the opposite side of his neck, feeling the veins pulsing in his throat as she bit.

Surprised by the sharp, piercing pain, he clenched her hair in his fist. Rather than try to pull her away, he pressed her mouth harder against his neck, her tongue sliding against his skin as his blood ran over her lips.

She sucked at the wound, the fluid salty and coppery, his cologne providing a sandalwood aromatic. He shuddered, the fingers of one hand weaving through her thick black hair, the fingers of the other folding into a pleasant hook as he penetrated her deeper. A flash of warmth rocketed through her core.

A chill brushed her skin as he found the zipper of her dress, the rending of metal teeth loud in the hallway. He fumbled at the door, then finally opened it and pulled her through, pressing her against the sink counter. She twisted free of the top half of her dress, hiking the hem over her hips, and he tore her bra loose.

Another moan ripped out of her as his hands grabbed at her breasts, and she watched the slow, dark trickle of red sliding down the open front of his shirt, a lazy river wending down his chest. Fumbling with the buttons of his pants, she freed him, pulling him inside her.

She lapped at the minor pool of fluid collected in the hollow of his collarbone and at the base of his throat, feeling the first faint tremors of orgasm approaching. She pulled at his hair, roughly, tearing small clumps free.

His tongue circled her nipple, and she demanded, "Bite me."

He took the raised nub of flesh between his teeth and bit down, gently at first, but her grunts demanded more, and he knew that she needed to bleed. He needed to taste her fully.

Grabbing the fleshy bulb of her breast between his fingers, he squeezed and bit down, the nipple almost chewy as his front teeth punched through skin, a bloody welt raising against his tongue. He bit harder and pulled, the pink tip popping free.

She screamed in pain, a delightful howl in his ears. Her nails raked away strips of flesh from his back as their mouths rediscovered one another, blood pooling between their half-naked bodies, gluing them together.

He took a fistful of her hair and rammed her head back against the mirror, his reflection cracking into a hundred new dimensions.

Reaching for a shard of glass, she dug the pointy area into his cheek, stabbing the mirror clean through, into his mouth. He spat in her face, and her tongue darted out in reflex, tasting the coppery, red emulsion against her lips. Tearing the dagger loose, the skin of her own hand sliced open around it, she stabbed him in the chest, again and again and again.

He grunted loudly in her ear, his hips bucking. She peppered his bleeding cheek with kisses, working her way down to the rhythmic pulsing in his neck, to the slow trickle she had begun. Her lips clamped over the bite marks, her teeth making fresh ruptures, and she bit down, hard and deep, opening his throat wide. He couldn't contain himself against the spasm of contractions as she came, and he drove himself deeper, gasping, until he was spent.

Emptied, he fell free of her grasp and crashed to the floor, lightheaded. The pain was beginning to register, and he noticed for the first time the odd reflection of himself at his chest. Dazed, Noel pulled the shard free, minor glints and reflections surrounding him on the floor. Coraline was sitting on the counter, licking the gore off her fingers from her ruined breast.

He watched as her rosy tongue curled around her slender index finger, their eyes meeting briefly before he fell into a pit of darkness.

Coraline pushed herself off the counter, her hand sliding across more broken glass, her palm opening with an acute pain as tendons in her fingers were destroyed. She studied herself in the mirror, a length of glass in hand, suddenly starved. The blade at her throat, cool against her skin, she pressed against the vein and opened it, drawing it full across. A smile bloomed below her chin, breaking open wide with a shower of red.

11

"THIS NEXT COURSE IS A VEGETABLE DISH. CHEF SCHAUER has prepared a kale casserole, roasted cauliflower with grapes, and Brussels sprout gratin. Enjoy."

Four dishes were plated as eyes turned toward the empty seats.

"Where are Noel and Coraline?" Peter asked.

"Bathroom, I thought," Joseph said.

"I wouldn't be surprised if Coraline is purging herself," Irene said, spearing a Brussels sprout. The dish was creamy and she nodded appreciatively at the taste of nutmeg and butter.

"Well, their loss," Joseph said, enjoying the cauliflower. The grapes added a nice, springy bite of freshness, the capers and lemon balancing the dish with a hint of tartness and acidity.

Although Peter avoided green bean casserole, he found the substitution of kale to be a particularly wonderful modification of such a tired and trite standby.

Casserole dishes reminded him of shitty Thanksgiving dinners with many of the same family members he diligently avoided the rest of the year. The noticeably canned flavors of gloppy mushroom soup always recalled past arguments over gay rights and liberal politics as he was dragged into the fray of heated shouting matches from the older, far-right religious conservatives of his clan. Most of the men he found himself annually surrounded by were dolts who considered him an abomination.

Biting into a crispy leaf of kale, he vowed to never attend another Thanksgiving dinner with his family ever again. The news would break his mother's heart, but heartache was a constant in life. He saw no reason to willingly inflict that…that *bullshit*…upon himself yet again. Truthfully, he'd let that annual charade play out for far too long.

Anyway, Aunt Muriel's casserole didn't stand a chance against Schauer's dish. The mushrooms were fresh and buttery, and the notes of garlic, salt, and allspice wove through the greens in symphonic harmony. Even the fried onions, battered with buttermilk and yogurt, seasoned with ancho chile powder, were crafted with precision, not that premade, store-bought crap in a plastic box.

Muriel's husband, Frank, was an especially atrocious sort. Rotund and big-mouthed, a bigot to the core. For the last six years, he'd begun every Thanksgiving dinner by praying to God that Obama's Kenyan birth certificate would be found and that the Good Lord would strike down that antichrist in a hail of brimstone and restore America's glory. Rather than bow his head as he delivered his micro-sermon, he would glare directly at Peter, an outspoken and registered Democrat, locking eyes with him, as if he were taunting him. He knew that Frank would love it just as much, if not more, if God would strike down Peter with a rain of fire and ash. The man was rotten with hate.

As he ate, Peter daydreamed of carving up Frank, as if he were one of Mom's predictably dry, dull turkeys. He would take a large butcher's knife to each of his joints, removing his legs and slicing open the flesh on either side of his breastbone, peeling away the meat.

He simmered in his rage, his face reddening.

"You all right?" Joseph asked him.

Peter blinked, as if he were awakening from a long, troubled sleep. He hadn't realized he was slouching and scooted himself up in the chair.

"Distracted, I guess."

"You were shaking," Irene said.

Laura leaned across the table, pressing the back of her hand against his forehead. "Shit, you're burning up. You sure you're OK?"

"No. I mean, yeah, I'm fine."

Joseph nodded, letting it rest. Each of them knew the false bravado was a lie, recognizing their own burgeoning wickedness with each passing course, a hidden undercurrent of rage that the food helped to fuel. But they pressed on in feeding their inner demons, and let the matter drop.

12

SCHAUER WATCHED THE SAVAGE COPULATION, MARVELING AT the gruesome affirmation of life as it bled out into death.

Noel and Coraline were fine dining companions, and he was struck by their loss. This he brushed aside, with the knowledge that they would be immortal soon. Their deaths would give way to ancient life, and their souls would be enraptured in a higher plane. The Old Gods would see to that.

Towering over the still-breathing, diminished husk of Baen'sollogotgartha, he squeezed the being's fleshy chest and promised him the world.

The Old God had been lost to antiquity, nearly entirely forgotten by mankind, but Earth would soon be reminded.

Rumors had persisted, as they often do. Back-alley gossip amongst certain types of collectors, the believers of the outlandish, hunters of the unknown. Mysticists, occultists, cult members, fetishists of paranormal Nazi experiments, whispering and wondering, each of them.

The seizure of this beast had not been cheap. Most of the rumors he'd followed had led to dead-ends. After an arctic research team met a mysterious and violent end, he had begun to wonder. With that wonder came an enormous amount of private funding for further explorations and excavations. Of the one hundred and twenty-seven people he had hired, all but four had lived to bring him this beast. The greatest hunt of mankind, conducted entirely in secret.

And this evening, a meal unlike anything ever known in the history of human consumption.

This was his sacrifice.

13

After clearing away their vegetable dishes, the waitress returned with four overly large saucer plates garnished with chopped mint. Standing in the center of the plate was a large, heavy, metal tumbler filled with a slushy white liquid. Beside the glass of frozen punch was a chilled coffee spoon.

Joseph dipped the spoon into the glass, taking a small sample. He immediately went back for more with a guilty rush, his endorphins singing.

The frozen drink was made of milk, bourbon, and vanilla, then dusted with freshly ground nutmeg. Heavy, but unabashedly appealing, the milk punch was the perfect cleanser after the earlier meals.

Unbidden, he thought of his mother lying on her deathbed, kept alive by the whiny susurration of a breathing machine. She'd been a violent alcoholic and a large part of the reason why Joseph rarely drank.

One summer day – he must have been seven or eight – he'd gone outside to play following a heavy rain. When he returned, his shoes caked in mud, he'd made one hell of a mess of the carpeting as he ran through the house. She'd been furious, and, at the end of a lengthy sermon that found him on the receiving end of a leather belt, he'd been dutiful in cleaning things as best he could.

That night, when he was sleeping on his belly, his mother came into his room, tottering on shaky, drunk legs, and pressed a hot iron against his left shoulder, ending his pleasant dreams with a painful burning, pressing hard despite his screams and the rubbery stink of searing flesh invading both their nostrils.

Spooning the punch into his mouth, he could almost feel the tight contraction of his scolded skin beneath the hot soleplate.

Pulling the cord on her life support was his fondest memory of dear old mother, watching as her thin chest deflated and stilled. Burning down the home he'd been raised in later that week was a very close second.

He smiled around the spoonful of punch, the bourbon heavy and warm against the back of his palate.

"It's good, huh?" Laura said, clearly pleased.

"Very," Joseph said, listening to the wheeze of the breathing machine whispering its last gasp.

What little of Laura's face that was unhidden by the demon's mask indicated a pretty woman. She was petite, small-breasted, and he had admired the curve of her shoulders and the line of her spine through the open-backed blouse when she turned away from him. He enjoyed her apparently good-natured and easily amused personality, her vivacious smile. Despite her being half his age, he wondered what it would be like to fuck her, her body writhing beneath his as he held an iron to her belly.

She ran her spoon across the top of the punch, skimming the frozen concoction away from the glass. With the spoon halfway to her mouth, she looked down and, her curiosity plain, asked, "What the hell is that?"

"Let's see," Joseph said.

Laura tilted the cup toward him, and he saw immediately what her concern was. Buried in the punch was a gleaming, black object, perfectly round.

He dug around in his own cup, unburying a similar object, and hoisted it up. Bringing it closer to study, he could make out the features better. The blackness came in varying shades, and he saw the imprint of multiple hexagonal shapes beneath the icy casing.

"I think it's an eye."

Laura went pale, her spoon clattering against the plate and table before shaking itself to the floor. She pushed the plate away, unable to hide her disgust.

"It sorta resembles a bug's eye," Peter said, having found the decorative eye in his tumbler. "But way too big for that, right?"

"Oh yeah," Joseph said, "way, way too big."

"I don't think I can have any more either," Irene said, pushing her plate away.

Joseph and Peter looked expectantly at one another, the same playful question in each of their eyes. "Well?"

With a small chuckle, Peter stared directly at Irene as he shoved the spoon in his mouth. Her face scrunched in disgust as she turned away, an audible, liquid pop coming from both men's mouths as they bit down.

Peter's mouth screwed up around the taste, his lips curving downward. His throat bobbed as he forced it down.

Joseph spat his out into the cup with a groan. He took the freezing tumbler and twisted to the side, spitting several more times. The taste was similar to bleach, but much saltier, and a thick sheet of the eye's jelly clung to his taste buds. He spent another minute half-gagging and spitting, then reached for his wine, hoping to drown away the putrescence.

"Maybe you weren't supposed to eat that," Laura said, looking for all the world as if she were seasick.

"I think I'll go join Coraline in her purging efforts," Peter joked.

"Where are they, anyway?" Laura asked, turning to Irene.

"Probably they discovered some other earthly delights to take part in," Joseph said, refilling his wine glass.

Surprised, Laura let out a quick laugh. "You think? Oh my god."

Joseph shrugged half-heartedly, kicking off his shoes beneath the table. His socked foot found her ankle and brushed against the bare skin, stroking upwards. She shot him a small smile, apparently not minding, and drew her chair closer.

14

THE EIGHTH DISH WAS JOINT MEAT WITH AN ARUGULA salad. The roast was herbaceous, the salad hitting a sweeter note with its honey and balsamic vinegar dressing, and topped with goat cheese and an egg.

"OK," Laura began, "what has horns, fucked-up bug eyes, and a shit brown egg yolk?"

Her stomach still roiled from the earlier eyeball incident, and the food was no longer sitting right with her. She felt bloated and gassy, the contents of her stomach shifting painfully, and an acidic burn lingered at the back of her throat. She picked at the food with her fork, moving it around the plate but unable to eat anything.

The egg appeared rotten and its odor was cloying. The brackishness made her belly lurch, but Irene, still feeling somewhat adventurous despite an upset stomach, and being unfamiliar with such an odd egg, sliced into half of it with her fork, spilling the brown yolk across the greens, and stabbed into the arugula. The bite was nutty and creamy, but held an unctuous flavor that she could not quite pinpoint. Greasy, certainly, and bitter, like lye.

As the treacly yolk slid down her throat, she placed the flavors with an unexpected connection. The taste reminded her of an abortion when she was two days shy of becoming a teenager.

The food carried with it a proprietary invasiveness, and she felt a too-familiar pinch in her cervix, a cramping deep in her core that she blotted her eyes shut against. A gorge rose in her throat, stuffing her esophagus, the muscles in her neck collapsing around this reaching otherness as it crawled up and up, stretching into her skull.

Gagging, she dropped her fork, a painful twitch in her eye. Something was pressing against the back of her orbital bone, and she could feel her right eye pushing up against the eyelid as that thing tried to shove it out of the way.

Gritting her teeth against the pain, she backhanded her fork to the hardwood floor, where it rang out with a metallic crash.

Startled, the other guests stared at her with concern. Blood was leaking from a tightly pinched eye, pooling against the inside of her mask. A sharp cracking noise echoed across the table as the suture that fused her maxilla and zygomatic bones fractured, and she let out a wretched, agonizing cry.

Peter shot up, his chair falling behind him, and bent to try to help Irene. He had no idea what he could do or what could be happening to her, but he was driven by the instinctual need to assist. His first thought was that she was choking, but that didn't make any sense. As far as he knew, choking people didn't bleed from their eye.

Irene's mask was askew, the shattered bones of her orbit punching through the skin and upsetting the balance of her leather mask as the geography of her face quaked and ruptured.

Her eye twisted through the mask's eyehole, dangling by the optic nerve across the side of her face.

Laura screamed, shoving herself away from the table, not knowing what the fuck was happening. In seconds Irene had gone from bad to worse and she could feel the electric hum of chaos as everything unraveled around her.

Joseph yelled a warning to Peter. "Get back," he said several times, but the words were lost. Either Peter was ignoring him or couldn't hear him over the increasing din of Irene's screaming.

Peter bent closer, seeing something writhing in the red-black hollow of her eye socket. A thin, bluish muscle was expanding, inchworming its way forward along the raw rope of optic nerve, its bulbous, multi-eyed face seeking the air, sniffing its way out of her skull.

"What the fuck," Laura shouted, now standing and rushing backward, away from the table. In her panic, she didn't realize she was going the wrong way until her shoulders slammed against the heavy panes of the window. Frost nipped at her, surprising her as her bare back pressed against cold glass. The doorway was now at the opposite end of the room, past the horror show Irene was inexplicably birthing.

Peter couldn't get away fast enough. The creature exploded free of Irene's face, her jagged bones opening long slits in its sides as it pushed free. He had time to see a disc-shaped mouth as it opened, springing at him, biting down on his large, fleshy cheek. He tried to tear it away, but the fucker was clamped on too tightly, and he could feel it sucking against his flesh, inhaling him.

Its tail grew larger, its body stretching as it wrapped around his neck. He pulled, but the tail cinched tighter, the skin slimy. His fingers slid off the damn thing, unable to find any purchase.

Joseph stabbed at it with a fork, sure that he could hear the abomination squealing in pain, even under Irene's tortured moans. Peter's face was going purple, and Joseph found himself surprised at how strong, and how much bigger, the creature was. Fucker's like a python, he thought.

He screamed loudly, forgetting about Peter's predicament in a flash of pain as Irene drove a steak knife into his shoulder blade and ripped it free. He turned toward his assailant, her cratered face unbearably close, and managed to dodge out of the way as she thrust the knife toward his belly. She howled in anger, and with her mouth open, he saw this waking nightmare expand even further.

They were small and multi-legged. No, not legs. Tentacles. They reached and grasped at the sides of her unhinged jaw, their bodies snaking across her tongue and teeth, seeking escape. Beneath her blouse, he could see something roiling in her large belly, pouches of fat rippling against the fabric.

He stabbed at her with the fork, burying the utensil in the side of her face, but it didn't even faze her. Irene was running strictly on autopilot, he realized, nothing more than a vessel for these monsters excavating their way free.

He stepped back as she threw a half-hearted swing his way, then doubled over with pain, a wretched tearing noise sounding from her abdominal cavity. Fluids slapped at the floor, and her blouse and slacks were immediately drenched. Paralyzed by fear, he watched as her intestines unraveled between her legs, slopping against the floor with a wet staccato as more of those tentacled, spidery creatures crawled free. Her body went slack and collapsed upon itself on the floor.

He felt faint, a wave of nausea sweeping over him as his stomach cramped. He fought back the urge to vomit, but could taste the knot of bile at the back of his palate.

Joseph glanced back, toward where Laura had been seated, but she was gone. He heard her scream and stared over his shoulder, finding her by the window, batting at her hair. Some of the spiders had reached her, were crawling on her. She managed to fling several off, their bodies sailing into the fireplace and exploding in the flames. He hurried her way, smacking away as many as he could and taking her hand, pulling her away from the window.

"Up," he said, leaping atop the table and pulling her with him. He kicked aside the dishes, rushing to the opposite end, flailing at the creatures as they tried to jump on him.

Peter fell to his knees, his fingers uselessly trying to pull at the thing coiled around his throat. He couldn't breathe, and the world was turning black at the edges of his vision, the dining room growing dimmer. His face throbbed, and he could feel hundreds of teeth grinding against his cheekbone. It had sucked away the flesh and fat and muscles and still buried itself deeper and deeper, consuming him, growing larger and stronger.

Small appendages tickled his ear, and he swiped at them. He was lethargic, but still cogent enough to realize that whatever was on the side of his head had bit him. Was still biting him, nipping at his ear. He wanted to scream at the unpleasant feeling of tiny legs stepping across the folds of his ear, dipping inside the ear canal. He tried to wave it away again and a searing pain flushed through his hand. Holding his arm before him, he saw that two fingers had been torn away, the small bones of his first knuckles exposed around ragged clumps of pale flesh. His eardrum ruptured as the creature burrowed deeper, a painful, fuzzy feeling as it rutted around inside his skull.

The snake constricted further, the mouth hinging open wider and darting through his eye with the horrible, wet burst of an exploding water balloon.

When the darkness came, he welcomed it.

15

Pulling Laura along, Joseph shoved through the first door they came to, off the right side of the dining room. He suspected the kitchen lay beyond, and had noticed their mourning-veiled waitress coming and going from there. He decided the time had come to speak to Schauer.

Rather than a kitchen, he found a large, empty room. The waitress was there, and if the cigarette butts at the base of the stool she sat on were any indication, she had been chain-smoking through much of the evening. A dumbwaiter stood open on the opposite wall behind her; the kitchen appliances were clearly unused. Dirty dishes were towered atop the counter, beside a disused, dusty sink.

"Where is he?" Joseph asked. He stifled a belch.

The waitress stubbed out her cigarette on the countertop, and that was when he noticed the gun. She held the revolver in her lap, pointed at him.

She raised it and fired, but he was already moving, slamming the door shut behind him. Two more rounds found their way into the door, the wood splintering and sending tiny shards at his face.

Laura was screaming, and he moved her farther away

from the door, briefly taking her in his arms. The bugs, or whatever they were, were preoccupied with the easy pickings in the dining room.

"We need to get out of here," he said.

"What about Noel and Cora? We should find them."

"They could be like Irene. Maybe what happened to her happened to them and that's why we haven't seen them."

She stopped dead in her tracks, pulling at his arm. "We all had the same food. What if that happens to us?"

The thought had lurked in the back of his mind, but he'd forcefully sent it to the side, ignoring it. There were enough problems to deal with.

"It won't," he said, but the words lacked the weight of assurance or conviction.

"I don't feel good," she said.

"C'mon," he said, dragging her forcefully along the corridor before she could protest or ask more questions.

"I overheard the waitress say the bathrooms were at the end of the hall."

"Forget them. We need to go."

"No, we can't. We can't do that. Are you crazy, we can't leave them here."

Nearly shouting at him, her voice went shrill. He hated the way women's voices took on that whiny, high-pitched tonal quality when they were upset, expecting the rest of the world to cave to their pathetic needs.

"Fine," he snapped, cheeks burning. He shook his head, but went along with it. If more of those things were waiting for them, it would be her fault, and he'd have no problem shoving her into the heart of the horror and running away. She was thin and small, not much meat on her, but enough to be a distraction. Easy pickings.

"Cora," Laura called. "Coraline!"

"Would you shut up, at least?" he snapped. "You're going to bring those things right down on top of us."

She rushed past him, peeking into the open doorways and finding empty rooms and sheeted furniture. "Noel?" she tried, moving on when he failed to respond.

Joseph took the next door, and she rushed past to check the one after that. Every few seconds he stared over his shoulder, worried he would find those bug things scrabbling against the walls, coming for him, fully expecting the waitress to pop around a corner and shoot him to death. He could hear the creatures wheezing in the air, the gasp of a dying old woman, the stink of bleach and ash hanging in the corridor.

The two bathrooms were on opposite sides of the hall. Instinct drove them together, Joseph opening one door while Laura, who he now noticed was awfully pale, her eyes glassy beneath the mask, crowded next to him. He closed the door on inky darkness and turned toward door number two, heart racing.

His slick palm grasped the knob, turning it. His brain spent a long moment absorbing the sight of blood-slicked floors and shattered mirrors. Laura gasped in his ear.

They were everywhere, hundreds of them, and much, much larger than their dining room kin. The largest of them fought one another, feasting on falling brethren, their massive tusks goring soft bellies, boney cages parting as their round, tubular mouths suckled at seeping, bluish-gray flesh.

He could barely make out the remains of Noel and Coraline, the latter splayed open and dismembered, thick, gory streaks trailing away from her body on the white ceramic tiles. The smaller spiders gnawed on her innards, while a larger beast tucked its snout into Noel's waist, clumps of his skin and plasma sheeting its enormous, abstract cranium, wet smacking noises echoing through the chamber of Noel's chest.

Laura bumped into him, her body flailing and shoving him forward. He turned to cuss at her, but saw the bathroom door being pulled shut, barely catching sight of black fabric before the lock clicked into place. He ran to the door, searching for a way to unlock it, but found no more than a solid brass plate. No lock. Not even a handle. The door could only be opened from outside the bathroom.

Sensing their presence, the beast kneeling before the dead diners looked up, gore trickling across the boney cages that hid much of its face, crouched on thickly plated knees, its arms like thick tree trunks, terminating in three long, ropey fingers that curved into serrated talons. Tentacles swam through the air, seeking them. The walls shook under the deeply resonant grunts, the bass of its guttural cries quaking through the floor and up the skeletons of Laura and Joseph.

They stood stock still, not even breathing, hoping they would somehow be ignored.

Joseph doubled over with a pained wince, his arm curving around his belly. A wad of phlegm lodged in his throat, and he tried to clear it. His other hand groped at Laura, and she bent to help, concerned.

"I'm sorry," he said, knowing that his death was imminent. Knowing that Laura's was, too. Still, even a few more moments of life were better than none.

He forced himself to stand upright, despite the agony. Grabbing Laura by both arms, he pushed her forward, toward the giant beast crouched before them. Tentacles snapped around her, and he heard bone crunch beneath their grasp. She was dead before she had time to scream, her head hanging at an unnatural angle, neck broken. The tentacles twisted and pulled, her head coming free, the rest of her body dragged toward those massive, parting tusks.

His stomach clenched and roiled as the muscles cramped and constricted. A sharp, stabbing pain shot through his core as his innards calved. He flung his mask off, then pulled free of his sweater and tore the button-down shirt beneath it open, buttons clinking against the slippery tiles.

In the mirror, he watched in horror as the skin of his torso rippled, as if a strong ocean current shifted through him. His flesh was nearly transparent, thin, and shot through with black piping. He pressed his fingers to his greasy belly, punching through the too-thin screen, and stretched it open. With a dazed sense of curiosity, Joseph watched a host of tentacles unravel and spill out of the ruined cavity.

The massive beast stopped eating, bits of Laura dangling from the ivory cage across its mouth. It stared at him, watching him with keen interest, waiting.

A slick wad, thick and heavy, climbed up Joseph's esophagus. Pinpricks of pain tickled the back of his mouth as the creature rose, entrenching its stingers in the soft tissue lining the inside of his neck as it dragged itself higher and higher.

Collapsing to his knees, he screamed in pain, his mouth full of blood and a repulsive, oily liquid.

Joseph had noted the taste in the previous dishes and was familiar with it now. He could finally pinpoint what, exactly, that particular flavor was. Bitter and ashy, unusually greasy, with the sliminess of okra. He tried to swallow it away, but that was of no use.

The taste of death flourished in his mouth.

16

Baen'sollogotgartha and the Old Gods of its realm promised immortality to those they consumed. Not on earth, but elsewhere, on another plane. A plane where mankind would be seen as gods in their own right, where their power over existence would be immeasurably strong.

Schauer craved no power, and cared little for the weight of life and death in his hands. As with any number of magnificent chefs, though, he sought the power of transformation.

Footfalls sounded against the stone steps as the waitress descended into the manor's basement, gun in hand.

"It's time," he told her.

She nodded mutely, removing the tricorn hat and veil, setting them neatly on the counter. She undressed and quickly folded her clothes, placing them beside the mourning wear. Schauer took her hand and gave it a gentle squeeze.

Opening her mouth, she put the gun barrel to the back of her upper palate and pulled the trigger with no hesitation. Matter exploded out of the back of her skull, smacking against the creature's face. Its ruined mouth opened and contracted, its forked tongue seeking sustenance.

If time allowed, he would prepare a meal of long pig for his final guest, here in this kitchen.

Good food did wonders for a soul, Schauer knew, and the mingling of a particular blend of flavors could bring tears to one's eyes. In the best instances, they helped another individual experience something communal, to share in the stories and cultures of another. Meals could inspire and lift a man.

In the best cases, ingredients were used in unusual ways

to elevate an otherwise common dish to something extraordinary. With that sense of respect and endearment, those meals became transformative in nature.

For years, he had sought the perfect guests. Those with palates of depth and subtlety, and a breadth of experience, who could appreciate mysterious, experimental meals and allow themselves to be consumed by the heady flavors of the dish plated before them. It had taken time, but Schauer was patient.

His patience had been rewarded. His skill had aided him well, and his dreams had been realized. With little more than his culinary know-how, Schauer had transformed his guests, elevated them.

Bending over the beast, he rested his hands flat against the shiny, sweat-slick cranium, and licked at the open wounds. The white sheen was coppery and burnt tasting, highly metallic and acidic, sulfurous almost. He ran his long tongue across the side of a fractured plane, and up to the hollow of an eye hole, allowing the cloying flavors to meld along his sophisticated palate. In return, the beast's own tongue sought and probed, longing for a taste. He dared not get close, though. Not yet.

For these beasts, consumption was a sex act. Their reproduction was predicated entirely on cannibalism and ruinous parasitical acts with other creatures. They were a driven species, their methods of satiation distilled into the simple act of eating, of devouring, the cycle of life reduced to a system no more complex than the rending and tearing of flesh and muscle with gnashing teeth and swallowing throats, followed by an engorged birthing.

He surveyed the husk of the creature. Plenty left, yet, for a feast. A knot bloomed and twisted in his belly, wrenching his guts in a violent twist. He doubled over in pain, gasping in agony. Still, he smiled, and thought for the last time of his assembled guests and the arctic surveyors before them.

Through the simple act of consumption, he had made each of them gods.

Soon, he would join them, and the world would change in their wake.

Let Go

Everett Hart hadn't set foot inside Brown's Fish & Chips in three years, not since his wife, Lucille, had died from breast cancer. When she was alive, they'd been regulars at the joint, coming every Sunday evening except during Lent, when they came on Fridays, which was when Brown's was at its busiest. Getting a table had often come with a long wait, regulars or not.

Brown's had been a staple in their relationship for going on twenty years, and it had seemed to Everett that the family-owned restaurant would always be there, same as his Lucille. She was gone; the restaurant remained.

Little had changed about the small restaurant. At the front was a glass display case with the counter on top, empty save for the single wooden shelf that divided its interior, with room enough for two cash registers, although he could only recall ever seeing one of them manned, even during peak Lent hours. Two walls of the dining room were lined with a row of brown vinyl booths, the upholstery shiny and spiderwebbed with white lines and the occasional crack where the stuffing hemorrhaged its way out. In between were blue Formica tables with four chairs, the metal rimming polished and bright beneath the overhead lighting. Everything about the restaurant screamed "relic," Everett included.

The walls were unadorned, save for a single clock mounted at the front over the glass display case.

Unassuming, maybe even dull, Brown's attracted the elderly, primarily, thanks to its cheap food and barren interior, although families and children were certainly welcome and occasionally even seen.

Everett did not consider himself elderly, even if retirement was fast approaching and he had his AARP card. He was well aware that death was close and that his birth was a quaint, forgotten notion that could only be smiled at, even if just with a meaningless, wistful smile. Lucille's passing had made that abundantly clear, more so than his hair loss—and the whitening of what little hair remained—and all the damnable wrinkles that marred his face and body.

"What can I getcha?" the waitress asked. She appeared roughly five minutes after a young Mexican boy had come to fill his water glass, not that Everett was logging the minutes. He didn't mind waiting and revisiting old phantoms.

Everett hadn't bothered looking at the menu. There was no need; he always ordered the same. "Fried perch. Coleslaw. Fries."

"You got it, hon," she said, making a quick scribble on the order pad and sauntering away.

She looked like that waitress from *Alice*, he thought. Her hair was a miniature peroxide-blond beehive, and her uniform was brown. She was larger, too, and older. And maybe she didn't look all that much like that one from *Alice* after all.

I think you're thinking of Mama, from Mama's Family, Lucille said from inside his head.

You know, I think you're right, hon.

The waitress's name tag said Maddie, and she had a big caboose that he watched with morbid fascination as it swung side to side with each step toward the rear of the dining room, to the swinging door that must have led to the kitchen. He caught a brief glimpse of activity beyond, bodies hustling back and forth.

He sat facing the inside of the restaurant because Lucille had always liked to take the seat facing the door and the front window. She was a people watcher and had always been oddly absorbed by who was coming in. Back then, he and Lucille had probably been the youngest customers Brown's had ever seen.

Lucille's parents had introduced them to the place. It had been her father's eightieth birthday—his last, as it happened—but the food had been good enough that they came back once in a while when neither felt like cooking. "Once in a while" turned into once a month, and that had turned into once a week.

Lucille watched the people, occasionally commenting to him on who was coming or going. He would listen attentively, sipping ice water with a wedge of lemon squeezed into it. A bowl of lemon slices for the fish always sat on every tabletop, and he always added lemon to his water, too. As the years slipped by, he began bringing a newspaper with him, hoping to stay up on current events, and she brought a book, and their table grew a bit quieter, their conversations and her observations a little less frequent. After nearly forty years together, how much did they have left to say?

If you were here right now, I'd be talking your ear off, he thought, imagining Lucille across from him. Even when they sat in companionable silence, reading, they always had a hand stretched across the table, breaking their hold only when necessary to turn a page, but their fingers always found one another again and settled into that familiar, reassuring squeeze.

Newspapers were too hard to read anymore, the print too small. And the world events always seemed to be so much the same with murder, wars, corruption, drone strikes, an unending pantheon of misery and finger-pointing and brutality. He didn't need that.

Instead, he read on an electronic tablet, losing himself in fiction. Stuff Lucille, a horror hound, would have enjoyed. Some of it he enjoyed in spite of himself. It was mindless entertainment, junk food for the brain, and Jesus, he could almost hear his mother's voice speaking those words. His son, William, had gotten the tablet for him two years ago, and he had learned how to increase the font size so he could read without his glasses.

He read more now than ever before. What else was he going to do? The kid was out of the house, and his wife was in the ground. TV bored him, and with his books, he could always make a mental movie if the words were good enough.

Since getting the Kindle, he'd bought most of Lucille's books in digital form—the type in the print editions she had owned, like that in newspapers, was too tiny for his tired old eyes. He now had a healthy library of titles by Brian Keene, Joe Lansdale, and Jonathan Maberry, from Ania Ahlborn to Stephen King—of course—and so many more he could hardly recall all the names populating his digital shelf space.

As his eyes drifted over the scattering of old folks at the other tables, Lucille's voice piped up again.

She's got a sort of Jacqueline Kennedy vibe about her.

It's the pillbox hat, Everett replied. Looking toward the woman's partner, a weathered black man in a blue windbreaker, he asked, *What about him?*

He looks like Ossie Davis, she said. *They were illicit lovers once upon a time,* she added with surety and because she always had a story about the people she saw.

Really?

Yup, she said. *She was a reverend's daughter and they started dating young, and when she got pregnant and then lost the baby it caused all sorts of controversy in that small rinky-dink town they were from.*

He fought in one of the wars, Korea probably, and gave more to his country than he ever got back, that's for sure. But she waited for him to come back home, and when he did they came north, settled here in this little town and made a home.

He found a job as a car salesman, but not one of those slimy used car salesmen you always hear about. No, he was one of the good ones, as honest as he could be and still cut a commission, fair and decent. She was a purebred housewife, maybe did some medical billing from home to help make ends meet. She was never able to have kids, and she went through a few miscarriages before they figured out it wasn't ever meant to be.

They love each other, though, a lot, and they're happy together. You can see it in their eyes, how they look at one another even after all these years. Ain't that something? Had she been there, she would have taken a long drink of water, a certain sparkle in her eyes as they drifted over the other people, seeking more stories.

He had always wondered where she came up with those stories, and regretted that he could never recapture their magic. He tried, though, simply so he could imagine her voice, and even as he looked over the other diners he knew he was tapped out, with no more stories to tell.

Everett shifted his weight then took out his Kindle and

resumed reading a Joe Hill novel while he waited for his fried perch. A few minutes later, the waitress came with a plate of hot buttered rolls, and he took one to nibble on. Mostly, he just needed something warm to occupy his free hand.

Lucille would have loved a Kindle, he knew. They'd have been able to read and hold hands and never let go to turn the page.

But he also knew that, eventually, one of them would have had to let go.

When his food arrived, he put the Kindle to sleep and closed its magnetic cover before placing it back in his coat pocket, the pocket with the gun. He folded his coat in half, burying that pocket, and turned his attention to the fish.

He savored the crunch of the crusty golden beer batter, and after the first bite, he squeezed a lemon wedge over the four filets. Even better, he mused. Satisfied, he reached for the ketchup set up alongside a greenish bottle of vinegar at the end of the table, against the wall. He spent a long time squeezing the bottle, piling ketchup into a tall hill beside the fries. He was saving the coleslaw, served in its own small bowl beside the plate, for last. He had always loved coleslaw, and Brown's made it just right. None of that vinegar base. This was all mayo, perfectly balanced and nicely chilled, the perfect endnote to the meal.

God, he wished Lucille were here. He wished they'd been able to come back together one last time, before the chemo destroyed her appetite and the cancer finally ate her up.

Since her death, food had become tasteless. No longer a thing of joy, eating had become another part of the daily grind, just some manufactured nutrients and chemical energy. He stopped cooking because with only him in the house, what was the point? He ate from boxes, all mass-produced stuff and mostly from the freezer and cereal aisles. This plate of fried perch was the first meal he had actually enjoyed in more than three years, and that, he knew, was mostly because he imagined Lucille across from him, enjoying her food, always a duplicate order of his.

"How about some dessert?" the waitress, Maddie, asked as he polished off the fish and spat out an errant lemon seed.

A police siren roared outside, the cop car screaming past. Everett and Maddie turned to look, although from his spot inside the booth, he couldn't see the car. Besides, by the time he got himself situated to see around the corner of the high-backed seat, the car was long gone.

"No, thank you," he said.

"When you're ready, then." She left a green bill holder on the table and scooted away.

Another siren wailed past, and then a third. Maybe more, judging by the volume of the noise, which was loud and sounded as though the car had stopped nearby.

Everett was curious, and he had to fish his wallet out of his back pocket anyway, so what harm could scooting over do? He wanted to take a look. The other patrons, most of them older than he was, seemed just as interested. Based on the hushed but animated conversations at the other tables, he figured this was probably the most exciting thing to have happened in their vicinity in quite some time.

He found his wallet, in his back pocket where it always rested, and dug out an unsigned credit card and his ID. In plain block writing, he had written on the back of the credit card, "PLEASE ASK FOR ID," but hardly anybody ever did.

The ID and credit card went into the small plastic pocket at the top of the bill holder, and he stood it upright at the edge of the table to catch Maddie's eye.

"What's going on out there?" he asked when she came by the table.

"Nothing to worry about, I'm sure," she said, a bright, cheery smile on her face. "Probably somebody ran a red light. We've had a few teens think they're in a drag race before, so could be that."

He was glad to see that she did check the credit card and ID first thing, and she even offered him a brighter, more authentic smile.

"Well, hey there, happy birthday!"

Everett blushed and smiled.

"Seventy-one?" she said, disbelieving. "You don't look it, hon. Good for you. How's retirement treating you?"

"It's good," he lied. Everett wasn't retired, but there was no point going into that with her. No reason to tell her how the crash back in '08 had wiped out a healthy bit of his retirement savings, and he'd had to work longer to save more.

He could tell she was about to say something, but then a gunshot rang out. And then another. A scream sounded too close and ended too abruptly. More shots were fired, and more sirens were approaching.

"What's going on out there?" he said, pushing himself out of the booth and forcing Maddie to step back. He turned toward the front of the restaurant and the cacophony outside. An officer stepped into view, pointing his gun toward something beyond the stretch of window, still hidden from Everett, the cop walking backward and pulling the trigger.

"Oh no," Everett said.

There was a crack in the sidewalk there, and Everett had tripped over it more than once. He'd never fallen, but the crack was just big enough to make him stumble and break his stride. The cop walking backward, though…

Sure enough, the officer's heel caught the break in the cement where part of the sidewalk jutted up, and he went down hard. The man he'd been shooting at lumbered into view and dropped below the window.

The screams were loud, and Everett could barely believe his eyes. It had all happened so fast. A bloody hand reached up, its fingers grasping for the edge of the restaurant's brickwork, but it found only the smooth stretch of glass before falling limply away. Four red lines ran down the window where those fingers had been.

Another flash of movement grabbed Everett's attention as two bodies hurtled themselves toward the front glass door, slamming their way through. A man and a woman, both in their twenties, he guessed. The man turned on his heel quickly, throwing the door shut and turning the dead bolt before collapsing. The woman was red-faced and breathing heavily, and she fell beside him, wrapping her arms around him.

"What the hell?" Everett said, his voice husky and confused.

A loud thump slammed against the window, gory hands and a dirty, bloody face pressing tightly against the pane. The man's mouth was working overtime, opening and closing, leaving fresh, wet streaks against the glass. The eyes were completely white, the retina milky, and the exposed flesh was pale. Deathly pale.

Behind Everett, a shrill scream drew his attention. Somebody fainted. Or at least, he hoped they had fainted rather than dropped dead. Maddie was standing over the prone body, yelling for someone to call 911.

As he drew nearer the door, he saw that outside was unbridled chaos. Whatever the two kids had been running from—and to Everett, they were just kids, even if in their twenties—the guy had been smart to lock the door.

The girl's mascara was running, and her blond hair had bright pink and green highlights. The boy's dark skin was lined with sweat, his afro, cut high and tight, shiny with perspiration. Both wore jeans and hoodies, and both looked terrified and in shock.

Everett was too old to kneel, but there was a cushioned bench opposite the door, and he lowered himself onto the seat, hunching forward to get a better look at them.

The girl had her face buried in the boy's neck, one hand holding the front of his shirt in a death grip. The boy had a consoling arm around her and appeared too dazed to even notice the old man across from him until Everett spoke.

"What's happening out there?"

"It's crazy," the boy said. He shook his head and screwed his eyes tightly shut. "It's like a horror movie or some shit, you know? Like the end of the world."

Everett's mouth fell open, at a loss for words. What could he even say to something like that? It was crazy. Right?

Looking out the door and window of Brown's, he wasn't so sure.

The scene was like something out of Lucille's crazy horror books. The books he'd begun reading to help keep Lucille around, the books he'd even kind of begun enjoying.

A police car braked and swerved, the tail end, with a stink of burning rubber, sliding around to block the road. The cops got out, drew their guns, and crouched beside the driver's side, using the car as a shield. They took turns popping up and firing, but Everett couldn't see at what.

Then the bloodied man at the window turned toward the noise and began to shamble off. One of the cops, the one nearest the rear tire, seemed to catch sight of the movement and shouted for the man to stop. The man kept moving, though, and the officer opened fire. A slug tore through the man's shoulder, and Everett watched as blood and bits of bone and pink tissue exploded out of the man's back, but the man didn't fall. No, he kept walking. Another bullet passed through his belly, and still he kept walking.

"This is impossible," Everett said.

The man was nearly on top of the car now, and the policeman stood up and took careful aim. The back of the bloodied man's head exploded, his skull whip-cracking back as he finally fell, finally stilled.

The policeman collapsed, too, pressing the side of his gun to his face, his shoulders shaking.

"Jesus," Everett said. "Okay, look. We need to get away from the windows. This is stupid to be so close. If one of those bullets goes astray…"

He stood, holding his hand out to the young couple. "Come on. Let's go back. It's safer in the back."

As he helped the girl to her feet, and then the boy, he saw a pair of raw, bony digits rise up in front of the window, seeking out the brick sill's edge. The hand was short a few fingers, the bloody stubs tapping against the glass. The crown of a head appeared, the hair clotted in a thick black sheen, and then a face. The nose had been torn away, and the cheeks were a pulpy mess. His lips were gone, revealing objectionably white teeth that opened and shut of their own accord, a loose string of frenulum dangling from the stripped gum of his lower jaw.

It was the policeman, the one Everett had seen trip and fall only moments before. He was somehow still alive.

Not alive, Lucille said, the echo of her voice in his mind sound and sure. She was convinced of what was happening, and he believed her. Trusted her.

The policeman was standing tall now, looking into the restaurant with too-large, too-white eyes.

"C'mon, then," he said, the couple both on their feet again. "We're going to the back."

Everett hadn't noticed the crowd of loose-skinned old-timers at the edge of the dining room. They stood well enough away from the windows, but the way they were all bunched up made passing difficult. He caught snatches of their worried, overlapping speculations as he huddled with the couple, passing them through.

"It's that Zika virus. I been hearing about that all over."

"Glenn Beck said the Rapture was coming. Listened to him on the way over. Ted Cruz was on there, talking about how we're due for a holocaust cause we've lost our way. Not enough Jesus, and 'cause of the gays getting married. This is what we get now."

"It ain't the gays or Zika or nothing like that," one man said. He sounded supremely confident, but if he had anything else to offer, Everett missed it.

"Terrorists then," the Zika guy said. "Or them Chinese."

Gunshots were coming fast and steady. Until they weren't. The dining room grew darker as a mass of bodies passed the restaurant, a crushing wave of people, deformed and disfigured, shambling by, practically falling over one another. Falling over the police, overwhelming them with their sheer numbers.

Maddie and Teeg—the tall black chef dressed in jeans, a white T-shirt, and apron—stood on either side of a pale old woman slumped in a chair. Maddie was helping her drink water, and Everett surmised it was the person who had fainted. A sweaty pitcher of ice water sat on the table in a pool of condensation, and he grabbed two empty glasses from another table and poured for the couple before sitting them down around a table farther back.

"We gotta get out of here."

"Let's stow that shit," a thick, deep voice said. The cook. "I can't let any of you leave now. Too dangerous. You see what's going on out there, don't you?"

"Teeg," Maddie said. "C'mon. Maybe the back is clear, and we can all leave."

"We ain't leaving," Teeg said. "We're on lockdown, far as I'm concerned. I want everyone to move back into the dining room, as far away from the windows as you can get. Come on, people, let's go."

When none of the old-timers moved, Teeg let out a drill-sergeant bellow. "I said, let's go!"

That got the old folks moving, if not quite scrambling.

The front window was crowded with leering faces, an entire row of milky eyes staring inside, watching them, smearing bloodied saliva and dirty hands all across the glass. Everett's eyesight was bad enough that most of this vision was a fuzzy blur, but right then and there, he'd have given anything to not see it at all, blurry or otherwise.

"What happened out there?" he asked, turning his attention back to the young couple.

"How the hell do you even explain it?" the girl said.

The mascara had buried her puffy eyes in black rings and left long, ashy streaks down her cheeks. Everett thought she would be prettier without all the piercings in her eyebrows and the tiny ring in her lower lip. She wore a baggy Oakland University hoodie, the cuffs of the sleeves badly frayed, presumably because she worried at them with her pointy nails, as she was currently doing. A nervous habit, maybe.

"I don't know what happened," the boy said.

The young man looked a bit more put together, but

one sleeve was bunched up high around his forearm, almost to the elbow, revealing a long stretch of ink that ran from his wrist and disappeared beneath the hoodie. His was a black OU hoodie, the large cartoon face of the school's Golden Grizzlies mascot prominent across the chest, and Everett guessed they went to school together. The boy's tattoo sleeve was devoid of color, but the black tones and negative space made the Grim Reaper plain, along with the row of tombstones and skulls rimming the work.

Kids these days, Everett thought, and he swore he could hear a bit of his father in that sentiment. And when had that happened, exactly? Probably around the time he'd had William, maybe. He should call the boy.

The boy, he testily reminded himself, was thirty-six. But Everett was at that stage in life when anybody younger than him qualified as a kid.

"You were running. What from?"

"What do you think from what?" the boy shouted, waving his inked arm toward the window. "From that, man, from that!"

"It's all right now," Teeg said, taking a chair beside Everett. "Just drink some water. You're safe in here."

Even sitting, Teeg was a tall man, his long arms hanging limply at either side, his fingers nearly touching the floor. And even though he was slender, his deep cannon-fire voice gave him instant command of the room.

"We're all safe in here," he said. He held eyes with one of the cotton-headed men until the retiree nodded, then Teeg nodded, too, as if they'd all come to some sort of agreement. Hell, maybe they had.

"This guy," the OU girl said, "I don't even know where he came from. Like from out of nowhere, right? We were walking down the strip, and we heard this scream. I turned around, we both did, and I saw this guy grabbing a lady."

"I thought maybe it was a mugging or something," the OU guy said.

"And this guy, he jerked the lady toward him and bit into her throat. Like really bit down hard. Tore her neck open with his teeth, and there was all this blood."

"There were more, though. I don't know where they were coming from. Four or five of them, maybe, and they were snatching up whoever was closest."

"And one of them grabbed this baby, and—" Fresh tears ran freely down her face, and she snorted back a glob of snot, palming her eyes. "Oh, God. I can't even."

"So that's why we were running. I don't even know why we stopped here. All those police coming, maybe. I mean, the door was unlocked, and it was right here, so…"

"You did right coming in here," Teeg said. "Locking that door. Smart thinking. That was good."

The OU guy picked up the glass of water and held it in his hands, his fingers tightening and loosening, alternately tapping against the glass.

"I'm Kara, by the way," OU girl said. "This is Mitch."

"I'm glad you're safe. I'm Teeg. Can I get you some food? A drink?"

"Nah," Mitch said. "Thanks."

Kara just shook her head, the tears still flowing.

"It's good to see you, too, man," Teeg said, looking warmly at Everett. "Been a while."

Everett nodded. It was all he could do. He struggled to hang on, the weight of the last few minutes hitting him all of a sudden. The fried food sat like an iron weight in the middle of his belly. Then he noticed Teeg's outstretched hand and took it.

"I was sorry to hear about Lucille. I'm glad you found your way back here, though."

Everett nodded again, his mouth dry and his eyes burning. He was surprised Teeg even remembered him. Surprised but gladdened, his heart heavy. They'd met only a handful of times, but it was sweet Teeg remembered them, even after all the years away and all the faces in between. Everett felt guilty he'd barely remembered Teeg until today, hadn't thought of the man at all, really. And here was Teeg, remembering both him and Lucille, remembering even her name, and holding onto a condolence for three long years.

Christ.

If Teeg was a mind reader, Everett wouldn't have been surprised. The chef reached over and, with a surprisingly strong grip, squeezed Everett's shoulder and, with his other hand, gave him a pat on the arm.

Maddie was bussing the tables, refilling water glasses. He watched her work for a moment, tracking her back through the swinging door to the kitchen. A moment later, she was back out and hitting up the tables she'd missed. Neither time had Everett noticed the bustle of activity in the kitchen, not like before, and he wondered why Maddie was filling water glasses and not the Mexican boy who'd greeted him at the table.

"You seem suddenly short-staffed," he whispered to Teeg.

The chef's brow crinkled, his mouth subverted into a deep scowl. He spoke softly, his words meant for Everett's ears only. "Lost a few bodies," he said. "Just me and Maddie now."

"Jesus."

"These two brothers, see, Philippe and Javier—busboy and short order—worked for me, decided they didn't want to hack it. Thought they'd be better off running. Took a bunch of knives and bolted out the back door before I could stop them. Wasn't too long later, they was screaming."

"Jesus," Everett said again.

"S'why I don't want y'all leaving if I can help it. Not yet. Not till it's safe."

"We can't stay here forever." The voice came from somewhere in the back, behind Mitch and Kara so Everett couldn't see who it was. Teeg's voice had been soft, and Everett thought it unlikely the man had heard, but he didn't know for sure. Maybe the old geezer had heard them, or maybe he was just awfully prescient in his timing.

"Police'll get it sorted out" came a soft-voiced woman's answer.

"We're not going to be here forever," Teeg assured them, speaking louder now to address everyone. "Just long enough to wait it out. Please, everyone, just take your seats for a bit, okay?"

The old-timers were compliant, and soon the scraping of chair legs against the linoleum was loud enough to blot out the noise of fingers drumming noisily and hands slapping loudly against the window and door.

"I gotta get cooking," Teeg said, rising from the chair with a groan. "Who's hungry?"

Nobody said anything, but he wasn't fussed. "Once y'all start smelling the food, your stomachs'll get grumbling, don't you worry. I'm making it on the house. We're all in this together, may as well eat."

Some of them murmured thanks as Teeg passed by a handful of elderly couples on his way back into the kitchen.

Not sure what else to say to Kara and Mitch, Everett slowly walked back to his table, keeping his eyes averted to avoid meeting those staring, dead gazes ahead. He wished he could blot out the sounds they made, the fleshy *thunks* against the windowpane and the growling, hungry sounds that went with them.

Absently, he resituated his ID and credit card in his wallet, slipped that back into his butt pocket, and slid into the booth. His knees and back protested slightly with achy twinges, and he let out a sigh of relief as he settled comfortably into the worn-out vinyl.

He closed his eyes, a pain in his chest blooming. This wasn't the way to die, damn it. Not like this. Not at all how'd he planned it or wanted it.

But no, it wasn't a heart attack but an attack of sadness and revulsion laced with dire, black humor. The absurdity of it, to have his long life felled by something straight out of an overripe horror cliché. There were still things to do. His job, for instance. He sorted mail for the post office, nothing glamorous, but it was his job, and he felt a sense of responsibility toward it. This was to be his last week, after all. Retirement was right around the corner.

And then what?

As he dug in his coat pocket for his cell phone, the backs of his fingers brushed the gun tucked in there, along with the Kindle. Ah, yes. What then? He'd already started thinking about that.

He couldn't imagine the shape of his life anymore, all the things that had passed and how little was left ahead.

Lucille was gone. His son had his own life, his job, his own family, in a different state. William visited for the holidays, usually, his wife and daughter in tow. Thanksgiving every other year, and Christmas. The occasional phone call, but those had grown more infrequent over the years. Lucille's death had brought an uptick in William's calls, but as time marched on, they settled back into their infrequent groove. Everett could have called him, he knew. Should have called him, in fact, but he hid behind the idea that he wasn't a phone guy when the simple truth was that he was merely lazy and stubborn. William had inherited that much from him.

And soon he wouldn't even have a job anymore. What would he do all day? Sit around the house, watching bad, mindless TV and reading e-books? That wasn't a life for him. Whenever he imagined it, it felt hollow and meaningless. He just wanted Lucille back; he missed her so much. So he'd begun thinking about the 'what thens' of retirement, of another cornerstone of his life being chipped away and tossed into the dustbin of his personal history, and he began to feel as though he knew the answer, and he carried it with him always.

The cell phone woke with a finger tap to the screen, the big white numerals of the current time set against the manufacturer's default wallpaper.

A few moments later, William answered with a breathless, "Hey, Dad, what's up?"

"Hello, son!" Everett found himself smiling, tears forming a burning, standing puddle that he had to blink away. Somehow he knew this would be the last time he'd speak to his boy. "I just wanted to check in, make sure everything's okay on your end."

"Yeah, things are good. How are you holding up?"

"Ah, you know. This weather."

Behind him, dead fists slammed against glass. He wondered if more police would come, if there would be more gunshots and whether William would be able to hear them through the phone and worry over his father.

"It's only going to get colder. I'm telling you, you should head to Arizona. You'll feel better."

"Maybe," Everett said. "How are Ellie and Tabby?"

"Both are good. *Tabatha*, though, has decided she hates being called"—he lowered his voice and whispered conspiratorially—"*Tabby*, so we're all on notice. The fits she throws, Jesus, you wouldn't believe it."

Tabby was three going on thirty and had little trouble making her presence and her demands known to those around her.

"Oh, I think I can imagine," Everett said. When William was his daughter's age, he'd liked to hide under the clothes racks when Lucille took him to the mall, and he proved to be a holy terror who fought against her, literally tooth and nail, when she dragged him out kicking and screaming.

"Ah, crap. Hey, Dad, I gotta go. Ellie ran to the grocery store for a bit, and the house is strangely quiet. I should go see what *Tabatha* has gotten into."

"Quiet kids are never a good sign. You better go check. Love you, son."

"Love you, too, Dad. I'll call you later."

William disconnected first, probably relieved to cut the call short. Everett exhaled slowly. He'd wanted to tell his son one last time how he felt about him, and while it hadn't been the talk he'd imagined, it was as good as it was going to get. "Good enough" was the best he could hope for. If Lucille's death had taught him anything, it was that there was always so much left unsaid and never enough time to say it all.

If he had time, and if William actually called him back, which he doubted would happen, Everett would tell him again how much he loved him. He would apologize, too, for not having been a better father. Everett didn't think poorly of himself as a parent, and he knew he'd done as well as he could, but always could have—*should have*—tried harder, striven to be a better father. He had wanted to be a better father to William than Everett's father had been to him. Mostly he'd been successful, but there had also been too many lapses on his part that could never be corrected.

If there was time, he'd talk William's ear off if allowed to.

Time was such a rare and precious commodity. William's birth had proven that to him almost immediately. Lucille's death had driven it home even further, a thick nail through his heart. He'd always thought they'd have more time, that there would be just one more day, and that tomorrow he would be stronger for her, less of a coward. He was going to apologize to her, too. Had meant to, had told himself he would do it tomorrow, before time ran out, but tomorrow turned into tomorrow into tomorrow, and time ran out for both of them.

When Everett was a boy, a teenager who had foolishly thought himself a man, his ill-tempered father had finally had enough. A petty argument between his parents had been the last straw, the final spark that ignited his father's short, thin fuse. Dad had never hit Mom, but the emotional and psychological abuse he'd left in his wake was violent enough. Sometimes words could do far more damage than a fist. Everett had learned that early in life, and sometimes his own tongue was a lash, and he wanted to tell Lucille he was sorry for that. His father had stormed out of his and his mother's life, packed up the car and left.

"Maybe one day you'll see I'm not so bad," Dad had said. His parting shot across the bow as the back door slammed shut behind him.

Everett had never seen his father again after that, and he had never had the chance to see if his father could be a better man. Everett himself knew he could be better, too, if he hadn't been so lazy, and he hoped that William did not think as poorly of him as he did his own father.

He'd never left William or Lucille, not like that. But too many times, he had checked out emotionally and mentally. Too many times, he had thought about leaving, oh yes. Had come so very close. But his son needed a father, and Lucille needed a husband. He loved them, and in the end that was a strong enough bond to keep him tied to them, despite the occasional urge and depressive insistence that he run and run far.

He'd stayed.

Now they had all left him. All the things that kept him connected, that made him and defined him, slowly detached, one by one.

Lucille. William. His job.

The pounding against the glass behind him reminded him that now, too, the world around him had become unmoored. Impossible things slammed against the glass and rattled the locked door in its frame, reality itself ungluing from all that Everett had thought he'd known. One last illusion undone and stripped away.

His hand fell onto his lumpy coat pocket. The gun in there.

The gun was always for just in case. In case he couldn't take it anymore. In case the loneliness became too unbearable, the weight of it too crushing. In case he decided he needed, finally, to see Lucille again. In case he lost one more goddamn thing.

Always just in case.

He didn't think he would use it until after Friday, his last day on the job. Not until after he was retired and cut loose from yet one more thing that defined his days. He couldn't bear the thought of having nothing left. And so he kept the gun in his pocket, just in case.

"We can't stay here."

The man's voice was gravelly, probably from too many

years of liquor and cigarettes. When Everett turned to see who had spoken, he saw it was the Ossie Davis-looking man in the blue windbreaker. The gentleman was older than Everett, with thinned hair and a scalp lightly stained by the coloring used to make his hair an impossible shade of black for a man so advanced in years. His face and hands littered with liver spots. Everett recognized his voice as the same one Teeg had shut down earlier.

"We can't stay here," he said again.

There were a few nods of agreement, a few whispers of dissent, and a loud silence from those who simply had no idea what to do and were too afraid to commit one way or the other.

The kid, Mitch, was looking at his phone, his thumb sliding up the screen over and over. Kara sat beside him, their chairs butted up together, their knees touching and her head resting on his shoulder. Whatever he was reading caused him to look incredulous.

"They're calling this a riot," he said, practically laughing at the absurdity.

"Who is?" Everett asked.

"The news, their *official sources*," he said, mockingly. "That's the party line, I guess. 'Authorities are urging people to remain in their home until the situation is resolved.'"

Mitch snorted then tossed his phone onto the table. "Riot. Yeah, right. A riot. That's what this is."

"How long until that glass breaks?" Ossie asked, tugging at the front of his windbreaker. "All of them pressing up against it like that?"

Everett turned to get a look around the corner of the booth. More faces were pressed against the window now. A lot more.

Brown's didn't have much in the way of safety features.

There were no bars on the windows, no security gates for the doors. Only a dead bolt, maybe an alarm system. The restaurant was situated in a sleepy suburb where crime was low enough to barely register as a concern. This so-called riot, though, may have been enough to single-handedly destroy the small town's police force. Everett realized it had been a while since they'd heard a siren or even a gunshot.

He worried over how widespread things were. William hadn't seemed to know about it, and that gave him some comfort. Hopefully his son and family were safe and blissfully ignorant of what was happening here.

It would spread, though. He knew that much. Lucille's books didn't seem so entertaining anymore. They felt more foreboding, more cautionary, like a warning they hadn't heeded. *Joke's on you now, guys.*

How long until the troops rallied? State police or National Guard would have to respond, wouldn't they? Or were things so bad already that even those resources were being applied elsewhere or diminished entirely?

"What about unofficial sources?" Everett asked, pointing Mitch back toward his phone. "Isn't there like a Tweetbook or something?"

His own phone had apps for those, but he'd never used them. He had a lot of things on his phone, all manufactured, installed stuff, but he hadn't opened a single one of them. As far as he was concerned, a phone was supposed to be a phone. Maybe an e-reader, if the Kindle died. Games, this so-called social media stuff—that was all useless. Or so he'd thought.

"Hashtag zombie apocalypse?" Mitch said. "Let's see."

Mitch's face slowly sank, a spark leaving his eyes. "It's not just us," he said, finally.

He kept talking, reading tweets and describing pictures and videos people were uploading, but Everett didn't listen.

He heard sobs as the older women broke down, a few of them digging their own cell phones out of purses so they could call loved ones.

Teeg rolled in a banquet cart piled with salads, fish baked and fried, onion rings, french fries, carafes of coffee, and hot water for tea. He looked around at the collective misery and said, "Eat up."

"It's spreading," Mitch said.

"We can't stay here."

Eyes turned toward Teeg, and he held their gazes for a long moment. Finally, he let out a deep breath, and an admission. "No, we can't. We don't know what it's like out there. I think everything's been turned upside down. Doesn't it feel like that? Feels like it to me. Which is why we all need to eat up, get our fuel, then we'll head out."

"I'm starving," Mitch said, as if realizing it for the first time.

"C'mon, y'all. Grab a plate."

Teeg and Maddie stacked each plate high with food and filled cups with coffee and tea. Nobody wanted to call this the last supper, but it sure did feel like it. Everett wondered how many of them were honest enough with themselves about what was happening that they even dared think of this as their last meal.

Conversations started and stalled and started again all around him, although Everett sat by himself, in the same booth he'd been seated at hours before. Night had fallen, but the coffee kept him alert. The young couple sat at a nearby table, but he didn't engage them, and their focus was entirely on the food before them. Kara was an eater, even if she didn't look it, and she worked through her meal with a contagious gusto.

The tartar sauce was freshly made, and Everett loved the tingle in his cheeks left by the finely chopped pickles and capers. Halfway through the dish, he heard a rising growl and pneumatic hiss from outside, barely louder than the noises of those creatures everyone was desperately trying to ignore. He knew with dreadful certainty that gunfire would commence.

When the shots rang out, they came with vicious, sudden loudness, startling the other patrons. The gunfire kept on, sustained in a way that made him think it must have been a machine gun, certainly a high-end bit of artillery.

The undead were packed deep, and the bodies in back protected those in front. The bullets managed to chew their way through the corpses, striking the glass. Between the assault from the shooter and the crush of bodies pressing against the pane, the glass exploded, and a tidal wave of corpses, animated and otherwise, flooded into the restaurant.

Bullets slammed into the walls and ceiling as the shooter tried to retarget on the shifting mass, maybe realizing living beings were still in the restaurant, and jerking up on the weapon to avoid hitting those inside.

Teeg's head snapped back, his body dropping. The food lining the table in front of him chipped and burst apart.

"Get down!" Everett said. His body protested the sliding movement he made to slink beneath the table. Kara was closest, and once he was safe beneath his table, he grabbed her arm and hauled her to the floor. Mitch was moving, too.

The other diners weren't so lucky. The Ossie Davis lookalike jerked and flailed in his chair, his wife, sitting across from him, covered in blood, both his and hers. Her pillbox hat was nowhere to be seen. The side of her skull had been blasted into a crescent, her eye dislodged from its cavity and dangling before her open mouth.

Maddie spun, a bullet catching her in the shoulder, and in her hip another that set her spinning back in the opposite direction. Her neck exploded, the large-caliber machine gun decapitating her.

Bodies began shifting by the window as the gunfire turned toward the door. More of the creatures outside were trying to get into Brown's through the front window. Some were lucky enough to climb over and land in the twisting heap of undead, while others were cut down by the machine gunner.

Zombies rose, their noses flaring as they sniffed out the fresh blood and became incensed.

From his position on the floor, Everett could not make out what was happening outside. The shuffling corpses blocked his view, but the sounds were a good indicator. A man's shrill scream pierced the air, and then came a screech as tires fought for purchase on the macadam, an engine roaring. Metal crunched, and loud *thuds* filled the air as he imagined hordes of the undead being plowed into by a Humvee. There was a wicked crash and bursting mortar, then more gunfire followed by a scream that ended in a shocked yelp and a cry for help. One last gunshot, and then the sound of running.

Everett watched as crooked feet lumbered closer, the walker nearly tripping over his own steps.

Everett, Kara, and Mitch were still far enough back in the dining room that they were not yet in immediate danger. They still had time to escape.

He reached up for his jacket and found the gun, the grip both strange and familiar in his gnarled, arthritic hand. It was a six-shooter, an old piece, fully loaded. He'd only ever planned on needing one bullet.

"Come on. We need to go," he said. He hoped the panic he felt wasn't apparent in his voice. Holding his Saturday Night Special, he definitely didn't feel like Dirty Harry or John Wayne, or any of those action-movie guys who always had a clever quip and true aim.

The kids looked at him as if he were holding a rattlesnake but quickly adjusted to the new reality. Kara nodded, then she took her boyfriend's hand and helped him out from under the table.

"Start moving," Everett ordered. "I'm right behind you."

That wasn't exactly true. His knees were flaring up, protesting the weight of his kneeling body, his hip tight and his back aching from the odd contortions. He had to crawl forward, then get a free hand up onto the seat of the booth, steady himself and raise one leg to get a foot beneath him, using his arm and fucked-up knee to push off, up into a standing position. The process was slow and sluggish and painful.

A scream erupted behind him, and although he knew he shouldn't have looked back, he couldn't help himself. A Q-tip of a woman was being jerked back by her poofy, cottony cloud hair, her feet wheeling back. Teeth bit through the wobbly folds of her turkey neck, boring down through the skin and veins to get into the deeper recesses of her throat.

Kara and Mitch were waiting for him, the boy practically waving him home. He had no idea why. They owed him nothing, yet Mitch's arm was looping around his waist.

"You need to get out of here," he said.

"We're all getting out of here, man," Mitch said, guiding him through the swinging door and into the kitchen. They all avoided looking at Teeg, their feet turning the destroyed food into messy slop against the blood-splattered tile floor. If not for Mitch's aid, Everett thought he might have slipped in the mess.

"We're the only ones left," Kara said.

"I'm slowing you down."

"None of that now," Mitch said. They were almost to the rear door, the employee entrance.

Only a few feet away.

A few feet too far, Everett knew, even before a surprisingly strong hand clamped down on his shoulder and pulled him off balance, his body tugging between Mitch and his assailant. He twisted funny, a hot, writhing lance of pain exploding in the center of his lower back. He gritted his teeth against the pain, but moving forward was impossible. The hand gripped the meat of his shoulder tight, hauling him off his feet.

"No!" Mitch screamed, fighting against the undead creature for supremacy over the old man's body, trying to pull Everett away.

"Let go," Everett shouted, but Mitch hung on, maybe thinking Everett was talking to his attacker. This close, he could easily see where the broken glass from the front window had lacerated the monster's face and neck, bloodied shards still buried in his skin and glinting off the overhead track lighting. He had an arm up between them, but it was sagging, getting weak and tired awfully fast. Teeth snapped too close to his face, pink drool dangling from the creature's lips and threatening to spill onto Everett's own face.

"Let go," he said again, finding the boy's eyes and nodding. Telling him it was okay to let go. "Just let go."

Mitch's hand loosened. Everett raised the gun, shooting the zombie point-blank in the skull. That was where all the books said to shoot them, in the head, the only way to put them down for good.

"Come on," Kara urged, reaching for Everett on one side, Mitch on the other.

His back screamed bloody murder, lightning bolts of agony arcing all through his spine, arms, and legs. He could hardly stand it hurt so much, and the fall, the way he had landed, had done something awful, broken something inside him. His legs wouldn't support him, and the two youths had to keep him standing upright, the edge of the prep counter pressed against the back of his thighs.

This is it, then, he thought.

"I think I broke my hip. Ain't that something?"

"There's more coming," Mitch said, looking nervously toward the swinging door.

The door was still moving, swooshing back and forth in slower, disintegrating arcs, but in those little flashes of insight toward the dining room, the three of them could make out the shuffling masses growing nearer. That door would open soon and stay open for a good while as the undead filled the kitchen.

"You two need to leave. Go on now."

"You gotta come with us," Mitch protested, tugging at his arm. Insistent, but why?

Because it was the right thing, because they were trapped together in some unbelievable horror and that was just what one did, or because human survival depended on trust and cooperation?

Whatever it was, it didn't matter.

"Here," Everett said, taking the boy's hand and pressing the gun into it. "You need this. Take it."

Even something as simple as passing a gun to the boy sent excruciating, knifing pains through the center of his lower back.

"We can carry you."

"No, you can't," Everett said. As if an afterthought, and more to himself, he added, "My burdens are too heavy."

"What?"

"Doesn't matter. Hey, you know the one about outrunning a bear?"

"What are you talking about?"

"When you and your buddies are in the woods, being chased by a bear? You don't have to outrun the bear. You only need to outrun your friend. You just need to outrun the slowest poke, let the other guy be bear food. That's what this is. You understand?"

Talking ached, but relaying this seemed vital. Everett had to get it through this boy's skull that he didn't need to be a hero, not on his account.

The swinging door slammed open, the entryway crowded with bodies working to shove past one another, hands reaching out before them and clawing at the air, reaching for the young couple and the old man. One body broke free and clumsily strode forward, and that was like breaking a levy, the rest pouring in behind.

"Go!" Everett screamed with all the energy he could muster. That simple, single-syllable command died in his throat as his back seized, and he choked on the word.

Kara and Mitch looked between him and the horde, uncertain and far too hesitant. The boy raised the gun and fired, clipping one of the zombies along the neck.

Everett tried to tell him to go for the head but couldn't drum up the words. He was busy coughing, which ignited new pains inside him. His hip throbbed, and he wanted to lie down and cry.

"There's too many," Kara said, grabbing her boyfriend's arm and pulling him with her. She looked back toward the old man, tears standing in her eyes. "I'm sorry."

And then Mitch was throwing open the rear door, pulling her through and into the alley. Her mouth opened to say something more, but it was forgotten as he grabbed her and nearly took her off her feet.

As always, there was never enough time to say it all.

Everett gripped the edge of the prep table with both hands, trying to keep as much weight as he could on a single foot, his arms keeping him up. His muscles were sagging, growing shaky. It didn't matter. The horde would be on him soon.

For all the times he'd imagined being with Lucille again, he had never considered this particular scenario as a means of being reunited with his wife.

He closed his eyes and waited.

He did not wait long.

Slowly, the tethers holding him to this world came undone, the detachments peeling screams loose from him until his voice ran hoarse and teeth found his throat and his mouth and tongue, and obliteration followed.

In his final moments, as the darkness descended, he saw Lucille. She was young and pristine, her blond hair full and ringing her perfect, beautiful, unlined face. Everett was young again, too, and when she opened her arms to him, he fell into her embrace. Her smile was golden, and her kiss even better.

She held him tightly and never let go.

The Marque

1

Darrell Fines pinched off the excess tobacco and finished rolling his cigarette. He lit it with the dying embers of the one already hanging from his mouth and took a hungry puff. With a fresh smoke in hand, all he had to do was wait.

"You been up to see 'em yet?" Hank Myrtle asked

He turned toward Myrtle and shook his head. "Nope. Not yet."

"They don't like waiting."

"I know it."

Fines looked down at the camp beneath them. The sound of working men straining poured out from the tunnel behind them, which Myrtle watched with a lazy eye. A rifle was slung over Hank's shoulder, never used. Fines's free hand rested on the butt of his S&W, used a few times too many.

"Shift's over soon. Let's get everyone back home in one piece, then I'll go up."

"They don't like waiting," Myrtle said again. There was worry in his voice, a pained expression on his face. He was nervous, antsy.

Worst still, he was right. The beasties did not like to be kept waiting. Whatever they wanted, they wanted it right then and there. Not in five minutes, not at the end of shift. It was all now or never with them, and the latter was simply not an option. Not if you expected to keep on breathing peacefully.

He'd heard the gossip over yesterday's attack at the farm. Lousy business, that.

"You got this, then?"

"Ayuh," Myrtle said, his northern Maine accent shining through. Fines had never heard anyone say "ayuh" until he'd met Myrtle a few years back.

"Fuck it then. I'm off."

Fines was two steps away when Myrtle hollered at him and said, "Good luck, man."

Fines nodded, not breaking stride, and waved over his shoulder. He kept a solid pace through the work camp and into the habitat ring, whittling his cigarette down between his lips.

A full-face respirator was hooked onto his belt, bouncing off his thigh as he walked. The women and children outside, either working on chores or playing, or maybe a bit of both, pretending nothing was wrong, all wore their masks. Most of those were half-face respirators, which left their eyes exposed. A dust storm would be hell, and hell was something there was plenty enough of around here.

Several camp folk watched him, baleful glares following him through the makeshift 'stead. He met some of their eyes and nodded back, not taking their open antagonism personally. If he were on their side of things, likely he'd hate himself, too. As it was, he hated himself enough.

He knew what they called him, and he knew, too well, that they were right. Traitor. Dog. Turncoat. Coward. A beat-up old bitch. Yes, he was all of that, and then some.

Dust hung in the air, large spores like dandelion seeds, spreading across the dead grey plains and the dead grey skies.

The children ignored him and carried on as they were. He watched a group of six kicking what looked like a rock between them in a pick-up game of soccer, through a brackish mix of dirt and pollution. As he drew closer, he saw they weren't playing with a rock at all, but a canine skull. Eventually his steps took him past and they fell out of view, while their commotion hung in the dusky air at his back.

Through it all, his hand rested casually on the Smith & Wesson.

His cigarette died before he reached the lift at the end of the camp, taking it skyward to the ship that hung above their daily lives, blocking the sun and casting a permanent shade over all that was beneath. The control box was a simple two-button affair – one for up, one for down. No words, no icons, simple reasoning stating which was which. Fines couldn't go any further down than he already was, so he hit the top button.

Much of the last few years was spent on the ground. Enough that he forgot how acrid the ship smelled, as if there had been a recent electrical fire.

A putrescent green skein clung to every surface, a thin vapor of it boiling off the floor in a heady steam. The stink of burnt metal and scorched wires offended his nose and he breathed through his mouth. The air itself was clean, if not nasty, and perfectly breathable, so he had no use for the respirator. Besides that, the beasties would likely be offended if they caught him masked aboard ship. They were mercurial enough without the extra risk.

He spent a few long minutes maneuvering through the dank, musky corridors. The heat was oppressive, and sweat pooled beneath the Stetson's headband. Dark circles formed on the chest of his chambray shirt, spreading out from beneath his armpits. More than merely the heat, his nerves were jumpy, making his palms wet. An uncomfortable, damp warmth had settled deeply in his groin, and his slick thighs rubbed against his jeans. His balls had curled up tight, butterflies knocking around his hollow belly, as he wondered what the hell they wanted with him now.

He'd played it cool in front of Myrtle, but the truth of it was, he was scared.

He hadn't been this afraid since he was a little boy and Daddy had come marching up the stairs to his bedroom, drunk and intent on working out some anger with a thick leather belt hanging from his fist.

Whenever little Fines had heard that front door slam shut and the engine noise and the rumble of tires escaping the driveway and turning onto the road, he knew. He'd spend the next few hours in a cold sweat, bed sheets pulled tightly around his small, too-thin frame, hoping, thinking to himself, *maybe not tonight.*

As the years went on and the pattern crystallized, and he was too young to escape, he knew. When Daddy came back, and he heard the loud thudding footsteps rising to greet him, he knew. He'd been conditioned to expect only one thing, and in time he began to cry and wail even before the metal belt buckle found his bare skin and the leather carved its long red welts.

After his first time on this ship, this mausoleum of

horrors, he'd spent many nights thereafter in bed, thinking to himself, *maybe not tomorrow*. But today, he'd been summoned, and there was no turning away. There was no escaping.

The hallway branched into arching corridors, multiple shafts bleeding off on either side, some sloping up, some down. He hooked a left, heading toward the bowels of the ship.

Two thirds of the way down, there was a cluster of beasts huddled off to one side, their bright, watery eyes studying his approach. Two craned their heads toward him, their beaks snapping. Dark thoughts pushed toward him, a fibrous grip encapsulating the membrane surrounding his brain, squeezing and probing. Their thoughts felt slithery in his mind, slick and wicked. Limp tentacles sprang to life, coiling and writhing in the air between Fine and the beasts, ringing their monsters' faces like a Medusa's head, oval slits at the end of each long cord snapping open and shut. The tentacle's mouths, he knew, hungering for fresh meat.

"Sorry, boys, the farm's downstairs," Fine said, moving past them. A deep throb blossomed in the centre of his head, then slowly drifted away. They were reading his intent, and after a moment his head cleared, which meant they had found what they were looking for.

One of the beasts threw out an arm at him, pushing him forward and away. He nearly tripped over his own feet, their barking laughter chasing his stumbling down the chamber. He tried to steady himself on the wall, but his hand slid in the green mucus-like sheen that covered all of the ship's surfaces. Globs of it ran in thick runners between his fingers, over his skin. He shook his hand and sent a web of it splattering to the floor. Disgusted, he wiped off the rest on his already soiled jeans. Suddenly, he'd give anything to be back down on the 'stead, away from those beasts, off this ship. He had lived too many of his years in the shadow of those monsters, and the 'stead was preferable by far.

A large oval archway separated his current segment of tunnel from the next. Stepping through, he found himself in an expansive, high-ceilinged room. He looked upwards, but the roof was too far away, out of sight. A disconcerting red glow pulsed through the room, mingling with the ever-present green fog.

A demon's version of Christmas, he thought, then laughed at himself for the peculiar notion.

He passed an ornamental display of human skulls, the stand itself made from various human bones. He knew enough to be able to identify the parts on sight, even though his days as a human anatomy instructor for Allen Park High were long over. The trunk of the stand was composed of a cluster of radial and ulna bones bound together with baling wire. The cups of the iliac bone carved loose from too many hips to serve as holders for the decapitated skulls. Rib cages that were repurposed to serve as feet for the base of the stand, propping up the entire morbid sculpture.

Rotting skin hung in the air, the stench of old, burnt human meat clinging to his nostrils. He fought the urge to throw up and moved deeper into the marque's sanctum. A deep thud broke the silence, and soon enough he saw what had caused the noise.

The marque held a young man in the air, gripped him by the face, the man's legs flailing loosely in the space between their bodies. As Fines entered, the beast flung the man to the ground. Bones snapped – the noise of the man's neck breaking on impact – and his legs went still. The marque chuffed, a sound Fines had come to recognize as pride, and ripped off the man's leg, biting into the calf, tearing free a stretch of muscle that Fines mentally identified as gastrocnemius.

The marque turned, as if sensing Fines's presence. For all Fines knew, that was exactly what had happened. The beast's thick skull leaned toward him, nostrils flaring as he took in large, windy breaths. Tentacles, each with mouth slits rimmed in red at one end, snapped at him, eager for a taste. The marque dropped the leg and shoved the corpse away, broadening his chest, arms puffing out at his side – a territorial display, although both knew damn well Fines wanted nothing to do with the dead body. The marque leaned in, dangerously close, and snapped his beak at Fines's face. But he held his ground, didn't recoil or even flinch, and the marque chuffed again.

Fines knew the routine and kept his arms at his side, empty palms facing forward to indicate a lack of hostility. He bowed his head slightly, but never broke eye contact. His head ached under the monster's mental assault, but it lasted for only a few minutes.

Sit, the beast ordered. The word did not take shape in Fines's head, so much as a general emotion of the command itself flooded into him. It was still disconcerting, even after more than seven years.

He hated to do it, but he sat. The greasy slickness bled through the seat of his pants and he fought to hide his disgust.

The marque spent another too-long moment staring at Fines before broadcasting his demands.

Boy. Find. You.

Cold fingers pressed into Fines's soul as dread crept up his spine. This was worse than he had thought.

"Why me?" he asked. The words tumbled out before

he could stop them, and he chided himself. Waited for the killing blow that belligerence should have bought.

The marque waved his hand toward Fines's hip. The gun.

Law. You. Boy. Find. You.

"I need information, then. Who is this boy? What happened to him? He disappeared?"

The marque slapped his chest, over and over, each time harder than the last, each hit making his snarling grow more rank and vulgar. A thick clot of spit hung from his beak by the time he was finished smacking himself.

Son. Find. You. Go. Now!

Fines knew he wouldn't get anything more. Not here. He was lucky to be leaving at all, and he didn't need to be told again.

He stood, the weight of this new mission pressing down on him. His foot fell into the green slime, which he thought was only appropriate. He was stepping into some serious shit.

2

"CHRIST, IT'S HOT OUT HERE," FINES SAID. HIS VOICE came out of the respirator muffled and scratchy.

"Ayuh," Myrtle said, holding loosely to the reins, his brown Criollo keeping pace with Fines's Spotted Saddle.

"Hey, let me ask you something," Fines said. Myrtle turned to him, his eyes hidden behind his respirator's faceplate and the reflection of lights from the camp. "Is that a real Maine thing, you always saying 'ayuh' or did you pick that up from too many Stephen King books?"

Myrtle snickered and said, "I wouldn't know nothing about that."

Although he'd cleaned up and put on fresh clothes, Fines felt dirty from his time above. His ass still felt clammy from sitting in the muck that covered every surface of the ship, and he wished he could wriggle out of his own damn skin, or take a nice, long bath in a vat of acid.

In the distance, a whistle blew. Night shift for the mines. The steaders had carved tunnels into the hillside, searching for coal to keep the lamps lit and to burn in their iron stoves for warmth. Looking around, Fines was reminded, and not for the first time, how far they had all fallen. And judging by the looks in other people's eyes, those looks reserved for he and Myrtle alone, they might have fallen further than most.

They rode and talked, Fines filling in his partner on what the beasts had wanted.

"The marque, huh? And his son." Myrtle let out a slow breath, briefly fogging the inside of his clear faceplate. "Shit, man."

"It's bad all right."

"Least it gets us away from the mines for a bit," Myrtle said. "That's something."

Fines nodded, trying to see the bright side. Working the mines was mostly a do-nothing job. Hang out at the entrance, hope there was no roof collapse, and break up the occasional fight. Still, it beat working the farms. Fines didn't have the heart for that.

He maneuvered his horse over to a hitching post outside a ramshackle bar. The raucousness from inside spilled out into the street. Sounds of laughter and shouting beneath which was an undercurrent of threat — the understanding that it would not take much to turn everything sideways, the tension that accompanied spilled liquor and drunk men seeking to blow off a heavy head of steam.

Both horses drank from the trough while the two men dismounted and adjusted their gear. Myrtle, as was his style, kept the Remington bolt-action resting on his shoulder, his hand gripping the stock. Fines hoped his friend wasn't feeling too jumpy, even as he unconsciously checked for the sidearm he always carried and knew was there.

He led the way, pulling open the makeshift door – nothing more than a simple piece of plywood with a hole carved into it for opening, closing, and padlocking the door to the frame – and entered.

If there was one thing the steaders had become good at over the years, perhaps even in spite of their loathing for them, it was ignoring the law dogs.

A few heads turned toward Fines and Myrtle, and then immediately dismissed them. There was no lull in the noise, the conversation, or the drinking. If anything, there was only a pronounced and studious effort at disregarding them entirely. Even the whores directed their attentions elsewhere.

Fines rested his elbows on the bar, waiting for the bartender to acknowledge him. He waited a while, long enough that when the bartender, a man he knew as Clarkson, passed by to deliver a drink at the opposite end, Fines grabbed him by the arm. "Whisky, neat."

He received a grunt in reply as the man pulled away. Clarkson returned a few minutes later with a small tumbler with two fingers worth of amber fluid. Fines laid down a small collection of weathered dollar bills and took a grateful sip.

"Anything else?"

"Some information would be good," Fines said.

"Got none to share," Clarkson said, folding his arm across his thick trunk and large, heavy belly.

"It's about the beasts. One of them's gone missing. I need to know where."

"Too bad for you, then. Good riddance to the fucker."

When Clarkson didn't move on, Fines knew there was something more he was holding back. Annoyed, he pulled loose another cluster of bills with the largest denomination on top.

"Spill."

The barman leaned in close, his mouth beside the lawman's ear. "Fuck yourself, nigger. I ain't helping you. And I sure as shit ain't helping *them*. Drink your drink, and get lost."

Fines closed his eyes, chasing the sudden burst of anger away with the flow of whisky down his throat. All the shit everyone had been through, and some still clung to the old ways, the deeply embedded veins of racism. Should have been that animosity toward the monsters would be enough to get people past skin color. That wasn't in the cards, though. Part of being human, he thought, was finding things to hate.

A dull throb bloomed in the centre of his brain. The marque was in his head, watching, and Fines felt the growing roar of the alien's bloodlust pulsing through his own veins. He was a puppet on the strings now, and any hope of a peaceful resolution was long since gone.

Why the fuck couldn't you just cooperate, Clarkson?

He thought briefly of Charlene, and tried not to think of how badly she would hate the man he'd grown into.

"I want you to remember, after, that it didn't have to go like this."

Turning from the bar, Fines stuck two fingers in his mouth and blew a shrill whistle that rang out over the din, catching everyone's attention.

"We got a missing beast," he said. "I need information. Five hundred to anyone that can help."

There was an uneasy silence. All eyes were on him now, and the only sounds came from the crickets outside and groaning wood stools shifting under the weight of drinkers.

"Five hundred," Fines repeated. "All we want is information. Your cooperation."

He watched them all, one hand resting easily on the butt of his revolver.

If it was going to happen, it was going to happen now.

His brain ached under the weight of the marque, the shifting sludge in his skull sending a spine-deep pain through him, nerves sparking and jangling with vibrant urgency. Wherever the marque was, Fines knew that the beast was salivating at the prospect of crimson mayhem.

His body was a powder keg. All that was needed was one single spark.

"It's easy money, people," he said, hoping it was still possible to resolve this peacefully. "We only need some information, and then we'll be on our way."

One man shifted, perhaps mustering the courage to speak, to be a peacekeeper and give Fines what he wanted. Before he could say anything, a drunk slurred a loud, "Fuck you!" from the back of the room, and that settled it good and proper.

He caught the first bottle that was thrown at him, and stepped outside the arc of the second. The bottle shattered against the bar top, spilling its contents in a frothy spray. More bottles were hurled at him, some going too high and slamming into the liquor bottles behind the bar. Clarkson hid his face behind his arms to protect himself from the exploding glass.

A bottle slammed into Fines's hip and pain shot down his leg, along with a warm trail of fizzing beer. The bristling chuckle of the marque's humour chilled his heart. The beast was getting his thrill now, delighted at the promise of killing.

Myrtle lined up the sights of his rifle and fired, once, twice, three times. One man's head exploded, another took a bullet straight to the heart, while the third caught one in the neck.

Fines drew his revolver and shot the man closest to him. Watched him topple over a table.

One of the customers drew his own gun, but couldn't clear the holster before Myrtle pegged him as well.

Fines leapt over the bar top, landing beside Clarkson, who was crouched beneath the cash box, surrounded by shards of broken glass and pools of spilled booze, the remnants of his livelihood.

"Should have told me what I wanted to know," Fines said. Myrtle's rifle blasted again and again, until the gunfire ceased and smoke filled the small tavern.

Fines stood, his gun tracing over the few men still alive. He caught a quick glimpse of Myrtle in his peripheral, cheek sliced open and blood leaking down his neck and beneath his shirt. Fines had a few cuts on the back of his hand and his hip would no doubt be sporting a bruise come morning.

He didn't like the fidgety look of the tall man in the back of the room, the way his eyes darted. Fines turned his revolver on him and fired, ending him before he might get stupid.

"I want information," he said to the few left standing. "Who's got it?"

Silence hung in the air, still and heavy. People exchanged glances, but nothing was said.

Fines picked a man at random and fired a round into his belly.

"It doesn't have to be this way!" he said. His eyes burned, and he told himself it was from all the gun smoke. The lurch in his belly gave rise to the lie, and he hated himself. *What the fuck have I become?*

The man squirmed on the floor, clutching his stomach with both hands and screaming loudly. Death would take a few good hours; until then, it was all only red-rimmed pain.

"Take him and get out of here," he told the others surrounding the squirming man. "All of you get out of here. Just go."

He'd lost the taste for this, hated the number of souls that hung over his head simply so he could go on another day and keep drawing air. He looked around at the barroom filled with the dead, absorbed the anguished crying of frightened whores with their make-up ruined by tears, and tried to remind himself there were worse things even than this.

"Get out, God damn it," he shouted again, but they were shell-shocked and too terrified to move. Eventually his screaming broke their paralysis.

With the tavern emptied, Fines reached over the bar and snatched Clarkson's shirt collar. "Stand up," he said, not caring how badly the man cut his hands on the glass, or how badly the liquor burned his open wounds.

"You're going to tell me everything you know, or you are not walking out of here. My generosity is at its limit."

"You – you," Clarkson stuttered. "You come in here, bust up my bar, shoot my customers, and you want to talk about fucking generosity?"

Fines grabbed him by the front of his shirt and slammed the butt of his revolver into Clarkson's nose, breaking it and sending a gush of gore and snot down the front of his face.

"The marque's son has gone missing. What do you know about it?"

"What makes you think I know anything at all?" Clarkson asked, cradling his face in one hand.

"Because you know things. You hear things. People come in here and they talk to you. And those that don't just talk to you buy skeeze. You're a man with connections, and I know you know something."

Myrtle shifted his weight, standing beside the entrance. A trio of dirty, soot-stained men approached and stopped at the door. "We're closed," Myrtle told them, shoving them off and away.

Clarkson reached for a towel and held it beneath his nostrils, the yellow cloth turning red where the blood darkened it.

"You know about the farm?"

Fines nodded, a tension headache building behind his eyes. *Shit.*

"Bastion's boys are the ones that did it. They raided the grounds, killed four or five of the beasties, took one of them. I figure that's what you're looking for."

"What about the people?" Myrtle asked.

Clarkson shook his head, his eyes downcast. "Bastion and them, they were too late."

"Aw, fuck," Fines said, feeling way out of his depth. The tension knotted his brain even tighter, a painful squeeze that threatened to turn the inside of his skull to pulp.

"The marque's son," he asked. "Did they know?"

Clarkson shrugged. "Don't know if they did or not. Can't imagine it mattered much. Payback is what it is."

Fines nodded. "Yeah. It's a bitch."

The raids were nothing new. This time of year, they'd even come to be expected. Kidnapping the marque's boy, though. That was a new level of aggression, a ramping up that could only lead to even more hostility on both sides.

Fines hated harvest season.

3

ALL THAT WAS LEFT AT THE FARM WERE EMPTY SHELL casings and large swathes of dried blood teeming with flies. Corpses littered the dirt. The large, squat husks of beasts steamed in the cooling night, their bodies reduced to burnt shells and cracked carapaces. The humans fared little better, many of them charbroiled. Friendly fire, Bastion would have called it.

Fines dismounted and turned to Myrtle. "Stay with the horses. Stay sharp."

Myrtle raised the respirator enough to clear his mouth, then turned and spat. Resettling the mask, he nodded in acknowledgement and turned his horse around to better view the perimeter and lines of approach, rifle at the ready.

Dust kicked up with each of his steps as Fines moved down the main trail. Some houses had been torched, some blown apart. Dynamite or grenades, it made no difference so long as it got the job done. He was thankful the respirator blocked out the smell.

The beasts wouldn't clean this up themselves. That dirty job would trickle its way down the chain, miners pulled from their regular shift duty to haul and bury bodies, rebuild the labs and stables. If the atmosphere weren't already threatening to boil over into open riots and more violence, it would be soon. Simply put, there was no good way things were going to end.

This wasn't the first time one of the beast's body farms

had been attacked. Human work crews would rebuild it, and everyone would ride out the lull until the next attack. Bastion wouldn't let it stand for long.

Fines strode up to the main building, situated at the centre of the lot in a foot-fashioned cul-de-sac. The path was lined with burned-down buildings, which he knew were primarily residential compounds. He kept an eye out for traps, worried that Bastion might have rigged explosives to notch up a few more dead in the aftermath of the attack.

The centre building had been torched down to the rafters in some spots, and he could see clear into the facility. He pried into the darkness with a flashlight, sweeping the beam around the four corners, across the ceiling and floor. The scorched earth was littered with broken test tubes, heat-shattered machines, ruined gestational tanks. Whatever liquid had been in the tanks had turned to a crystallized powder that glittered across the burnt floors. Small, curled shapes dotted the floor around each tank, and as he stepped closer he realized what they were. Intellectually, he knew, but his mind still rebelled against the horror.

He bent to study the shrivelled forms of fried embryos and cooked fetuses, their tiny, unformed bodies constricted from the blaze that had ended them. Few were fully developed, but some were sufficiently close to human in appearance, nearly infants. Only one was far enough along the growth phase to be considered an actual baby, and its flabby body was an overcooked, blistered horror.

Fucking Bastion, he thought.

The other buildings, the breeding kennels, offered much of the same. The people inside had tried to flee, but Bastion's men – hell, maybe even the beasts – had taken to firing at the few windows and solitary entrance, preventing anyone from getting out. A number of couples had been shot in the face, head, or torso. A far better, less cruel way to die, Fines thought, wondering if maybe Bastion had tried to wrap his cruelty in something resembling dignity. Immediate salvation prior to the cleansing flames.

Did anybody make it out? Were there any survivors? Or was Bastion's mission purely rage and mayhem?

Whatever his motive, it made no difference. Everybody was going to pay for this in one way or another.

"We're all condemned," Fines whispered. "We're all going to burn, eventually."

He reached out, his fingers nearly touching the deformed hand of the dead woman lying before him, but stopped short. Her fingers were slightly curled, her bare skin lacerated in various places from where the subcutaneous fat had popped and burst, the entire length of her blackened.

Wiping his sweating palms on the back of his jeans, Fines headed back to the horses. Myrtle handed over the reins and Fines saddled up.

"Well?"

"They're all dead," Fines said. "Whatever breeders they had stocked up are gone now."

"Not like the beasties will go hungry anyhow."

"No. No, they won't," Fines agreed, thinking that fact made all this even more reckless and stupid.

Families were going to be torn apart as the beasts forced scores of fertile men and women to the other farms, caring nothing for mating selection or choice. Genetics weren't any kind of concern; so much of it was random. As long as the women could push out a child regularly and frequently and the men planted their seeds, the beasts would have food and the farms would keep on running.

"We need to find Bastion," Fines said.

"You ever think that maybe he's right?" Myrtle asked.

"Of course I do," Fines said, spurring the horse forward. He was eager to put distance between him and the remains of the farm. "It's a question of lesser evils."

"And who do you think does more damage? *Them*, or him?"

Fines breathed faster than the respirator could handle and his mask fogged up. "Let's get out of here."

The ride back to camp was going to be a long one. Fines stretched in his saddle, looking up at the lights above. They were miles away from the stead, but the ship reached across an enormous amount of land, blotting out the stars he knew were far, far above.

Nights now were spent below the winking orbs of reds and blues and greens and yellows, the vessel's running lights and lit-up offices, rooms, restaurants, bars, recreation centers, anywhere the beasts might spend their downtime.

He didn't quite realize until this moment how strongly he missed the moon's glow and constellations.

Day or night, it didn't matter. The ship cast a constant grey pall over the landscape.

"Looking back on things," Myrtle began, "you still believe we made the right choice?"

"What choice is that?" Fines asked, knowing perfectly well what Myrtle was talking about. Or, rather, *still* talking about. He sighed. "Weren't no choice, man. It was live or die, was all. And you made the same choice I did."

"I know that. Just thinking that if we stayed with him…"

"Well, staying wasn't an option, now was it?"

Myrtle shook his head, face darkening behind the respirator shield. The way he was talking, the questions he was asking, took Fines down a mental avenue he'd rather avoid.

He could remember the day as if it were yesterday. Seven years since the beasts arrived, their ships knocking out the Earth's satellites, killing communications the world over and sending out massive EMP pulses that killed everything digital. A thousand-plus ships breaking through the atmosphere of a planet technologically sent back into the dark ages.

There was panic, rioting, wars against the aliens, and when that proved futile, wars against one another. Words were spoken of a united front, but they were hollow and meaningless. Nothing more than mere words that fell apart before they even passed the lips of frightened officials.

The ships tore through skyscrapers, reducing entire cities to rubble, their afterburners incinerating whole neighborhoods and districts. They were an overwhelming force, and humanity had little to fight back with.

Fines and Myrtle had been a part of the resistance, their old lives as dead as the planet, blood on their hands and faces, their souls dirtied. They had fought alongside Bastion once upon a time, until their insignificant guerrilla army was outmatched and overpowered by the invaders. Most fled, Bastion among them; a number died; and a few, like Fines and Myrtle, were rounded up and given an impossible choice.

"What's got you bringing all this up now, Myrtle?"

Fines slowed his horse to a halt and dismounted. He found a handful of carrots to feed the Spotted Saddle. The horse needed a rest, and Fines wanted to stretch his legs. Besides, Myrtle tended to speak more freely with both feet on the ground.

"I'm tired of all the looks," he said, scratching at the skin beneath the edges of his mask.

"None of us like it," Fines said. "All of us made the same shitty choice, and all of us hate ourselves for it.

Everyone's looking for somebody else to blame. That's all it is."

Myrtle took off his respirator and rubbed his face, pinching the bridge of his nose. He looked haggard, and dark circles hung beneath his eyes.

"Maybe it's just being out here, away from it all. Makes it harder. My thoughts are getting all jumbled up, having too much time to think."

"Yeah, well, thinking never was your strong suit," Fines said.

Myrtle laughed without humor. Then, his throat burst open, a wet splash striking Fines in his face before he ever heard the gunshot echoing across the plains.

Carrots fell from his hand and the horses reared. Fines moved out of the way to avoid getting kicked in the face, adrenaline surging. Another gunshot followed, striking Myrtle's horse. Fines tripped over an outcropping of rock, falling backward. Pain shot up his back.

Myrtle was still alive, clutching at his neck. Blood ran between his fingers, a dark stain on the parched, cracked earth beneath him. He croaked, a pink bubble bursting on his lips. He stretched out his free hand, his fingers clawing at the dirt, trying to find a grip to pull himself forward. All he did was make long trails with his nails and uproot buried rocks.

Fines reached for his gun, searching the horizon for the shooter.

A hiss rattled loose from behind him, and then a voice telling him, "Wouldn't do that, Darrell. Hands free, please."

Fines obeyed, keeping both hands loose and away from his body.

Myrtle looked up, beyond his partner, and shut his eyes. His face had gone pale, and he seemed to settle.

Boots crunched their way past Fines, a pair of men flanking him.

Myrtle's lips were moving, speaking a final prayer for salvation between himself and his god. Bastion raised his gun and fired twice, his bullets punching through the clear plastic shield and turning the inside of the mask red. Myrtle's foot twitched, an odd jolt that kicked up a small plume of dust, and then settled.

Bastion turned to Fines, holstering his gun. The other three men kept their weapons trained on him.

"I hear you've been looking for me," Bastion said.

4

THE BITTER TASTE OF ASH COATED FINES'S TONGUE, ALONG with a coppery metallic tinge from his split lips, cut cheeks, and broken teeth. He sucked at the sore empty gap where his molars had once been. The last thing he remembered was Bastion standing over him and the blur of a rifle stock crashing into his face, again and again, until he passed out.

He rolled over, his ribcage screaming, howling. When he coughed, the taste of copper grew stronger and sharp fragments from his chest stabbed into his lungs.

On the bright side, he could no longer feel the bone-deep bruise on his hip from where the base of a beer bottle had socked him good. He was only seeing out of one eye, the other hidden behind a dense mountain of swollen flesh. The fingers of his right hand – not his shooting hand, thankfully – were bent in unnatural directions, blackness beneath each fingernail.

Slowly, he maneuvered himself into a sitting position up against the far wall, his movements rattling the chains.

His hands were cuffed in front, and the chain led to a metal hoop that had been spiked into the earth a few yards above his head. He wasn't going anywhere, apparently, and it took a while for his one good eye to adjust to the darkness.

He was alone in a small, empty room. Really, little more than a cubby hewn into the rock. No bed, no place to sit, not even a pot to piss in. Apparently, his time on this earth was less than the time until his next bowel movement.

At least I won't have to wait much longer, he thought.

When he closed his eye, he saw Myrtle dying again.

He tried not to think of Charlene, or their daughter, Ruby. He missed them both. Every day his heart ached, and he thought of them before sleep each night, and on waking each day. Back at camp, on the small table beside his bed, next to the oil lamp, was Charlene's Bible. At their home, before the beasts came, Charlene had stuffed the entire top row of their bookshelf with all her religious paraphernalia. The Bible, a crucifix, religious-themed movies like *Noah* and *The Passion of the Christ*, stuff like that. When the time came to evacuate, she took only the Bible and a single family photo, which she tucked behind the front cover. That picture was still there, capturing a younger, vibrant couple, and the two-year-old Ruby, sitting in a park, years before the fire had scorched it from the earth.

Fines had never read the Bible, and never planned on doing so. He was a man of science. He'd kept the book only because Charlene had cherished it, and it was all he had left of her, aside from the faded photograph. There were nights when he held it close, and he could convince himself that he could smell her in the musty, yellowed pages. A hint of her perfume, the scent of her skin lotion.

The book and the photograph were both stained with his tears, his family reduced to dying memories.

Both Charlene and Ruby perished in the first wave of attacks. Fines lived only because he'd been faster. He'd tried to encourage them to move, to keep up, but his legs were longer, and Charlene had insisted on carrying Ruby, who was crying and afraid. He'd been carrying a bag loaded with canned goods, what few provisions they had on hand, like bottled water and lunch meat, some diapers, and Charlene's Bible. The beasts had stormed the city on foot, mauling everyone in reach and shooting anything they drew a bead on. Neither his wife nor daughter had seen it coming, which was for the best. He was grateful for that much, at least. But, Fines … Fines had seen it all. A Good Samaritan had pulled on Fines's arm, grabbed him, twisted him around, and forced him into a run.

Fines kept on running.

Cold water on his face, snapping him awake. Fines looked up to see Bastion standing over him with an empty bucket.

"Sweet dreams?" Bastion asked.

Screams echoed in Fines's head, the sound of agony that lasted seconds before being abruptly cut off. "No," he said, "not particularly."

Bastion nodded at this, his tongue rolling against the inside of his cheek and puffing out the side of his face. "You gonna behave if I unchain you?"

"Where are we?"

"A cave. We're about half a day's ride from the farm." He pointed at the hoop overhead. "How's 'bout it?"

Fines nodded, his head fuzzy. He snorted, moving his legs to get his feet beneath him. "Sure, I'll behave."

Bastion gave him a long look, then reached up to unlock the chains. "The beasties don't usually come this far out," he said. "So we're in a bit of a dead space."

"I get it," Fines said, scratching along the inside of his busted nose. "Don't even think about running, in other words."

Bastion laughed through his nose, his lips puckering a bit in the process. "See you're still smart, boy. That's good. C'mon."

Bastion turned his back on Fines, seemingly unthreatened by him, then led him out of the tiny cell and into a wide artery in the tunnel system. A few torches lit the way, small ringlets of light in the solid blackness beneath the earth. Fines looked both ways but saw no opening into the cave in either direction.

He kept close to Bastion as he took them deeper. There was barely enough light to see. Bastion had optical upgrades from his time in the Army – a standard-issue, blink-powered nanotech injection. His retinas were infused with graphene, which translated infrared light into a visible image. The irregular placement of the torches helped him amplify the low-level ambient lighting. Bastion's eyes were a relic of another time, before the entire world was reduced to cinders.

Fines had to bend his knees a bit to keep his feet from sliding out beneath him as the tunnel took a precarious drop, both men's strides turning into a near-run. The tunnel evened out again and, ahead, Fines made out a ring of light from another torch-lit checkpoint.

"It's just up ahead," Bastion said.

"What is?" Fines asked, but received no reply. He guessed he would find out soon enough.

There was a small alcove dug out of the wall, and even before he saw the beast, Fines could feel the thick fingers slicing into his mind. The assault was sudden and the world briefly went black, blinding him. His knees weakened, and Bastion had to help him stand.

The beast chuffed as it left Fines's head, a thunderous assault left in its wake, banging across the insides of his temples.

"You shouldn't have brought me here," he said, blinking the blurriness away. His head ached, and even the dim torchlights were much too bright.

"Had to," Bastion said. "You're going to make a choice, right here, right now."

"No," Fines said, nearly doubled over from the pain, cradling his face in both hands. "You don't understand. I'm a beacon."

Although he couldn't raise his head, he could hear the shakiness in Bastion's tone as the man fought to control himself. "What?"

"The marque. He's tapped in to me." Fines stood, lifting the front tails of his shirt to show the network of scars that ran across his left flank and up his torso, beneath the fabric. He winced in pain, everything suddenly much too bright, as the beast fired a fresh lance into the centre of his cerebral cortex. "He's sounded the alarm. They know where we are."

Bastion's eyes went between the man and the beast. The flickering torchlight made it hard to tell, but Fines's swore the man had lost some color.

"Then I guess you're going to be in a hurry to choose."

"Choose what?"

Bastion held Fines's gun in his hand. Another man – Fines hadn't even had time to realize he was there – pressed a cold metal barrel to the back of his head.

"Us or them."

"It isn't like that," Fines tried to say, but his heart wasn't in it. The words stuttered pathetically.

Bastion took his hand, shoved the gun in it, and curled Fines's fingers over the handle. The gun felt good in his hand, the worn grip familiar and comforting.

"You're either a human, or you're a monster, Fines. You need to decide which it is. Us or them."

His thoughts drifted back to Charlene, and he wondered what she would think of him now, the way in which he eked out another miserable day of life. The cold centred in the back of his head from the gun's push, raising the hairs on the back of his neck, and he knew there was no choice to make. Live or die, those were his options. Bastion could gussy it up all he wanted, as if there were sides to be chosen. The truth of it all was even simpler, though. Choose life, or don't.

He looked at the monster, hanging from chains and splayed against the wall. The snakes that had surrounded its skull had been cut off one by one, leaving only jagged, seeping stumps. Its beak was fractured, a clean break running down the centre. Segments of its carapace had been torn away, exposing raw flesh covered only by a thin veil of webbed, milky fat. It hung there, still, half its exoskeleton torn away to leave denuded, muscled slabs. It breathed heavily, as if each inhalation were torture. Probably it was, given the severity of the damage.

Fines wanted to ask why. What had been Bastion's purpose in abducting and maiming this beast, the marque's son? With Bastion, he knew, there could be any number of reasons – attempting to gain intel, maybe – or no reason at all, other than because he could.

The weight of the marque pressed heavily against his mind, his sides burning in rhythm with his rapidly beating heart. When he raised the gun and pointed it at the beast, his hand was steady, and that, at least, was something.

The first shot rang out, deafeningly loud in the enclosed space, and Fines's ears rang in its wake. He fired a second time, to be sure. The marque's rage flooded through him and the gun fell from his hand as he collapsed to his knees.

The inside of his skull felt like a thousand micro explosions detonating against the soft tissue, obliterating the spongy mass of his mind. His vision reddened as veins exploded in his eye from the pressure. He curled into a foetal ball, pain wracking his entirety, waiting to die.

After far too long, the world went black.

GROGGY, FINES AWOKE TO FIND BASTION KNEELING OVER him. He tried to sit up, but Bastion pushed him back down, gently.

"Lay still a minute."

"Now you're worried about me, huh?"

For a very brief moment, Bastion almost looked sad. "I need to know what happened there. How bad is this?"

Fines realized his words were slow and slurred. His face felt funny, his whole body sluggish. He reached to his cheek and found drooping skin, the corner of his mouth pulled downward by deflated muscles. It had been a stroke. The marque had detonated an aneurysm in his brain.

"How long was I out?"

"Few minutes."

Fines nodded. It felt like he'd been unconscious both much longer and hardly at all. In the span of an eye blink, he'd gone from standing in pain to lying in pain, as if no time had elapsed.

"The marque played you good," Fines said. "Me, too. P-p-played me like a fiddle."

"What do you mean?"

Fines made to sit up, this time unimpeded. A steady drip plinked against a shallow puddle of blood behind him, the pulped remains of the monster's head hanging forward and whatever fluids were left inside slowly leaking out.

"I s-s-s-saw it, when he was in my head," he said, hating the neurogenic stutter to his words. "The marque, he knew. He knew everything, ex-c-c-c-cept where his boy was at. He knew you took the beast, knew that you and I were acquainted a while back. He knew our p-paths would c-c-c-cross eventually, one way or another."

"How'd he know I'd let you live?"

Fines shrugged. It was a good question, and he only had a simple answer for it. "He didn't. He took a ga-gamble."

"How'd he know I had his son?"

"They're telepaths, Bastion. There's no s-s-s-s-secrets between the lot of them. Only distance."

Bastion fingered the scars across Fines's abdomen. "And this is what, like a signal booster?"

Fines nodded. "Also a bit of a leash, a sort of GPS tracker."

"And now they're coming here."

"It'll be a b-bloodbath," Fines said.

Bastion sat beside his old comrade, the two of them gazing at the tattered remains of the beast. "Which leaves the question of you, I suppose."

"I can't go back," Fines said. His voice was distant and soft, his thoughts drifting back to the hut he'd come to call home, and Charlene's Bible beside his bed. For the second time in his life, he'd lost his family.

"You're still a traitor, Darrell. You still spent too many years working the farms, doing the beasts' bidding."

"And what would you have done?" Fines asked, picking at the skin around his nails out of nervous habit and tearing off small slivers of flesh. "Taken the bullet? If I recall right, you r-r-r-ran. You ran and left us behind. Me, M-M-M-M-M-Myrtle, S-Sanders, Henry, P-P-P-Pauline, Sa-Sa-Sandra, McCormick. You even recall any of those n-n-n-names? You call me a t-t-t-traitor, and that may be, but at least I wasn't a c-c-c-coward."

Bastion face was red, but he kept his voice even. "You don't think you could be both?"

Fines opened his mouth to speak, but thought better of it. Truth was, he knew he was both. A traitor and a coward. There was one other truth that he gave voice too, the cold realization steeling his spine.

"Either way, I'm a d-d-dead man now, aren't I? Either you kill me, or they kill me."

"Doesn't make much difference where the bullet is coming from, does it?"

Fines shrugged. "Not in the end, maybe. But I c-can help you. If I have any choice at all in this, I'd m-mu-much rather go down swinging and take out one or two of them if I can. And I suspect you could use an extra gun."

Bastion shrugged, then snorted loose a dry chuckle. "Fuck it. Not like any of us are making it out of here alive, right?"

He stood, then held his hand out to Fines, a wry smirk plastered to his lips. Fines took it, their hands slapping together, the sound of a pact between desperate men, and stood. Bastion handed him his gun, and again the S&W grips felt comfortable and inviting.

Together, they strode up the tunnel, their fates sealed. Fines used the time to mentally say his piece to the dead, hoping that he would see Charlene again soon, and Myrtle, too. Hoping that all this was not all for nothing. Even if there was no Other Side, no Heaven, waiting for him, he hoped that, at the very least, their sacrifice wasn't utterly meaningless.

5

STANDING AT THE EDGE OF A ROCKY OUTCROPPING, FINES ran his tongue over the edge of the rolling paper, pasting it down with his spit. The motions were clumsy, his face aching and cottony. He struck a match off his boot heel and took a long draw, enough to give his head a pleasant spacey feeling.

"Reckon we-we-we've got about an hour, tops," he said. Bastion nodded, but said nothing, staring off at the horizon.

Fines could practically hear Myrtle's voice, quietly reminding him: *They don't like waiting.* He could feel the pressure of time escaping, each passing second bringing him closer and closer to death and absolution. Closer to judgement.

Below them were at least two score of people. The tunnel entrance was not too far above them, and Fines could easily see the scars of disease on their skin. The beasts had brought with them a lethal, shingles-like virus that many had taken to calling stitches. Puckered black lines flecked across areas of the body, usually sprouting thin, pointy stems and giving them the appearance of surgical sutures. Plenty of disfigured men, women, and children moved below, the dark viral networks shiny against their pale skin.

Stitches spread like wildflowers in the farms, where so

many people were confined to enclosed spaces and forced to share bodily fluids during their obligatory breeding.

"I thought you'd killed all of them," Fines said.

"We're not the monsters, Darrell," Bastion said. His eyes finally left the horizon to look at the mass of bodies. "We got out who we could. The beasts set the fires, killed anybody who tried to leave the breeder sheds."

"They don't have much time left, from the looks of them."

Bastion shrugged. "Maybe not," he admitted.

There was no cure for the stitches, no way of treating its victims. Fines was thankful that the disease wasn't airborne. The plan was to move them into the tunnels and, hopefully, keep them away from the monsters for as long as possible. Still, he was skeptical that their defensive lines would last longer than a few seconds.

"Keep your respirator on, you'll be OK," Bastion said. To make his point, he pulled his own mask down and, wearing long sleeves and gloves, made his way down the shallow gradient to start leading people up into the caverns.

Fines finished his cigarette and brought the mask down over his face, then fitted his Stetson back on his head. He touched the shoulders of each person as they passed, taking a mental headcount of their numbers. Forty-eight people, most of them naked, frail, and unkempt from their prolonged imprisonment at the farm. A few had blankets around their shoulders from Bastion's crew, but spare provisions were limited and the vast majority went without. Inside the tunnel, Bastion's men led the breeders deeper into the mountain, sending them down different arteries in the hopes that keeping them separated into smaller groups would increase their odds of hiding and surviving.

A few were near death, but, then again, weren't they all? Him and Bastion especially.

Movement above drew his attention, the lights across the gargantuan ship overhead blinking to life. In the distance, he saw a cluster of black dots against the polluted skyline. They were too far off, but soon they would grow larger and larger, until they were right on top of them.

"Let's get inside," Bastion said.

Fines nodded, his hand resting on the butt of the gun holstered at his hip.

THE RIDERS DREW CLOSER, THE MATTE GREY FINISH OF their individual speeders plain against the constant gloom. The sky behind them was a wall of heat vapor, pulsing against the thrum of the vehicle's engines that kept them aloft.

Fines could feel the pressure of time escaping, the burden pressing against him, tension stiffening his shoulders. His mouth was dry and his heart was beating like a caged animal.

"They're here," he said. He cast a quick glance over his shoulder and saw Bastion nod in acknowledgement.

Even against the desert warmth, Fines could feel the heat of the approaching riders. With a sweaty palm, he unholstered his gun and stood ready. Bastion was beside him, rifle raised, watching the beasts' approach through a scope, his finger resting against the trigger.

Fines watched a line of sweat work its way down the side of Bastion's face. Fines wiped a dusty forearm against his forehead, the hand itself limp and lifeless, smearing a thin paste of sand and sweat across his face. His own breathing was ragged through the respirator, and he struggled to keep his fear under control.

Closer and closer, the riders came. Their skiffs were all sharp angles and pointed edges, talon-like as they cut through the atmosphere.

Already Fines could feel the darkness of their probing minds stabbing into his own thoughts, digging and seeking for his resolve and how to best destroy it. There, and then gone, as if the brief mental assault had been nothing more than the flame of a dying wick, snuffed out.

The boom of Bastion's rifle surprised him as the edges of his vision slowly resolved and he came back to the world. A rider fell, smashing into the desert, a small mushroom of dust blooming upwards around its corpse.

A sudden cacophony erupted behind them. Howling and gunfire echoed through the cavern as Bastion's men were overrun. Pale, naked bodies collided with the shooters, the breeders snapping and suddenly attacking.

Not snapping, Fines realized too late. Possessed. He thought of the beasts' thoughts slithering over his mind and reaching past him, and knew that the marque's soldiers had taken a tight grip over the broken, tortured minds of the breeders.

A young woman, her body marred by stitches that reached across her trunk and stretched up her face, reached out for him, her nails raking uselessly against his mask. He grabbed her by one wrist and tried to wrestle her away, to put distance between them, but she was surprisingly strong. The mental push of the beasts added a frightening level of viciousness to her struggle, and the long, sharp nails of her free hand raked against Fines's cheek and across his eye. The pain startled him and he let go of her. The woman was quick and hurled herself at Fines, tackling him to the ground, her thumbs hooking around each of his eyes, nails pressing hard against his eyelids. A painful pressure throbbed through his skull as his eyes pressed against the muscles that held them in their sockets. He pulled his gun between their bodies and felt the barrel jab into her belly. His finger eased the trigger back and the loud boom partially deafened him.

Her body went limp and he was able to push her off. She scrabbled against the rocky floor, reaching for him, and he fired another round through the top of her skull.

Ahead, gore splattered against rock as Bastion's men fought against the swarming forms of the possessed. There were too many of them. Far more than the small posse of raiders that had freed them.

Behind them the beasts hovered outside the mouth of the cavern.

"We need to k-k-k-k-kill *them*," Fines shouted, trying to draw attention toward the monsters. Nobody could hear him over the savagery. Turning, he nearly stumbled over Bastion. The man was curled on the ground, clutching his face. His respirator was missing and a thick redness poured from between his fingers.

Fines snatched up the man's rifle and took aim. To him, the monsters all looked alike. Only the marque was distinguishable by his large frame and the network of scars that crossed the ugly planes of his face.

Take out the leader, Fines thought.

The marque reeled to the side, maneuvering his skiff into a vertical rise and canting to the left as Fines fired. The bullet grazed the monster's thickly muscled leg and he grimaced.

Fines ejected the spent round and prepared to fire again, knowing that his chance of taking out the marque was lost. The beast had broken formation and his soldiers were preparing to do the same. As Fines took aim, a meaty thump in his back rocked him off his feet and sent him sprawling. His arms shot out to break his fall and the rifle scattered away from him.

Fingers pulled on his hair, yanking his head back and then slamming his face into the ground. Silver streaks flashed across his vision and he was too dazed to stop it from happening again. He moaned, blood on his lips, large hands wrapping across his neck and throat, squeezing.

A gunshot rang out, too close, and the pressure eased off him. He rolled onto his back, going for his pistol, but Bastion stood over him trying to suppress a cocky grin. The left side of his face was slashed to ribbons, so maybe it hurt too much to smile.

To his left, another dead breeder with a network of stitches on his body and a bloody pulp where his face had once been.

"Th-Thanks," Fines said.

Their posse was still defending itself, some of the men grappling with the possessed breeders while others fired round after round into the thick mass of bodies, felling as many as they could to thin the herd and keep back the line of attackers.

Bastion had a look in his eyes, the kind that Fines recognized too easily from staring into the mirror every damn day. A look of failure.

"There's n-n-no-no reasoning with them," Fines said. "We have to put down the beasts."

"Once the breeders are dead," Bastion said, "they'll turn us against one another."

Both men had seen that particular tactic before. The weakness of humanity's minds had made the end of the world too damn easy. Right now, the beasts were having fun, using the men and women in the tunnels as playthings, softening up and fatiguing those with weapons. To make them more pliable for manipulation.

Fines grabbed hold of his gun again, while Bastion scooped up his rifle. With the stock against his shoulder, he moved forward to the gaping mouth of the cavern. Fines followed, hoping the men at the opposite end could sort things out with the breeders. He and Bastion had to focus on the beasts.

Sidling up against the cavern wall, Bastion took a quick look outside, searching for the monsters. He was greeted by a high-speed energy bolt, which glanced off the rock and sizzled past.

The skiffs gave the monsters permanent high ground and a wide view of the combat below.

Wind kicked up a thin swirl of dust, the grit stinging Fines's eyes as he neared the opening and took shelter behind a rocky outcropping. He poked his head around it, looking for the skiffs. The air beyond the cave's mouth shimmered from the heat radiating off the beast's airships, but he couldn't spot them from that angle.

"They're up there somewhere," he said.

Bastion nodded, the wounds on his face seeping and pooling against his shirt collar. He took a quick look back toward the battle. The noise of fighting was dissolving into an eerie quiet. He lowered his head and shut his eyes for a brief moment.

Fines looked back, muttered, "Shit."

The possessed were regrouping, striding toward the two men. Even in the darkness of the cave, Fines could make out their blood-slick, scarred flesh, and the prone forms of Bastion's men beyond, pulps of flesh littering the ground and gore streaking the cave walls.

"I go," Fines said, "you c-c-cu-cu-cover me."

"We go down swinging," Bastion said, his voice trembling.

They moved together, guns forward and seeking a

target. Fines broke into a run, half-sliding down the curve of land and hitting the arid expanse below. Overhead, Bastion fired a series of rounds at the skiffs, forcing the beasts to scatter.

Fines was an easy target on the open landscape, each footfall chased by gunfire from above. The marque was in his head, a vulgar, raw cacophony grating against his grey matter. The seams of his skull felt ready to pop wide open, his brain squeezed between a needled vice. Pain nearly dropped him in his tracks, but he kept moving. One foot quickly in front of the other, always moving.

Then a searing blast tore through the back of his leg, obliterating his knee, and he fell, face sliding against the rocky ground.

He screamed, the pain overwhelming. Through wet eyes, he stared at the ruined limb. The lower half of his leg was gone, the skin and bone a messy paste staining the earth. The severed half laid near his other foot, the soles almost touching. He writhed on the ground, his fingers hooked into painful claws around his thigh, trying to stop the gushing blood.

The world faded around him, the marque's infiltration of his mind a dull roar against the agony of the injury. He had to stop the bleeding, or he would die.

A blast of heat washed over him as a skiff landed nearby. Staccato bursts of gunfire rang through the air, but he couldn't tell how close Bastion was. His mind was addled, the strumming screams of his pulse thick in his temple.

The marque stood over him, the tentacles ringing his scalp snapping hungrily. Slowly, the beast crouched, its mental assault unrelenting. Each beat of Fines's heart sent a sonic boom through his skull, his brain nearly liquefied.

He forced his eyes to meet the monster's ugly glare,

forced his good leg to work, trying to push himself away. A last, desperate act for survival, even though he knew full well that it was a pointless effort. The raw sinew of his sputtering, ruined thigh dragged in the dirt. Rocks sent pinpricks of fire through his nerves.

The marque crouched beside him, the tentacles stretching toward his face, mouths snapping greedily. One tore a thin strip of skin from his paralysed cheek, and he watched, with an awful detachment, as the snakes writhed and fought over the scrap of tissue.

He felt around the ground for his weapon, but found only mealy earth. His fingers brushed against something solid, but he didn't dare look, didn't dare take his eyes off the marque. He groped for the object, slowly rolling it toward him, trying to get a sense of the shape. A rock, or a stone, maybe. The edges bit into his skinned palms and he swung his hand around, smashing it into the marque's face.

The clod of earth broke against the marque's ugly visage. Not a rock, just a loosely packed clump of dirt.

The tentacles seized the opportunity, grabbing ahold of his wrist, wrapping themselves around his hand and taking bites of his fingers. The snakes swarmed, swallowing entire digits and leaving a ruin of stubs. One burrowed into his wrist, biting through the radial and ulna, digging into the small carpal bones. His arm was trapped in a nest of greedy, hungry vipers, and they feasted.

The marque traced his thick fingers down Fines's chest, the long talons digging lines from his breastbone down to his belly. The wounds instantly welled with blood. Dread anticipation froze Fines, and he tried to steel himself, but it was impossible. The stabbing pain tore through whatever resolve he had.

The nails dug into his soft belly, slowly, and he could feel the marque's delight echo in his skull. All Fines could do was watch as the monster's distal phalanges pierced his skin, sinking into the flesh over his abdominal muscles. It sank deeper, grabbing his intestine and squeezing into a fist, then tearing out his innards.

Fines watched as his belly uncoiled through the ruined cavity, screaming so long and hard that he felt something pull and then pop in his neck. His whole body was drenched, in sweat and plasma, and he forced himself to look away.

But the marque wanted revenge and blasted the sights into Fines's head, forcing him to watch through their telepathic connection. Even with his eyes tightly shut, Fines saw it all. He heard the wet smacking noises of the marque's feast, as he dug through Fines's body for the sweetest treats. Fines felt the unreal sensation of those long tentacles slipping around his stomach and prizing away his liver and gallbladder.

Finally, his heart gave out, his last thoughts buried beneath the marque's glee and hunger, denied even the peace of his own escape.

Bastion hadn't managed to fell any of the beasts. He took his potshots, heard a round ping the side of a skiff, but they were on him too quick. Whatever dreams of accomplishment he'd had were torn away in an instant.

The mental assault drove him to the ground, fluids leaking from his nose and ears, the signals in his brain clamped down tight, leaving him frozen.

He was forced to watch Fines go down, an observer of the whole nasty affair. He bore witness, the death of his old brother in arms meant to be both a lesson and a punishment.

New world order, one spoke, the words like gristle rubbing against the caul surrounding his brain.

The tears ran freely, Fines's screams deafening as they echoed through the canyon.

The possessed were rounded up, their fate beyond his ken. There were only two options for them − serve, or die. They'd either be sent back to the farms, or they would be killed. *New world order,* he thought.

Kneeling on the rocky ground, the mental hold the beasts held him in slowly loosened. The shadow of the marque fell over him, the large-bodied monster silently passing judgment.

One of the beasts yanked Bastion's head back, forcing him to look up at the marque with eyes wide open. There stood the horrific elder, face limed in gore and the tattered remnants of organ meat and torn flesh, snakes coiling around his skull and seeking sustenance, their hunger undying.

He wondered if Fines was with Charlene and Ruby. He hoped so. And he now knew the weight of Fines's decision, the same choice that fell to every man, woman, and child that was left of the human race.

Serve. Or die. Either way made little difference to these beasts.

Law, the marque said. *You.*

Bastion met the monster's glare, and found himself oddly relieved. He was a coward − Fines had been right about that. But he was a living coward. He looked at his comrade, still in an uneven circle of dark earth, his body lumpy and gutted. He felt a twinge of guilt, but he accepted his fate.

All of his men were dead, his friends nothing more than history. For whatever reasons, he had lived, and now he was given the option to keep on living.

This was the new world order, he thought, and he nodded dumbly.

The beasts returned to their skiffs, and he watched them fade into the horizon. Then, he began walking, following their trail into town.

There were mines to watch over, farms to tend to. That was his job now. Fines had realized that the difference between freedom and oppression was defined in between heartbeats, and now, so too did Bastion.

He owed penance and was due punishment. Serve or die. He was the law, his badge an emblem of his own dishonor. A watch and warrant built off gore and guilt, but mostly fear.

Bastion had plenty of work to do.

Stupid Girl

Her headlights cut through the black velvet of night, the only source of illumination on this stretch of US 72. There were no streetlights, no traffic lights, not even any other drivers on this long and lonely road.

Heather had been driving for hours and the last signs of civilization—a small town called Grayling—were nearly an hour in the rearview mirror. She was more than an hour away from Traverse City, a northern Michigan tourist hotspot that sat in the webbing between pinky and ring finger of the mitten state. Although the weather was warm, it was still off-season for the tourists and she looked forward to taking in sparsely crowded beaches, vineyards, and the various restaurants lining Front Street. Even more, she looked forward to doing these things alone.

Mark had been out of her life for the better part of two months, but this morning made it official. The divorce was final, the paperwork signed and agreed upon. Finally. Even the circlet of pale skin where her wedding ring had once sat was tanned over. This trip north was her surprise gift to herself.

Fuck you, Mark!

She turned on the radio, needing a blast of music to keep awake. She'd gotten a late start on her spontaneous road trip and it was nearing midnight. She hadn't bothered to call work, but she'd get up early enough to call in sick, then go back to sleep. After that, it was a book on the hotel beach and whatever drinks the outdoor bar was slinging. After a minute of cycling through the local FM stations, Garbage's "Stupid Girl" flooded her speakers.

You certainly were stupid, girl, she thought ruefully. Shirley Manson sang on about wasting all you had and selling yourself lies, and Heather couldn't disagree. The song wasn't a perfect match for her marriage, but close enough.

She tapped her fingers on the wheel, her eyes flicking between the mirrors and windshield. The woods on either side of this two-lane stretch of highway were home to all kinds of wild animals, she knew, and the last thing she needed was a deer running out in front of her. She tried to stay aware of what was around her, even if she couldn't fully see into the darkness beyond the conical beams of light. Hell, she could barely make out the trees she knew were there.

A flash of movement caught her attention, her head snapping toward a pair of glowing eyes at the edge of the road just as the Escape crested the top of the one of the many hills that rolled under 72. And then it was gone, quick as it came. She turned back to the road, eyes forward and—

"Shit!"

She slammed on the brakes, white flashing light filling the cabin of her SUV. Her tires squealed loudly against the asphalt as she cranked the wheel, the front of the vehicle pulling onto the rumble strip.

Another vehicle was pulled halfway off the road, its back end jutting into the street with its hazard lights on. She kept her foot on the brake as she fought to calm down, adrenaline pumping through her. The car was empty, the driver's side door open, but no signs of the driver anywhere.

She looked on either side of the road, waiting for the glow of lights from another driver, somebody who could help. A minute passed. Then two. Nothing. Her fingers found the cold metal of the door handle.

What are you doing?

What if somebody's hurt?

You can't just stop here and get out! Who knows what's going on?

You should call the police!

A sensible suggestion, if she hadn't forgotten her phone. Her trip north was so impulsive she hadn't bothered to pack any clothes and had forgotten her cell at home. She'd grabbed her keys, wallet, and nothing else. *Stupid girl.*

Her door opened with a sharp squeal and in the quiet night air rocks crunched like gunshots beneath her shoes. She slowly walked to the other car, looking between it and the woods that stood revealed in its headlights. She reached the door and stopped, drawing in a shocked breath. A dark arc of liquid stained the road less than a foot away from the deserted car, leading toward the trees. Her throat clicked as she swallowed.

"Help." The word came weakly from somewhere beyond the headlight's reach. A man's voice. "Please," he said, struggling.

She couldn't see him, but she stepped forward, slowly, cautiously. Whatever exhaustion she'd felt was absent now.

"Where are you? Are you hurt?" Stupid question, she

thought. The way he sounded, she'd be surprised if he *wasn't* hurt.

The leaves and grass at her feet were slick, and as she stepped farther into the woods she could hear the panicked cries of an animal.

He hit a deer, she thought, understanding now. Hit it and was dragging it into the woods.

Something moved in the dark and she could just barely make out…a pod, maybe? A cocoon? Swaying from a pine tree's branch ten feet overhead. As her eyes followed the contours of that strange shape, she saw the deer within, kicking its legs and whinnying. Blood ran in sheets down the structure, raining onto grass below. And there was the man. Most of him. Gore burbled from between his wet lips and her mind struggled to make sense of the mess of torn flesh and scattered organs. His tongue pushed out as his single remaining eye fell upon her.

Deeper in the shadows, something large moved toward her. Multi-limbed, almost spider-like, but the configuration was all wrong. More like a praying mantis, but with more and bigger arms. And teeth. So many teeth, like the maw of a leatherback turtle. She saw hundreds of teeth encircling the inside of its mouth as it reached toward her.

She screamed, and she cursed herself for not staying in the car.

Stupid girl.

Back Soon

GABRIEL EVANS WAS SIX YEARS OLD, OLD ENOUGH TO understand death, and he was pretty sure his father, who was much, much older, was dead.

Only a few minutes before, Gabe had come out of his room, hungry and searching for somebody to help make him breakfast. Of his mother, there was only a piece of scrap paper left on the kitchen table, her chicken scratch writing on it. He paid it little attention and went off to find his dad, instead, his heart set on pancakes, or maybe some eggs.

He wondered if Daddy had been alive when she left, or if his death was the reason she had gone out. Gabe stood at the threshold of his parents' bedroom for some time, watching in nervous apprehension. He wasn't sure what had made him stop, some kind of instinct that was older even than his father, a subtle change in the air itself that froze his feet to the floor and ground him to a halt. Then, the smell hit his nose, and he knew. It smelled kind of like a bathroom, but there was another smell mixed in with all that awfulness that he couldn't identify. Still, he stood quietly, watching, waiting.

Dad lay atop the bedsheets and blankets, sprawled facedown, perfectly still. Gabe kept hoping to see the subtle rise and fall of his back and shoulders that would indicate the man was breathing. He'd seen it before, lots of times, when he would silently creep into this room before they were awake and just watch them for a bit before crawling onto the mattress between them.

Rooms with the living felt different than rooms with the dead, as if when somebody died they took more than just their lives and souls with them.

A noise like nails skittering against the glass window made Gabe jump, a scream peeling loose from deep inside him. Shadows flickered across the pane, the wind moving the tree's low-hanging branches, and he kicked himself for being stupid.

Slowly, he moved into the bedroom, tears welling in his eyes. He was grateful that his father's face was turned away from him. The smell was worse up close, and when Gabe put his hand on his dad's arm, intending to shake him awake, to bring him back to life, his father's skin was cold.

His hip pressed against the edge of the bed, Gabe became aware of a tacky coolness pooling against his waist and stepped back, gasping in surprise. His pajamas were wet, sticky against his skin.

After a moment, his brain finally caught up with his eyes, made him realize the bedsheets were the wrong color, that it wasn't just a trick of the light, but…something else. It was a color he knew well from all the summers of scraped elbows, knees, and hands. Curiosity pulled him forward again, put one foot in front of the other, and marched him around to the other side of the bed.

His father had settled into blankets soaked in blood.

The early morning light, while still gray, came through the window shades just enough to show him a corner of dad's wide smile, right below his chin. It was a dark and wet smile, and everything about it was all wrong.

Gabe screamed then, and ran out of the bedroom, back to the kitchen. His empty stomach was rebelling inside him, trying to jump straight up and out of his throat, and he hit the sink counter just in time. Nothing came up, though. Instead, he dry-heaved into the metal basin, ropes of spit hanging from his lips while black dots danced in front of his eyes.

Drool pattered on the chef knife beneath his mouth, the blade covered in red.

He shoved away from the counter, his feet skidding across the floor, and fell on his butt. He wiped at his wet lips with his forearm, his heels digging into the linoleum and pushing him back, away from the knife, away from more of his daddy's blood. The tears came easily as the reality of it all sank in, hitting him like a leather belt across his belly.

Gabe was wobbly and his legs shook as he stood, grabbing onto the kitchen chair for support. He sank into it with relief and buried his face in his hands as he sobbed, wondering what he was supposed to do now. He thought about having to dig a great big hole in the ground and hauling his daddy into it, and it only made him cry harder and harder. Or was he supposed to call someone? Call 9-1-1? He didn't know. Dads weren't supposed to die like this, not when their kids were so young, and he just didn't know how to do anything but cry and cry and cry. Tears ran a trail from his palms, down his wrists, warm and salty, to pool against the table at his elbows.

He tried to get himself under control, tried to wipe away at the tears, but that only made fresh ones. Through blurry eyes, he saw the note on the table, the one his mother had left, held down by a thick roll of black garbage bags. Red splotches stained the edges of the small scrap, Mommy's fingerprints clearly defined in the stains on either side of her jagged and sloppy handwriting. Although the words were short, the printing was worse than her usual chicken scratch. Maybe she'd been crying, too, when she wrote it.

Gabe pulled the note out from under the garbage bags and held it close. It said only, BACK SOON.

Meme

The Karma's A Bitch meme challenge was one of the hottest video fads to hit the internet a year or two back. It was actually based on another meme, a fan edit of the TV show *Riverdale*, in which the show's character Veronica utters the infamous phrase "Karma's a bitch." In the fan edit, Veronica is then shown in various outfits and styles through a series of quick cuts. The meme challenge borrows this editing style, with the people appearing one way, saying "Karma's a bitch," and then a quick cut to a radically different appearance. For instance, we'd see them in their pajamas one second, and then the next they're dressed in heavy make-up and leather, ready to conquer a nightclub. The meme challenge was big in China, but I don't think it ever caught on in the States. Not after the first murder, anyway.

The death of Mallory Rabbens gained its own sort of notoriety and went viral for reasons far disconnected from a cult teen TV show. In her video, Mallory appears in her bedroom, lying in bed, wearing cozy looking fleece pajamas. Her mascara is streaked, her eyes puffy, and even in the dim lighting of her room you can see the jagged red lines in the twenty-year-old's sclera. You can't help but wonder why she had been crying, what had made her voice so fragile and broken as she said those three little words.

"Karma's a bitch." She sniffles, wipes at a tear, and then quickly pulls the covers up and over her face.

The flash of fabric serves as the single moment of continuity between Mallory Then and Mallory Now. It's like a magic trick, the way she transforms in that seamless instant of video manipulation. Even the scene itself has changed. The snow-white comforter falls and she's sitting now, bound to a chair by thick ropes, in front of a bare concrete wall. Duct tape seals her lips and winds around her head in a thick matte gray loop. An enigma dressed all in black stands behind her. You can see one black gloved hand grab a fistful of her shockingly red hair to pull her head back, exposing the long, narrow line of her neck. In an instant, a second black hand slashes across her throat and the bright overhead light glints off the large blade her killer holds.

All told, the video is exactly twelve seconds long. The recording ends on a grisly note as that first spray of blood ejects from her severed carotid. Twitter removed it, as did Facebook, Instagram, and even Reddit. You can still find it, though, if you look hard enough. Mallory Rabbens, and others too.

There are currently three Karma's A Bitch murder clips floating around online, each posted roughly a month apart. Some Internet armchair detectives have noted that the bedroom Mallory is first seen in, the one where she's crying in bed, looks eerily similar to the bedroom Gloria Gentry and Lisa Stevens were in. Both are even wearing cozy fleece pajamas, which they argue cannot be coincidental. The three girls do not look even remotely alike. They have different builds, different hair colors, and different eye colors. Visually, there's nothing connecting them. Yet they all appear in the same bedroom, and all are crying as they utter that singular phrase: "Karma's a bitch."

What are they crying about? What's going through their minds at that moment, before they pull the bed sheets over their heads? Do they know what's about to happen after the sheet falls? Is any of this even real, or is it all just an elaborate hoax? You can't help but wonder.

Maybe one day I'll tell you, or I'll let one of them tell you. But not today. I need to finish editing video number four.

Ministrations

If you want to take revenge on a man, send him a really beautiful woman.

Arabian proverb

No one rejoices more in revenge than woman.

Juvenal

MARTY HARSHOK COULDN'T TAKE HIS EYES OFF HER. THE long-haired brunette in the gray cotton dress with spaghetti straps and skirt that ended just above mid-thigh was absolutely tantalizing. Mesmerizing, even.

He'd been discretely following her around the grocery store for the better part of ten minutes, blindly pulling goods off the shelves to fill his cart. He'd forgotten what he had come into the store for, but whatever he had needed then was of far less importance than what he wanted now.

From the end of an aisle he watched, mouth wet, as she stretched to reach a box of cereal from the top shelf. Pushing off the balls of her feet, her heart-shaped calves popped, the muscles of her strong, lean thighs flexing. He followed the line of her extended arm from wrist to the paler hollow of her shaven armpit, down to the top edge of the dress's corset that fell just beneath the white athletic bra she wore under the simple garment. Stretching, the cotton pulled tight over her ample breasts.

Marty thoughtlessly licked at his lips, his palms sweaty against the handlebar of the grocery cart. He had never seen a woman so goddamned beautiful, so enchanting. She could give the world's hottest model a run for her money, and she wasn't even fucking trying. She was just standing there, in the middle of a grocery store aisle, grabbing a box of cereal, and Marty had never seen anyone quite like her before. She had a carefree, unselfconscious air about her that he found intriguing, as if she were the only woman in the store. She existed in her own bubble and the other shoppers had responded in kind to that ethereal otherness radiating off her. They didn't just give her space and room to maneuver, but seemed to treat her with deference, as if she were royalty. They, too, recognized she was extraordinary but when her eyes made contact with one of them she was quick with a wide, charming smile. She was absolutely exquisite.

And then she turned, her shockingly bright blue eyes meeting his. He'd been caught staring and quickly looked away, a red flush heating his cheeks. As he suddenly found something of interest by his shoes, he thought he had seen the flicker of a smile play across her full lips. When he looked back up, hoping to confirm it, her back was to him and she was moving further down the aisle. He watched as her toned, ripe apple-shaped ass shifted beneath the cotton, the hem of the short skirt gently rippling with her movements, fluttering against the lush curves of those perfect cheeks as her hips swayed.

He had to get out of here. The crotch of his jeans had grown unforgivingly tight and his erection strained painfully against the zipper. Grateful to have the cart as a shield, he turned it around, the wheels shrieking in protest. The cart was noisy and wobbly, but it hid his arousal well enough, and once he'd gone flaccid he was able to ditch it.

In the parking lot, he sat in his car watching the store's entrance. His engine was running hotter than the car as he thought about seeing her one more time. The radio played, but he didn't hear a single damn song it broadcasted. He was too focused on the grocery's exit doors, waiting to see her again. He didn't think she had left before him, but he wasn't one hundred percent positive, either. Shoppers came and went as he shifted uncomfortably in his seat, tugging the material of his pants and his boxer shorts away from his groin. His underwear was soaked with precum, the fluid cold and tacky, and all he wanted to do was rub one out as he daydreamed of the girl in the gray dress, her mouth against his, her lips steadily moving downward over his naked chest, lower and lower still....

Marty knew he was being foolish. No way in hell was he going to be able to live with but one last look at her. He needed to see more of her, wanted to know more about her, where she lived, what she did at night. Did she live alone? And if so, how did she keep herself occupied in the long, lonely hours of the night, in an otherwise empty bed? Or maybe she had a roommate or significant other, a man or a woman who helped sate her every desire. She was a puzzle, a total mystery, and he had to learn about each and every single piece of her existence, all the various aspects that made up her private life.

Thirty-five minutes later, he saw her again. She raised a slender hand to tuck hair behind one ear before the wind could snatch it and blow it across her face. The breeze was gentle and it did wonderful things to the thin cotton fabric, pushing the loose corset flush to the smooth expanse of her stomach, the billowy veneer of the skirt pulling taut over her hips and briefly diving between her legs to punctuate the perfect triangle of her crotch. She walked confidently, the loose dress maneuvering around her toned, tight body, the slight wind playing with the fabric and spot checking her curves as she headed to her car.

She stopped at the bright yellow Jeep Cherokee parked the next aisle and two spaces over from his own Nissan. He enjoyed the view while she unloaded, thinking the Jeep's smart paint job would making following her that much easier. This was clearly a woman used to standing out in a crowd. He thought maybe she liked being watched, then wondered what else she might enjoy doing while others observed, and his hard-on roared back to life.

He had to force himself to calm down before he did something stupid. He'd been stupid before and it had made portions of his life very uncomfortable. He'd been busted four times for peeking while loitering, a misdemeanor offense that had, initially, netted him probation and a handful of days on a court officer-supervised work program picking up garbage on the side of the road. His third and fourth offenses had come with jail time in addition to probation.

The number of times he'd been caught, thank God, paled in comparison to the number of times he'd gotten away with secretly watching women in their homes. It was a crime he'd committed frequently as a teenager and young man, but the excitement had eventually worn off and he had needed more danger and risk to get off properly. A bolt of anticipation shook his spine watching this brunette, and even a minor dash of fear. He hadn't prepared properly and hadn't dressed for the occasion.

But he didn't want to lose this singular, majestic opportunity. He had to follow her, that much he knew, no doubt about it.

The Jeep reversed out of its parking spot and made a beeline for the closest exit. Marty waited a moment, trying not to be obvious, and then followed. They turned right and he was careful to keep enough distance between them while making sure he kept her vehicle in sight.

Following her was trickier as she turned onto a side street and navigated the various twists and turns that led to her neighborhood. For blocks, theirs were the only cars moving and his heart hammered against his ribs with a furious nervousness.

At one point he was certain he'd lost her, arriving at a stop sign with her nowhere in sight. Turning his head left to right and back again, clutching the steering wheel tightly in his sweat-soaked hands, he swore. And then he saw her. Two-thirds of the way down the street to the right, her bright yellow Jeep stood in a driveway, the hatch open. She collected a few bags and made her way up the porch of a ranch-style house, keys in hand.

He wanted to leap out of his car, run up behind her, and bend her over the trunk, taking a handful of her silky black hair in his fist and pulling her head back, watching the mix of pain and pleasure as he rammed into her. She would beg him to fuck her, he knew, right there in broad daylight, too lost in their mutual lust to worry about the neighbors as she pleaded for him to cum inside her.

Instead, he drove on, finding no signs of life on either

side of the street. No kids playing, no dogs barking. Later might be a different story, but at the moment this was a sleepy little neighborhood. He could have her any way he wanted, right here, right now. But no, he decided. No, he would be a good boy for now. Later…well, he wouldn't make any promises about later.

He caught sight of the house numbers beside her front door as he drove past. Through the glass screen door, he spotted a flash of movement as she came back into the entryway to retrieve the rest of her groceries. By the time she made it back outside, Marty was already turning off her street.

He returned that night, dressed more appropriately for the occasion. Black sweatpants, black shoes, black gloves, a black long-sleeved tee, and a black Carhartt 2-in-1 hat with a pull-down face mask. He would get hot, even as the warm day gave way to cool night, but that was OK. It was all part of the game.

The neighborhood, late at night, now past midnight, was even deader than it had been during the day. This, too, was OK. Preferable even.

He parked at the end of the block, close enough to run back to if necessary, far enough to appear discreet. He walked, keeping his head low, wary of the night's noises. All around him were dark houses, save for one. Hers. He couldn't help but smile beneath the face mask, his thumb fingering the grooves of the utility knife's blade release button in his pocket.

A flood of saliva washed over his mouth as his eagerness grew for what was to come.

He'd been busted for peeping, but so far that had been it. The police hadn't picked him up for the rapes, and that was because he was careful. In his opposite pocket was a condom, which would be leaving with him, along with its wrapper.

The peeping was merely prelude. When he was younger, it had been the main event, standing outside a girl's bedroom, watching her undress, maybe doing something more if he were really lucky, and fondling himself until he climaxed in his pants, withdrawing his sticky hand and wiping cum on the legs or ass of his jeans. Eventually, he'd needed more. It was like going from *Playboy* to hardcore porn. An easy transition to make, but going in reverse? That was too tame, too dull. He needed the action.

One light switched off as he approached, the curtained window going dark. A moment later, a golden light filled the windows of a different room further down the side of the house, facing him. It was like she was inviting him over, directing him where to go.

He cut onto her lawn, following the brick siding and crouching beneath the window. Her bedroom, but it was empty. The door was open and he could see the glow of a light from just down the hallway beyond. He crept to the back of the house, following the light. A small rectangular window sat up high in the wall, and he could hear the rush of water from the other side. The bathroom shower. Images of her perfect body came easily to his mind, her skin glistening wet, her erect nipples capped with soapy suds.

Moving to the back porch, he tested the latch of the screen door and found it unlocked. Cautiously, he pulled the handle, the door opening surprisingly quietly. He looked around at the neighboring houses, saw all was still dark, and tried the door knob. It turned easily and the back door swung open soundlessly.

His heart was pounding, his erection tenting the front of his sweatpants, leading the way for him.

He closed the door and followed the soft glow of the hallway to the bathroom. The door was open and he caught a glimpse of her in the mirror, distorted by the frosted glass of the reflected shower. She sang softly as she washed and rinsed her hair, but he couldn't make out the words.

Marty crept further down the hall, enjoying the otherwise empty feeling of the house. She lived alone, no pets that he could tell, certainly no dog, thank God. The floors were hardwood, so his shoes left no tracks in the carpet. This truly was his lucky day.

The woman's tastes were Spartan, her house hardly furnished beyond the bare essentials. Her bedroom held, of course, a bed, nightstand, table lamp, and a few books. Aside from the dresser, the TV and streaming service puck atop it, and closet full of clothes, she had little else. Perhaps she had only recently moved in, he thought. It didn't matter, not really, but he still found it curious.

Her day's clothes were piled in a heap beside the bi-fold door of her closet. A pair of gray panties sat discarded at the top and he snatched them up quickly. He pulled down his mask and brought the crotch of her underwear to his face, inhaling her musk. He nearly moaned, his cock aching for release. He dropped the tiny garment, then stepped to the closet.

The door gave a small squeak as its hinges folded, but it moved smoothly enough in the track. The closet was nearly as empty as the rest of this woman's life and he found more than enough room to stand comfortably inside, closing the door. A cobweb dangling from the clothes rod brushed his face, and he swatted it away, his heartbeat spiking suddenly in a way that had nothing to do with his lust. The unbidden thought of eight hairy legs crawling over his arms or up the back of his neck gave him the shivers. He hoped there weren't any spiders in the closet with him, hiding in the dark recesses beside him, waiting for the perfect moment to strike. He shivered again, cursing his overactive imagination. He was scaring himself. *Stupid.* He had to focus. Standing opposite her bed, he could see the scope of the room before him perfectly through the bi-fold's pine slats. All he had to do was wait. And not freak out over stupid shit.

The noise of water rushing through pipes inside the walls stopped abruptly. The shower was off, and he couldn't help but smile. The creaking of floorboards and the soft padding of her steps indicated he would not have long to wait.

His fingers curled around the handle of the utility knife as he tried to control his breathing.

Sʜᴇ ʜᴀᴅ ɢᴏɴᴇ ʙʏ ᴍᴀɴʏ ɴᴀᴍᴇs ᴏᴠᴇʀ ᴛʜᴇ ʏᴇᴀʀs. Nᴇᴍᴇsɪs, Rhamnousia, and Adrasteia were but only a few, and the most infamous, at least during a particular time and in a particular society. She called herself Ada now, a modern take on one ancient name.

As she stepped out of the shower, she caught a whiff of him, his scent lingering in the hallway. She had known he would be here, just as she had known when and where he would be out shopping earlier in the day. She had seen him first at the market, his weak mind so simple and transparent that his personality and memories were laid open before her like a lavish buffet. Ada knew him better than he would ever know himself. She was privy to all his secrets, including the ones his own mind had fought to suppress, and those memories he had filtered through the lies he told himself to feel important and powerful. His sense of entitlement was exhaustingly common to the men of this species, a genetic flaw engrained so deeply in the fibers of their being it was unlikely the world would ever be rid of it.

But at least it kept her busy.

Regardless of how strong they thought themselves, men were ultimately weak. Susceptible. *Oh so predictable.*

She knotted the towel above her breasts and went to the bedroom. He was exactly where she expected him to be.

He wants a show, she thought. He was lucky she was feeling playful. Let him watch then, she decided. Let his sins build and multiply. It would give her that much more to savor later.

She turned on the television. Briefly, as she let the towel fall away, she saw herself through his eyes, saw the fantasy playing in his head. It was all so pathetically male she almost laughed.

Ada saw two options. She could ignore the script he was fantasizing about, as all the previous women he'd sought dominion over had, or she could give him what he wanted. He expected to take that what was not his, but in his delusions it was offered freely, wantingly. She knew well how the scenario would play out in option one. The second, though...that, she found curious.

A gasp of female ecstasy came from the television as the studio logo of a pornographer dissolved on the screen.

Ada settled into bed, the soft sheets cool against her bare skin, airy pillows fluffed to help prop her up. A part of her wanted to storm the closet and gut the cowardly man hiding in there. Another part of her, the stronger part, wanted to have fun. Wanted to toy with him...and, she had to admit, toy with herself as well.

She sat through ten long minutes of character introductions as the porno's set-up was established. She wanted to fast-forward to the good stuff, but crazy Marty, he wanted to watch her watching it. He was enthralled at the build-up, the ten minutes for him over in the span of a few heartbeats.

As the women onscreen began to fool around, though, she set aside her reservations, allowed herself to relax. Ada began to grow aroused as the couple's foreplay grew more heated and a man joined them, and one hand slid down the flat plane of her bare torso. Her fingertips curled through the patch of hair between her legs, then reached further down to the sensitive folds of skin and the sudden gush of wetness leaking from her core. With her other hand, she squeezed one breast, her fingers pinching the erect nipple, and gasped in pleasure almost in time to the actresses. As the blonde began to go down on the brunette, Ada penetrated herself with two fingers, biting her lower lip against the wave of ecstasy.

She couldn't wait any longer. Instincts far older than her were taking over and she allowed herself to surrender. At least a little. As she rubbed at her clit, she looked to the closet, her mouth open in a slight O as a ripple of pleasure shot through her, her eyes finding his through the pine slats and the darkness he slunk in.

"Come here," she whispered. Then again, louder, firmer, the invitation unmistakable.

She could read the curiosity in his mind, the confusion. The *What The Fuck Is Happening?* of it all. He was so, so predictable. She reached toward the closet with one hand, the other still rubbing at her pussy, and said again, "Come. Here."

The door opened and the black clad figure stepped toward her, his knife in hand, blade extended. She smiled, pulled her fingers free of her opening, and extended the shiny wet digits toward him, inviting him to taste of her.

SHE'S SO FUCKING PERFECT, MARTY THOUGHT. WATCHING as she, still damp from the shower, laid on the bed, feet flat on the mattress, legs bent at the knee and opened, one finely manicured hand roaming toward her sex. Her fingers tugged at the black curls of hair, slipping through her mound, and then disappeared behind the shield of one muscular thigh. He imagined her a runner, given the graceful fluidity and build of her body. She was toned, but not ripped. Her stomach was flat, but she didn't have a six-pack. She had sex appeal for miles and miles.

Forgetting himself, he slipped off the glove and dropped it. He loosened the drawstring of his sweats and reached inside, gripping his cock. His fist pumped, and he nearly shot his load all over the closet door when she moaned and turned toward him.

And then she spoke to him. But that was impossible. She couldn't know he was here. But then she told him to come to her, extending her arm as if in invitation.

He'd only ever fantasized about such a thing. This wasn't something that happened in real life. Not to him. Ever since he was a boy life had taught him one thing above all else. If you want it, you have to take it. Nothing is ever given to you.

Yet, here he was, being offered more than he ever could have possibly imagined. He did the only thing reasonable. He opened the closet door.

She pulled two wet fingers free from her crotch and presented them to him. He pulled away the face mask, tucking it under his chin, and grabbed her wrist as he took her fingers in his mouth.

"You're delicious," he stammered. He felt uncomfortably nervous in a way he'd not felt in a very long time. Nervous, and afraid. Those feelings, though, were of less immediate importance than licking the juices from her fingers. She *was* absolutely delicious, like honey. He wanted to taste more of her.

She twisted toward him, her legs spread wide to either side of him. A line of sweat beaded the center of her chest, trickling down to the triangle of short black hair at her crotch, the glistening pink folds of her opening startlingly bright amidst the darkness. He sank to his knees, clumsily dropping the utility knife on the nightstand, and inhaled the smell of soap and the musk of her arousal, and pressed his tongue into her.

He lapped at her sweet wetness, her fluids soaking his lips and chin. Her fingers grabbed a fistful of his hair, pulling his face in even tighter against her, and she began to grind against his face.

Her slit pushed down hard on his mouth, his nose buried in a tangle of pubic hair. He pushed two fingers into the warmth of her hole, his tongue encircling her clit. Her thighs locked his head in place as she fucked his face, smearing her wetness across his mouth and nose, grinding harder and harder against him as she neared her climax. Her pussy clenched around his fingers, the pulses of her orgasm squeezing his digits, a fresh wave of honeyed fluid squirting against his lips and into his mouth. The hair of her labia and the insides of her thighs were so soaked a dark wet circle had spread across the bedsheets beneath her.

She took his face in her hands and kissed him, her tongue dueling with his, and then she began to lick his lips and chin and cheeks, everywhere she had drenched him. She tugged at his shirt, demanding he stand. Before he was fully straightened her hands were at the waist of his sweatpants, her fingers curling into the elastic band of his underwear, pulling off the bottom half of his clothes while he worked out of the shirt.

Her mouth swallowed his cock hungrily, one hand gripping his thigh while the other went to his balls, massaging them, gently pushing and pulling the loose sack of wrinkled flesh. As she worked him with her mouth, one finger crept behind his balls, to the soft line of flesh that lay on the road to his anus.

He moaned a sigh of encouragement and she dipped that finger back into her wetness, lubricating it well before returning it to the tight, puckered knot of skin. There was a moment of resistance as the tip of her finger sought entry, and then it relaxed, the muscles grabbing ahold of her finger, drawing the digit into him. He moaned loudly as her lips rode his shaft, her tongue gliding across the sensitive head of his penis, and her finger rhythmically went in and out of his asshole.

She sucked his cock so hard there was a wet pop as she pulled away from his glans. "You like that?" she said, her voice husky with desire.

He could only murmur his reply, gasping as her finger twisted slightly in his rectum. Oh yes, he liked that indeed. He couldn't believe this was happening, even as he thrust deeper into her mouth, fucking her face faster as he grabbed her hair. She pulled away, giggling as she slowly slipped her finger free from his anus, the muscles tightening as they pushed against the digit to eject her.

"Not so fast," she said, chiding him with a warm smile. She pushed herself off the bed and, taking his hand, encouraged him to move to the mattress. "Lay down."

"You're incredible," he said, breathlessly. "A goddess."

In his mind, he heard a voice that was not his own. *Her voice.* In his head, speaking to him.

You have no idea, she said, wordlessly, her lips unmoving as she continued to smile down upon him.

HIS DOUGHY BODY SANK ONTO THE BED SHEETS, HIS COCK jutting stiffly toward the ceiling. He wasn't a fat man, but the lack of muscle definition or toned features told Ada exercise hadn't been of much interest to him since leaving the Army. His appearance ultimately meant nothing to her, and soon there would be little to distinguish his outside from his insides.

He made to reach for her, the muscles of his shoulder tensing as the sheets sucked at his flesh. Threads of Egyptian cotton stabbed and wove through the underside of his body, stitching him into place, enmeshing him until his backside was indivisible from the bed upon which he lay. Snake-like ropes wound around his arms and legs and neck, further pinning him in place. As he realized what was happening, the impossibility of it all, his eyes widened in panic.

"I can't," he gasped painfully, "I can't move!"

She stretched atop him and dragged her fingernails across the side of his stubbled jaw. "That's the idea," she whispered.

"I can't move," he screamed, as if she hadn't understood.

Ada only smiled, straddling him and taking his frightened, flaccid dick into her. Looking down on him, he was so much like an insect trapped in a spider's web. That thought gave her an idea, and her smile grew wider. The idea really should have come to her sooner. Marty, after all, was an arachnophobe, a fact she had gleaned while pilfering his mind and luring him toward her with gentle suggestions.

She placed a hand upon his chest to better feel the fearful racing of his heart as her body stretched and elongated. Long, segmented arms grew from her torso, lined in fine hairs. Her legs fused together, the tops of her thighs melting into her buttocks, the flesh molding itself into a large, bulb-shaped spider's abdomen. Her cheeks ballooned into massive hairy sacks that drooped from either side of her mouth and ended in massive, wickedly pointed fangs. She snapped these fangs at Marty's face, a rough laughter bellowing from within her as he screamed. Eight large eyes grew through the melting skin of her face, and her breasts grew larger, the rust-colored areola expanding to the size of dinner plates.

She laughed as his heart pounded against his sternum, the vibrations of his ribcage powerful beneath her palm. She rubbed her bulbous, bristly-haired abdomen against his crotch, her extra arms pulling his legs up around her, the fabric suddenly pliant and putty like.

"I want you to come deep inside me," she purred, breathless. Marty had screwed his eyes tightly shut, hoping to protect his sanity from the impossibility of her transformation. She lowered her torso toward him and, cupping one breast, brushed her nipple over his lips. His mouth parted and his tongue tentatively flickered over the stiff nub. She sent a soothing suggestion into his mind, a hypnotic feeling of safety, and felt him grow hard inside her.

"Yes," she whispered. "Oh god, yes."

Men, she thought, *were all so damnably alike, it was pathetic.*

A spill of warmth blossomed between them as her gyrations drew an orgasm from him, his semen washing over her hairy abdomen. She continued to grind her distended bottom half over him, slowly retreating from his mind, those feelings of safety and security departing with her. His grunts and gasps of release became an agonizing wail that grew ever louder as the friction built and the fine, sharp hairs that covered her speared the sensitive flesh of his genitals. His eyes snapped open at the blistering pain, and she could see that fleeting hope that this was all a dream simply fall over and die.

"That's it, baby," she said, "just like that." She couldn't help but laugh, using his words against him. He'd said those words to the women he raped, just as he neared climax with them.

She ground harder, rubbing his hips raw as she lined up her oviduct with his anus. "Hmm, yes. Just like that." She threw her head back as a fit of uncontrollable laughter shook through her, her fangs snapping at the air. She pushed his legs higher up into the air, creating a tighter seal between them. The lips of her oviduct kissed his asshole like a lover, and she came with a wet gush. Hundreds of eggs ejaculated from her opening and jetted into his rectum.

Panic shook his heart into a dangerous gallop. Beneath her palm, his chest shook like a cornered and frightened rabbit.

Slowly, Ada crawled off him, her body returning to its natural state. Marty's lower half was a sticky mess, pearlescent egg sacs clinging to his thighs and anus. His genitals were a red, pulpy soup from the scouring of her spidery form's sharp, bristly hairs.

She curled besides him, drugged by the afterglow of her climax but too wired for sleep. Although his head was immobilized, his eyes tracked her movements. His mouth was screwed up in a rictus of pain, hanging open as he fought to control his breathing as a wave of painful spasms shook through him.

"Close your mouth," she said, pushing up on his lower jaw to seal his lips. "You'll catch flies like that."

She laughed at her joke, reveling in the reflection of herself in the tears forming in his eyes.

His mouth fell open again, a window-rattling peel of agony escaping his lungs before turning into pained coughing. Pink bubbles formed against his lips. His eyes bulged, threatening to pop loose from their sockets, and his face grew empurpled.

"What you're feeling now are birthing pains, Martin."

His eyes shot to her, widening in unmistakable horror as more pained and panicked screams ripped free.

"Congratulations. You're a father now."

Marty's stomach swelled, waves of movement rippling the skin from below, from within his guts. He howled as his belly split wetly apart, hundreds of spiders disgorging themselves from his innards in a hairy wave of black and red. More lingered inside of him, feasting on the meat of his organs.

Abruptly, his screams died, and Marty died with them.

When he awoke, it was to a world of pain that ensnared his entire body from the top of his head to the tips of his toes.

"Where am I?" he croaked. His mouth was bone dry and his throat felt bruised, the taste of copper lingering on the back of his palette.

The woman laid beside him, her fingers curling through his chest hairs. He recoiled, a lightning bolt of agony ripping across his backside as he tried to move, freezing him in place. Slowly, the pieces of it all began to reassemble and the fog of sleep lifted to reveal the nightmares of memory.

He hadn't imagined any of this, hadn't dreamt it. All of it was real. He had died, for a time at least. He could actually remember dying, the flash of impossibly bright white light that followed the most brutalizing pain he had ever experienced. And the spiders...dear God, those...*things*, and what they had done to him. What *she* had done to him.

"Who are you?" he said, the words a whimper.

"I have had different names from different people," she said. She gave him a halfhearted shrug, her eyes staring past him as she recalled the various titles she had been granted.

"Some have called me Justice, others Nemesis. I am both Invidia and Mesperyian. I am Rhamnousia, and Adrasteia, goddess of retribution." With a sing-songy inflection, she added, "I am yours and you are mine, now and forever and ever."

"Why are you doing this to me?" he said. "I didn't...I didn't do anything wrong."

Her eyes darkened and her lips twisted into a scowl. "You broke in here with rape on your mind. I know what you had planned. The same as what you did to Amirah, that poor crippled girl in Afghanistan—you do remember her, yes?"

"Who?" he said, lamely. "I don't know who —" One look from the mysterious woman was all it took to silence him. Tears leaked from Marty's eyes. *How could she know?*

"I know everything, Marty. Amirah was so despondent that she told her father about how you raped her. He and her brother beat her to death for bringing dishonor upon them. You raped her, and you are responsible for her murder."

"No," he said. His voice broke upon that single word, his plea releasing in a two-toned whine.

And then he saw her. Amirah. Not as she was when he had attacked her, or how she would have looked in her final agonizing moments of life as her swollen face bled and the bones of her skull fractured and collapsed. He saw her as she had been, before Al Qaeda bombs scarred and dismembered her, plucking loose an arm and a leg from the left side of her body, before a religious fanatic threw acid in her face, melting her skin and blinding her in one eye for the simple offense of going back to school after she had healed from the explosion that had miraculously failed to kill her.

Martin had seen her pushing herself, alone, to class in an old, squeaky, hospital-grade wheelchair. He hadn't seen a terribly wounded young girl, barely into her teens, though. He had seen an easy mark. Easy prey. Grabbing ahold of the worn rubber handles on the back of her wheelchair and hauling her into an abandoned, bomb-blasted store had been simple.

Now, she stood before him on two muscular legs, thick black hair cascading in waves over her bare shoulders and across her chest. She was a whole woman, unscarred, unblemished. A goddess.

And then she smiled at him and all of her beauty was lost.

"You don't like her now?" Rhamnousia said, her lips making a fake pout. From the shadows behind her, another woman stepped forward. "I'm sure you remember Sara Lagana, no?"

Olive-skinned Sara came to his bedside so that he could see her more clearly. He remembered the thick mane of black hair, her large brown eyes, and prominent Greek nose. She had been a real beauty, but death had malformed her in odd ways. Her mouth was misshapen, and as her lips peeled apart he understood why. Large pointed teeth filled her gums, the bottom set overlapping the top, the set too big for her. She raised her hands over his face and the underside of her forearms unzippered from wrist to elbow. A crimson waterfall sheeted down over his face in a torrent, her blood filling his lungs, making it impossible to breathe.

"She lived with what you did to her for two months before finally taking her life. Her mother found her, and the note she left behind. Sara's mother had left behind the ancient beliefs of her forebears, but her grandmother...she's Smyrnaian and she still follows the old ways. She prayed to Nemesis for her *engoní*, her granddaughter, to be avenged. Now you, Martin, will pay. You will pay for all of eternity. You will suffer as you made these women suffer."

He tried to protest, but as he opened his mouth, more blood flooded into him and he choked on the taste of copper as he drowned in a red river. His lungs ached for air but found only more and more of the thick red plasma.

"I will leave you to their ministrations, Marty. Do make yourself comfortable. This is your home now."

For a brief moment, even as Sara bled into him, he couldn't help but wonder where she was off to, why she was leaving him.

Rhamnousia laughed, a full-throated and deeply unpleasant noise. "There are always more men like you, Marty, far too many, and more women demanding justice. As such, my calendar is awfully full." She shrugged and offered him a wan smile. "But don't worry, you'll have plenty of company to occupy you for all of your days, this I promise you."

He watched Rhamnousia through cloudy red eyes, saw

her nod to Sara and Amirah, and gently wave her fingers in goodbye. And then he saw no more.

Sara and Amirah were still there when he awoke. He gasped for air, his skin stretching painfully as he tried to move and found he couldn't.

This can't be happening, he thought yet again.

"But it is," Amirah said. A forked tongue slithered between her misshapen lips and journeyed over the wicked, metallic instruments that had replaced her teeth. Too-long fingers with far too many knuckles folded around his cock, and she began stroking him, a cruel smile ruining her face.

The soft skin of her palm grew rough, her grip tighter. Martin's moans of pleasure turned sharply toward pain as her hand turned sharp and gritty. Looking down the expanse of his body, he saw grains of sand clinging to his member. As she worked him, more sand clung to him, and soon she was scouring the thin layer of skin off his rigid member. Pimples of blood blossomed along his shaft, dribbling a lazy trail to his pubic hair.

"Please stop," he groaned.

Amirah only smiled that awful smile. Her thumb encircled the tip of his glans, the head of his penis swelling at her touch. With the flat of her thumb she flicked at the opening of his urethra, her smile growing wider.

"No," he begged. "No, please, don't. Whatever you're thinking of doing, don't do it, please, God, don't. Please."

The more he begged, the harder she laughed. Her laugh was far from pleasant. Rather, it was guttural, foreign, animalistic. And her smile...he'd never seen anything so primal, so evil.

Her grip tightened, the empurpled head of his cock

swelling, and it felt like his dick was wrapped in sandpaper. She pumped her fist, the skin of his shaft peeling away.

Despite the agony, his erection never flagged. It stood tall and bloody, fully engorged and refusing to go flaccid. If anything, he grew harder with the pain, until the erection itself became yet another focal point of discomfort, the need for release a physical ache as tormenting as any of these women's wickedness.

His cock was raw, the flesh of it degloved. It looks like a skinned raw sausage, the shaft weeping blood and sticky with sand. Amirah bent toward the ruined organ, her mouth opening with seductive promise but delivering only more pain upon him. The heat of her breath stung his flayed member, like salt on his wound.

Her knuckles hardened and cracked, the skin turning dry, a roughness spreading across her hand and up her forearm. Her thumb, now jagged and sharp, rubbed tight circles over his raw glans, the tip of her nail pressing into his opening. Something wormed its way into him, fierce points biting into his abused skin, chewing their way deeper into his urethra. Martin howled, the cords of his neck straining.

Something was scraping along the delicate inner flesh, moving inside of him. He was able to angle his head just enough to see...sand. Sand was pouring into him, a steady stream of it trailing from Amirah's thumb and into the core of his shaft.

"Please stop," he whined.

Her eyes met his, but he found no remorse there, no compassion. Only a steely determinedness, and even a hint of self-righteous satisfaction.

"I'm so sorry," he said.

But it wasn't enough. It would never be enough.

An aching fullness blossomed in his bladder, a painfully

urgent warning signal that the organ was in desperate need of emptying. Urinating was impossible, though, and the sense of fullness only increased as more sand pushed into him, soaking up his blood and piss and turning to heavy sludge inside him.

Like some kind of fucked up hourglass, sand roared through him, scouring him from the inside, filling him, getting everywhere. Martin had always hated going to the beach. Afghanistan, fuck, the whole entire Middle East, was like one giant steaming ashtray of awful, gritty sand. He'd hated it there. He fucking hated sand. Hated the way it got into everything, his shoes, between his toes, in his clothes and hair. Hated the way it felt.

Amirah smiled at him knowingly. Of course she knew. She knew everything.

His bladder stretched to its limits and ruptured. Sand flooded into the cavities of his guts, turning muddy with blood inside of him. He gagged on it, on the clumps of blood-mixed sand rising up his throat to choke him.

Amirah's other hand came to his face, two fingers stabbing into his nostrils and turning grainy. Sand shot up his nose, into his sinuses, his head filling with it even as he coughed up more. He couldn't breathe, couldn't get any air into his lungs. He was drowning on earth.

He wanted to apologize one last time, tried to say it with his eyes. But Amirah was beyond caring for anything other than vengeance.

Martin's body bloated and shifted as sand crept into all the vacancies left within him, his eyes bulging as sand pushed against them from within his skull. His heart slowed as sand filled each of its chambers, and then that too exploded under the building pressure and Martin was, again, no more.

.   .   .

When Martin woke, he screamed immediately.

"Please, stop," he shouted. "You have to stop! I don't know these women! I've never met them! You have the wrong man! Listen, this is all some kind of mistake, I swear! I swear to fucking God you've got the wrong guy!"

He carried on like that for some time, until his cheeks burned red with exasperation. He was met with only silence.

Sara sat beside him, and she caressed his face. Amirah sat opposite, and her hand, too, gently touched his cheek.

"I'm sorry," Martin said. "I'm so sorry. Please, you have to stop. I'm begging you! Please, stop, stop."

Amirah smiled and his heart leapt in fear at the sight of the wicked metal implants hidden within her mouth.

"I remember begging you," she said.

"How many times did I ask you to stop?" Sara said. Her nails dug into his cheeks as she forced his face toward hers. "Do you remember?"

"You took from us what you wanted, Martin," Amirah said.

"Now it's our turn," Sara said.

"You belong to us now."

"You wanted us so badly…"

"And now you have us," Amirah said.

"Forever and ever and ever."

Martin screamed as they began their latest round of ministrations, the taste of copper welling in the back of his throat as it bubbled up into his mouth. His mind fought to rebel at what was happening, but he knew it was useless. There was no doubting it, not any longer. He was in hell, trapped with the demons he had made of these women. The torments he had paid upon them for the sake of his pleasure would be repaid to him a thousand-fold and more.

He died again that day. And again that night. He was reborn over and over, into a life of torment everlasting. He existed only to die, loudly and painfully and bloodily, over and over.

It was exactly as Amirah and Sara had said, as Nemesis or Rhamnousia or whatever her name truly was had said before them.

This was justice—their justice.

And he was theirs. For all of eternity, he was theirs.

Forever and ever and ever…

Stay Away

ALL AROUND THE WORLD ARE PARTICULAR PLACES THAT possess strange dualities, existing not only on this plane of existence but elsewhere and, on occasion, else*when*. Not many, mind you. They are few and far between, and hidden—most often—in plain sight. On certain days of the year the power these locations possess are at their strongest, bridging one dimension to another, allowing some to pass through doorways from one reality to another. Curiously, most are repelled by this power, like matching ends of a magnet. Some, though, might find themselves attracted to it, or at least cajoled into ignoring their own best instincts.

Take, for instance, Mya Hernandez, as she stands outside the large Victorian home on East Ferry Street, her friends on either side. The house is dark, its windows unlit, unwelcoming, and with nary a decoration in sight save for one. Mya holds in her hands an old pillowcase, its opening frayed and fat with candy. She's dressed as Elsa from the movie *Frozen*, a costume she's worn for the last five

Halloweens, and like the pillowcase it too has seen better days.

"C'mon Mya, you gotta," Sherene says from her left, dressed as Evie from *Descendants*.

"It's your turn," said Maxine on her right, dressed as Mal, also from *Descendants*.

Mya could have been Audrey—*should* have been Audrey, if her parents had any money at all. Part of her wonders if that's why her friends are daring her so strongly, pushing her into climbing the steps of the big orange-bricked house. She follows the line of unlit casement windows to the third story, to the steeply pitched and sharply pointed gabled roof and the widow's walk that tops the tall turret on the eastern side of the home. It's been vacant longer than she's been alive. She knows of the rumors, the gossip, the local legends of ghosts and goblins. They say it's haunted, but other quieter voices speak of darker things than mere spirits, and when they do it is with a far off look in their eyes, their voices turning to whispers before trailing off into silence.

She's the odd man out in her old costume, but Max is right. It is her turn. Maxine had gone last year, and Sherene the year before that. Both had crept up that flight of steps to the porch and come running back down, not quite screaming but clearly afraid. And no worse for the wear. Nothing to be afraid of.

Still, butterflies jangled in Mya's belly and she felt a light presence pushing her away. She couldn't explain it, but she knew she had to stay away. She knew, too, that she couldn't, or else she'd never live down the torment from her two best friends.

Nobody was even inside the house to give out candy and reward her for scaling her way to the top and striking the door. Not that knocking on the door was her main objective, anyway. No, she had to touch the pumpkin that sat on the top step. That strange, incongruous squash that had been lovingly carved and placed just before the door on the porch landing. A candle flickered inside it, giving life to the triangular eyes that watched her, making the jagged toothy lines of its mouth into something mischievous. Nobody ever seemed to know who carved the pumpkin or placed it there. No one ever saw. It was simply there after sundown on Halloween and gone by sunrise.

Mya swallowed a dry lump in her throat and looked to Maxine.

"Do it," Max said, giving her a gentle shove. "Blow out the candle."

"Blow me."

"C'mon," Sherene said.

"Hold my bag at least." Mya sighed and shoved her bag at Max until the girl took it.

She looked down either side of the sidewalk, noting the utter absence of any other trick-or-treaters. The street had been so vibrant only moments ago, but suddenly the girls were alone in the dark. Her heart pounded in her chest like a scared rabbit as she stepped onto the paver stones leading to the steps. To the pumpkin. She tried not to walk too fast, nor too slow. She didn't want the girls to see just how afraid she really was.

"Sometimes, things come through," old lady Gerlach had said once upon a time. She'd been cutting Mya's hair and they'd gotten to talking about Halloween and how excited Mya was to score loads of candy. As they chatted, the contours of their conversation eventually led to talk of the Victorian house and the Ferry Street legends. She remembered that snippet of conversation now, but little else from that day. That was all old lady Gerlach would say, and when Mya pressed for more all she got was a simple, "Never mind now."

The flicker of flame shifted, and it seemed to Mya that the pumpkin's smile grew larger as she approached. It seemed to welcome her even as she felt the urge to run away, her body charged with an odd energy that screamed for her to flee. She wouldn't look back at her friends, though. Wouldn't give them that satisfaction, not even as another strange urge took her.

She reached out with shaky fingers and felt the hard, wrinkled skin of the pumpkin. It was surprisingly warm. Its eyes seemed to follow her hand and just as she made contact it moved, lightning quick. Jagged teeth clamped down hard on her arm, the inside of its mouth furnace hot. Her skin blistered as flames boiled her fingers and she screamed. Her costume ignited, the fire spreading fast, engulfing her as she pulled away the stump of her ruined, chewed-up wrist.

Max and Sherene screamed, too, and took off running as Mya danced and writhed in the dry grass to the music of the pumpkin's insane laughter. As the fire consumed her, she remembered one other thing old lady Gerlach had said about the house.

"Stay away from it."

White and Black

THE SMELL OF ROT PERFUMED THE AIR. HER THROAT
ached. Her stomach cramped in hunger. She had no idea
how long she had been locked away in this too-white room.
No memory of her abduction. She remembered the things
that had happened *around* her being taken, the final exam
she knew she'd aced, the celebratory too-many drinks that
Friday night, and the cute guy she'd been flirting with
while toying with the idea of kissing him if he didn't make
the first move.

He'd made a move all right. And that was the last thing
she remembered. A gulf of blackness bridges that memory
to the next, of waking in this room some indeterminate
time later. She didn't know how much time had passed, but
it *felt* like a while. Days, maybe. She'd asked and been met
only with silence. It was impossible to say how much time
had elapsed as the lights were constantly on. The scrubs
she had awoken in had been startlingly white but were no
longer. Fresh stains marring her clothes were the only sign
of time's passage. Those stains, and the rotting stink.

She'd been in this white room, wearing white clothes,

sleeping in a white bed long enough for her fighting spirit to grow into a cooperative attitude, her resistance worn down to a dull, weary nub. Somewhere along the way, she'd stopped asking what he wanted, where she was, why he drew her blood at intervals so goddamned random it made the passage of time impossible to judge.

Meals came at irregular intervals, as well, sometimes multiple times a day and other times only after prolonged absences. All she knew for certain was that he kept her deliberately off balance, her mind and body utterly deprived of stimulation beyond the odd visit when he entered and jabbed a needle into her. She'd been strapped to the bed initially, until it was clear she was no longer a threat and her resistance had been eliminated. Then she was allowed to move freely about the room. She thought maybe – *maybe* – a month a month had passed by then, and she was physically and mentally weak, her body a catalog of blistered sores and aching limbs.

Her cell was an eight-by-eight cube, occupied only by her, a bed, and a toilet. When he came in, she had tried to look past him but saw only blindingly white light. She knew, too, that the door locked behind him because she had tried to escape the first time she'd been allowed to roam. It was a long time after that before she was allowed to move again. The scars on her face had healed poorly.

She'd had to regain his trust, all the while wondering why she was here and what was happening. He never said, but over time he grew more comfortable as her compliance grew more apparent and came more readily. Until she bit into his throat and he bled out on the floor.

Nobody came. There were no more meals after that, and eventually she worked up the courage to eat. She tried to tell herself it was like shredding pork with her bare fingers, but it didn't work. The meat was too raw and bloody to convince her, even when she pretended it was Carolina style. She had choked on the taste of decay, gagging on the putrefying meat and the stench of shit and piss his body had evacuated as his muscles relaxed in death.

She wondered if the world had come to an end. Maybe a plague had wiped out civilization and she was among the last survivors, being poked and prodded and tested by Earth's last scientists for a cure to a plague only she was immune to. Or maybe a meteor had come and sent humanity the way of the dinosaurs. She imagined a horde of zombies on the other side of that door, the cute guy from the bar decomposing beside her and giving her fantasy life by way of Smell-O-Vision.

And then, with maggots squirming on the white floor and wriggling in their death spasms beneath her feet as she stepped across them, she thought, *What the hell?* and tried the door.

It opened.

Beyond was a void of perfect blackness, so thick and pure in pitch that the glaring white lights of her small, perfectly white room could not penetrate. She could see nothing, nothing at all. Light refused to enter and no sound came from within its depths. It was like looking into a black hole, or staring into the abyss. Outside of her prison was nothing but black emptiness.

Behind her, whiteness interrupted by splashes of red on the walls, a larger pool of it dried and tacky on the floor, and the prone corpse the varying colors of death and decay. Before her, darkness. And in the middle: her, dressed in filthy nurse's scrubs that had once contrasted perfectly with her ebony flesh.

She stared into the gloom, waiting for her eyes to adjust to the lightlessness before her, but the black remained absolute. It remained pure and perfect, two things she had never been, not even as an innocent child.

She looked back at the once-cute guy, remembered wanting to kiss him, wondering at his taste. By the time her lips finally met his flesh, he tasted of salty copper.

The black was still and quiet. Almost welcomingly so. She reached a shaking hand into the space before her and felt coldness. Her hand lingered there, and she realized she was waiting to be bit, as if a shark swam in those murky depths.

She stepped into the void, directionless and blind. A chill met her flesh, but also, strangely, a warmth. Even though she had taken little more than two steps, she could not find a single trace of light from the room she'd left only a moment before. The light was gone. Only the dark remained.

She was released.

Sundown

Hannah Ford could feel the stares on her back, her sides, all around her. She sipped her coffee, then turned on her countertop stool, slowly, deliberately, to meet the glares of her watchers head on. Instead, she found hurriedly averted gazes as heads turned away to study other, less interesting, facets of the diner. Six others were in the diner with her, all white, and while she had felt them observing her seconds ago only a few had the temerity to meet her head on now. She met the eyes of those bold enough to look at her head on and refused to look away first. She stared them down, coolly, sipping her coffee, one elbow propped up on the counter behind her.

"Morning," she said. The white man nodded, his lips a thin line, but said nothing in return. He held her stare a moment longer to save face, then turned his attention to the menu.

One of her other observers was quickly typing out a text on his cell phone. These men had been brave enough to stare her down when her back was turned, but each lost their courage in the time it took her to complete one revolution. They looked away, red-faced, one by one.

Hannah wondered if any of them had the nerve to rope themselves a young black boy named Harlan Reynolds, hitch him to their pick-up truck, and drag him through a mile of rocky fields to the Centralia Cemetery and the hanging tree he'd been strung from. Most of these men were middle-aged, but not exactly fit. Still, it was possible she was sitting among some tired-looking, pot-bellied murderers. A few were older, approaching retirement age, and it felt safe to rule them out, but only tentatively. The 80-year-old with thinning hair looked awfully spry, and she couldn't help but chuckle to herself at that.

Reynolds' demise had been, incredulously, ruled a suicide, until parties unknown leaked the coroner's report detailing the extent of the damage inflicted upon Reynolds prior to being lynched. The public outcry was sufficient to force the Nemaha County Sheriff's office to reopen the case, "in light of these additional details," and promised a complete and thorough investigation. The leaked reports pointing toward an attempted cover-up made Hannah's blood boil, for so many reasons. She suspected, too, that the promise of a deeper investigation was nothing more than lip service given the nationwide attention the case had received following the leak. In the two months since Reynolds's death, though, the news hadn't even bothered to follow-up and report on the sheriff's supposed investigation, and no arrests had been made. For all intents and purposes, Reynolds was just another dead and forgotten Black man, lost in the shuffle of bigger headlines to captivate a nation's short attention span.

And yet, that wasn't why Hannah had come to Centralia, Kansas. Not entirely, anyway. Odds were, she would have been quietly stewing over the news, or rather, lack of news, at home, alone and angry at the injustice, but content to let others get involved in her place. A lynching wasn't her usual type of business. Not exactly, anyway. The photos she found online changed all that.

She hadn't wanted to look at those images, although she had certainly seen worse in her days, but a morbid curiosity drew her attention. She felt responsible for bearing witness, to try and absorb some of the pain Harlan Reynolds had experienced in his last moments. Although Anonymous had leaked the photos all over social media and they had spread like wildfire from there, that wasn't where Hannah had first seen them. She first encountered the photos capturing Reynolds murder in a private occult group she had been a part of for a number of years now. The poster had been asking if anybody recognized the symbols in the tree trunk. The image had been cropped, in-camera most likely, and much of the carving was incomplete and out of frame. What was visible, though, was clearly arcane. The few responders didn't seem to know much about it, but promised to return when they had more information.

Hannah hadn't bothered to wait for updates. She'd packed her gear, loaded up her Jeep Wrangler, and made the twelve-hour drive from Ann Arbor, Michigan to Centralia, Kansas on little more than a whim. She didn't know what the cut-off symbols meant, but she knew the minute she saw them that this was her kind of job after all.

She finished her coffee, not expecting a refill from the disinterest waitress and not getting one, either. The waitress had been brusque, but she'd poured Hannah the coffee before finding something at the other end of the counter to busy herself with. Hannah set the empty cup down, left a few bills under the saucer, and stood. She turned around and nearly slammed into the wide, too-close, brown-shirted chest.

Her eyes roamed over the Nemaha County Sheriff patch on his sleeve, the badge on his chest, and a name tag that read MORELL, up to the hard, lined face staring down at her. He looked like he'd been carved from a hunk of granite, and his eyes were the coldest blue Hannah had ever seen.

"Sheriff," she said.

"Miss," he said. He stepped around her, taking a seat at the counter next to the one she'd been occupying. Sitting, they were nearly eye to eye. He looked her up and down, the toothpick between his lips bouncing. "What brings you to Centralia, you don't mind my asking?"

"Just passing through," she said.

"Well then, I hope you have a nice, quick visit."

Hannah nodded, and began to turn back to the door when his icy voice stopped her again.

"Word of advice, miss, if you'll allow it. You'll want to make sure you're out of town come sundown, you here? Folks round here, they don't take kindly to people like you come dark, you understand? They get skittish."

Hannah's blood went cold, and she nodded, stiffly. "Oh, I understand, Sheriff."

Centralia had been a sundown town back in the day, and Blacks had been prohibited from living within the town's borders. The laws might have officially been struck down, but attitudes were a lot harder to change. She knew of plenty of predominantly white cities and towns all across America where sundown policies were still in effect, even if only unofficially, and the police in those areas had little trouble coming up with various reasons for stopping a Black person. A broken taillight that mysteriously appeared as the officer made their way to the driver's side window of a Black man's car, flashlight swinging, or stopping somebody because 'they fit the description' of a supposed suspect.

The sheriff's warning, on top of Harlan Reynold's murder, was impossible to ignore. As was the fading sunlight.

She tucked her cellphone into the hip pocket of her blue jeans as she pushed through the diner's door. Her yellow Jeep was the most colorful thing around for miles, and as she approached, she saw the long slash of grey steel that cut its way from the gas cap up to the hood. Somebody had keyed her car while she'd been inside. Hannah shook her head and swore to herself, wondering if the sheriff had been responsible for this. Aside from Morell, nobody had come in or out of the diner during the time it had taken her to drink her one cup of coffee. Or maybe it had just been somebody offended by her Michigan license plate and the U of M faculty parking sticker in her windshield.

Walking around the Jeep, she studied her vehicle for any additional damage. Only the driver's side had been keyed, and the soft top was still secure. The doors were all locked, but she double-checked the cargo compartment to be sure. Her camera equipment was safe, and her small duffle bag with books, clothes, and toiletries didn't look like it had been disturbed.

Hannah checked her watch. Only a little more than twenty minutes until sundown. She had wanted to make it out to the Reynolds crime scene, but she also needed to find a place to bed down for the night. The tree would still be there in the morning, she decided, as she climbed into the Jeep and pointed the vehicle toward the town's borders.

Once she passed the quaint "YOU ARE NOW

LEAVING CENTRALIA" sign, she said, "Hey, Siri, what's the nearest motel?"

Settled in her room, Hannah booted up her laptop and logged into the message board where she'd first learned about the Reynolds murder. She had saved the posted images but was curious to see if any new insights had been made since she'd last checked the prior evening.

As soon as the thread loaded, she was confronted with the crime scene photographs. The very first image at the top of the page showed Reynolds as discovered by the police, hanging from a tree in the town's cemetery, his arms limp at his sides and feet pointing lifelessly toward the short, scorched grass and headstones below.

The symbols that had been carved into the tree were barely discernible, but a second, low-resolution image showed them more plainly. The sigil had been carved high up the tree, and part of the top had been cut off in the photograph. Whatever eagle-eyed observer had originally spotted the carvings had cropped the image in an effort to better showcase the symbols. Unfortunately, it was so heavily cropped, and the carvings themselves were rather small, and an even smaller element of the photograph's larger composition, that it was difficult to make out much detail. To complicate matters further, at the time the photo had been taken the sun had cast a long, deep shadow from the tree's higher branches over the etchings. The cropped photo was hardly bigger than a thumbnail, and when blown-up to larger dimensions it was too much of a pixelated mess to make any sense of.

The only thing Hannah could read clearly about this image was the desperation in the OP's search for help: "Can anybody make any sense of what this says???"

What followed were the same unhelpful comments she'd seen last night. People telling the OP his image was too small, too illegible, and the shadows too dark, to be readable. Others offered to help in any way they could but given the amount of digital artifacting in the low-resolution photos, the promises rang hollow.

Not for the first time, Hannah wished digital photography manipulation worked like it did on those TV crime shows, where you could crop and enhance, and pull out even the smallest details in the most brilliant ultra-high definition resolutions possible. Unfortunately, *CSI* was a fucking joke when it came to getting such details right and took an awful lot of dramatic liberties in order to shortcut reality for entertainment.

Less than twenty-four hours old, and the thread looked like it was already a dead topic. No new posts since last night. She sighed and put the laptop to sleep, not having really expected a different outcome than this. This was why she was in Centralia in the first place, to see those symbols firsthand, figure out what they meant, and why they were carved into a killing tree that a young black man had been lynched from. The fact that there were symbols carved into the tree bark at all was enough cause for concern, and it made the hair on the back of her neck stand on end. Although she had no idea what the symbols were, she could make out just enough in those deep black shadows to know it wasn't a simple John Loves Jane devotion. What she had seen was enough to send her into a twelve-hour drive across five states, and it made clear to her that the Reynolds murder, as heinous as it was, was not just a racially motivated killing. It was a ritualistic murder.

· · ·

Hannah woke before her alarm, intent on getting an early start. What she thought of as her "normal life" as an academic allowed her a fairly flexible lifestyle, but she was accustomed to rising early, going to bed late, and operating on little sleep and a fairly high volume of caffeine. She figured she could kill the roughly two hours before sunrise in a local diner, reading over breakfast, before she crossed the city limits back into Centralia.

She was so eager to lay her eyes on the symbols carved into the hanging tree that she was tempted to skip breakfast and drive directly back into town. Her stomach rumbling and concern over what the Centralia locals might do if they saw a Black woman in their midst while it was still dark out was enough to dampen her enthusiasm. Besides that, she was very much looking forward to digging into the latest in John Connolly's Charlie Parker series, which she was enjoying and thought she might enjoy more alongside a plate of runny eggs and hash browns. Certainly, it would be more enjoyable than having the Nemaha County Sheriff sicced on her again, and she wasn't aiming to start her day off by getting arrested or worse. And she certainly wasn't planning on getting an eyeful of those symbols in such an up-close and personal manner as had befallen Harlan Reynolds, rest his soul.

Breakfast at a nearby diner was cheap and filling, and she was able to lose herself for a time in her Kindle. The coffee wasn't bad, not great by any stretch of the imagination, but the waitress was quick with the refills and with enough cream and sugar Hannah was able to drink four cups of the stuff without complaint. From her booth, she watched the sunrise through the clear glass window as she polished off the dinner plate-sized serving of hash browns, then read a couple more chapters over coffee to give the world some extra time to wake up for her.

Finally, bill paid, she unplanted herself, dropped the ereader back in her purse, and pulled herself into the Wrangler. The morning sun was already warming the earth, promising to make life miserable with its heat as the day wore on. She was glad she'd already taken the soft top down, but if the heat kept up, she'd be putting it back on and blasting the AC soon enough.

Hannah was careful to observe the speed limit as she worked her way back into Centralia, crossing over the Black Vermillion River on Old Number 9. Farms and long stretches of cornfields eventually gave way to the small suburbs of the town proper, until the flat stretches of land, woods, and farms took hold again at Centralia's edges. At the northernmost edge was the cemetery where Reynolds had been murdered, but not buried. According to the news, his body had been interred a few miles away in his hometown of Seneca.

Reynolds had been discovered at the northern edge of Centralia Cemetery, where the graves were sparser and the land less heavily trafficked by visitors and mourners. The site of his demise was far enough removed from the heart of the cemetery that the four roads looping around the more central burial plots didn't even extend that far and the asphalt gave way to dirt well before reaching the hanging tree.

The Wrangler bounced over the rougher terrain of the narrower dirt road, but the cottonwood came into view soon enough.

She pulled to a stop and retrieved her camera gear from the cargo compartment in back. Although it had grown hotter in the short time it had taken her drive from the diner to the cemetery, a cold chill enveloped her as she stepped closer to the tree. Her breath bloomed before her in a smoky cloud and goose pimples rose across her arms.

Cemeteries were a common locale for hauntings, populated by the dearly departed such as they were, but this tree in particular was a virtual hot spot, so to speak, for the restless dead. She couldn't help but wonder how many people had been strung from the cottonwood's limbs and left to die, kicking uselessly and struggling against the noose. Her stomach lurched, and she felt sick imagining the lives lost on this desecrated land.

The cuneiform symbols had been carved into the bark, high-up, and not very recently. The edges of the shapes were worn and rounded, but whatever magic it invoked was unbroken. Hannah imagined that in this tree's heartier years, it's foliage would have easily hidden the carvings. Secrets were like that, though; given enough time, they became exposed.

Hannah held her Canon digital camera overhead, snapped a photo, and checked the display screen to see if she had gotten any of the carvings in-frame. The result was surprisingly good, and she smiled. Although it was broad daylight, she used the camera's built-in flash to eliminate the shadows of the branches, and the symbols stood out in stark relief. She took a few more photos, hoping to improve her luck a bit, rotating the zoom on the lens to get a closer shot. Satisfied, she let the camera hang from her neck and walked around the tree, studying the trunk for additional markings. She couldn't find any, which was for the best.

What she had seen already disturbed her enough.

Harlan Reynolds's mother was in her late forties but looked much older. Her wrinkles were more like deep caverns and her hair had bypassed premature graying and ran straight to shockingly white.

Mathilda had cracked the door just enough to peer out and stood silently waiting for Hannah to speak first. The younger woman introduced herself and held out a business card, which Mathilda read with equal silence, taking a moment to digest the admittedly obscure information printed upon it.

"Dr. Ford. A symbologist, hm? With the University of Michigan? And on my doorstep why?"

"I'm here because of your son, Ms. Reynolds, and the rather unique symbols that were carved into the tree where he was found. First of all, though, let me express my deepest condolences. I'm so sorry for what was done to--"

The door closed in Hannah's face, her next words caught in her throat, stillborn. After a moment, though, as she was ready to turn around and leave, she heard a rattling of chains from inside the house and the door reopened.

If it were possible, Mathilda looked even older than she had only seconds before, and deflated. She stepped back as the door opened wider and she nodded her permission for Hannah to enter.

The small house stank of cigarette smoke, and Hannah noticed a number of discarded beer bottles near a worn recliner. Mathilda settled into the chair and adjusted the billowy mumu around her large legs.

"Thank you for your kindness about Harlan," Mathilda said. "I'm sorry I cut you off there. This is all rather much of a shock, you understand."

"I do, and I know this is unusual." Hannah opened her bag and fished around for the photos she'd had printed at a drugstore on her way to Seneca. "I won't take up much of your time, but I thought you would want to know I was looking into this. By any chance do you recognize these symbols?"

Mathilda stretched forward to receive the photos and peered at them closely. Her cheeks puffed out as she let out a long breath of air. "Do *you* know what they are?" Mathilda said.

Hannah nodded. "Yes, I do. What I don't know, or more accurately what I don't understand, is their relationship to Centralia and why there were cut into that tree."

"They not just in that tree, honey. They all over that town, you look close enough."

Hannah felt like she'd just been punched, and the news left her reeling. "Why?"

"To keep us out. And, when they can, to kill us."

"Centralia was a sundown town. You know what that was?" Mathilda said.

They had taken their conversation, and mason jars of iced tea, to the porch, needing some sunlight to shine over their dark conversations. Hannah sympathized, knowing it wasn't easy to sit alone for long in a home left suddenly empty by death. Sometimes you needed the light.

Hannah nodded, having learned this much about Centralia in her cursory research into the tiny community. A sundown town had laws prohibiting Blacks from being within its borders after sunset and prohibited their living there. It had been, for much of Centralia's existence, a legal method of segregation designed to protect the sensibilities and fears of its all-white citizens toward The Other, giving them a nice warm racist blanket to keep them safe and coddled.

"Saw pictures my grandma had," Mathilda said, "from back in the day. 'No Blacks Allowed.' 'For White People

Only.' That kinda shit. She even had her Green Book, still, and I said, 'Grandman, what's this book?'"

Hannah sat quietly, sipping on her tea as Mathilda spoke. She knew of Green Books, or, as they were published in the 1930s to the late 1960s during the height of America's segregation and the proliferation of sundown towns throughout the country, *The Negro Motorist Green Book*. The book was a resource to warn Black motorists about sundown towns and segregated areas where Black lives didn't matter a single bit.

Mathilda shook her head. "She told me about this book, how the places listed in it were places where Black people just up and disappeared, never to be seen or heard from again. I was born just a few years after the Jim Crow laws were killed, and grandma, she'd kept all that stuff as a reminder, and as a warning, too. Told me they may have taken the laws off the books, but they'd still find ways to kill us, grind us all down into the dirt. Grandma was right about that, weren't she?"

Mathilda took a healthy sip of tea, her throat clicking as she swallowed.

"Anyway. Centralia. Back in 1901, Grandma was just a little bitty slip of a thing, too young to remember what happened, but she liked her history, you know? She knew she'd been just a little baby, so she'd asked her momma and daddy about what happened in 1901 and they told her, and she told me. And now I'm gonna tell you, because you got to know. I told Harlan all about this town, its history, but, fuck, what did I know, right? I'm just his mom. Kids're like that, I suppose. I'm sure I was. Anyway. 1901."

Mathila wiped at the tears standing in her eyes and took another drink.

"Back then, if you were Black, you couldn't live in Centralia. A man named Whitmire tried to make a go of it, though, and when the whites found out about it they shot up his house, drove him and his family out of it, and burned the place down. Whitmire and his family, they had to flee out into the night with only the clothes on their back before they burned or got shot. Well, Whitmire returned," Mathilda said, a small smirk crossing her lips, "and he brought some friends with him.

"They shot the fuck outta that town," she said, laughing now. "Drove all them white folk back inside, made them taste a bit of that fear they tried to pay off on Whitmire. Papers back then had stories about it, 'Negroes Hold A Town,' course it was all shaded, you know, because being Black was a crime back then, and the whites were being unfairly targeted by this mob of angry Black folk they'd just tried to kill. Crazy innit?

"But Centralia was a sundown town, and in some of those sundown towns, Black people had a way of disappearing. Just, poof, gone. Never to be seen or heard from again."

Hannah thought of the symbols on Centralia Cemetery's big, old cottonwood tree, how they had looked aged and weathered, a part of that tree for a very, very long time. She wasn't an arborist or an archeologist, but she didn't think that carving could have been more than a century old. But she did suspect that it had been re-carved, the scarring made deeper, fresher, over the course of the last 120 years.

"Grandma didn't know what all happened exactly, because her parents didn't know either. All they had was rumors and guesses. But those Black people that went into Centralia with Whitmire, not a single one of them ever came back out. Not one of them. Nobody knows what happened, and eventually Black people learned that if they valued their life, they stayed the fuck out of Centralia.

"Now and again, you get some cocksure young fool, thinks he's all that, gonna try and mess with things, thinks just because there ain't no sundown laws on paper no more that it's all oh so copacetic, he can do what he wants. Centralia, that town reminds us it ain't so. It makes examples out of them such folks, gives us public reminders of how we need to mind our Ps and Qs, know our place. And Harlan…my boy…he just the latest in a long, long line of reminders going back to the day that fucking town was founded.

"That town is evil, Dr. Ford. Its people is evil. I was younger, I mighta said that town was cursed, but it ain't cursed for *them*, and it's a curse they made. We the ones that're cursed."

Hannah leaned forward in her chair slightly, her elbows resting on her knees. "Do you know what these symbols mean, Mathilda?"

"I don't, not exactly. Neither did grandma. She just said they was bad juju, and I can't say I disagree none."

Calling the carvings in that tree *bad juju* was an understatement, and Hannah debated how much to share with Mathilda. She was used to being met with skepticism by many, even those who had deliberately sought her help or advice regarding abnatural occurrences, like various officials in law enforcement at both federal and local levels. But Mathilda had a right to know, she decided. The woman's only child had been brutally murdered. And given some of what Mathilda had just shared with her, and, more importantly, those things she had left unsaid, Hannah suspected the woman would be open to what she had to say.

"Well, they are definitely bad," Hannah said. She took a deep breathing, stalling just a bit to collect her thoughts and brace herself.

"And you're right, they are a curse on outsiders, or at least those that were defined as outsiders by whoever made these carvings. Are you at all familiar with a group of people called Thule?"

"Uh uh," Mathilda said, shaking her head.

"Over the course of human history, there have been various cultures, groups, and organizations identifying themselves as Thule. To the ancient Greeks, Thule was a place that existed beyond the borders of the known world. Nazi occultists believed Thule was also a place, one they called Hyperborea, and that it was where the Aryan race originated.

"The symbols carved into the tree where your son was found, they're a language. They're Hyperborean."

"You saying Nazis killed my boy?"

Hannah shifted uncomfortably in her lawn chair. "Not precisely, although I'm not ruling it out. Thule cults have existed in a variety of forms for a very, very long time, and although the Thule Society and the Nazi Party were closely aligned due to common, shared beliefs regarding white supremacy, not all Nazis were Thule, and not all Thule were Nazis. Thule obviously predates the Nazis, and has survived quite well on its own following World War II. And the words etched into this tree are most certainly a Thule language."

"What do they say?"

"I can't speak to specifics -- I'm not well-versed in Hyperborean -- but they point to a sacrifice being made to feed their gods."

Mathilda's mouth opened, then closed. She looked ready to say something, but at a loss for words, she drank from her jar. After the quiet stretched on for a time, a tear falling down her deeply lined face, she said, "What're we gonna do about it?"

The question had been on Hannah's mind since she'd first seen the pictures online, and it had only grown more persistent after she had verified the veracity of those photos with her own eyes.

"You got a ladder I can borrow?" Hannah said.

RETURNING TO THE CEMETERY DURING THE DAY WAS TOO risky. Hannah didn't know if any services were scheduled, but she imagined the graves would have visitors or groundskeepers tidying up, or fresh holes being dug for future burials. The day brought too many unknown elements that could hinder her ability to break the spell cast upon that tree by those runes. The night brought its own share of risks given Centralia's enforcement of their still lingering, but unofficial sundown rules. She could still hear the sheriff warning her off the town, telling her about how skittish people got after sundown when it came to non-whites.

She spent much of the morning with Mathilda, although they spoke little. The grieving woman showed her pictures of Harlan, from the time he was a chubby little baby right on up to his high school senior photos. He'd been an athlete during his school years, playing baseball and basketball. Hannah watched the years melt with each turn of the page, and Harlan shed the baby fat as his tiny boy's body became that of a man's. And then they hit the end of the photo album and there were only a handful of blank pages left in the book.

Eventually, Hannah excused herself, telling Mathilda she had things to prepare and that she would return later for the ladder. She hadn't lied but had still felt guilty leaving this woman alone with her broken soul and the pain of memories. The quiet had gotten to her, had grown too thick and uncomfortable, and she couldn't figure out a way through it.

She spent several hours driving the streets of Centralia, trying to spot the Hyperborean runes that Mathilda claimed the small town was rife with. They hadn't been easy to find, but she did manage to spy several artifacts hiding in plain sight. The cuneiform symbols had been used as decorative flourishes for the door and window mouldings around City Hall. There were additional decorative runes on the plaques of statues, or over the entrances of local shops. By themselves, the carvings had little magical properties and acted more like an amplifier or reinforcement for the Hyperborean magic carved into the cemetery's cottonwood. That tree was the focal point, a sort of antenna, for the magic.

Turning to her computer, she spent a few hours engaged in research. After some deep web work, she was able to link the cuneiform runes to certain spells mentioned in the *Oera Linda*, an ancient occult manuscript from antiquity that had been rediscovered in the 1860s and was eventually dubbed "Himmler's Bible," due to the Nazi officer's obsession with the tome. Himmler so fully believed in the ancient writings from *Oera Linda* that he founded the Ahnenerbe, a think tank that primarily concerned itself with utilizing the occult to fulfill Hitler's goals of achieving racial purity. Between the mid-1930s and mid-1940s, the Ahnenerbe had conducted a number of expeditions across Europe, Africa, and the Arctic and Antarctic to trace the influence of Hyperborean legacies on Earth, and record pagan and witchcraft rituals in an effort to summon their Thule gods and divine the future.

The links to Nazi occultism likely weren't relevant at all, but they did provide her with a path toward understanding Thule society and their beliefs. If what

Mathilda's grandmother had said about Blacks disappearing in 1901 was any indication, then Thule activity in Kansas predated World War II by several decades. As a researcher and academic, though, she knew that in order to understand what happened in the past, you sometimes had to look at what followed and examine subsequent events.

Thule occultists existed long before the rise of Adolf Hitler, and the Nazis had merely popularized and adopted those ancient beliefs for their own diabolical ends. They were ancillary to what had happened in Centralia in 1901 and were occurring still to this day. America was a country of immigrants, and those people brought with them their own cultures and beliefs. It wasn't much of a leap to recognize that somebody along the way had brought their Thule customs to the shores of the US, and that they had, eventually, settled in Centralia and weaponized their racist ideology. Although the timeline of events made it clear that person or group of people couldn't have been Nazis, it was the Nazi's obsession with Thule occultism and lore in the decades that followed that allowed Hannah to gain a deeper insight into that fringe legacy. If it weren't for the horrors of World War II, she might not have recognized these 1901 carvings for what they were.

Sometimes you had to go forward to go back.

Harlan Reynolds had been sacrificed. Hannah had told Mathilda that much, but she had not told the boy's mother the full truth. His body had been sacrificed, but his soul was still bound to this realm as an offer in waiting to a destroyer god the *Oera Linda* referred as "The Masked God." Hannah could only imagine the torment the boy must be experiencing in such confinement, trapped and unable to pass, and she hoped that by breaking the curse that bound him he would be able to move on to whatever peace awaited him in the afterlife.

She felt a fresh surge of anger toward the men that had lynched Harlan. It hadn't been enough to kill him. They'd denied him a long life and a peaceful death and continued their torment of him even after his physical self had been extinguished. They had tortured him, and they kept on torturing him, even as he moved beyond this realm and into the next. She curled her fists at the injustice, the atrocity of it all, and wanted to slam her hands down upon the computer, to break it and fling its pieces across the room. Instead, she forced herself to breathe, forced herself to relax. There was nothing that could have been done for Harlan in life, but she had a chance to help him in death, and she would do everything she could for him.

By the time she finished her research and stood, her body stiff from having sat for too long, she noted the sun was setting.

THE CEMETERY WAS EMPTY AFTER MIDNIGHT, BUT HANNAH kept her lights off as she drove down the marked path between the tombstones. Centralia Cemetery wasn't gated, which struck her as odd, if not downright archaic, having grown up in the city. It was just a simple plot of land defined by Cemetery Road and the trails that looped around the graves.

After only a few minutes, she was back at the too-familiar cottonwood. In the golden light of the full moon above, the ancient, gnarled trunk and its thick limbs reaching toward the heavens looked downright sinister. Mathilda's breath caught in her throat as she took in the sight. This tree was one of the last things Harlan would have seen.

"You ready?" Hannah said.

"Yeah."

Hannah squeezed Mathilda's thigh, and the older woman put her hand on Hannah's to squeeze her back. Mathilda offered a weak smile, one that wasn't strong enough to reach her eyes.

"Let's get that ladder, then," Hannah said.

As she unfolded herself from the driver's seat, Hannah put her bag over her shoulder, reassured by the weight of its contents. She tapped the leather, cool from the Jeep's air conditioner, and felt the outline of the Sig Sauer pistol that she carried as a general precaution. Satisfied that she was as prepared as she could be, she opened the back hatch and began pulling the ladder out. It was a long piece of equipment and they'd had to stand it on its side and work it between the driver and passenger seats, so Mathilda helped guide it from the front and made sure it didn't snag and tear up the interior.

Hannah unfolded and extended the ladder and set it up against the trunk of the tree, the top step coming to rest just beneath the sigil. She was careful of the surrounding branches as she climbed, not wanting to get poked in the eye or have her face scratched up. She couldn't help but notice the broken branches from where Harlan had unwillingly, painfully, and violently ascended this same tree. The mental imagery was disturbing, but her mind ran through the ugly scenario despite it, and she could all too easily imagine the noose being tossed around the tree's thickest upper limb, the white men below pulling on the other end, or using one of their cars to haul the rope, as Harlan's body rose, hands uselessly trying to pry loose the coils of rope from around his neck, legs kicking at the air. His flailing body would have snapped the younger, thinner branches on the way up as he struggled against his approaching end.

The temperature plummeted, her breath fogging the air. She took a quick look down at Mathilda, who seemed untroubled. Likely, the poor woman hadn't noticed the change at all. Hannah knew she was more sensitive than most to the abnatural, and spirits recognized and responded to this. In a way, she was a conduit for them to make themselves known. Others, like Mathilda, would go their entire life never suspecting the presences that surrounded her. But Hannah, she spoke for them when she could, helped them move on if possible, and so she climbed, not daring to look down again.

She came eye-level with the Hyperboran writing and could feel the electric charge of the magic, the hair on the back of her arms and neck standing on end. She swallowed, her mouth dry and heart hammering, and reached into the purse, her hand sweaty despite the chill only she felt. Her fingers coiled around the knife handle and --

The roar of engine noise break through the midnight silence, followed by the grinding of tires rushing to a stop on dirt roads, rocks plinking against metal and earth.

Hannah risked a look over her shoulder, needing to work fast. The sheriff's car was in the lead and Morell was the first one out, hand going directly to the pistol on his Sam Browne belt. She couldn't see Mathilda below her, but she knew the gun was aimed right at Harlan's mother.

She freed the knife from her bag, her arm rising with it just as the ladder shook. She tumbled sideways, her hands snatching at the air for something to hold onto, and then she was falling. Pointy fingers snatched at her face, and warm blood spilled across her cold skin. The air came out of her in a pained gasp when she hit the ground, a flash of lightning shooting through her jolted spine and hips. The back of her head cracked painfully off the ground, rattling her brain. It took her a moment to breathe again, and in that time a lean white face filled her vision. She recognized him from the other day at the diner. Sheriff Morell. Recognition flashed in his eyes, too.

"Y'all never can listen and do what you're told, can you? I told you to stay out of this town come sundown, but here you are." Morell shook his head. "I ain't surprised, though. Fact is, I was counting on it, you see. I bet if I'd told you to look both ways 'fore crossing the street you'd just barrel head-down straight into rush hour traffic, wouldn't ya? That's how you people are, all of ya. Never listen, no respect. And now we gotta do this the old-fashioned way."

Hannah watched the frozen plumes of her breath break in the air as she gasped and struggled to roll over. The fall had fucked with her back and every movement was a fresh surge of agony. Hell, even breathing hurt.

Morell watched her struggle with a wry smile, then reared one leg back and kicked her hard, right in the ribs. Not hard enough to break bone, but she instantly knew that breathing wouldn't get any easier for her.

Mathilda was down on her knees, hands raised in the air over her head. Lying in the dirt, Hannah saw five others forming a half-circle around them, guns drawn. The headlights of the sheriff vehicles they'd arrived in had all been doused, but the moonlight provided enough to see by. She could see their goofy grins, the excitation plain on their faces as they gawped at their fresh catches for the night. The current of violence was strong in the air, and she knew, just *knew*, that everything was going to tilt sideways soon. She knew, with that self-same conviction, that she was looking at the lynch mob that had killed

Harlan and had claimed the lives of many of the other restless spirits that lingered here and were bound to this massive, scarred cottonwood.

Morell stepped around her, holstering his service weapon, then knelt with his knee pressed into her aching spine. She grunted as rough hands pulled her arms behind her back, looping a plastic zip tie around one wrist, then the other. He continued to kneel on her, his weight pushing her down on the unyielding ground. He was suffocating her with his weight, and her entire torso protested in pain.

"Get off," she gasped.

Morell shifted slightly, putting even more of his weight on her and screwed his knee harder into her back. "Jenkens, you cuff that big one. I want both of these ready to go. Rest of you get your stuff together and get us prepped."

Hannah struggled to inhale, and each breath made her ribs ache. Morell kept her pinned to the earth until Jenkens was finished and Mathilda was left lying in the dirt on her stomach, her helpless eyes boring into Hannah's.

"I'm sorry," Hannah mouthed. Mathilda shut her eyes and seemed to nod before she was hauled to her feet.

Morell stood, then grabbed ahold of Hannah's biceps and hauled her to her feet. "Move," he grunted, pushing her into a walk as he led her to the patrol car. Hannah was shoved into the back of his patrol car while Mathilda was deposited in another.

She watched as the men moved between their vehicles, opening and closing the trunks, removing items that they carried over to the tree. Hannah had lost her folding knife in the fall, and her bag was in the grass near where she'd fallen, but she didn't consider herself helpless or the situation hopeless.

Hannah rotated her wrists in the too-tight zip ties, her

hands already feeling numb from the loss of circulation. In a way, it was good Morell had squeezed the plastic loops around her as securely as he did. It made cutting herself easier, but the job was still time consuming. She just hoped there would be enough time to prepare.

As she worked her skin raw, she kept an eye on the policeman as they went from their cars to the tree. A large noose had been tossed over one of the tree's upper branches and candles had been arranged in a wide circle and lit beneath it. The men pulled on dark robes, the hoods obscuring their faces, and they knelt in prayer, hands joined. Hannah couldn't make out what they were saying, but she doubted it mattered. She'd seen sacrificial rituals before and while the gods and entities the practitioners worshipped varied, they all seemed to follow a similar process. The men were just getting warmed up, hyping themselves up for what was to come and working to shift their mental processes away from their jobs as police officers and into a more reverential mindset.

Warm blood slicked the plastic around her wrists, pooling between the zip ties and her skin. She continued working her hands back and forth, letting the plastic bite her deeper. She winced against the pain, compartmentalizing it as little more than a nuisance and gritted her teeth against it, the better to ignore it. The blood slick was growing thicker, her wrists turning more easily with the lubricant, and her palms grew wet.

Hannah dipped a finger against the opposite palm, as she shifted her butt closer to the edge of the hard plastic seat. There wasn't a lot of room to work with here, but it would have to do. With her wet finger, she began to draw on the seat behind her, leaving a trail of bloody shapes and signs built from memory. As she drew, she spoke in a dead language.

The car door opening interrupted her before the spell could be completed and Morell was grabbing her by the arm, hauling her out of the vehicle. He'd heard some of what she'd spoken and saw the mess she'd made of his seat.

"What the hell are you doing?" he asked, getting in her face so that they were chest to chest.

She said nothing and just let him fume. His face was hidden in shadows beneath the robe's hood, but she imagined he was red-faced and angry. She couldn't help but smile.

Morell slapped her across the face, then shoved her ahead of him, pointing her toward the tree. Jenkins came with Mathilda and the two women were led in a procession toward the noose that was awaiting them.

Hannah stared into Morell's eyes as he fitted the loop of rope around her neck. He was intent on securing the noose and she hoped her shoulders didn't move enough to signal she was drawing again, this time on the back of her shirt.

Morell stepped back and nodded toward somebody that Hannah couldn't see from somewhere behind her.

An engine started and an electric whine cut through the air. It didn't take her long to realize the noise was that of a winch and the rope was being pulled taught over the thick branch. The rough hemp bit into her neck, squeezing tight against her windpipe, and she was yanked off her feet. She rose into the air, kicking uselessly, trying not to panic and failing. Hannah couldn't breathe, and the weight of her suspended body was pulling on her strained neck and aching lungs. The rope tightened over her carotid arteries and she felt like she was slowly drowning. Her legs flailed, the primal part of her terrorized and seeking solid ground to stand on, and she had to fight against the fear to continue her bloody drawing. She just hoped the symbology was cogent enough and not too badly drawn to be useless. Blackness crept in around the edges of her vision and her mind swam. She tried to speak the words around a thickened tongue jutting between her lips, her eyes bulging and threatening to break free of their orbits.

A cold hand pressed against hers, and her first thought was Mathilda. But she knew that was wrong. Mathilda was still on the ground, and the hand was too immaterial. It was less a hand and more a suggestion of a hand, but it was comforting, nonetheless. She hated to pull away from it but had no choice. She had to keep drawing before she passed out.

Below, the men moved, but their actions were as indistinct as the words they were chanting. The language they spoke was guttural and ancient, but it had power. Hannah could feel the magic of their words as the air around her changed and grew hot. The hair on her arms rose in response to the building electric charge. It felt like the onset of a lightning storm.

She couldn't drag in enough air to speak, but she tried to gasp out the dead words as best she could, hoping it would be enough. The ephemeral hand squeezed hers, the cold fingers chilling her to the bone. Although the touch was deeply unpleasant, Hannah found a measure of reassurance in that touch. The hand grew stronger, if only briefly, and the plastic around her wrists snapped. Her hands felt heavy, as if they were filled with sand and needles. Dully, she reached overhead and grabbed onto the rope above her, trying to pull herself up just enough to relieve some of the pressure and let her breathe.

Lightning cut through the air, arcing through the branches of the tree. When Hannah had been little, her grandfather had bought her a ball lightning lamp, and she remembered staying up late to play with it, watching in awe as the electricity responded to her touch. Now, she felt like she was inside that lamp, hanging right in the middle of those arcing blasts of electricity and pulsing lights.

She was too weak to climb up the rope to the branch above, but what little movement she was capable of was enough to panic the men behind her. She couldn't hear the winch speed up, but she certainly felt it as her body shook in stops and starts as the rope was jolted lower and then back up again to repeat the process. They were trying to create enough of a drop to snap her neck or decapitate her.

Hands pressed against her, trying to help hold her up. She could only make out the faintest images of their beings, and there were more of them, this restless community of the dead, than she had suspected. While the little bit of magic she had worked wasn't strong enough to free them from the binding spell that held their souls in place, trapped within this tree, it had been enough to give them some degree of agency. She could feel their anger and pain as they swirled around her, and others rose above her.

A streak of lightning danced too close, the heat of it burning a line across her shins. She needed to get down and away from this mess. Above, a loud cracking noise rose above the electric howl of the storm swirling around her and she was falling again. This time she was ready for it. What she wasn't ready for was what she saw as she fell.

High above the tree, the sky had broken apart and instead of stars she saw a strange and foreign land. The earth above was bleached white and built there were monochromatic structures that defied human geometry. Her brain ached to look at them, unable to process the imagery her optic nerves were transmitting. The shapes and lines made no sense, and she turned away from the portal, screaming, as she hit the ground.

The thick branch landed nearby. Chaos had erupted in the men, and some of the Sheriff's deputies were fighting with their robes to free their guns. Hannah knew she wasn't out of the woods yet, and she spied her knife and bag, dropped near the fallen ladder. She reached for the knife and unfolded it, and then was jerked back, the noose tightening again around her throat.

Her feet kicked for purchase in the soil as she was dragged backward. Somehow, she'd held onto the knife, but only barely. The handle was greasy with blood and mud. Rocks bit into her back and shoulders as the winch pulled her, and she reached overhead with the knife. Hannah sawed back and forth against the rope, struggling to breath. Just as she began to lose hope, the rope snapped and she slid, painfully, to a stop, gasping for air.

Lying still for a moment, in the hopes that she could collect herself, get her racing heart under control, and fill her lungs, she grew aware of the fresh aches in her back. The rocks and hard earth she'd been dragged across had left her feeling skinned, and the back of her shirt was wet and sticky. She looked toward the tree but saw only lightning and the confusing sight of an alien realm. Whatever spirits were trapped by the Hyperborean magic were confined again. Her minor spell had been broken, but it had at least served its purpose. She was alive, and she had to get moving before she squandered that small opportunity.

Ignoring the catalog of aches and pains and bleeding wounds, Hannah forced herself to her feet. Small explosions marked each footfall as Morell and his deputies opened fire on her. Lucky for her, their aim was terrible. She tried to run, but after nearly being hanged and dragged to death her body was in too bad a shape. The best she could do was lurch and try to keep herself low, making as small a target of herself as her battered ribs allowed.

An awful noise broke over the sporadic gunfire and she couldn't help but look toward the sound. It came from above, high over the tree. She immediately wished she hadn't sought out the source of that noise, her mind reeling as her brain struggled to make sense of it all. The shapes of the buildings and, now, the creatures were too much of a confusing, jumbled mess. It wasn't just that she was looking at something so plainly alien and inhuman, but that her senses were trying -- and failing, badly -- to translate structures and lifeforms that existed and operated at a higher dimensional level than the three-dimensional space her brain inhabited and understood. The Hyperborean portal Morell and his men had opened was extra dimensional, a gateway to anti-de Sitter space.

And something was coming through it.

Suddenly, Hannah realized just how quiet the night had fallen. The sounds of gunfire had lapsed and even the electric hum of the portal's light show amidst the tree's branches was muted. Morell and his men stood gaping at the portal, watching as a massive, churning, bone-white blob of flesh pushed through. Witnessing this being's intrusion into three-dimensional space was supremely disorienting and Hannah's head ached trying to make sense of it. A throbbing pain pulsed behind her eyes and lit up the entire pathway of nerves deep into her brain. It felt like her mind was melting, and she wanted to drop to her knees, drive the blade of her knife into her throat and saw open the veins and arteries there and bleed out into the grass, welcoming the peace of oblivion and

NO!

She shook her head, trying to rally her sanity amidst the insane. She heaved herself forward, toward her handbag and the ladder. She had to destroy the Hyperborean sigil and close the gateway before things got any worse.

Gunfire erupted into the night once more, and she ducked her head low. The shots weren't being aimed her way this time. She twisted her head to see what the sheriff and his men were doing, then wished she hadn't. They'd all lost their damn minds.

Jenkins had executed one of his fellow deputies and now stood watching the white blob breaching dimensions, his mouth agape and arms spread wide. Blood leaked from the orbits of his eyes like ruined mascara. As he shouted insensibly, he took his gun in both hands and shoved the barrel beneath his jaw, tight up against his throat. When he pulled the trigger, Hannah saw the back of his head come off.

"God!" she screamed, looking away too late.

She wiped blood out of her own eyes, felt more pooling in her ears, afraid to look at the seething tumor of flesh birthing its way through the portal above. Morell was screaming at his men, ordering them to stop firing, to put their guns down, but he was being ignored. His men were too afraid, their minds too far gone for rational thinking, and they were shooting in a craze-fueled panic.

The fleshy blob drooped lower and began to unfold, reaching toward Morell and his men. It hadn't even touched one of them when a man's tortured scream rose over the gunfire. Hannah's gorge rose and she dry heaved into the grass at what she saw. The cop's innards were pulled free of his body and splattered across the graves behind him, his hollowed-out skin flopping uselessly to the ground.

It didn't even touch him, her mind shouted, *it didn't even touch him*. Over and over as she stumbled forward.

Finally, she reached her handbag and freed the Sig Sauer from it, tucking the gun into the back of her waist. Then she was righting the ladder, a metallic clang ringing in the night as it smacked against the tree.

"Didn't even fucking touch him," she said, unable to believe it. She understood it, but she was goddamned if she could believe it. A few years ago, she had attended a theoretical physics seminar at her university about higher dimensional space. The group of panelists had spent some time discussing the possibilities of mankind existing in higher dimensions and what would happen if higher dimensional lifeforms inhabited three-dimensional space.

"Because a four-dimensional creature exists outside the boundaries of three-dimensional space, they would be able to see everything in our realm, the same way we can look down on a 2-D object and see everything. They would be able not only to see you, but to see *inside* you," the faculty member had said. Then, flashing a wicked smile, he added, "They'd be able to reach down inside you and pull out your organs without even breaking your skin!"

There were laughs at that, along with some gasps and squirms, and the faculty member had looked rather pleased with himself for his gross-out moment of the seminar. Hannah had laughed, too, thinking it was little more than bullshit theatrics from a young professor enjoying the limelight.

"Son of a bitch had been right," Hannah said, climbing the rungs as fast as she could. She occasionally looked back to see what was happening, worried that Morell or his depleting stock of cops might start shooting at her again. She turned away before she had to watch another one of the deputies kill himself, but not before she saw him kill another fellow officer. Morell's homicidal Thule cult was quickly devolving into suicidal sacrifices to their inchoate god. Clearly, this night had not gone as they had planned.

The hair all along Hannah's body stood on end, responding to the blanket of static electricity covering the air. Flashes of lightning danced all around her, but, blessedly, refused to make contact. It felt like when you tried to push matching ends of a pair of magnets together, her whole body thrumming in repulsion to the currents surrounding her. And her head – god, did it ever ache! Her brain felt like a throbbing, clenched fist, like it was ready to punch its way out of her skull.

Reaching the top of the thick cottonwood tree, she raised the knife and stabbed it into the gnarly bark, twisting the blade to break away pieces of the old, thickly lined skin. She hacked deeper, drawing new lines into the ancient sigil, corrupting its meaning, transforming it -- destroying it.

Lightning flashed and there was a massive crack as a tree limb snapped. The bushy head of the cottonwood went up with a *whoomph!* of flames, fire spreading across the dry limbs and leafy greens.

Hannah scrambled as best she could back down the ladder, the smoke already growing thick and making her cough. The summer had been dry in Kansas and the flames spread fast. By the time she reached the ground, fire was dancing all across the top of the tree, thick, black smoke billowing into the air, reaching toward the portal and the unfolding blob of flesh above.

A moment later, the portal was gone and the white flesh was falling. It landed in the flames, sparks and ash flying as it tumbled through the blazing vegetation that had become its funeral pyre. Hannah watched it burn, satisfied. And then she remembered Mathilda and Sheriff Morell.

The latter laid still in a pool of blood. He'd taken his own life, and the top of his head was a grisly, pulpy mess that her eyes refused to linger on.

"Mathilda!" she cried. Hannah couldn't find the woman, and she called for her again.

"Here!" Mathilda shouted back.

Hannah followed the older woman's voice, heading toward the police cruisers. Mathilda was struggling to rise above the back end of the Ford. Hands still bound, she'd run off and taken cover. Smart.

"Turn around," Hannah said. "Let me get those damn things off you."

She flicked the knife and the zip ties came off Mathilda's wrists with ease.

"My god," Mathilda said, watching the fire burn, an orange glow lighting up the cemetery and its field of fresh bodies.

Hannah led her back to the Wrangler, helped her inside. "I owe you a new ladder."

"Nah, don't worry about that." Mathilda looked like she wanted to say more, and Hannah waited, her eyes silently encouraging the woman to speak her mind. Finally, she did.

"I thought… I thought I saw Harlan there, under that tree. Saw him, and… and felt him."

Hannah smiled, and the two women hugged, Mathilda softly crying into Hannah's shoulder.

"I did, too," Hannah said. "He's at peace now."

Mathilda cried freely, and in her tears she thanked Hannah Ford for that.

. . .

AFTER THE WOMEN SAID THEIR GOODBYES, HANNAH returned to the motel for a few hours of sleep. She was looking at another long drive back to Michigan and needed rest before she hit the road again. Sleep wouldn't come, though. Lying with her head on the pillow, her mind kept racing and refused to slow down, until, finally, she pulled out her laptop and began writing a case report detailing the last two days in Centralia.

Her thoughts were a jumbled mess and it was a struggle to make sense of it all in an orderly, let alone coherent, fashion. She was still having difficulty processing all that she had seen only a few hours ago. She'd never seen a dimensional breach before, although she knew they had happened a number of times previously over the course of humanity's legacy. There had been plenty of small breaches conjured, and even a few on larger scales in places like New York and Arkham, Massachusetts, but those events had been more than two hundred years ago if she recalled correctly.

She recalled thinking that Morell and his men had been taken off-guard by this evening's (or was it this morning's?) occurrence, and they had certainly been susceptible to the mind-shattering nature of dimensional intrusions. She thought, too, of Mathilda's grandmother and her stories of the missing Black men and women that had violated Centralia's sundown laws, and the hanging of Harlan Reynolds. Hannah felt it was extremely likely those earlier disappearances were linked, that those poor people had been sacrificed and lost to another dimension, or else were killed and buried, never to be recovered.

Human sacrifice was risky business, and it didn't always capture the attention of the intended deities. Most often, mankind was simply ignored. Portals were opened and closed with little attention paid by the target audience on the other side. Lives were sacrificed with nary an eyebrow raised, and people like Morell got it into their heads to keep on trying until they got it right, likely unsure of what, exactly, they were trying to summon.

But the more they kept trying, the more dark psychic energy that was built up over time upon the altar of death -- in this case, the hanging tree at Centralia Cemetery -- the more likely this primitive human race was to finally be noticed, like the annoying fly circling the head of a greater creature, buzz buzz buzzing until they finally got swatted.

The more Hannah thought about it, the more confident she felt that this was exactly what had happened. Morell, and the generations that had preceded him, had killed as many Black folk as they could to honor their Thule gods, but whatever portals they had opened had gone unheeded by those in Hyperborea. Eventually, after 120 years of bloodshed, 120 years of Black lives lost to these white men's racist rituals, the Hyperboreans finally took notice.

Guess the Thule weren't impressed by all that so-called white superiority, she thought, a wry smile cracking her lips. She couldn't help but laugh, although she found none of it funny. It was either laugh or go crazy, and she'd already gone half-crazy once this evening. So, laugh it was.

When she finally got herself back under control, she wiped away a tear, her sides aching.

Hannah finished her briefing, gave it a read over and added some additional thoughts and clarifications as they came to her, then read through it a second time. Satisfied, she saved it to her hard drive, uploaded it to a cloud storage service, then emailed the report to her handler with herself CC'd as an additional backup.

She closed the lid and put the computer back in its

carry-bag. Sunrise was only a few hours away and she was exhausted.

Sleep came easier now that her mind was unburdened, and she sank into a deep rest, her alarm set for early afternoon.

When she woke, she loaded the Jeep, settled her bill, and drove, putting Centralia behind her forever.

Hannah vowed to never fucking return to fucking Kansas.

Above the Earth, Below the Ground

"To live is to war." I'm giving short shrift to Henrik Ibsen, of course, who continued that thought with "To write is to sit in judgement on oneself." Both sentiments, I believe, are accurate. I'll keep my judgements to myself, though -- I'm sure your mother has shared plenty of her own about me and there simply isn't enough time to go into all that.

I don't have much time, Carmen. My war is nearly finished, you see, and they will be here for me soon.

I was there at the start of it, did you know that? It was spectacular, all those meteors blazing bright white lines across the night sky... It was beautiful for a time but beauty never lasts, does it? I suppose what followed had a certain kind of beauty to it, if you tilt your head just right and look at it from a peculiar enough angle.

We were so goddamned conceited. Humans, I mean, although I suppose I'm just as guilty as anyone. We fancied ourselves at the top of the food chain, but that was hubris. Pure fucking hubris, my dear. Remember that, will you?

Don't ever think yourself bigger or better than you really are. I know that sounds bad, but if there's a lesson to be learned from all this it's that, and it goes for every single one of us that's left. We were part of a system – humans I mean – and we deluded ourselves into thinking otherwise. There are bigger systems than us. Only the most mentally deficient that are left would try to argue otherwise.

The Earth itself has systems of its own – water cycles and weather, things you learned about in elementary school, I imagine (was that really so long ago?) – but even our world is part of another, even grander, cosmological system.

The Earth is a living, breathing organism, Carmen, and we spent hundreds of thousands of years stabbing and pillaging and raping and polluting it, thinking we owned the lands and seas and skies, that it had been given to us, that we held dominion over all of it. God, how could we ever have been so stupid?

Fitting, isn't it, that the first signs of new life began to grow in what used to be the Arctic? We had melted so much of the ice that had once covered those northern reaches of the planet and the soil was so soft and hungry. The seeds sank right in and took root. They grew elsewhere, of course, but we didn't know that, not then anyway. All those greens and purples and blues blossomed in the Arctic first, big and bright enough to catch the eyes of our satellites and space stations. It took longer to notice its emergence in other places, but by then it was already too late.

By the time we realized we were at war, that we had been invaded, we'd lost the high ground and were in retreat. The whole damn planet had been pollinated and we didn't even know it! And we think we're so goddamned smart, don't we?

I never believed in God – another thing your mother grew to hate about me – but I did have a certain kind of faith. Not the kind she drummed into your head every Sunday morning, but one that most people seemed hellbent on denying and persecuting in our waning days as a species, but it was a faith in its own right. I believed in intelligence, you see.

We have all these systems within systems. Ecological systems, food chains, wind, diseases, planetary order, evolution – it's all connected, no matter how disparate it appears. We never could see the forest for the trees, though. An order exists, even at its most chaotic, but the real key is this – the system is alive. It thinks, it responds, it adapts. And it communicates.

The world itself is an organism, host to innumerable other organisms, plants, humans, insects, you name it, we got it. (Or we did, until we fucked it all up). We deluded ourselves as a species into thinking we were the big, bad alpha dog. What we were doing, though, was ignoring the massive apex predator all around us. It was too big to see, but we'd managed to wound it anyway.

And what happens when you attack a wild animal, Carmen? Back it into a corner, bleeding, scared, and angry? What does it do?

It defends itself.

That's right. Bravo. You always were smart, girl.

Systems within systems, you see? And a grand, marvelous intelligence above it all. We're a disease, Carmen, humans are. We invade and inhabit the Earth the same way parasites and viruses inhabit us. Our bodies fight off the infection, until it simply can't anymore. Why wouldn't a living, breathing world do the same? To so large a celestial body, we're little more than gnats. But think about those systems, the immune system especially, and how it looks and operates within the human body. Viruses attack us all the time. We are constantly under assault, our bodies primed for war immediately from birth. But where do those viruses come from? The Earth itself! Yes! Along with hurricanes and tornadoes, hail and snowstorms, heat waves and the killing cold washing over us like fevers.

What happens when we get too sick for our bodies to fight off an infection? We get help, don't we. We go to the doctor. We have them inject us with vaccines and pump us full of radiation.

Do they even teach you in school anymore about all the things we did to this world? Hell, do you even go to school, or something like it? Does so simple a thing even exist anymore? Fuck it, that doesn't matter. I mean, it's not like you're ever going to read this. Christ, you're probably not even – NO. No no no no no no. Not going down that road, not now.

The wars we fought, in between dumping all our trash in rivers and into the ocean (did you know we had dumped so much garbage into the ocean that the trash actually made brand-new islands? It's true!), burning up all the world's gas and oil reserves until we had changed the composition of the atmosphere enough to make the sky an oven all its own? Of course, that wasn't ever enough for us, was it? We had to keep on dropping bombs, to combat everything from water scarcity to immigration, because that always works out so well for us, doesn't it? And I mean, we knew what we were doing and what the effects on this world would be. We did it anyway, deliberately, willfully, just to spite ourselves, and we denied all of it every fucking step of the way, even while our cities were drowning. We elected politicians who promised – literally promised – to make the world worse, to make all these systems more unstable, to make the climate more destructive and harmful for human life.

What I'm saying is, we got exactly what we deserved.

If somebody did that to you, if somebody kept hurting you over and over with the singular intent of destroying you, of killing you, you'd fight back, wouldn't you? Maybe even throw some rocks at them, right, like you did to Libby Carmichael, maybe? You remember that? God, whatever happened to her? Do you still stay in touch? Is she even stil—

I didn't get to name this thing. That honor went to Giannina Rudolpho. She was Brazillian, exceedingly smart. Her brain was like a knife it was so sharp. You'd have liked her, I think. But she wasn't very creative. That's how this new lifeform got saddled with the name *Hominemque comedere*. That's Latin for man-eater, which was a bit too on the nose for my tastes, not to mention ridiculous, even if it is all-too accurate. Naturally, the press loved it… Normally the honor of naming a new discovery would go to the person who actually found it. That would have been Scott Richardson, an American, but he didn't last long enough to name anything, did he?

Scott, Jesus. I haven't thought about him in a while, and when I do, it all comes down to those final moments. Sad to say, it's really all I remember about him.

We didn't know what we were dealing with. Not then, at least. I mean, really, how could we? *Hominemque comedere* was an entirely new species, largely unlike anything we'd ever seen here on Earth. Some analogs existed, of course – the venus flytrap springs to mind immediately, along with pitcher plants and flypaper traps. You should look up some stuff on the evolution of carnivorous plants, it's fascinating stuff! Before *Hominemque comedere*, there were nearly 600 species of carnivorous plants. When I was your age, nearly a quarter of them were on the brink of extinction because of mankind (and most of us would have been hard-pressed to even name something other than the fucking Venus flytrap – HA!). Things have changed quite a lot since, haven't they?

Used to be, evolution was seen as a long, slow, gradual process. Funny how quickly that changed. You wouldn't even know the world I grew up in. Less than one generation was all it took to change everything. Think of it as a much, much smaller Big Bang. Oh, look up the evolution of peppered moths, too, while you're at it. That'll give you some idea to work with here.

For Scott, everything changed in the span of a heartbeat, that poor, dumb sonofabitch.

We'd all been wearing protection, of course. Bulky hazmat suits like you see in the that were like big rubber suits with thick plastic face masks to see out of. Standard operating procedure. We were there primarily just to observe, take samples, monitor the air and soil. Scott wanted to take some photographs, that was all. Those plants, they looked so beautiful. They were so large, tall and wide, with thick pointy stalks. Well, you've seen them. But that's how it's supposed to work, right? That's its system. It looks nice in order to attract you, to get your attention, make you curious and then

CHOMP!

Hominemque comedere is fast, Carmen. It's so goddamned fast. It was on Scott before we even knew what was happening. Blink an eye and he was gone, that's how quick it happened. The attack didn't come from the front, though, that's its trick. That's how it gets you. It draws you in with those good looks, the sexy beast, and it springs up on you from below. All these… these tentacles, these vines that are like tentacles almost, explode up from under the soil, sending up a massive cloud of dirt and rock, and SNATCH YOU RIGHT UP! They're sharp, too, those vines. The edges of them are like razors and they cut through Scott's PPE like it was nothing…and then they got inside the suit…inside Scott, and I swear I can hear him screaming all over again as I write this, the notes of fear and panic all wrapped up inside brutal agony and…

I'm sorry, hon. I just… God, I don't even know.

But that's how it started.

Has anyone told you how it's going to end?

Do you know about *Ophiocordyceps unilateralis*? The so-called zombie-ant fungus? Horrific pathogen that one – it attaches itself to the ant and then pierces its exoskeleton. Once inside, it takes control of the ant's body, overriding the creature's nervous system and refining its behaviors in ways needed to suit the invading fungi. Eventually, the fungus begins to grow and sprouts <u>through</u> the ant's body, bursting through its head to release additional spores.

Nature is a monster, my dear. A beautiful, horrendous monster, one that is completely without mercy.

But the thing about *Ophiocordyceps unilaterali* is that it <u>only</u> affects ants. Oh, to be sure, people have tried to make variants of it to use against other people in the hopes of satisfying our universal death fetish. Terrorists would have loved to use it in the middle of New York just as much as the Americans would have loved to fit it into warheads and drop zombie-making fungus bombs all over the Middle East. Times were so much simpler then, when all we did was kill each other, rife with the promise that there wasn't anything to one-up us.

Until *Hominemque comedere* came along and made *Ophiocordyceps unilaterali* look like a case of the sniffles…

For as nightmarish as it was – as it still is! – to hear

Scott's screams, it was even worse to hear the silence that followed. *Hominemque comedere*, what it does to people, is quiet. So, so quiet… When it needs to be, at least. When it doesn't want you to know. <u>It lurks</u>, the son of a bitching thing does. <u>It lurks</u>.

It's good at keeping its secrets too, *Hominemque comedere* is. Look at how long it laid in secret, and then baited us after biding its time, hiding in the ground. I know what it did to Scott, and to imagine that happening on a global scale, catching the whole damn world, so to speak, completely unaware, springing its trap on us. By the time our leaders and armies and scientists knew what was happening, it was already too late. As they say, the best defense is a good offense, and *Hominemque comedere* had the best offense of them all. All our napalm and MOABs and nuclear weapons proved useless, but don't think we didn't try. For a species with so keen a survival instinct, it's really quite extraordinary just how suicidally driven we are when push comes to shove. You'd have thought we were competing with *Hominemque comedere* to see which of us could shorten the human lifespan the quickest.

My own time is now almost up, sweet child. Besides, my hand is beginning to cramp. I can hear them approaching, drawing close, their roots moving through the soil above me, the steady march of borrowed bodies above that. I'm in a root cellar, if you can believe it, Carmen. Bit ironic, isn't it? I thought it might be deep enough down, protected enough that maybe, just maybe…

Hominemque comedere has left us no safe quarters, has it? Entire villages wiped out, cities laid low, skyscrapers wreathed in vines… Above the earth, below the ground, it is everywhere now, this Earth's new custodian, its new protector and guardian. Its vaccine for the human plague.

We had our chance, you know, and look at what we did with it.

Perhaps these man-eaters will prove to be more sensible inhabitants. One can only hope, at least. If this is what the world called upon to save itself from us, I dare not imagine what shape life beyond *Hominemque comedere* might take.

Revolver

1

THE PRICE TAG ON MY HEAD WAS $5,000. EASY MONEY.

I followed the bald man down a long corridor lined with closed doors and framed black-and-white studio portraits of the station's newscasters. I turned away from their glossy-print gazes, focusing on the producer's back. He wore a long-sleeved blue button-down and black khakis that had sharp creases on either side of his legs. Sweat beaded his forehead from the brief moment he'd spent outside to allow me access to the building. The overhead lighting made his shoulder-holstered gun gleam.

He deliberately kept a few paces ahead of me, and I caught the downdraft of his cologne. He smelled nice. I didn't. Too much time in the heat, dressed in too many layers, wearing most of the few clothes I had to my name all at once. I didn't want them to get stolen and find myself fucked over by the winter.

Not that I was going to live that long.

"We're through here, Ms. Stone," the producer said. I forgot his name. Stevens or Stephenson. Whatever.

He held the door open for me and tilted his head back, nose up, holding his breath as I walked past. I imagined he worked with a lot of the desperate filth, and wondered how he hadn't gotten used to it yet. Fuck him. Let him enjoy his false sense of security. Truth was, he was living on the edge between prosperity and desolation, a good two weeks' notice away from losing everything. Eventually it would happen, and he'd be blindsided by it, same as everyone else.

"Should I leave you my coat?" I asked.

His lips curled in a funny, sour sort of twist and he primly shook his head. "You can hang it over there," he said, pointing to an overly elaborate coat hanger.

I shook myself free of the carpenter's coat, and then peeled off two oversized sweaters, down to a dirty, sweat-stained and once-white tank top. I thought about taking off my boots to fuck with him, smirking at the idea of smacking him across the face with a toe-jam-soiled sock. Smug prick.

Stevens – if that was his name – stood at an end table, next to a fancy bar stool with a thick leather seat. A large wooden box the color of dark walnut was opened on the table. The revolver sat enshrined in plush velvet and he motioned me toward it with an artificial air of ceremony.

"This is a Remington New Model Army Revolver, first produced in 1858," he said with a reverential tone. "Fully loaded, six shots, with .44 caliber rounds."

I nodded, admiring the gleaming gun metal and polished wooden grip. I sidled up close to Stevens to deliberately invade his personal space. His distaste was apparent, but I'll give him credit for not moving away.

Instead, he breathed shallowly through his mouth, lips slightly parted.

"It's a nice gun," I said. "Why six bullets, though? I'll only need one."

He shrugged. "Dramatic effect. We'll have you open the cylinder, show it to the cameras. Let the audience know this is for real." He licked his lips, staring at the firearm as if it were an old lover. "Did you want to hold her?"

Her, I noticed. Not *It*. Christ.

"Sure."

He passed it to me with the gentleness he might use to handle a newborn. I'd never held a gun before and the weight was surprising. Even though it was only a few pounds, it seemed heavier. My fingers curled around the handle, and my index finger closed on the trigger. I'd never held a gun before, but this felt surprisingly natural, and a little too easy. I pointed it, away from Stevens, of course, and tracked the room through the sight at the end of the barrel.

I can do this, I swore to myself.

After a minute of mustering confidence and expelling doubts, I resettled the gun in its box and took a deep breath.

The Remington came from the Open Carry Association for Armed Americans, a "proud sponsor" of the *Revolver* webcast. OCA3 had a lot of politicians in their pockets – enough to pass mandatory open carry laws for all citizens in virtually all of the red states. Stevens was the third man I'd seen in the broadcast house that carried, and I knew there were plenty more I hadn't seen, behind all those closed doors and in the studio set.

As a media employee of a far-right-leaning broadcast, Stevens was considered to be in a high-risk profession; along with police, firefighters, airline pilots, military servicemen and -women, educators, mail delivery, cable and internet service providers, doctors, construction workers, jewelers, librarians … The list seemed endless. OCA3, and their bought-and-paid-for shills across the nation, insisted that "a right ignored is a right lost forever", and that it was the duty of all 'real Americans' to exercise their Second Amendment right and bear arms at all times.

"Don't put the gun to your temple," Stevens said. "You'll want to put it here, behind your ear." He pointed to a spot behind his ear lobe, where his skull met his neck. "Give that trigger a nice, long, steady pull and that'll do ya."

"Why there?"

"We want to avoid any accidents." He licked his lips, as if he were salivating at the promise of a gun going off. A fucking Pavlov's dog of the open carry movement. "Don't want the bullet to glance off the bone of your skull. Had this guy one time, the bullet circled his skull, blew off his scalp but didn't kill him."

He stared at the box, plainly lusting. "Or you can stick it in your mouth, put the barrel up against your upper palate."

I made the mistake of shifting my gaze downward and noticed the growing bulge tenting the front of his khakis.

"It's been cleaned already, and it's a reliable gun," he said. "You're all ready to go."

He licked his lips again, and then, for the first time, really looked at me.

"There's a bathroom through there," he said, pointing at a door behind him. "You can get cleaned up, and we'll have make-up get you ready for your big debut. Fresh set of clothes in there for you, too."

I nodded numbly, unable to remember the last time I'd had a decent shower. He stood stock still, as if he were waiting for me to undress in front of him. After way too long, he rolled his eyes and let out an exasperated sigh, put out by my modesty. I waited until I couldn't hear his footsteps anymore, then went into the bathroom and closed the door behind me. There was no lock.

Hot water cascaded down my body for a good, long while, and I held my fingers under the powerful spray to wash away the grime that had collected under each fingernail. Shampoo wrung all the excess oil away from my long hair, and I rediscovered the joyous feeling of fingernails against my scalp as I worked up a lather. A women's razor had even been left for me, and I went about shaving my legs and armpits, if for no other reason than a brief return to a mostly forgotten routine.

I held the razor tightly at first, controlling my impulse to cut deeper. The razors were embedded in a safety cap, allowing for a surface-level, injury-free shave. Not like the single-edged razor blade that left the shallow pink lines on my left wrist, and then years of therapy and medications in its wake. "My cry for help," according to the shrinks.

Finished, I stood in the steam-filled bathroom, wrapped in a terry cloth towel that I could happily live forever in. I wondered how gauche it would be to die in it.

A black clothes bag hung from the inside of the door. I cracked the door open to let the steam out, then dressed. The white blouse and blue capris were both ironed – all sharp creases and crisp fabric. They fit well enough, but felt a bit loose, either because I wasn't used to dressing so lightly or because weight loss from too many missed meals had left me little more than a skeletal frame covered in taught skin. I left the socks in the bottom of the bag and stepped back into the main room. Or was it a dressing room? Green room? Guest suite? Did it matter?

Walking barefoot against the plush throw rug, I balled

my toes into fists. I'd picked up this trick from some old holovid that pre-dated even my dad. It was oddly relaxing, and I paced for a few minutes, telling myself again this wasn't a serious mistake.

I can do this.

Along the back wall was a long counter of freshly polished oak. The tang of Lemon Pledge was barely discernible beneath the thick stink of bleach. Glass shelves filled with bottles of amber and clear liquids caught my eye. A square tumbler waited on a coaster, inviting me. Something to steel my nerves wouldn't hurt.

I reached for the top shelf and pulled down a bottle of bourbon. Knocked back two fingers, neat. It took a minute for the burn to blossom behind my breastbone and deep in my belly, but the warmth spread pleasantly. The booze was much better than the stuff I'd been drinking for most of my meals of late, and I poured off another two fingers. Fuck it; I made it three.

The walls were all white, and if I caught the right angle I could make out the dark tinge of stains, barely visible. The bleach had done a good job, but the cumulative effect of so many *Revolver* crowdfundings had left its indelible mark.

On the opposite side, at the front of the room, were three liquid holodisplays. Two were running stock photos – a polar bear standing on an ice float, hummingbirds, Earth from space, massive steel-bodied trucks with customized chimneys spewing columns of black smoke into blue sky.

The middle screen was running what passed for the news these days. Talking heads argued back and forth, digging deep into the disused history books and reaching all the way back to the nation's only black president to focus all their angst and hate on. With complete, straight-laced seriousness, they laid all of America's ills solely on that long-dead once upon a time president, exclaiming that he had been personally responsible for bringing Middle Eastern fundamentalist terrorists into the country across the Mexican border. One speculated that the ex-president had bought the cell leader a first class ticket with his own creds, but so what? It was still all taxpayer money, anyway.

A viral outbreak was sweeping through Plano, Texas, and had left more than a hundred people dead. Apparently, also the former president's fault. They never blamed the current president for the tumultuous mudslide the country had been lost under, and had, for the better part of a decade now, been arguing which of his former liberal rivals, whether in office or not, had done the most grievous harm.

When the newsfeed switched cameras, to show the men in full and sitting across from one another, I saw that they were both armed. Naturally.

In a segment they called 'Secular Murder Spree', they ran the names of women who had received abortions that week, and vented their frustrations over the continued existence of underground women's health clinics. This in spite of the personhood amendments that stripped women of most of their civil rights. It took the broadcasters a surprisingly long time – nearly a full minute – to get around to comparing the clinics to Nazi extermination camps. In a ticker at the bottom of the screen, the names and addresses of each woman scrolled in an endless loop. I couldn't figure out a way to shut off the display, but the rant was a convenient reminder that I was doing the right thing.

I'd known what a shit-fest this faux news network was going in. Last week had been sweeps week, and to bolster ratings while also celebrating the anniversary of the Religious Freedom Restoration Act all of the state-run media reveled in bigoted debauchery. *Revolver* brought in a revolving door of LGBTQIA contestants who had no other options. Each had been given a choice – life in prison, chemical castration, or a chance to win their family some money and, maybe, give their deaths a smidge of meaning.

The zealots in office told us often enough, and loudly enough, that this was a Christian America. They just never bothered to clarify if we were New or Old Testament. And eventually their claim was repeated enough to win the perception of truth. Now, everything was a Holy War.

I covered my ears to block out the noises of such earnest hatred, but whoever was monitoring me was a spiteful little fucker, and the volume on the display rose and rose.

This world was way too fucked up to keep on living in. Especially with people like that – the so-called reporters, the so-called politicians, all of them just radical fundamentalists beneath it all – given so much power and influence.

Without knocking, Stevens opened the main door and popped his head in from the hallway. "Eyes are up here, bub," I said, after his leer failed to drift much further north than my chest. "And quit drooling."

He came into the room, but spoke back into the hallway. "Come on in."

"Sure, that's fine," I said, like I'd been given a choice about who I socialized with before the main event. Stevens kept on ignoring me, but the woman that followed at least said 'hello', and seemed to recognize me as a fellow human being, if not a compatriot.

"I'm Tracy," she said. "Why don't you have a seat?"

"Here?" I said, pointing at the barstool.

She nodded – way too perky for me. "That's fine, yeah."

I straddled the leather seat, feeling the weight of Stevens's gaze all the while. Starting with a manicure, Tracy decorated me and got me all dolled up for my first, and last, time on TV.

"I don't think I could do this if I were in your shoes," she confided.

She kept her voice low, throwing Stevens a sideways glance every now and then. I caught him staring at the both of us more than once, licking his chops. He kept his arms folded across his chest, one hand lingering near the grip of his holstered pistol.

"That's because you haven't hit rock bottom yet," I said, rotating the tumbler between my fingers.

While Tracy worked, I tuned into the newscast. Always a mistake. A supermodel had been shot to death in LA after staging a 'Get Out The Vote' campaign. Two female anchors – both blonde, full figured, and virtually indistinguishable from one another, as if they'd been plucked fresh from a cloning tank – had joined the men and were taking turns mocking the model's life and her murder.

"She was a supermodel," one woman said, "so, obviously, she didn't have much in the brains department."

"She didn't get it," the other said. "We're at war with the Middle East, and she's speaking out against gun rights and demanding gun safety for people here in the States. She's part of this campaign to turn the country into a communist state. She got what she deserved."

"Ladies," the first woman said, speaking to all of us now, her voice deepening into condescension, "you shouldn't vote if you can't control your emotions. If you can't vote properly, if you can't vote conservatively, stay home. Play with your apps and your phone and stay home. Make some cookies, find a date." She threw the collection of paper she'd been holding at the table, clearly disgusted. "Do literally *anything* else."

"That's right," the other woman said, nodding vigorously and glaring at the camera. "Our soldiers aren't over there dying so you can go out to the polls and be completely clueless. Get a clue. Stay at home."

"Let her life be a lesson. She should have kept her mouth shut and her clothes off. Learn something from that, ladies."

A dull throb was building behind my eyes, and I pinched the bridge of my nose trying to drive it away. "How can you stand working for these people?" I asked.

Tracy shrugged. "It pays the bills," she said. Stevens coughed to attract her attention, and she shut her mouth.

Instead, she said, "Close your eyes."

I felt the soft press of a brush against my eyelids, and then a few sweeps across each cheek. She did my lipstick, then had me blot with a Kleenex. Finally, she did a light bit of curling with my hair. Something simple, but it finished off the appearance she was going for.

"What do you think?"

For the first time in a long while, I felt – maybe even looked – beautiful.

"Gonna be a shame to splatter half my head against the wall and ruin all your good work."

My words took the shine off her perkiness, her beaming smile cracking then eroding in stages; first crestfallen and then downright plummeting off her face entirely until her lips turned into a thin, barely-there crease. I couldn't muster up enough of a shit to care. The bravado was false, and my suicide was still enough hours away to not feel entirely real. I watched her smile wither and die with a small bit of satisfaction as she packed up her gear without another word.

Stevens was on top of me, clipping a wireless lavaliere mic into place.

"You need to undo a few more buttons."

"Excuse me?"

He held both hands out, his empty palms cupping the air in front of my breasts. "Show more skin. C'mon, this is your last night on Earth. Let's see those tits."

"Get the fuck out of here," I said.

"It'll bring in more money. You want to raise enough creds for your family, right? So?" He shrugged. "Show your tits. You'll make a killing."

My face burned and I told him again, "Get the fuck out of here," my words edgy and clipped. I fought back the desire to throw my drink in his face, not wanting to waste it.

He huffed, his cheeks ballooning as his face turned red. He twisted away from me and stomped back to the door, talking all the while: "Hey, it's your life. At least what's left of it. You don't want my advice? Fine. Don't take it. Fuck you too. I've only been doing this for five years, you hear me? I know what I'm talking about. And before this? I worked on *This Evening, Tonight*. You want to get all stuck up over me trying to help? Fuck you, lady. Enjoy your fifteen minutes of fame. Fucking psycho bitch."

The door slammed behind him, shaking in its frame. The holodisplays shimmered in the wave of his frustrations.

I shot back the bourbon and poured another. Free booze was a luxury I hadn't enjoyed in ages.

I nursed my way through round number three, letting the liquor cut through the fog inside my head. I felt downright swimmingly all of a sudden, and the world was clear enough to me that I wasn't sure if I needed to laugh at it or cry because of it.

My fingernails were too neat, too shiny. I'd given up weeks of accumulated filth for that French mani, trying to shut out a memory that came to me, unbidden – my fingers scoring the earth as I tried to kick myself away from the weight pressing down on me. My heart raced and my hand started shaking. I had to set the glass back on the bar. My tough-girl routine could only carry me so far, but I'd almost died this morning. And how fucking ironic would that have been? To check out before I could do it on my own with cash in hand?

I thought of the stranger's oppressive weight bearing down on me, my fingers scrabbling, nails carving shallow scars into the dirt, its blackness pressing into the nail beds and crowding the corners of my vision. His breath had been hot and putrid, heaving forcefully into my face, his stink invading my nose and mouth. He'd held a makeshift knife – a long shard of glass with one end wrapped in electrical tape – to my throat and had finished before he'd even unbuckled his pants. The thrill of it, the physical power he had over me, had been enough for him, and it had been more than enough to leave me shaken and violated.

I'd been through worse, so I wasn't sure why I suddenly felt so shaken-up by this particular attack. Maybe it was Stevens, and his oafish, ripe sense of entitlement; the way his eyes had lingered and the way he'd held his hands before my breasts, not touching me, but making his thoughts plain enough.

The bourbon made me feel less like a piece of meat, and forced my hand to be still.

As I glanced around the room again, the truth of it finally sank in. A truth I had known in a largely academic way, without examining it too deeply; like knowing that the sky was blue. The reasons why weren't important. It was a fact of life. But suddenly it carried new weight and settled into my brainpan, taking root in my mind with a new clarity.

I was alone.

Not too many people get a glimpse of how their own funeral will be, but I knew. All I had to do was take a look around this room and I could see the end so clearly. It was only me. No friends, no family. Not even motherfucking Stevens.

Me and a gun. Somehow, I always knew it would end this way.

2

THERE WERE NO WINDOWS IN THE ROOM, BUT I COULD hear the rioting outside through the walls. Angry shouts, hostile screams – the sounds of discontent, of pain and resistance. I didn't need to see it to know what was happening. I'd seen enough on the way in, as the *Revolver* security team picked me up from the displacement camp and delivered me here. This evening's riot had been birthing then, but was in full swing now.

Three floors up and on the opposite end of the street, I could still hear the loud engine and clacking of treads against asphalt as police combat carriers, mobile assault units and tanks rolled into place. The gunfire was sporadic, but I knew it would grow as the evening progressed. It always did.

A week ago, I'd been on the outer edges of a riot that had engulfed the entire city square. I'd been scavenging for food and wound up with a mouthful of tear gas. That was before the police began firing their automatic rifles into the crowds. I'd been lucky to escape.

As the bourbon settled, my mind drifted. I couldn't help but think of good old Ravencroft. When I was sixteen and Dad demanded to know what had happened to my wrist and why it was wrapped in gauze I had lied – told him I cut myself on a bush ... best I could think of at the time. Stupid, I know. He demanded to see, and when I tried to weasel out of it, he grabbed my arm and tore the bandage away. Then he found the razor after digging through the garbage can in my bedroom. After that, we were off to the ER and a week-long stay in the psych wing where they pumped me full of drugs that made me want to kill myself even more, and then medication that numbed my brain and turned me into a zombie during the very few hours I was awake.

It had felt as if my mind was disconnected from my body, and that I was living in a frail shell where everything was slow and sluggish. I had existed for a time on two planes, both myself and not myself, a familiar stranger in my own skin. Another batch of pills made my heart race and the world sped up into a nauseating, dizzy spin. Eventually, they sorted it out, but not before a lifetime of cardiac irregularities had set in.

Like this guest suite at the news station, my room in Ravencroft had been windowless too. Except there I had a roommate who spent most of the time muttering to herself and drooling across her hospital gown. I'd sit in the rec room with drugged-up horrors who stared blankly into space. There was a window there, at least, providing a wonderful view of the lower adjacent wing's roof.

"The attempt was serious," I had argued in my earliest group therapy session. I had been exquisitely pissed off to have my aborted suicide brushed aside as a 'cry for help'. I didn't need help. I needed to not be such a fucking coward. I needed to not have a fucking last minute epiphany about all the things I'd miss if I were gone.

"Then why not do a better job?" the doc had asked. "Why try to hide the razor in plain sight? Why not have a better excuse for your injuries?"

No planning, no follow-through. A cry for help. I sat there crying, hating myself for living and having to sit through this shit. Officious prick.

When I started drinking and collecting DUIs, my probation officer asked me what alcohol was supposed to solve. She didn't get it either. None of them did. None of them understood the one, single, basic fucking fact of it all. Alcohol wasn't going to solve anything – it didn't have to. It simply needed to help me feel like a goddamn human being. It needed to make the world bearable.

But that was the one thing the world could never be again – bearable. Things only got worse. The bottom fell out of the whole place completely after the last market crash; a total downward spiral, and those of us with too little had even less. Displacement camps were set up for those who had their homes seized by the banks, or the police, who became increasingly aggressive in their stop-and-seize practices, even in the total absence of a crime, in an effort to prop up their local governments and demand additional funding.

I poured off two more fingers of bourbon as the gunfire went from erratic to almost continuous. I'd have to find a new bottle soon, and I wasn't even trying to get hammered. I needed to be clear-headed enough to pull the trigger.

Rioting had become such a common practice, a backdrop of daily life, that it hardly even made the news anymore, unless there was a significant body count. The mention of rape hauled me back to the broadcast.

"Reports coming out of a college in Madison, Wisconsin where a young woman is claiming to have been raped by the football team. We've obtained some photos from the party she was attending, and look at that," the journalist said.

He was young, his hair a black Brillo pad. The photo, blown up to focus on the girl in question, occupied the right side of the display.

"You can see her holding a red cup, probably filled with booze, and wearing a midriff T-shirt and a miniskirt. I mean, what did she expect going there, to some frat-house sorority mixer like that?"

"Beyond that," the other reporter said, gesticulating with both hands, "it's a football team, right? These guys need to blow off steam before the big game. Right? She shouldn't have been dressing so provocatively."

"You know how it is," Brillo Pad said, "These women want sex so badly, and if they're not satisfied they call rape. That's how they are. It's ridiculous."

"Next time, ladies, be sure to cover up. Dress sensibly, this kind of stuff won't happen to you."

Right, I thought, *dress in layers, wear your entire wardrobe. That'll stop 'em.*

I hunted again for a way to shut this bullshit off, but it was impossible to escape the state-sponsored news.

"This is a Christian country," Brillo pad continued. "And if you're a good Christian, this kind of stuff doesn't happen."

"That's right," his co-host chimed in. "She needs Jesus. That's the only man she needs to let inside her, not an entire football team."

"She's a whore, that's the bottom line. And we know what happens to women like her."

"Yeah, they end up standing on the street corner, expecting taxpayers to pay for their abortions."

I threw the crystal tumbler at the display. The broadcast rippled slightly as the glass passed through and shattered against the wall. Still they prattled on, their poison inescapable. "Fuck you!" I screamed, my heart racing. I wanted to turn this off, to shut them out, to be rid of them. Alone in this room, and I still couldn't even get rid of these two men and their twisted ideals. Why couldn't I be alone? Why?

The newsman brought on a rotating gallery of talking head politicos, all of them men. The Wisconsin state rep reminded viewers that rape was God's gift to women.

"If this cheerleader," the rep said, "gets pregnant, then, you know, that's a gift. This gift of human life. God knows all of it, from beginning to end. He has a plan for each of us, and, look, you know that life begins at conception. A beautiful new life could come from this ugliness, and that's just a gift from God. It's a wonderful thing, really."

I twisted to the wooden box and opened it. The long barrel of the revolver shone beneath the lights. I could do this. I could do this right now and blot out all their voices.

But no, I couldn't. Not yet.

I inhaled deeply and shut my eyes against the tears, forcing myself to listen to the gunshots and maimed screaming from outside, focusing on the distant noise instead of the sadistic, filthy machismo pouring from the display. I wished their voices weren't so loud. *A little while longer*, I told myself. *I can do this.*

3

THE BUILDING SHOOK, THE CONCUSSIVE THROB OF explosions outside dulled by distance and the thickness of the studio. The talking heads appeared oblivious to the troubles rising outside their windows. They were either used to ignoring it, or had their heads so far up each other's asses that the plight of the people made no difference to either of them.

I ignored the tiny voice in my head warning me to stop and rifled back two more fingers of bourbon, finishing the bottle while the room spun and vibrated. I held on to the bar's edge as I looped around back to the shelves of liquors.

There were no mirrors in the room, and I studied my distorted reflection in the line-up of booze, my face curling around the curved edges of thick glass, bright in the overhead recessed lighting. I was wobbly, but cognizant enough to chide myself for being a stupid drunk. I counted the bottles and found twenty-eight more reasons to die, not including the gin.

Christ, I was pathetic.

Stevens popped his head in the door, again troubling neither of us with so much as a knock. "Five minutes," he said.

"Sure," I said, the word thick and palsied as it slurred on my tongue. "S'great."

I saw his eyes land on the empty bottle behind me, the weight of silent judgment in them as I took down a bottle of Balvenie. He said nothing, but he didn't need to.

"Oh, fuck yourself," I said, nearly falling over. He was a fucking hypocrite.

I grabbed the empty and threw it toward him, but missed by a mile as it glanced off the cabinet door in front of me and dropped to the ground. I nearly fell over. Could barely stand. Couldn't even aim straight. Two more things to add to the list of things 'Cara Stone sucks ass' at. Already a long, long list of failures, with decades of recriminations behind each single fucking one of them.

When I finally felt solid enough to stand, I saw Stevens was gone. Good. Fuck him. I didn't need him. Who the fuck was he anyway? Asshole.

I took small steps back to the plush bar stool, nudging the empty bottle gingerly with my toe to push it out of the way. Why didn't the stool have a back, at least? I was going to fall over. I propped myself up on top it, using the Balvenie on the end table as support to keep myself upright. Why was everything so spinny and tilt-a-whirl? My eyes were heavy.

"Stay with Sean and I," Brillo Pad said, "as we return with a new episode of *Revolver*. First up, though, a word from our sponsors."

The two men were replaced with another man, this one dressed in combat fatigues and carrying an assault rifle in one hand, and a large wooden cross in the other. A number of other men stood behind him, each armed with a variety of guns, rocket launchers, bazookas, and knives. I wasn't focused enough to listen to the rambling Sovereign Citizen recruitment speech, and the world dimmed as I tuned the speaker out.

"Miss? Hello?"

I opened my eyes to Brillo Pad's smirking gaze. I'd hate to wake up to his condescending bullshit on a regular basis. Shit. Did I pass out? A hand squeezed roughly at my left breast, pinching the nipple through the blouse. I shoved the hand away and shot daggers at Stevens. Fucking pervert.

"Hello, hello, hello?"

"Oh. Hey," I said, lamely. My tongue felt fuzzy. I

wanted to sleep. I made a show of smiling, feeling absolutely none of it.

"Two minutes in, and you're already a drunk skunk. That's gotta be a new record, hey, Sean?"

"I think so, Brian. But, you know, women don't have the fortitude for this kind of fundraising. Men are able to muscle through it pretty well, but the ladies get too emotional to stay clearheaded. I'm not surprised by her inability to stay sober."

"Can you hear us OK, Miss Stone?"

"You two are assholes, you know that?"

"Wow, language," Brillo Pad Brian said. "You wouldn't talk to Jesus that way, now would you?"

"I'm sure it's that time of month," Sean added, giving a sage nod and a smirk to the camera. A real yuckster.

Stevens was standing beside me, and the weight of his unforgiving stare bored into me. How many times had I seen that disappointed expression on others?

I stared at the scars on my wrist as I set the empty tumbler aside, trying to screw up some courage for this. I wanted to get it over with, go right to the 'bang bang, goodnight' part of the show. I felt so small under their stares and wanted to curl up and bring an end to it all. I hated myself for being so pathetic, but was somewhat relieved that I could still at least have enough control to finish myself off. There would be peace at the end of all this, finally.

"OK, so," Sean said, "let's talk money. Something I know women can never get enough of. You're here to raise five thousand dollars for your family, is that right?"

"That's right," I said, keeping my answers short.

"You've come to the right place, then. *Revolver* is all about helping the unfortunate. Our corporate sponsors, the Kay brothers, Johnnie and Donnie Kay, have matched your fundraising goal as they always do. Your five thousand is guaranteed. What we're going to do tonight is see how much more money we can earn your family, and help get a few more folks out of the breadlines tonight. The Kay brothers recognize how much of an enemy poverty is to society, what a blight it is on this country, and they're working to eliminate it one person at a time. Tonight, Miss Cara Stone, their war against poverty begins with you!"

I could hear canned applause through the piped-in speakers surrounding me. The clamor made my head thrum painfully. The noise of slapping hands gave way to the muffled roars of explosions, and I smelled a too-close chemical stench. I dimly wondered if the factory town on the city's outskirts was burning, and how close those flames might come to us.

"What's happening outside?" I asked.

My question seemed to have taken Brillo Pad off guard, and he flashed an arrogant smirk at the camera. "Nothing you need to worry about. You're surrounded by an awful lot of strong menfolk, and our building's security team is top notch. We'll keep you safe."

I opened my mouth to respond, then noticed the small green light on the lavaliere wink out. I spoke anyway, asking, again, "What's happening out there, though? Shouldn't you be reporting on this?"

"You're off-air, Miss Stone," Stevens said, as if I were brain dead. Shit, maybe I was. And even if I were, he still had no right to look at me like that, as if he was so goddamn patronly and concerned for me – the kind of concern that was wrapped in a haughty sense of superiority.

"What's going on out there?" I waved an arm toward the far wall. "And you keep your fucking hands off me, you hear me?"

He shrugged, clearly bored. "The usual riots. Soup kitchen ran out; too many mouths and not enough food. Entitled fucks decided to start something, and now we gotta put them down. Nothing you need to worry about." He patted the pistol under his arm to emphasize the point. "They'll calm down once the show gets into the swing of things," he said.

I thought of the massive jumbotron in the city's center square, and the metal bleachers lining the courtyard around it. My mug would be blasted large over the park grounds, while people gathered to watch and warm their hands around their bowl of hot food.

"People like you," he pointed at me, then flapped his hand in the general direction of the building's north end, toward the park, "nothing you all love more than free handouts and cheap entertainment."

Something to the left of me gurgled and gave off a steamy belch. The scent of coffee perfumed the air, and I noticed the maker in its final stages of brewing.

Stevens grabbed the bottle of Balvenie and poured two cups of coffee, black. He set one on the table for me, and then left the room without another word. The door closed on a trail of hot steam.

4

THE PRETTY PICTURES BLANKETING THE OTHER TWO holodisplay feeds dissolved into a stream of ranting vitriol. The *Revolver* social media stream. I read the comments with a glazed detachment, as if I were studying a train wreck.

Icons sat beside the vulgar text of supposed men hiding behind usernames that were rife with sexual innuendo, swear words, or obscure movie references. Most of the users' icons were cartoon images or video game stills; a rare few were actually vain or brave enough to slap their face beside words they should not have been proud of.

One user hid behind the façade of a cartoon mouse and wrote:

> RAPE THE BITCH TO DEATH! #REVOLVER

Another:

> UGLY BITCH. SHE LOOK LIKE A HOMELESS SKANK.
> #REVOLVER BEST THING TO EVER HAPPEN TO HER.

And:

> FAT ASS #REVOLVER DESERVE TO DIE TONIGHT.
> GET HER FAT ASS OUTTA BREADLINE.
> LEAVE THE CRUMBS FOR SOMEBODY ELSE!

Not to leave out this gem:

> SHE GONNA SUCK DAT #REVOLVER WISHIN IT WAS MA DICK.
> #DIESTUPIDBITCHES #KILLALLDABITCHES

The coffee was too hot and too bitter to enjoy. It went well with the stream of ugly consciousness scrolling across the display. Very briefly, I thought about spiking the coffee, but knew that I needed to be alert. The demons were running rampant, inside and outside my skull, and no matter how badly I wanted to stay drunk, I knew that I needed to sober up. Last thing I needed was Stevens's big, ugly hand tweaking my nipples again.

A dulled *whoompf!* rattled the bottles over the bar. Plaster dust fluttered down through the beam of recessed lighting. The holodisplays and lights flickered briefly before regaining full strength. I was missing a hell of a show, apparently. Had to be better than this state-run filth.

I opened up the walnut box that held the revolver and hefted the gun's weight again. I couldn't deny the sense of power it imbued me with, even as I doubted my ability to follow through. My final moments would be coming up soon and I wanted to be clear-headed.

I can do this.

But, could I really? The artifacts on my wrist said otherwise. I closed my eyes and took a deep breath. All I needed to do was put the gun to my head and pull the trigger. Not that difficult. Barely any thought required at all. Then, I would be good and truly free. I could escape. That was all I really wanted, and how I went about achieving that didn't matter. I was in control, and I could do this. The news hosts, the *hashtaggers*, the rape-loving politicians, Stevens, all of them – they didn't matter. They could try to degrade me and strip me of my worth and individuality. I didn't care about them. I was in charge of my fate, and this was my choice.

I cradled the gun in my lap, holding tightly to its grip, steeling my nerves with the weapon's utter indifference. Then the left-most holodisplay snapped and flung a new face into place, and it felt like a rivet gun was firing into my belly and twisting my intestines in a vice.

"Dad?" I said, noticing the tiny green light splashed against the white fabric above my breast as I looked down. Live and on-air now.

Through the watery haze of the standing puddle that formed against my eyes, I saw an extra fifty dollars had accumulated on the tally display. Five thousand and fifty dollars, my life's worth.

"You don't have to do this, sweetie," he said, imploring me. His bottom lip quivered, making the loose skin beneath his chin shake. I had the same eyes as him, and I saw the same watery gaze reflected in his, both of us holding back tears at the sudden reunion.

I'd expected this. Known it was coming, that it was part of the *Revolver* gimmick. Still, it took the wind right out of my sails and shook me to my core. I'd tried to prepare myself emotionally, tried to lock away all the feels, but my stomach still quivered with butterflies and my heart raced. My throat burned as I choked back the sobs. I hadn't seen my father in ten years, and now this.

He was here to watch his little girl blow her brains out on state TV. How could I not cry? How could I not hate myself?

"Mr. Stone," Brillo Pad said, "thank you for being here tonight for your daughter. Is there anything you want to say to her?"

"It's not your fault, Cara. You don't have to do this. I don't need the money. Please, come home."

"I—," I began, my voice hitching. My mouth flapped open and closed of its own accord, and my throat swelled enough to make sounds difficult. I think I squeaked. *Don't fucking cry, you shit. Don't.* "I can't," I said.

The truth of it all was plain and simple – it *was* my fault.

After my 'cry for help', after the antidepressants made me feel so good that I decided I didn't need them anymore and went off my meds, I went straight into a downward spiral. An underage DUI bust, and pissing dirty with THC, was more than enough for the state police to seize my parents' home and all their belongings, even though the charges of Contributing to the Delinquency of a Minor filed against them didn't stick. They were tossed out on the street and it was me who left them there.

There were harsh words, to be sure, but Dad didn't disown me. He didn't need to. I'd invented enough arguments in my head and went through all the potential back-and-forths, and they all ended the same. I knew that reality wouldn't be any different than the lousy movies I dreamed up in my head. So I left.

He and Mom spent months searching for me. I stayed hidden, though, and I lied to the shelters and to the bums I decided to cohabit with. He *touched* me, I said. A year later, I learned through the hobo network that he'd left a message for me at one of the shelters.

Mom was dead. Massive heart attack.

That sealed the deal. I was poison. I didn't even know where they'd been living, or where she was buried. I was too busy staying drunk and avoiding the police for the warrants I knew were out there from skipping out on my probation officer. At that point, the fewer people I was involved with the better. Fuck everyone, you know?

"I can't come home, Dad," I repeated, stronger now. I sat up straighter, still holding the gun in my lap, index finger curled around the trigger.

"There's a better way, sweetheart. It's not too late. Let me help you, please. I can get you help, and we can turn all of this around."

But in my head, his voice said what I knew to be the truth: *You killed your mother. You're beyond hope. You might be cleaned up right now, but we both know you're nothing more than pure filth. You don't deserve my help. Kill yourself. Get it over with.*

"Mr. Stone, did you know that your daughter has active warrants for her arrest? She has multiple misdemeanors: counts of drunk and disorderly, operating while intoxicated, resisting arrest. And, of course, soliciting. Mr. Stone, your daughter is a whore. How does that make you feel?"

Dad's face went red as the blood rushed to his ears. I knew he was seething. "What? What kind of question is that? She's my daughter! How do you think that makes me feel?"

A burning lump crawled up my throat and I stumbled off the stool before rushing headlong into the bathroom, a hand clapped tightly around my mouth. I couldn't stop it, couldn't contain it. Vomit sprayed between my fingers, and I was running and gagging as my stomach emptied itself of everything. Booze, coffee and bile burned against my tongue. My foot hit the puddle and skidded against the sick-slick tile and I went down hard. My back crashed into the bathroom floor, the back of my head bouncing hard off the tiles. Muscles seized up instantly, a tight shock of pain all along the length of my spine and in my hips. I twisted, half-screaming, half-gagging, to finish throwing up. Hot, sticky liquid dripped down my neck from the side of my face. I could hear myself repeated through the room's speakers – an unpleasant, discordant echo.

I lay there for too long, in my nasty waste and humiliation, reeking of bourbon and spent coffee, utterly dazed. I could hear Brillo Pad and his ammosexual co-host laughing at me. Their words were lost amongst the whirling ringing in my ears and flashes of silver that lingered in my vision with every blink. I couldn't make out what they were saying, but their mocking tone was unmistakable.

Slowly, I got to my knees, using the bathroom sink to haul myself to my feet, my back screaming all the way. The pain kept me from standing up straight. My whole body was shaking, and a thick caul of mucus covered my chin, darkening the neckline of my stained blouse. I washed in the sink, ignoring the condescension of the *Revolver* crew and the concerned pleading in my father's voice.

If I needed another reason to kill myself, I guess I had it.

My eyes lit upon the social media stream. More men laughing at me.

Sick whore, one said.

That was funny, another said. Now suck off that gun.

Lost amongst it all was a lone voice of reason. A single person that wrote:

#REVOLVER IS DISGUSTING AND
IRRESONPSIBLE.
DON'T LET THESE PEOPLE WIN! TURN IT OFF!

It didn't take long for the message to get buried in the noise, or for other users to attack that one voice of dissent and threaten them with arson and rape and death.

"Honey, please," Dad said, openly crying now. Begging me. I saw #Revolver #FAG out of the corner of my eye and my ears burned. Another trait I shared with him. "There's other ways. We can fix this. I promise you, we can fix this. We can start over. We can change things. Don't do this."

"I'm sorry, Dad. I didn't do enough for you. I wanted to help."

"There's better ways for you to help than this. C'mon, sweetie. Cara. Please. I'm begging you, sweetie, please. Not like this. You have to listen to me. I—"

"Turn it off," I said, turning toward Brillo Pad.

He nodded and Dad disappeared in a dark wink.

"Your dad obviously loves you very much," Sean said. "You can walk away from the money, the money you earned for your father, and leave with nothing. Or you can continue to participate."

"We're up to sixty-five hundred," Brillo Pad said, a shine in his eyes. He licked his lips, slowly, as if anticipating the blood spill. My life nothing more than a cheap game to him.

"What's your choice?" Sean asked.

I can do this.

My lips were dry and my back ached scornfully. I brushed aside Dad's televised lip service and said, "Let's go for seven thousand."

Both hosts smiled, revealing toothy fangs, their leering eyes brimming with hatred. I was in the devil's sandbox, digging my hole deeper. That was my choice.

5

BITCH. SLUT. WHORE. HUSSY. I'D HEARD IT ALL BEFORE. Been called all of it and worse. Still, I was surprised at the amount of repetition in the media feed, and the frequency with which these words arose, as if cultivated from some collective, self-loathing hive mind of insecurity. There wasn't even an attempt to muster something approaching creativity in the insults. The whole display was pathetic vitriol.

Brillo Pad and his boy-toy eventually got around to my medical history. The Kay brothers owned seventy percent of the nation's healthcare providers, and obtaining a complete record of my past was an easy feat for them. The social feed filled with hashtag poison.

Mine: Hashtag Go Fuck Yourself.

"What do you have to be depressed about?" Brillo Pad asked, apparently in all sincerity. But it was a loaded question. I'd been down this road too many times, too.

My probation officer: "You're sixteen. You skip school, no job, you drink all day. What do you have to be depressed about? You want to be depressed, get a job."

Dad: "Why did you do this to yourself? Are people at school making fun of you? What's wrong? Talk to us. Tell us why you're so moody lately."

Ravencroft therapist *and* post-Ravencroft shrink, Dr. Tilbury: "How do you feel?"

It was all chemical shit, and I went through rounds of cocktail drugs to find something to even out the dopamine receptors and uptake my way to normalcy. Depressed was just what I was. I didn't need a particular reason, and anything could set me off, and oftentimes did. Why the fuck did I stop taking the pills?

Because you're an idiot, something dark and slithery told me, an all-too-familiar voice perched on my shoulder.

Nobody understood. Everyone thought they were miserable, that they had shitty lives, that their minor inconveniences were epic disasters. *My raise wasn't big enough. I stood in line for over two hours for a loaf of two-day-old bread.* Well boo-fucking-hoo. Cry me a river.

My brain chemistry is fucked up, and that's the bottom line. There's no cure, only prescribed placations for the demons inside me. If I took the drugs, I was weak. If I tried to solve matters on my own, say with a Remington New Model Army 1858 revolver for instance, I was weak. And if I let nature run its course, my disease was illegitimate and unearned. I was another homeless fruitcake, my depression somehow less than *real.*

But, people have their own problems. Nowadays especially. That's a hard hump to get over.

I shrugged and said, "Life sucks. That's all."

I saw the glare in Brillo Pad's eyes. The one that said my answer was a cop out. Maybe it was.

"How many sexual partners have you had?"

"Excuse me?" I asked, struck off-guard. I took a second to recompose. "How is that at all relevant?"

"Well, I'm reading over your medical chart," he wiggled a microtablet at the camera, "and it says you've had two abortions. That seems like an awful lot. And both before you were twenty."

"I was raped," I said, my tone hollow. I had to shut myself down inside. It was the one way I could go on. "I was … I don't need to justify myself to you."

"But you are promiscuous, aren't you?"

"Hey, I know you and your pals think rape is great and rape babies are God's gift to women, but—"

"But," Sean interrupted me, "you're a murderer! You're a sinner! You're a maniac and a serial killer and a whore." His was a toothy strike, and he craved his pound of flesh with theatrical zeal.

"Whatever." Defending myself was useless. I made a point of not glancing at the social feed. I needed a cigarette.

"So after you've killed two innocent babies, you think you can simply take other people's hard-earned money and kill yourself? Take the easy way out?"

I laughed. "You think this is easy?"

"Isn't it?"

"Honestly?" I said. "Listening to your hypocritical bullshit and *not* pulling the trigger on this here gun is one of the hardest things I've ever done."

"Why do this? You know you're going to Hell, right?" Brillo Pad jumped in, probably worried that Sean was hogging too much of his camera time.

"I guess we'll see." Not that I believed in Hell, or Heaven for that matter.

That little diatribe brought in another hundred bucks. I yawned.

"I hope we're not boring you," Brillo Pad said, smug as ever.

"I want to know about the riot outside," I said.

"There is no riot outside," Sean said.

"What's with the gunshots, the explosions? I can smell shit burning. Why don't you report on that? This city is falling apart."

"Those are a bunch of hoodlums getting what they deserve. What do you think *you* deserve, Ms. Stone?"

"You're deflecting," I said, sipping coffee, trying to be cool.

"You learn that word during your time in Ravencroft?"

I shrugged. "I heard tanks earlier. There's real life happening right outside this studio, and you're willfully oblivious."

"There's nothing happening outside." Brillo Pad was turning red and inching toward the edge of his seat, ready to fly off. If I were in the studio with him, he probably would have throttled me.

"Except people getting what they deserve, right?"

Another hundred bucks came in. "Maybe people actually want to hear the truth for once," I said. "Seems there's some real money in the news."

"That isn't your money," Sean said. "You didn't earn that."

A huge concussive blast hit too close, shaking the building. The lights dimmed and, this time, took too long to self-correct. The *Revolver* hosts did a fair job of keeping their cool, still holding on to the pretense that nothing was happening.

"An explosion just rocked the building, Sean," I said, putting on my best reporter's hat and mimicking some old-school journalists I'd seen on TV before the Kay brothers bought up the entire nation, one politician, one lawsuit, one television studio, and one piece of legislation at a time. "We are at the epicenter of something very serious, and very dangerous."

The green light winked out. The mic was dead. Brillo

Pad cut to commercial, but I still had the camera studio feed on the left-most display while the adverts played out on the center console. I watched the hosts talk animatedly – yell, in fact – at one another, at their producers, at everyone in the room with them. There was no audio, but their wide mouths and violently red faces told me everything I needed to know.

I couldn't help but laugh. For once, I actually felt OK. Somehow, an inner reserve of strength had helped prop me up in a way all the bottles of booze in the world never could.

The door blew open as another explosion erupted outside, even closer. The walls shook, but I didn't know if it was from the blast or from Stevens's furious stampede into the room. He took long, quick strides toward me and backhanded me across the face. The inside of my cheek cut open against my teeth and filled my mouth with a coppery tang. The blow toppled me off the stool and sent me to the ground. Hot coffee scalded the underside of my forearm and the back of my hand. Somehow, I still held onto the gun; even more miraculously, it didn't go off.

He flung the stool aside, sent it crashing into the wall, and delivered a swift kick to my stomach.

"You stupid whore," he screamed, kicking me again. "What the fuck do you think you're doing?"

I raised my head, tried to sit up, but he grabbed my face in one large hand. His fingers pushed my cheeks into my teeth, making my lips pucker in pain. He smashed my head into the floor, screaming in my face, an incoherent rage.

"You trying to ruin the whole fucking show?" he yelled.

Saliva peppered my eyes and forehead. His fingers loosened and I took in a massive, painful breath. My ribs burned with the inhalation. He punched me square in the face and I felt my nose depress inward with a sickening crunch, snot flooding the back of my throat in a bloody glob.

I tried to blink, but saw nothing except swirling stars.

"I'm going to teach you a good goddamn lesson," he said, one fat hand going to his belt and unbuckling the leather. I tried to scoot backward as he unbuttoned his pants and pulled the tail of his shirt away from his waist.

"You ain't ever gonna forget this lesson," he said. "I can promise you that much, you mouthy little shit."

"Get away from me!" I dug my heels into the carpet and pushed myself away. My shoulders banged into the wall, and his hands were groping at my pants, fumbling with the button.

I raised the revolver and pulled the trigger. Time slowed and I watched the immaculate details of horror, as the flash of superheated gases puffed against his hair and bubbled the scalp to bursting. A gout of red exploded from the opposite side of his skull, messy chunks of grey and white mixed in with the blood, making a noisy, wet splash against the carpet.

His eyes went soft as he collapsed against me. I spent too long trying to get out from under him. I spent a long time sitting against the wall, my breath ragged, pointing a relic of a revolver at him, waiting for him to move. He never did.

My heart was racing, and I couldn't quite believe what I'd just done. I wanted to cry, wanted to run, but I was stuck here in the 'off' position, exhausted, reeling and unable to catch up with reality.

I can do this, I thought. And then I wondered what *this* was supposed to be.

What did you say earlier, Daddy? That we could fix this? We could change things? Maybe we can.

I had five bullets left.

Another explosion, this one right outside. Close. Very, very close. The noisy, heavy treads of tanks rolling into the city square.

Blood seeped from Stevens's skull, a standing pool too thick for the carpet to absorb.

Five bullets and a promise. We can change things. Maybe.

For the first time in a long time, I felt good. For the first time in forever, I smiled a real smile. Not like I had anything else to lose, anyway, right?

6

THE RIOTS, THE EXPLOSIONS, THE GUNSHOTS — IT KEPT people on edge, nervous. I heard the shuffling of bodies behind closed doors, but nobody came out as I strode down the hallway and into the broadcast studio. Or maybe, since it was a Saturday night, the building was short staffed, operating on a skeleton crew. What kind of accountant wants to die a hero while pulling some weekend overtime?

I strode into the studio and marched past empty cubicles. Brillo Pad Brian and Sean were sitting right where they had been for the last few hours. An array of cameras surrounded them, but only one was operated by an actual human being; the rest were automated or controlled remotely from the control booth.

The cameraman turned, saw my gun, and reached for his own weapon. I shot him in the chest before he could pull on me.

Then I walked towards the hosts.

Brian and Sean both panicked. Brillo Pad went for his

gun, his hand shaking with nervous energy, and before the barrel cleared the shoulder holster the gun went off, punching a hole in the green screen behind him. The unexpected shot rattled Sean further, but he was at least able to get his gun out.

I shot him first, blowing away half his face.

Brillo Pad raised his hands in surrender, forgetting about his weapon.

"Any more guys with guns around?" I asked.

"Please, don't kill me."

"I don't know, man. I'm an irrational, shitty little bitch. Who knows what I might do."

"Those were just words. You need to get a thicker skin, that's all. This is a man's world. It's not anything personal."

"Seemed pretty fucking personal to me." I squared the front sight of the revolver with the centre of his forehead, and decided to get a little bit closer. I kept walking until the barrel was pressed to his skin and his eyes went cross looking at the metal shaft.

"You're not a man," I told him. "You're a weak, insecure child playing at being a man. And not even a real man, at that. You're trying to live up to some outdated, old-world Hollywood ideal of a man, playing dress-up with all your fancy little guns, like you never grew out of playing cops and robbers. You're not a man, and you don't know shit about what it means to be a man. You're a coward who's afraid of the whole damn world, and nothing more.

"You think this," I pressed the gun hard against his skull, "gives you power. Until somebody with some actual balls steps up, and then your true colors run, and you beg and you grovel. You had all kinds of shit to say about me, about how weak I was, about how awful I was. Where's your fucking righteous indignation now? Where's that smug superiority, that grandiose sense of entitlement you broadcast to the nation? Huh? Where is it?"

"You don't understand," he said. "That's what they pay me for. This is a show. It's entertainment. That's all it is. You need to understand."

"I understand entirely." I pulled the trigger and watched, dully, as he slumped in his chair, the back half of his head obliterated.

Two shots left.

I looked toward the control room, at the still cluster of open-mouthed people stationed behind the long stretch of clear glass. The center camera, now unmanned, went auto, drifting smoothly toward me of its own accord. I watched a woman barking orders, snapping her fingers at people, giving directions to her crew.

Over ten thousand dollars were on the board. The figure kept climbing by the thousands as the seconds ticked by.

Another explosion rocked the studio, and heavy footfalls stampeded through the anteroom. Shouting and gunshot were plainly audible, and too, too close.

"This isn't a man's world," I said, to the camera, feeling the need to speak.

"This is *our* world. Forget the Kay brothers. Forget their bought-and-paid-for politicians, and their Bible-thumping propaganda, and this *Revolver* shit. Forget them, and move past them. They want you to hate, they want you to fear. Because *they* hate, because *they* are afraid. They want us divided, and they want all of us to be as insecure and insignificant and as fucking petty as they are.

"Outside, this riot they've been ignoring. It happens every day. And you know what? It isn't a riot. It's not. It's a war. And it's at your doorstep right now. This is supposed to be our country, our home. This is *our* world, our lives.

We can fix this. We can change all of this. We can make it better.

"We *have* to make it better."

Boots hit the floor, getting closer and closer. *Revolver* security, or state police, or sisters-in-arms, I didn't know. I didn't much care.

I'd come here to die, and I still had two bullets left.

The tally board ran over twenty-six thousand, America eager to revel in its bloodlust and throw money at it? Or something else? It was more money than I'd ever seen in my life, more than I'd ever earn picking bottles out of the trash for their return. More money than my father had seen in ages. Blood money, earned in death.

You've had your fill.

"This is *Revolver*, signing off."

I shot at the center camera. The electronics exploded and glass clinked to the floor.

Smoke drifted inside, thick, grey and noxious with a chemical stink. Gunfire behind that, and the dull thud of far-off explosions. The moans of a dying city.

I listened to the rattle of armed bodies working their way through the outer work area, maneuvering through the maze of cubicles as they neared the studio.

I hoped that my father was right, and that things could still be fixed – some of it at least.

I made my choice. I did the only thing I could do. I sat. I listened. I waited. Come what may, I waited, the gun in my lap, finger at the trigger.

One bullet left.

Black Site

1

Skin sloughed away from the subject, dissolving in the synthesis chamber. Watching the pink tissue drift through the solution, Alpha was reminded of fish food flakes. He'd never had a fish tank, but Papa had. Because he carried the memories of Papa in his own skull, he was able to make the comparison by proxy.

"Subject Uniform failed to maintain cohesion," he said for the benefit of the record. His voice was dispassionate and wooden, no longer burdened by the personal sense of failure he had once felt during earlier projects. The lack of success, though, was not necessarily a failure. Rather, it carried the potential of a lesson, new data to study and build from.

Echo stood beside him, her hands hanging limply at her sides. Her fingers fidgeted against her thighs, patting out a tiny rhythm against her slate gray slacks, occasionally pinching at the fabric. As far as Alpha could tell, none of the others, himself included, exhibited such nervous habits.

Not for the first time, he thought Echo was simply unique, and not just because she was the only female of the project. That, in and of itself, had been an aberration. A fluke. An oddity that he enjoyed studying, frankly.

"Victor appears to be gestating regularly," she said. "Systems are normal."

Even Victor, though, was marred by irregularities, far more than Uniform had been. Yet Echo was correct – Victor, for all intents and purposes, was developing as planned, even if the term 'regular' was a bit of a misnomer. The project was on track, and that was the most important aspect. The loss of Uniform was a disappointment, but hardly more than a minor misstep in Papa's grander designs.

Drawing closer to the chamber, he studied the developing fetus. The only thing separating the viability of Uniform and Victor were slight alterations in protein sequences. A slight change in carboxyl groups, an alteration in an amino acid that made one's protein either active or inactive, turned a hormone on or off and, in turn, meant either doom or survival for one's genetic sample.

Victor was nearing the equivalent of its fifth month of development. In a normal fetus at this stage, the cellular formation would have taken on a shape plainly recognizable as human. Yet, Alpha failed to recognize much that was uniquely human in Victor's development. A clearly designed face, arms, legs, and torso were all plainly familiar in terms of categorization but far from human. In fact, the aberrations were so pronounced that studying the subject gave him a mild headache.

Echo put her arm around his waist, rested her head on his shoulder. He pressed his cheek against her hair, enjoying the warmth radiating from her body.

"Do you think this is it?" Echo said.

In the tank, Victor's arm unfolded and smacked against the glass, an eye swiveling toward them. The fingers were strangely elongated, and already they could make out the tip of a sharp, dagger-like nail as he pressed his palm against the thick encasement.

"We're getting closer," he said.

Despite the apparent physical differences, Alpha felt a strange kinship to the piebald creature. They did, after all, share a common genetic sequence, albeit one now far removed from each other. He had to still himself against pressing his own hand against the glass, so strong was the urge to make contact in even that minor way.

Slowly, he led Echo away, back to the work stations where Bravo, Charlie, and Delta monitored the synthesis chambers.

"Purge Uniform's tank and begin prepping the chamber for Subject Whiskey. Continue monitoring Subject Victor and alert me immediately if any other irregularities arise."

He couldn't help but notice his headache subside now that Victor was out sight and out of reach. If this current headache were a single instance, he would not have been so troubled by it. The fact that a slow burning pain began to encase his brain each time he personally examined Victor was enough to convince him that their current subject was, if not the direct cause, then at least more than casually related. This oddity was curious enough on its own, but he mentally filed it away for the moment. His growling stomach reminded him of more pressing matters.

He moved to the door, Echo following beside him as she so often did.

Leaving the lab, he was greeted immediately by Papa's face. His own face, in fact, albeit one that was substantially older and wizened, the shared furrows of their brows and the lined recesses around each side of their mouths far more pronounced in Papa's features.

The corridor was lined with imagery of Papa. In each of the photos, Papa proudly displayed his Raëlian pendant, the large silver icon of the Star of David intertwined with a swastika hanging loosely over his chest from a long gold chain. There were photos of the orbital mining magnate christening his latest asteroid platforms—one of which Alpha knew was this very same base—more of the man shaking hands with UN representatives and various presidents and dignitaries, and images of him with staff, researchers, lab workers, and miners.

There were no more rock pushers at this facility. No more researchers and lab techs, aside from Alpha and his team. The veins of this particular asteroid had run dry ages ago, and the platform had officially been shuttered for more than twenty years. Papa's deep pockets, though, and some fanciful accounting kept the lights on and the equipment running.

As they passed through the corridor highlighting Papa's achievements, Alpha was again struck by the disparity in Echo's appearance. While she carried many of Papa's features, she was unmistakably softer and appealingly feminine. Her skin carried a more youthful appearance, the laugh lines around her lips gentle and more charming than the severe set their old progenitor was marked with, and which, in time, would mar Alpha's own features. For her part, Echo looked as if she had merely inherited his features, as if she were Papa's daughter rather than a genetic duplicate. A mishap with the protein loads, some fat-fingered amino acid sequencing, and a minor dose of genetic gap filler during the earlier stages of synthesis had flipped a few too many switches. This was not to say that the production of Echo was a failure so much as it was a decidedly welcome outcome.

Alpha was, strictly speaking, the purest of Papa's clones. He was the original, second only to the progenitor. As they worked further down the line, each successive generation grew a bit more distant from Alpha and Papa, and were nurtured to be more distinct. Echo had been the apex of that distinctive cultivation, and Alpha had been convinced they were edging that much closer to the truth, stripping back the layers of genetic impurities to achieve something nearer an answer to a question that was virtually indefinable by admission.

Where did humans come from?

That was the question. Papa believed he had both the answer and the method for discovery. And that the necessary research could be conducted here, in this defunct orbital mining station operating as an off-books, privately funded black site.

Sometime during their walk, Alpha realized that Echo had hooked her hand around his and that their fingers were intertwined. When they reached his quarters, his hunger was momentarily forgotten and replaced with an equally base desire.

Their lips pressed together, her hands pulling his body close. In the tight confines between them, he worked loose the buttons of her blouse and slacks, and she shimmied out of her underwear while he stripped.

Not for the first time, he questioned the nature of their lovemaking. They had been partners for a handful of years, nearly the entirety of Echo's life. At the start of their affair, Alpha had been hesitant to pursue her, struck by the strangely incestuous nature of such a fling. Being nearly an exact genetic duplicate, he began to view sex with Echo as a nearly masturbatory experience. Although she possessed female anatomy, Alpha was keenly aware that he was, in essence, making love with, and to, himself.

While the nature of their relationship was an intellectual curiosity, the physicality was unbridled and shameless. They enjoyed both their own bodies and one another's with frequent abandon.

Even as her body bucked against his, his mind turned over the riddles of Uniform's failure and Victor's early achievement of cohesion. There was so very little separating success from abortion, and the genetic lines they used for replication were altered only slightly. The aim was to reach an answer that was as genetically pure as possible. To discover and recreate the common ancestor that had made progeny of *Homo habilis*, *Homo gautengensis*, *Homo rudolfensis*, *Homo erectus*, and down through the evolutionary chain that led to *Homo floresiensis* and, finally, *Homo sapiens*.

As Alpha and his kin carried out their work, this latest iteration of Victor and its achingly unfamiliar construction appeared to be proving Papa's hypothesis correct.

Whatever had given rise to those early attempts at humanity had not been a purely simple act of evolution. Like Papa, he was hesitant to call it creation, for that carried many unseemly religious connotations that spoke more toward fantasy than any scientifically proven reality. He preferred to think of it more as *manipulation*.

Witnessing the trajectory of Victor's development, though, a single negative, but pervasive, thought began to wriggle through his mind. He couldn't help but wonder if, perhaps, given the gross disparities between Victor's form and the modern human, that the answer may ultimately be even simpler. Certainly not creation, perhaps not even manipulation. He worried that the answer boiled down to pure tragedy. That Papa's hypothesis was only party correct in its presumptive capacity, but less so in its explanations.

Laying in the heated afterglow, with Echo pressed tightly against his side and lightly snoring, her head resting on his chest, he began to wonder at the possibility that the answer to humanity's rise had come as a result of nothing more than a simple mistake.

2

A COLLECTION OF MISTAKES LINED THE WALLS AND SHELVES of a defunct ore processing station that had been converted into a storage facility.

Alpha normally enjoyed spending time in this section of the black site, despite the plainly macabre nature of his surroundings. Here, he could gaze upon their past efforts, a mixture of wild successes and stunning failures.

Uniform's termination had left him in a rut, more focused on their past errors than usual. And the questionable viability of Victor continually twisted in his mind as he pondered if the physical aberrations of that particular subject were deformities or a natural occurrence of the subject they were attempting to replicate. Or, perhaps, "recreate" was a more accurate term, as he had never seen nor heard of such a creature in his life.

He slowly roamed through the maze of storage racks, occasionally stopping to soak in the details of their research. Beneath the overhead lighting tract, the liquid preserving the relics of disused flesh and tumorous lumps that vaguely resembled bipedal creatures radiated a warm, amber glow.

The other subjects varied in size and shape and genetic lineage, as did the maladies that had provoked their termination either naturally or through a systematic elimination conducted by the research group. In a large cylinder, Alpha studied lidless eyes that were too familiar, surrounded by a lumpy, misbegotten skull resulting from Proteus syndrome. The lips were far too large, the nose a violently configured clay-like structure, the bones of his cranium stretching the skin and twisting it into overinflated knots that buried one ear beneath a tumor covered in a patchwork clump of hair. The subject had died before reaching full maturity, but the cause had been a deep vein thrombosis rather than a complication from the physical disorders he had suffered.

In another smaller jar was a fetus that had begun showing its trauma at the accelerated equivalent of eight weeks. Because this subject's phonetic call sign was Juliet, the gene structure had been coded to produce a second female. However, the protein structures had been incorrectly sequenced. In normal fetal development, by eight weeks the embryo develops eyes, eyelids, arms, legs, fingers and toes, mouth, lips, fingernails, and detectable brainwaves. Slightly above the now-shortened umbilical cord, a small arm grew from the subject's belly. Its second arm was in the correct position, but grotesquely shortened, with fingers blooming from the shoulder joints. The mouth had failed to separate properly, cutting a small slit of an orifice into the creature's transparent and reptilian visage. Alpha had elected to terminate rather than proceed any further, accepting that they were clearly on the wrong track with Juliet.

Echo had actually cried that night, and he'd held her in his arms, crying with her even though he could not quite articulate why.

Some jars he studied intently, others he gave barely a glimpse. His pace increased slightly, his steps growing heavier, as he recognized the futility of coming to this room.

Victor was unique in his aberrations, his mutations. There had not been anything similar in all the decades of research that had been conducted at this facility. Nothing.

Rather than finding comfort in their years of progress built off these past errors, Alpha found himself further lost and troubled.

His sense of disquietude spiked sharply at the blaring of the emergency klaxon, a notification of trouble in the lab scrolling onto the translucent display overlay grafted across his forearm.

"PUT DOWN THE GLASS," CHARLIE DEMANDED. HIS VOICE carried a sharp edge, both hands open and stretched out before him in a plea.

Delta held Bravo in a chokehold, a large sliver of broken glass gripped tightly in his free hand. Blood pooled between the shiv and his palm, dripping down in solitary drops across Bravo's chest. The remains of a drinking vessel lay scattered across the floor.

"We can talk this out, Delta," Alpha said. "Just do like Charlie asked. C'mon. There's no reason for this."

Delta's lips peeled back from gritted teeth, a high-pitched moan curdling deeply through his throat. His eyes were red and watery, and he violently shook his head.

He jabbed the pointed edge of his makeshift blade into Bravo's cheek and drew a jagged line upward, to his temple.

Bravo gurgled a scream, both his hands clutching at Delta's forearm, trying to pry the limb away from his empurpled face. The glass continued up, into his hairline, digging a trench across his scalp and over his ear, up higher across the crown of his head. Blood sheeted down his face.

"Jesus Christ," Charlie said. "Fuck!"

Echo took a tentative step forward, but Alpha blocked her with his arm. He gave her a quick shake of his head.

"Delta. Listen to me."

"NO!" Delta shouted. And then he spun Bravo around and shoved him away, his clone tripping over his own feet, slipping in the pool his blood had made, and fell hard. His hands reached out in reflex to break his fall, his palms slamming into shards of glass tinkling in the widening crimson bath.

Alpha stepped forward, Charlie doing the same but from Delta's flank. If they could get Bravo out of the way, or maybe tackle Delta together, one of them securing the arm he held the weapon in –

And then Delta reversed his grip on the shard of glass and shoved it into his eye at a violently upward angle. They could hear the pointy shard break through the thin shelf of orbital bone and pierce his brain.

Delta roared and tore the improvised blade loose, taking his eye with it. He flicked the eyeball off, then took a deep breath and stabbed himself in the face once more. Then he raised his head back and rammed the glass into his carotid, twisting it on its edge and drawing it across his throat.

He choked on his blood, sputtering it out between his lips as he fell to his knees.

A moment later, he was dead.

Bravo had rolled onto his back with a shuddering moan. One hand reached out, his fingers curling in the gore until he found another shard of glass. Over and over and over, he punched the shard into his throat. By the time

Charlie and Alpha were able to restrain him, he was gone, it had happened so fast.

"Jesus Christ," Charlie said again, his face white as a sheet, he was nearly ready to faint.

Alpha turned away and looked toward the synthesis chamber. Toward Victor.

That…*thing*…seemed to be watching them. A sharp bolt of pain dinged across the inside of Alpha's skull, forcing him to look away, to look back toward the grisly chaos of Delta and Bravo's bodies lying prone only a few feet in front of him.

ALPHA AND THE REMNANTS OF HIS TEAM OF DUPLICATES gathered around a semicircular conference table. A steaming cup of coffee sat before each member. The display monitor projected information from Delta's autopsy report atop the center of the table.

"The glass shard entered at a forty-degree angle, and pierced Delta's brain. However, you'll see a rather severe abnormality to the surrounding region of tissue."

Echo leaned closer to the projection, her slim fingers hovering over the imagery. "It almost looks like—"

"Jelly," Charlie finished. "But…from a stab wound? That's not likely."

"No, it's not," Alpha agreed. "The amount of physical trauma is highly inconsistent with the findings. Yet, somehow, the frontal lobe is nothing more than mush."

"What about Bravo?" Echo said.

"Nothing outside of what was expected. His injuries were consistent with what we observed. This," Alpha waved toward the projection, "was the only abnormality I could discover."

"Maybe a degenerative condition?" Charlie said.

"Could it be a sequencing failure, some type of genetic breakdown?"

Alpha shrugged. He had another theory, but not one he was quite ready to share. He was more curious about the path of this conversation and whether or not his duplicates would arrive at a similar conclusion.

"We can rule out suicide," Echo said.

"That was never really on the table to begin with," Alpha said.

"Why not?"

"I've never felt suicidal. Charlie, have you?"

Charlie shook his head. Each of them had been curated from the same genetic source, Papa, and each had the same cerebral mapping and memories of their progenitor. Papa was not genetically predisposed to depression and had never had suicidal impulses, which meant that his progeny had never experienced either. With the genetic factors largely accounted for, that left only environmental factors, and the mining station was kept as relaxed and comfortable as possible. A psychotic break of this scale, in the case of Delta, was simply improbable, if not outright impossible.

"So, what then?" Charlie said.

Alpha took a deep breath, steeling himself. "Victor."

His duplicates exchanged glances, and a slight, fleeting wash of relief swept across him. *They knew*, he realized, chiding himself for feeling surprise. Of course they knew. They had to.

Echo pursed her lips, incredulous. "Are you suggesting that Victor telepathically controlled Delta and Bravo? That he used some kind of mind control to manipulate them into killing themselves?"

"Not just manipulated," Alpha said. "Consumed them. Whatever control Victor was able to exert over Delta was enough to turn a part of his brain into pudding. We cannot simply allow this level of power to continue unchecked."

"For fuck's sake," Charlie sputtered, turning toward Echo with venomous intent. "Victor is still developing. He's not even reached post-birth viability and already he's able to mentally dominate another organism and exert his will."

"If that's so, then we've created the first legitimately viable telepathic humanoid," Echo argued. "The potential research applications of this are extraordinary! And you want to flush it all away?"

"Yes, I do," Alpha said.

"We can't."

"What are your thoughts, Charlie?" he asked.

Charlie merely shrugged. "The project is a failure."

"Or a remarkable success," Echo said. Alpha noted the way she occupied her chair, her body slanting in his direction, one leg tucked beneath the other, her hand gripping the sole of her bare foot. She'd kicked her shoes off onto the floor, as she usually did at the start of meetings such as these, another unique habit unshared by either Alpha or Charlie.

Despite himself, Alpha let loose a sharp bark of laughter. "You're both right, in your own ways. Victor represents both a success and a massive failure. Regardless, what we must do next is clear. Purge Victor."

Charlie nodded.

Echo shook her head, eyes wide. "No! This is it. This is the breakthrough we've been looking for."

"It's not," Alpha argued. "This is larger than that, and goes well beyond our mission parameters."

"We cannot simply destroy him."

"We have two dead crew!" Charlie nearly came out of his chair.

"We're looking for answers about the origins of

mankind," Alpha stressed. "Our common ancestor, the so-called missing link. This isn't it."

"The Creator," Echo began, but Alpha cut her off immediately.

"Victor is not the Creator. Victor is an aberration writ large."

"Wait. Just wait." Charlie shoved away from the table and stood. "All of the experiments have used human genetics as a baseline. We've been steadily regressing backwards in each subsequent experiment, filling the gaps with a variety of *Homo* genetics predating modern man. We should be getting closer to a less complex, less evolved ancestor."

"Victor certainly looks less evolved," Echo said.

Charlie paced the length of the table, his hands gesticulating rapidly with his words. "Yet if we're saying he's the cause of Delta's erratic behavior, that implies a certain degree of complexity that would not exist in a lower-level ancestor."

"Even that's not entirely accurate." Echo's eyes rolled, "And you know it! The evolution of communication is remarkably complex. There have been plenty of studies regarding telepathic communication in animals, communication through pheromones and non-vocal signals, the way they somehow innately know when disaster is about to strike, like an earthquake, and prepare to flee. They possess a certain something that we don't, or perhaps no longer possess. We merely evolved to possess vocal communication, rather than telepathy. We cannot rule out its absence in these so-called 'lower-level' beings."

Alpha cleared his throat, interrupting them. "We've been working our way back through generations of genetic drift. Yes, we are looking for a common ancestor. And I think we have found it, actually. We've just not found the right one."

"Explain," Charlie said.

Alpha shrugged. "We're looking for a direct ancestor to man. I think what we've found is much, much larger than that."

Charlie stopped his pacing. "You think Victor is an ancestor to—"

"—to all life," Alpha finished. "Yes. And I think this aberration goes back much further than just life on Earth."

Echo stared at him, open-mouthed.

"Jesus, you're even crazier than she is."

Alpha had pondered the question of Victor on his own for quite some time. Each of them had, and it had allowed them to think freely and arrive at their own individual assessments. Although they oftentimes reached the same conclusions, occasionally one of them managed to surprise the others with an out of the box scenario. Alpha realized now that his was the most out of the box bit of speculation at the table.

He sipped at his coffee, taking the time to savor it while he thought of the best way to approach his explanation.

"Our universe is but a single strand in the multiverse. We know of eleven dimensions in the multiverse, and it's extremely likely that there are many more in any one of those possible universes within the multiverse. Within all of those various dimensions, within all of those various strings and strands of the multiverse, imagine the enormous—the seismic, really—potential for life. We're so keen on how life began on our planet, whether or not there's other life in our universe, but just stop and consider. Consider life beyond either of those things and think about life outside of our own realities, just for a moment."

Echo paled. Charlie looked flabbergasted and sank

slowly back into his chair. He crossed his arms over the tabletop and stared hard at Alpha, but said nothing. What Alpha was describing was Papa's supreme hope – a discovery of not just Elohim, humanity's cosmic father, but perhaps even of Elohim's creator.

"More than thirteen billion years ago there was an explosion, which led to a singularity. The question has always been, what caused this explosion. Of course, we have no answer, no way of knowing, really, but we do have plenty of what ifs. What if this singularity originated elsewhere in the multiverse and caused a breach, or a quantum explosion, an entanglement of some sort, and whatever life existed at that point of origin was turned into the same stardust each of us are made of?

"Victor is not a human ancestor. Victor is *the* ancestor, his genetic construct blown apart and seeded across our dimension and reborn in the primordial ooze that gave rise to life itself. And we've corrupted it, perhaps not knowingly but certainly willingly, giving it shape and form. We've taken something far more alien than us and twisted it to our own designs. Whatever Victor was originally, it wasn't like us. We've stripped away generations of the *human* genome, seeking an ancestral baseline based off our own junk DNA, junk DNA that Victor, in whatever small way, was a part of, DNA that helped guide the way we evolved.

"And now we've tried to recreate it, and we have made a considerably sizable mistake. Victor is not a pure ancestor. He's not a pure anything. Not anymore. Right now, he's a mistake, and we have to destroy him."

Quiet descended following his words. His throat surprisingly dry, he took another long pull of coffee.

"The amount of progress this signifies, though," Echo said. "The years of research we could build off of this. You say he's not pure, but what if this is only a start. We could make him pure over time with enough synthesis and enough finesse."

"There's a factor you're not considering, Echo," Charlie said. Alpha could see in the man's eyes where he was going before the words were spoken.

"If Alpha is correct and Victor is an extra-dimensional being, things can only get worse from here if we persist. We can only visualize three dimensions. We have no idea how many dimensions Victor inhabited, then or now, and what limitations we would be placing on him if we forced him to exist in our three dimensional world. Imagine all of the things he could see or do that we couldn't. Delta and Bravo already got a taste of that in the lab. Whatever it is that might be created from this failed gambit is not worth pursuing. Not if we value our own sanity, and, more importantly, our own fucking lives."

"This meeting is over," Alpha said. He turned toward Charlie and nodded. "Purge Victor."

3

ECHO'S FOREHEAD WAS PRESSED AGAINST THE GLASS, AS WAS her hand, which laid atop Victor's, his webbed fingers splayed in perfect alignment to her own. Both had their eyes closed, and Alpha felt a perverse pang of jealousy at the sight, as if he'd caught them in post-coital basking.

"Does it hurt you?" he asked, indicating his head. This close to Victor, his head was dully throbbing and he wondered what Echo must be feeling.

"It's a strange sensation," she said after a long moment. "But not painful. It's more…cottony."

She opened her eyes and slowly pulled away from the

synthesis chamber. Each movement was subtly marred with the hesitancy of regret.

"What was he to you?" Alpha asked. He was troubled by Echo's display, and the way she was acting was entirely inappropriate. He was glad that Charlie had stepped out to get fresh coffee after initiating the purge and could not see this display. Victor was a test subject, nothing more. So why was she acting like this was a personal loss?

More to the point, what had she been hiding?

What don't I know here? Alpha wondered.

"He was a part of me," Echo said. "All of us are each a part of the other. Do you not feel a kinship to him?"

"No," Alpha lied. Echo merely rolled her eyes, reading him clearly.

The truth of the matter was, even after all that had happened over the intervening hours, he still felt a sincere, and strange, sense of familiarity with Victor.

There was no other option, though. The incident with Delta and Bravo illustrated that quite clearly.

Victor's eyes sprang open, his mouth flaring painfully wide. The nanites circulating through the amniotic protein bath, responsible for genetic assembly and growth acceleration, were now operating in reverse. Rather than constructing their cloned subject, the nanites were now in an aggressive pattern of destruction.

Victor's thick hand slammed against the glass, abnormally large. Far larger than it should be for the fifth month growth plan. Bubbles erupted from his contorted mouth, and the hand came down hard against the glass.

THUD.

THUD.

THUD!

Victor's legs rapidly twisted in the fluid, creating tiny vortexes as his body turned, his heel smacking against the glass. Small patches of flesh came away in thin, splotchy layers, the cells circulating through the disruption his writhing motions made in the bath. Alpha was again reminded of fish food flakes, an impossible image to shake.

The aberration's face smashed into the chamber, his nose pressed flat against the glass as another scream erupted, fingers curling long talons against the glass.

Did he---?

Alpha looked closer, and…yes. Victor's nails, his *claws*, had dug a shallow trench into the glass.

THUD!

THUD!

THUD!

Closer this time. On this side of the glass!

Echo was slamming open palms against the chamber glass, her actions exciting Victor further, stirring his commotion into a frenzy. Limbs flailing violently, smacking into the glass at four different points, legs and hands working forcefully to free himself from the attacking nanites.

"Echo! Get away from there!"

Alpha spun, wrapping his arms around her waist from behind and tearing her away from the synthesis chamber.

"What the hell are you doing?" he screamed.

She twisted in his grip, the sudden force surprising him, and she tore free from his arms. She turned, cat-quick, her nails raking across his face, pain lancing through his face as curls of skin peeled away from his cheeks.

He stepped back, reflexively, raising a hand to ward off another assault. A painful burn radiated across the side of his face, and a pulsing tremor tore through his skull.

Echo kicked, her foot landing squarely in Alpha's crotch. He grunted and went down on his knees, hard, a projectile of gut-warm coffee bursting from his mouth to splatter against the floor.

Cold steel pierced the center of his brain, superseding all other pains afflicting his body. He cupped his head in both hands, elbows digging into the floor, and screamed.

From a nearby terminal, Echo grabbed the seatback of a chair and turned on one foot, slamming the chair into the glass chamber.

A crack appeared, a small fractured circle radiating through the thick shell.

She swung again, harder. Then again. And again.

Again.

Glass exploded, pointed shards stabbing into Echo's frame as a thick, warm bath of liquid splashed across her. Sirens erupted, warning lights flashing...too late.

"No," Alpha groaned. His vision was reduced to two small slits, the brightness of the lab facility far too bright. The light pierced his brain, stitching a web of pain across the entire surface of his skull with the staccato of a tattoo gun. Through the thin slits of his eyelids, he saw Echo stumble back, watched a thick, piebald foot stomp heavily onto the floor.

Echo was crying, but he couldn't discern if it was in pain or fear or joy.

Alpha rolled onto his back, grunting his way into a sitting position. He cradled his head in both hands, eyes pinched shut, a tacky fluid leaking from the corner of both eyes. He felt a sticky wetness leaking from his ears to pool against his palms. His heels scrambled for purchase, finally able to kick himself back, scooting on his ass away from the monstrosity before them.

He couldn't be seeing right. He knew that. What he was seeing was impossible.

Victor's flesh was bubbling outward, expanding,

shimmering with an upset watery appearance before hardening into solid, wine-stained colored flesh.

He's growing.

Alpha forced one eye to part, at least as much as the aching light allowed, and demanded of himself that he bear witness.

Victor was no longer a baby. No longer even a child. Victor was immense, and growing larger.

The nanites should have disrupted this, but—

Oh, Echo. What did you do?

He realized then that she must have reversed the purge. Rather than disrupt the synthesis and promote a breakdown of the genetic material, she had found a way to hack the purge protocols Charlie had enacted. Alpha hadn't seen her leave her own station, which meant she'd carried out a deliberate assault against the program from her own terminal. Rather than eliminate Victor, she had accelerated the growth program.

Whatever human similarities Victor may have possessed during the fetal stages of growth were absent in his adulthood. The alien DNA was supremely abundant now, those characteristics fully apparent in their total domination over the genetic code.

Even through the patchwork hide of its body, Victor's muscles stood tautly, cording his arms and legs, chest, and neck like steel rebar. Tall and hairless, easily more than six feet, his wrists and ankles thick, his limbs as dense as tree trunks. His face was expressionless, a smooth plane of thick gray tissue over an immense skull ringed with pointed protuberances and large bony shelves over its eyes.

Victor lumbered toward Echo, though she stood her ground, her mouth open in surprise. A piercing scream erupted from deep in her throat. Alpha wiped tears away from his eyes in time to see blood drip from her ears. She cupped her head, mirroring Alpha, and fell to her knees.

Victor reached toward her, his face still impassive even as his fingers wrapped around her skull and gripped tightly. The thick skin of his hand muted the rustling tissue paper noise, but Alpha could still hear it and then he realized with gross fascination that the sound was the tectonic shift of the bone plates of her skull cracking loose and crumpling in Victor's grip. Then the monster raised the deflated skull and jerked his hand, the noise of her neck snapping was sharp even over the emergency sirens.

"No," Alpha moaned, honestly unsure if he was protesting her death or the looming eventuality of his own.

A dark cloud enshrouded his mind, the ache in his brain growing impossibly tight. He felt as if his brain were swelling, boiling and bulging against its bony case and threatening to break through. If his skull were to crack open, though, relief would surely follow.

He reached toward the shards of glass, his palm slicing open in the debris as he sought out the perfect sliver.

"No," he said again, this time in protest. He was not in control of his own arm, his movements not his own but Victor's. The beast was in his head, manipulating him.

As he reached for the glass, he felt his brain peel open and the horrors that only Victor was privy to flooded in. What Alpha saw was beyond comprehension, and he felt the fundamental foundations of his reality crack and erupt, breaking beneath new knowledge that had no words and could only be expressed through his loud, agonizing screams, screams that turned his throat raw and left a coppery taste in his mouth. His eyes widened, the light brutalizing him, his face contorting into widespread agony.

The glass nearly slipped loose of his grip, his hand slickened with blood. He forced his fingers tighter around the shard, the blade slicing through tendons as he embedded the glass into his hand, demanding his grip to tighten further even as nerves fired and died, leaving his fingers frozen and useless. He raised his hand, the glass an arm length's away, and focused on the glittering point that he would soon impale himself upon.

Not like this. Please, not like this.

Not like—and in the span of eternity between thought and words, Alpha witnessed stars collapse, eaten alive by black unending mouths, supernovas climaxing and devouring solar systems whole, suns cradled in the cups of enormous hands, the bodies of beings so large he could not process them, could not meet their eyes lest his skull implode upon the sight of them, civilizations rising and falling in milliseconds, all of it broadcast into his brain in a complex system of visions, fractured and divided and spread across a complex web of information shaped like a spider's eye and shoved through a prism, more than his meager mind could handle, and his sanity burst like shattering glass into a hundred thousand pointed shards, and he screamed, coughing loose flecks of blood that danced across his forearm like rain—*Delta and Bravo.*

A booming noise rang out behind him, deafening him. His eardrums burst, and the second explosion was a muffled *whompf!* Victor staggered back, a hole blossoming in the center of his torso, and then a second, higher up and to the right.

The fog in Alpha's mind cleared, the darkness parting. He tried to release the glass, but it was buried too deep in his skin, his fingers refusing to budge. He had to pinch the point of the shard tightly between the fingers of his opposite hand and pull it free, screaming all the while in agony as he found fresh nerves to ruin.

And then the darkness returned, and his body collapsed to the floor.

A SHRILL DRONING IN HIS EARS RETURNED ALPHA TO consciousness. The emergency alerts, he realized, but they were quiet, too quiet, as if he were listening to them from deep below the water.

Charlie's lips were moving, but he couldn't make out the sound of the words. Those lips were a strange pale blue color, and Charlie's flesh was a stark, unnatural gray.

Alpha was wrapping his hand in medical gauze to halt the bleeding, and the skin itched from the surgical glue that had been used to seal the lacerations.

His ears were plugged, he realized, in addition to the deafness from ruptured eardrums. He could feel the thick bullets of blood lodged in both ear canals. In between those was a horrible, rending pulsation as his brain beat against its skull cage, pounding fiercely. His nose ran, leaking a curdled, gray substance over his lips, down his chin.

His brain was fighting to be free of the awful visions trapped in its folds. He wanted to shut his eyes against them, but that only gave those sights a fresh reality. Unbidden, the impossibilities returned to him and he stared again upon a drowned city and the massive figure sleeping over the flooded remains. That enormous, hulking piebald beast, its skull overlarge and barren, bony ripples distorting the slick flesh coating its skeleton. Red, massive supernovas for eyes, their brightness burning through the seams of closed lids, unable to contain the burning heat trapped beneath. And its mouth, a wicked bony cage set atop writhing tentacles that grew from its jaw and chin. This beast, this monster – a devourer of entire cities, a world killer whose belly was filled with the remains of entire planets it had gorged upon.

"We were so stupid," he said.

Charlie's lips halted and he stared at Alpha, a hard and curious gaze.

"That thing…a hybrid abomination, and we made it. It's old. So, so old. Older than anything. And we made it. Willingly, we made it. Stupid. So stupid."

Charlie said something, but the movement of his lips only confused Alpha further. Ignoring his clone, Charlie let his head loll to the side, his eyes rolling toward Echo. Alpha followed his gaze and saw she was splayed across the floor in a sheet of crimson, lying terribly still. In her, he saw his own demise and wondered again at how they could be so oddly different.

Idly, his fingers drew shapes in the blood pooled around him. He knew only a hint of the importance of the symbols, but his hand was compelled and moved of its own volition. Forcing himself to focus, he realized he recognized the imagery, an ancient language half-glimpsed from a Victor-induced fever-dream only moments-hours-eons before, these same symbols adorning the buildings of the drowned cities beneath the sleeping god. He sensed a certain weight behind the alien words, the threats promised in each stroke as he connected lines and circles in the gore. A hidden knowledge told him these words were far older than the conceptual universe surrounding him, his fingers drifting through entire dimensions joined together by a language that, if he were able to speak it, would deafen him and contort his tongue so deftly that the muscle would become dead in his throat and he would choke upon it.

Would Papa have approved? he wondered. There was Charlie, of course, who, despite having the same memory load as the rest, had somehow imprinted on Papa's younger, brasher self, an angry, arrogant twenty-something Raëlian ready to burn down the world with his proofs and theories.

Alpha believed he had been the purest. The first clone of Papa, and the most complete. He had shared Papa's belief that technology would bring mankind closer to their god, and that the process of cloning and genetic engineering and DNA synthesis would allow them to recreate the progenitor of all mankind and reunite humans with their alien Elohim ancestors.

Victor was supposed to be Elohim, but this was impossible. Rather than a prophet to shepherd mankind through its final days, they had unleashed a gross mistake, a frightening trespass across dimensions. Whatever Victor was, it went by a different name, a far older name.

"The realm of perception he operates on," Alpha whispered, more to himself than to Charlie, "this is wrong. We have made a horrible miscalculation."

He wanted to blame Echo, wanted to lay their deaths at her feet, but found that he could not. She was Papa, and Papa was her, and perhaps she was the purest incarnation of them all. Or maybe Victor has simply manipulated her to his own ends. Now she was dead, and it was impossible to blame her for any of it.

When Alpha closed his eyes, he strained to not imagine the horrors Victor had funneled into his head. That kaleidoscopic display of perception across dimensions that his addled brain could not handle. He may as well have been a one-dimensional figure thrust into the 3-D realm, so out of sorts and twisted upon a new reality that fractured his mind and broke the core tenants of the all. All that he thought he knew, all that he thought he was, shattered, and now he struggled to reassemble the various pieces of the self, to unravel the crumpled paper ball his brain had been twisted into. He was only dimly aware of Charlie dabbing a cloth at the corner of his lips to wipe away the drool leaking down his cheek. All he knew was pain.

"Where is he?" Alpha asked. If Charlie answered, he didn't know. He forced his eyes open and asked again, forced himself to watch Charlie's lips and to focus on the words, to hear those words past the shrill, soft droning of emergency alarms.

"He went into the ductwork," Charlie said. "He hit me with a tablet, then went up into the ceiling."

Alpha followed Charlie's eyes upward, to the gaping hole above Echo's body. The displaced lighting flickered in a strobe-like fashion, hanging limply from the damaged ceiling.

A fresh pulse of pain ripped through his brain, forcing him to double-over. A thin, bloody line of drool crept from his lips and he spit onto the floor.

His side was tacky and wet below the ribs. He couldn't remember why.

"We have to destroy him," he sputtered. The words were a revelation entirely his own. Something in his soul cracked and shifted, as if a weight had come loose and freed him from rusty chains.

He noticed the bloody script he'd lined the floor with for the first time then, and wondered when and how he had done this. Gibberish, all of it. Strange and arcane, like nothing he had ever seen before. Slowly things shifted in his mind and he began to see clearly, clearer than he thought he had seen in quite some time, although he could not pinpoint exactly when things had grown oppressively cloudy.

Turning toward Charlie, Alpha saw, for the first time, the angry gash and the long, ropy wound across Charlie's forehead. A deeper, wider tear marred his throat.

"No shit," Charlie *(no, not Charlie)* said.

(Charlie's dead.)

"No, no, no." Alpha screwed his eyes tightly shut, palm pressed tightly to his temple. A horrible scream ripped through the inside of his skull, angry and misbegotten. He was seeing things, hearing things. Talking to himself. *That was it*, he realized. That *had* to be it.

"The mining drones," Alpha stammered. "We need to bring them online."

Charlie's mouth hung open in a rictus of pain, but after a moment he nodded. Or perhaps his head simply lolled as his body slumped. Alpha wasn't sure, not entirely.

A dozen decommissioned drones had been mothballed on base. After the veins of ore ran dry and the site shuttered, the drones had simply been deactivated and warehoused. Papa had not been concerned with their resale value; it had been easier to simply shut them away than deal with more trade deals and selling used mechs. They could be used now, though, and set loose across the base and its ventilation grid to hunt and destroy Victor.

Charlie-not Charlie was already working on the tablet, fingers moving nimbly despite the pain contorting his features. One hand was frozen stiff by paralysis, fingers curled into a tight fist. A moment later he slammed the tablet to the floor beside him and screamed, "Fuck!"

"What?"

Charlie-not Charlie laughed, but there was no humor to be had, only mania. "The power cores. The fucking power cores."

Of course, Alpha realized. They would have stripped the drones of their energy cells while they sat dormant. "I'll go."

Charlie-not Charlie looked at him, somewhat

confusedly, but nodded. "Yeah. Yeah, good. Get them plugged in and I can control them. God, my head!"

Alpha stood on shaking legs, his whole body weak, and took three shuddering steps to the door, fumbled his way into the corridor beyond. A sticky mess poured from his nostrils and he wiped at it with the back of his good hand, barely curious at the odd coloration and the chowder-like consistency of the lumpy fluid. The pain ricocheting inside his skull diminished the further he got from the lab, but a noisy hum remained, forcing his eyes into half-open slits. He kept his wounded hand pressed to his belly, blood leaking a long trail down the hallway to mark his passage.

The mining drones were primarily autonomous, but there were also manned EVAs. Both would be useless for long-range space flight, and there were no shuttles off this rock. The black site was their home, and, when the time came, it would be their grave as well. Alpha and the rest were all illicit human experiments, and if they ever made it off the rock, Papa would be complicit in any number of crimes against humanity. Papa had left them no way off the asteroid, and they never had any intention of leaving.

As he made his way into the elevator that would carry him into the mech bay, he thought about these implications and the realization that he would die here solidified. What had been merely theoretical and shapeless with the distance of time was suddenly and achingly concrete in its newfound immediacy. If that was what it would take to stop Victor, then so be it. He would see this operation razed and sucked into the vacuum of space rather than risk that abomination being discovered.

4

Echo lay with her head resting against his chest, her arm splayed across his narrow hips.

"How do we know what's real?" she asked.

The question was a common refrain from her, the discussion one they'd had many times. She'd begun asking this question soon after her decanting as she began to explore the memories – Papa's memories – that were interlaced across her mind. She had spent several days initially disoriented by it all, unable to reconcile the memories of a man with her female features, struggling against the imprint and demanding that her life be her own until she had to be sedated. Eventually, the struggle eased, yet the question remained.

He had no answer for her, then or now.

"Alpha, you have to listen to me," she said. Her voice rang in his ears, inside his skull, across the open communications channel.

He shook his head. *No, no, no. Impossible!* He had watched her die. She was dead. It was impossible for her to be speaking with him. He was imagining it, hearing voices.

Victor, he realized. That son of a bitch was playing with him now, distracting him.

He moved down the row of deactivated mining drones, verifying their hull integrity before inserting their power cells. This was going to stop Victor. It had to. And Victor knew it, and was now trying to stop him with cheap fucking parlor tricks.

It wasn't going to work, though.

"I know who you are!" he screamed, whirling around in the semi-darkness as he screamed to the heavens. Victor was above him, somewhere, and inside him, too, deep inside his head, twisting his consciousness and his memory against him and projecting old thoughts, old desires, old questions.

"I know who you are and I will kill you, do you understand me?"

"Alpha, stop it. Stop and listen to me," Echo said. "It's Victor. Victor is inside your head. Do you understand?"

"No fucking shit!" he screamed. Victor, manipulating him, trying to trick him. He recognized the buzzing sensation, the spidery crawl across the surface of his brain, which was the clone's hallmark. He'd been feeling it since the synthesis began, standing beside the cloning tank while Victor took form. That should have been enough of an inkling to prompt an abortion, to purge the hybrid relic from the tank and reconfigure the systems for projects Whiskey and X-Ray.

But no. He saw now that he possessed every inch of Papa's hubris and his dangerous, wanton need to always be right, damn the cost.

"Victor is still in the tank, Alpha," Echo shouted. Her voice quivered in its awful pleadings, stained with tears and a jagged sobbing. "You're not well. We – I – can help you."

He curled one fist tightly, the pain and the bandages preventing him from curling both. All his effort brought his injured hand was fresh blood.

He was on the right track, then. If Victor was this worried, would go to these lengths to prevent him from activating the drones, then he was most certainly on the right track.

He was going to start up these fucking drones and sic each and every one of them on Victor, and he was going to destroy the whole goddamn asteroid while he was at it.

Gritting his teeth, he pulled open the battery compartment of the nearest drone and lodged the power cell into place. Managing this was difficult with only one hand, and his shoulder throbbed. The battery was large and hadn't been easy to maneuver. Pulling the hatch back down, he was forced to use both hands to bear the lid's weight.

His hand lit up in a brilliant, fresh spike of pain and he saw Echo even as he tried to blot her words out of his mind. She was lying on his chest, a pink bubble forming on her lips. His hand burned from the lacerations the glass had opened in his flesh, and he could feel her blood pooling between them.

Not like this, he'd thought. *Please, not like this.*

"Alpha. You need to remember. You need to get a grip."

The lid slammed down into place, and he buckled at the searing pain in his belly, forcing him to collapse to his knees, his useless hand pressed tightly to his stomach. His shoulder burning.

"Charlie," he said. "That's one done. Start her up."

He knelt beside the mech, panting heavily. A thick, coppery taste lingered in his mouth and throat.

"Charlie. Start her up," he said again.

The machine was lifeless, though. He began to second guess himself – did he forget something? Was there a start-up sequence or something to go through? Some method of priming the drone he'd failed to realize?

"Charlie's dead," Echo said. "You killed him."

"Fuck. You."

He forced himself to his feet, dragging the cart stuffed with batteries behind him. He felt terribly weak from the blood loss and knew it was only a matter of time before he died. He couldn't let Victor live, though, couldn't risk somebody trying to salvage the station's remnants and coming across the creature. Find him and dying at his hands. Or worse. God, what if, somehow, Victor made it off the mining platform? With his degrees of perception and ability to deceive, to play such twisted mind games with his prey, what would he do to the sky colonies on Venus, or on Mars or Earth?

At the next drone, he repeated the process of battery installation as best as he could. Two down and already he was significantly weaker. Sweat poured down his face, yet he felt frighteningly cold.

The lid slammed down like a gunshot and he felt an explosion in his torso. A second in his shoulder, and he staggered back and fell, the hallucination so vivid. He tripped over the cart, upending it beneath him and sending a cascade of large, heavy batteries across the floor. His bony hips crashed into the corner of a battery, sending fresh agony through him, his head cracking against another.

He lay there a moment, moaning. And remembering.

Charlie with his prohibited firearm. Guns were banned from the station, had been even as a fully operational mining colony. In the depths of space, a gunshot inside an enclosed facility was too large a threat. Somehow Charlie had come to possess one, likely pilfered from the remnants of station security from ages ago.

Charlie had shot him, twice. In return, he had opened Charlie's throat with the glass shard. Alpha had passed out briefly, and when he woke Charlie was staring at him, a gory hand wrapped around his ruined throat, lips moving but making no sounds. And then his lips had stilled.

"No," he said. "No, that isn't what happened."

He fought against the memory, his own mind rebelling against it, dueling factions within him screaming for and against.

"We tried to purge Victor," Echo said. "You attacked me with a chair, busted up my terminal. Do you remember?"

"No," he said, but with no trace of conviction.

"There was glass everywhere from the monitors you

destroyed. You stopped us from purging Victor, and then you came at me with a glass shard. Do you remember?"

"No," he lied. Tears ran freely down his face.

"Charlie tried to stop you, and you killed him."

"I—"

"I'm dying, Alpha."

"I'm so sorry," he said.

Breathing through his nose produced a gravelly noise as liquid roiled deep in his nostrils. His nose and sinuses were so clogged, he had to breathe through his mouth. He wiped again at his face, drawing away moist gray clumps lined with red stains against the back of his wrist.

So this is what happened to Delta. The thought made him chuckle.

He forced himself to roll into a sitting position, his guts squelching and he could swear he felt the rubbery bulge of intestine threatening to spool free from the hole in his belly.

"I don't know what's real," he said. Echo whimpered over the comm channel. He thought she may have been trying to laugh.

Hallucination or not, he understood Victor's plan. Such a simple plan. They had tried to kill him, and so Victor had, in turn, tried to kill them. Alpha had been his weapon.

He saw it all now with awful clarity. Victor, in his tube, small and piebald and deformed, barely human. He wasn't growing, hadn't broken free of the tube. The purge had begun, and he'd lashed out in self-defense. Delta and Bravo had been killed after Uniform had failed to achieve satisfactory synthesis and had been purged. Had that been a warning, or revenge? He didn't know, but he knew Victor had been responsible for manipulating the men toward their deaths.

But information, intended or not, was a two-way street. Alpha had learned things no human mind should be privy to.

He saw, too, what Victor had ultimately realized was the only possible outcome, and what Victor's manipulations of him had been aimed toward.

He dabbed at the wound to his belly, digging his fingers into the ragged hole torn into him. Fresh paint for his brush, he thought, and he drew new marks across the floor beside him. Ancient sigils that put the god to sleep, even if too late.

Alpha slowly, painfully, got his feet beneath him, shoving himself upward from the prone cart for balance. He and Victor had a similar end-goal now, and he was quite content to deliver the creature's final wishes.

His steps were aching shuffles and it took him far longer than it should have to make his way toward the computer terminal. He keyed in the necessary sequences to start up two of the mining drones, their battery cells weak but carrying enough of a charge to carry through one last assignment.

Their thrusters powered on, their large insectile bodies unfolding from their resting racks to deploy. They arced through the warehouse and turned toward the freight elevator to carry them higher up and into the station, to the laboratory where Victor waited.

The mining droids would kill Victor, and then they would destroy the station.

Murder-suicide. That was Victor's endgame, and now Alpha's as well. He accepted that as his legacy. Echo was on her way to dying, Charlie already there. Delta and Bravo, both finished. All because of him, because of Papa and his – their – experimentation, their curiosity. All of it their fault in equal measure.

And so he would die.

"I've spent my life being a tool," Alpha said. "An instrument, constantly manipulated. I thought that Papa's goals were mine simply by virtue of memory, of the inheritance of thought. My life has been a meme, though, nothing more."

"It doesn't have to end this way," Echo said. "We could rebuild. We could—"

Her words were lost in a wet-sounding coughing fit that eventually trailed off into a moan and then an unsettling quiet. He could still hear her breath, though, shallow and rapid, and he knew her moment of expiration was close at hand.

"No," he said, eventually. "There's no coming back from what I've done. Or from what has to be done. This entire project has been a failure. A mistake. I see that now."

"Victor played you," she said, her voice nearly a whisper.

"Victor, Papa. What difference does it make?"

"I forgive you."

Her last words. He could no longer hold back the tears, and sobs racked his body. His wounds ached and leaked, and he cried and cried.

Communications with the lab had cut out, the mining drones doing their job diligently and destroying everything. The alarm sirens found a new vigorous energy as they blared. In his mind's eye, he saw the drones deploying their pick axes and torches as they went to work on Victor, plucking away his limbs, immune to his control and suggestions. Victor was small and baby-like, and it would not take long for him to be disassembled.

The pressure doors slammed into place. The drones had succeeded in breaching the facility to open space. The last gap safety measure would only hold for so long, but Alpha wasn't sure that he would live long enough to see it fail. Odds were, the blood loss would finish him well before.

Or so he hoped. If some part of him recognized that to be a coward's way out, then it forced him to cling to life by a tether of unadulterated agony. Eventually the lights failed and, as he lay bleeding in the dark, he heard the metallic pounding of mining tools working against the doors.

A short time later, an explosive breach of depressurization lifted his body off the ground and sucked the air from his lungs. His death came seconds later, only moments before his corpse would be left to drift in the orbit of a disused asteroid he'd once called home.

In his final seconds, he wondered if perhaps he would discover Elohim after all.

A Note From The Author

Thank you for choosing to read my book – it's greatly appreciated, and I hope you enjoyed the journey!

If you would be willing to spare a minute or two, please leave a brief review of this work and let other readers know what you thought. Reviews are incredibly helpful, particularly for an independent author and publisher such as myself, and can help determine the success of a novel. Reviews do not need to be long — twenty words or so should suffice — but their impact can be enormous.

I look forward to your thoughts, and thank you, once again, for taking the time to read this story.

If you would like to know about upcoming releases, I encourage you to subscribe to my Substack at https://michaelpatrickhicks.substack.com/

About the Author

Michael Patrick Hicks is the author of several horror books, including *The Resurrectionists*, *Broken Shells: A Subterranean Horror Novella*, and *Mass Hysteria*. His debut novel, *Convergence*, was an Amazon Breakthrough Novel Award Finalist in science fiction.

In addition to his own works of original fiction, he has written for the online publications Audiobook Reviewer and Graphic Novel Reporter, and has previously worked as a freelance journalist and news photographer in Metro Detroit.

Michael lives in Michigan with his wife and children. In between compulsively buying books and adding titles that he does not have time for to his Netflix queue, he is hard at work on his next story.

For more books and updates on Michael's work, visit his Substack at https://michaelpatrickhicks.substack.com/

Also Available From High Fever Books

HIGH FEVER BOOKS

ABOUT FRIDAY NIGHT MASSACRE

NIGHT OF THE DEMONS MEETS *OLYMPUS HAS Fallen* in this novel of White House horror from "one of the supreme rulers of delivering unsettling, gore-filled bursts of violence" (Steve Stred, author of *Ritual*).

AFTER SUCCUMBING TO A DEADLY VIRUS AND INCURRING the wrath of voters in the 2020 election, the President of the United States makes a deathbed deal with the devil.

Imbued with supernatural power, President Tyler Coleridge refuses to surrender office after being defeated by his rival candidate and rings in the New Year with a White House bloodbath.

After turning against the press and his own Secret Service detail in a violent display of savagery, it's up to the lone survivor of Coleridge's protective detail, Mike

Hutchinson, to put a stop to the U.S. president's reign of madness before the nation is utterly crippled.

Inspired by recent events, *Friday Night Massacre* is a splatterpunk horror action novel in the grindhouse fashion, with a dash of comic book sensibility.

FRIDAY NIGHT MASSACRE CONTAINS GRAPHIC CONTENT that may be upsetting to some and is recommended for readers of extreme horror.

Available in print, ebook, and audiobook

Buy Friday Night Massacre now!

"*The Resurrectionists* is a stunning achievement — an effective historical novel AND a brutal horror story. Salem Hawley is a fantastic protagonist I look forward to following in future stories." **- John Hornor Jacobs, author of *The Sea Dreams It Is the Sky: A Novella of Cosmic Horror***

"Gritty, grand and grotesque, *The Resurrectionists* is a mind-bending, Lovecraftian myth set in the murky underbelly of post-Revolutionary War Manhattan. It played out in my imagination in a palette of reds and browns like a lush Hammer horror film. Salem Hawley is a riveting avenger, and I'm eager to follow him on further macabre adventures." **- Chris Sorensen, author of *The Nightmare Room***

"As terrifying and action-packed as a slasher flick, but also saturated with literary merit at its core, exploring social issues like racism, classism, and the ramifications of medical experimentation. It was such a fun, provocative read. I can't wait to see what direction he steers the plot in the second book." **- Jeremy Hepler, Bram Stoker Award-nominated author of *The Boulevard Monster***

ABOUT THE RESURRECTIONISTS

Having won his emancipation after fighting on the side of the colonies during the American Revolution, Salem Hawley is a free man. Only a handful of years after the end of British rule, Hawley finds himself drawn into a new war unlike anything he has ever seen.

New York City is on the cusp of a new revolution as the science of medicine advances, but procuring bodies for study is still illegal. Bands of resurrectionists are stealing corpses from New York cemeteries, and women of the night are disappearing from the streets, only to meet grisly ends elsewhere.

After a friend's family is robbed from their graves, Hawley is compelled to fight back against the wave of exhumations plaguing the Black cemetery. Little does he know, the theft of bodies is key to far darker arts being performed by the resurrectionists. If successful, the work of these occultists could spell the end of the fledgling American Experiment... and the world itself.

The Resurrectionists, the first book in the Salem Hawley series, is a novella of historical cosmic horror from the author of *Broken Shells* and *Mass Hysteria*.

Available in print and ebook

Buy *The Resurrectionists* now!

"WITH *THE RESURRECTIONISTS*, MICHAEL PATRICK HICKS introduced us to Salem Hawley in a fresh take on cosmic horror. With *Borne of the Deep*, Salem has taken the crown as my favorite new horror hero. Compelling characters, a unique setting, mythology building, shocking horror--this series is the real deal for readers who want to be thrilled and terrified." - **Cullen Bunn, author of *Harrow County, Bone Parish, The Sixth Gun***

"IN THE MUCH ANTICIPATED RETURN OF SALEM HAWLEY, Hicks dials everything up to eleven. The pace is intense, the cosmic horror delivers, and Hawley takes his place as a hero to root for. As long as you're well out of reach of what's coming for him..." - **Laurel Hightower, author of *Whispers in the Dark***

. . .

"An adrenaline-fuelled adventure rich with gruesome detail and human hardiness. A very worthy sequel to The Resurrectionists." **- Somer Canon, author of *The Hag Witch of Tripp Creek***

ABOUT BORNE OF THE DEEP

Emancipated during the American Revolution, Salem Hawley is a free man--until he finds himself indebted to a doctor for treatment for injuries incurred during the New York Doctors' Riot. Recruited to recover the stolen grimoire, *Al Azif,* Salem embarks on a journey north, to Arkham, Massachusetts.

Plagued by rain and the incursion of strange, otherworldly creatures, the seaside town of Arkham has become a dark and dangerous place. Unable to trust the locals, Hawley is forced to rely on only his wits to track down the thief. He must also contend with Louise LeMarché, an outcast and suspected witch who is searching for the missing tome, as well.

Time is against Hawley. Something ancient and evil is rising from the depths of the Atlantic, and if *Al Azif* is not recovered quickly, it could spell doom to Arkham... and all of humanity.

Borne of the Deep, the second book in the Salem Hawley series, is a novella of Lovecraftian cosmic horror and continues the story that began in *The Resurrectionists*.

Available in print and ebook

Buy Borne of the Deep now!

"A fun and nasty little novella...If you're a big creature-feature fan (digging on works like Adam Cesare's *Video Night* or Hunter Shea's *They Rise*) you're going to love this book." — **Glenn Rolfe, author of Becoming and Blood and Rain**

"Lightning fast...high octane fun." — **Unnerving Magazine**

"An adrenaline-fueled, no punches pulled, onslaught of gruesome action! Highly recommended!" — **Horror After Dark**

ABOUT BROKEN SHELLS

Antoine DeWitt is a man down on his luck. Broke and recently fired, he knows the winning Money Carlo ticket that has landed in his mailbox from a car dealership is nothing more than a scam. The promise of five thousand dollars, though, is too tantalizing to ignore.

Jon Dangle is a keeper of secrets, many of which are buried deep beneath his dealership. He works hard to keep them hidden, but occasionally sacrifices are required, sacrifices who are penniless, desperate, and who will not be missed. Sacrifices exactly like DeWitt.

When Antoine steps foot on Dangle's car lot, it is with the hope of easy money. Instead, he finds himself trapped in a deep, dark hole, buried alive. If he is going to survive the nightmare ahead of him, if he has any chance of seeing his wife and child again, Antoine will have to do more than merely hope. He will have to fight his way back to the surface, and pray that Jon Dangle's secrets do not kill him first.

Available in print, ebook, and audiobook

Buy *Broken Shells* now!

"Brutal horror. Raw. Animalistic. I couldn't put it down!"
— **Armand Rosamilia, author of the Dying Days series**

"*Mass Hysteria* is a hell of a brutal, end of the world free for all. A terrifying vision of a future gone mad with bloodlust, *Mass Hysteria* will haunt your nightmares." — **Hunter Shea, author of Just Add Water and We Are Always Watching**

"Fun, horrible fun, from start to finish." — **Horror Novel Reviews**

ABOUT MASS HYSTERIA

It came from space...

Something virulent. Something evil. Something new. And it is infecting the town of Falls Breath.

Carried to Earth in a freak meteor shower, an alien virus has infected the animals. Pets and wildlife have turned rabid, attacking without warning. Dogs and cats terrorize their owners, while deer and wolves from the neighboring woods hunt in packs, stalking and killing their human prey without mercy.

As the town comes under siege, Lauren searches for her boyfriend, while her policeman father fights to restore some semblance of order against a threat unlike anything he has seen before. The Natural Order has been upended completely, and nowhere is safe.

...and it is spreading.

Soon, the city will find itself in the grips of mass hysteria.

To survive, humanity will have to fight tooth and nail.

Available in print, ebook, and audiobook

Buy *Mass Hysteria* now!

www.ingramcontent.com/pod-product-compliance
Lightning Source LLC
Chambersburg PA
CBHW061042190726
48286CB00006B/1573